Copyright © [2022] by [Rebecca Amiss]

All rights reserved.

Book Cover Design by ebooklaunch.com.

No portion of this book may be reproduced in any form without written permission from the publisher or author, except as permitted by U.S. copyright law.

CONTENTS

CHAPTER ONE

July 1946

Boston, Massachusetts

The sailor at the bar was a dead ringer for Gene Kelly. I couldn't say the same for his dancing, however. He flung me around the dance floor, the smile on his beautiful face wider than the entrance to Fenway Park. I could tell by his thousand-watt smile that he had no idea he was such a dead hoofer.

I had only met him moments ago. He came up and asked if I would like to Jitterbug with him. I instantly said yes, draining the last bit of my Ward Eight cocktail and putting the empty glass back on the bar top. He took me by the hand and pulled me so hard toward the dance floor, I thought my hair might fly right off my head. His dancing initially caught me off guard, and I burst into laughter at the sight of him bouncing around, his body stretching and moving like a rubber band. His large grin made it even better. It's like he thought he *was* Gene Kelly.

The music came to an end, to my relief, and I put a hand over my aching stomach.

The band leader wiped his brow and took a sip of whiskey from his glass.

The sailor put a gentle hand on my back. "Want another drink?"

"Is the sky blue?" I said, already one step ahead of him towards the bar. I leaned forward. "Another Ward Eight, Rudy," I said to the bartender.

"Gee, Maggie," the sailor said, "you're a swell dancer. You could be the next Ginger Rogers."

"Thanks." I took a sip of my Ward Eight, enjoying the taste of rye whiskey and maraschino cherries. "I took some classes as a kid."

The sailor continued to keep his gaze on me. What was his name again? Hank? Bill? Did he even tell me? Either way, I didn't think I could take another dance with him, handsome as he was.

"What do ya say?" he asked, adding a suave wink. "Another dance?"

I nearly choked on my drink. I looked at him and gave him a tight-lipped grin of my own.

"You know, this has been fun, but I really gotta find my girlfriends and get going. Thanks for the drink…and the dance." I hopped off the bar stool.

"Do you have to go so soon?" he asked, taking my hand in his. His dark eyes creased together like a basset hound's. "One more dance."

"Sorry," I said, backing away. "I really ought to catch up with my girlfriends."

"Well, nice to have met you, Maggie." He gave the back of my hand a kiss.

"You, too…" *What was his name?* "Anyway, goodbye."

I rushed off, pushing my way through the throngs of men and women dancing. I searched around until I saw my best friend, Ellen, talking with a man who was clearly much older than she was.

She was giggling like a schoolgirl. Her tight, blonde curls bounced as her shoulders shook from forced laughter.

The man practically had her pinned against the wall. He held a glass of whiskey in one hand and leaned against the wall with the other. He bowed in close and whispered something in her ear, which made her go into one of her giggle fits where she ended up snorting.

I rolled my eyes.

The man gave Ellen a light kiss on the cheek.

She held her hand against her blushing cheek as he walked off.

I moseyed over toward her.

Her eyes were still dancing as if Clark Gable declared his love to her.

"Having fun?" I said.

"Oh, Maggie!" Ellen gushed. "I just met my future husband!"

"Did he propose to you?" I asked.

"Well, no. Not yet, at least. But, oh, didn't you see him? Wasn't he handsome?"

Her cheeks flushed, both from the kiss and most likely from the three gin and tonics I saw her nursing throughout the night.

"Yeah, he was a real Casanova," I said.

Although she didn't seem to hear, as her gaze was still dizzy with enamor.

"Where's Norma?" I asked.

"I'm not sure," Ellen said, finally out of her daze. "Shall we go find her?"

Yet again, I pushed through the hordes of Jitterbugging couples with Ellen close behind me.

A loud shriek came from across the room. Our heads turned to discover Norma dancing with a young man who looked to be no older than twenty, possibly even nineteen. He lifted her up in the air and swung her around like she was a rag doll. Her raven black hair danced along with her as he twirled and dipped her about.

Norma continued to let out loud whoops and thrilling shrieks as she danced, hiking the skirt of her dress up and waving her hand. When the song ended, she gave the young man a big kiss on the cheek.

He walked off, a fresh red imprint from her lipstick and a goofy smile on his face. The pure look of a man who had died and gone to Heaven. Norma always had that kind of effect on them.

"Hey there, crazy legs," I said to her.

"My goodness!" Ellen said. "How do you not get dizzy?"

"It's nothing," Norma explained with a wave of her hand, letting out a few quick breaths.

Norma could easily be on Broadway or in pictures with the likes of Ginger Rogers and Ann Miller, with her looks and talents. Her dancing left other women jealous, and while her singing was passable, she had a flair for the dramatic, being able to produce tears quicker than Greta Garbo when needed.

She chose a career in retail, however, earning a job as the head sales girl at Jordan Marsh department store, where I did some modeling for the sketches for their catalogs every now and then. I never quite understood her silly choice in career, given how she could be rubbing elbows with the rich and famous if she had gone the other way.

"How about you two?" Norma asked. "Meet anyone good?"

"Oh yes!" Ellen was the first to answer. "His name is Mortimer, and he…well, he really didn't tell me what he did for a living, but I'm sure it's wonderful."

"What about you, Maggie?" Norma turned to me. "I saw you talking to that handsome sailor at the bar."

"Yes, he was handsome," I said. "But the guy has two left feet!"

"You're never satisfied with anyone," Norma said with a light chuckle.

"That isn't true!" I folded my arms tightly across my chest. "He was lovely. I just prefer not having my neck snapped off my body!"

"Relax," Norma said, her tone still light-hearted. "I was only teasing. Anyways, what do you say, girls? Ready to head out?"

"Yes, I'm bushed." Ellen yawned. "I need to be up early tomorrow. I have to be at the hospital at six AM."

Ellen had been a Candy Striper at Boston Hospital for three years now. She was studying to become a nurse; her calling came to her after her brother was killed during the war.

"Sure," I said.

Even though I had nowhere to be tomorrow like Norma and Ellen, the two Ward Eights I had caught up with me, and I felt drowsy.

We walked through the overcrowded bar and out onto the sidewalk and headed toward Beacon Hill. The fresh July night air—although humid—was a nice relief from the smoke-filled bar.

Norma told us about her dancing partner whose name was Jimmy. The smile never left her face as she recounted how he mercilessly flirted with her.

"He told me he liked older women, even though he's two years younger than me," she said. "He kept complimenting my eyes, saying he had never seen eyes so brown before."

"How romantic!" Ellen gushed.

"Sounds like a cornball," I said.

"Maggie!" Ellen scolded.

"I'm sorry, Norma," I said, even though I really wasn't, "but that's the oldest trick in the book. He clearly has to brush up his reading skills."

"Well, I found it charming," Norma said, a hint of haughtiness in her voice.

"So, what shall we do next time?" I said, shrugging off Norma's salty attitude. "Oh, I know! Let's go shopping on Newbury Street. Then, we'll go out on the town that night and show off our new duds. Same place?"

"I've been wanting to buy a dress to match my new black Tam hat," Ellen said. "That's a wonderful idea, Maggie."

I turned to Norma. "Norma? Does that work for you?"

She nodded. "Yes, it should. I'll have to make sure I'm not working too late that day. Perhaps we could go when I finish."

I rolled my eyes. As much as I enjoyed Norma, she could be so silly sometimes. Didn't she realize that shopping on Newbury Street was practically a sporting event in itself? It took time. I surely wasn't going to be rushing from store to store just because Norma had to work beforehand. I would take my time if I damn well pleased.

Once we got to Beacon Hill, we said our goodbyes and parted for the night. I lived in a luxurious row house in the Louisburg Square neighborhood, while Norma and Ellen lived in lovely row houses not too far down on Acorn Street.

Everything about Beacon Hill was perfect. It was quiet, and no matter what the season was, it always looked beautiful. The cobblestone streets always reminded me of the rich history of the city and how it's shaped into one of the greatest places to live. I loved everything about Boston and couldn't imagine being anywhere else.

I opened the door slowly, so the creak wouldn't wake anyone up. The ornate hands on the grandfather clock on the side of the foyer said it was almost one in the morning. I shrugged off a yawn. This was nothing. I had come home much later before.

Before heading up the stairs to my room, I crept down the hallway and quietly opened the door to my Uncle James' bedroom and peeked in. He was dead asleep, lying flat on his back, his arms at his sides. His wheelchair sat next to him.

I wished he were still awake. I wanted to tell him all about tonight. How hilarious the sailor at the bar looked dancing to Ellen, yet again, flirting with a man twice her age.

I took one last peek at him as he snored, a light smile curling at my lips. I could wait until the morning. He needed his sleep anyway.

I shut the door softly, tiptoed back down the hall, and headed upstairs to get ready for bed. I went through my nightly ritual of taking off my makeup, putting my hair up into rollers, and applying night cream to my face before settling into bed and turning out the light.

The image of the dancing sailor drifted into my mind. I stifled a giggle, remembering his wacky dance moves. What a sight he was. Although his smile dazzled me, his hoofing skills made me nervous that I would have to bring an extra pair of underwear. I wondered if he would be there next time I went. Would I dance with him again was the question. While I would much rather be in the arms of a man who knew what he was doing, I figured I could give this guy another shot. He was by far one of the most handsome men I'd ever laid eyes on. After all, I could always use a good laugh.

I sat at the breakfast table nursing a strong cup of coffee that our house-keeper, Siobhan, had made. In between making breakfast and serving coffee, she also had the task of waking up my Uncle James and getting him ready for the day. She asked me to keep an eye on the bacon sizzling in the pan while she helped my uncle get up and advised me to shout out to her if it crackled or if I smelled it burning.

She scurried back in and wiped her hands on her apron.

"Did it give ya any trouble, Miss?" she asked me.

I looked up from the magazine I was reading, holding the coffee cup just under my mouth ready to take another sip.

"Oh, sorry. I was reading an article on how to get Joan Crawford's signature makeup look. I didn't notice." I craned my neck slightly. "Looks fine." I went back to reading my magazine and took the sip of coffee.

Siobhan let out a light sigh. "Not a problem, Miss." She flipped the bacon in the pan, cracked a few eggs in another, and scrambled them up.

My Uncle James came in, still in his pajamas. He wheeled his chair to the empty spot at the table across from me.

"Hey, kid," he said to me as Siobhan promptly put a fresh cup of black coffee in front of him.

"Hi." I put my cup down. "Sleep well?"

"Eh," he said. "You know how it is. Some nights I sleep like a baby, others, I can't fall asleep until the sun is almost up."

I nodded, remembering how peaceful he seemed when I checked in on him before going to bed. It must've been one of his "medium nights," as he called it.

"Any disturbances?" I asked.

He put his napkin on his lap. "No. Just dreamed about Lana Turner." A sly smile crossed his lips.

I smiled too, glad that he had a good night. It was the nights where he had flashbacks to those days in Germany, where the only thing he could hear were the screams of his fellow men crying for their mothers, and the sounds of bombs going off that kept me up as well, wishing that my uncle didn't have to suffer through such torment.

"Lana," I said. "That's a new one. Usually, it's Rita Hayworth."

"Oh, she was there, too." Uncle James smiled.

I laughed but stopped short when I heard my parents stomping down the stairs. They entered the kitchen in a swift, unison fashion.

My dad, as usual, was discussing how to continue expanding his grocery store chain within the Northeastern region with my ma, who had some ideas of her own.

"I think that we should go with Maryland before New Jersey," Ma said as they walked in.

"Mary," my dad said, taking the cup of coffee Siobhan held out for him, "New Jersey is our best bet for now. We just sealed the deal with New York—our biggest deal so far. If New Jersey sees that we've secured New York, they'll practically come crawling to us. Trust me, I know what I'm doing." He smoothed out his tie and sat down. "Is breakfast ready, Siobhan?"

"Yes, sir," she said, putting a plate of steaming eggs, bacon, and baked beans in front of him.

He grabbed a piece of toast from the center of the table and practically ripped it with his teeth.

My ma sat down next to him, and Siobhan placed a dish in front of her. They both ate with gusto.

"Jeez," I said, "is it your last meal or something?"

My dad looked up, then back down at his breakfast, and continued to shovel it in his mouth.

"No, Maggie," he said. "We have to get to work."

"It's Sunday," I said. "You don't normally go into the store on Sundays. You just hole yourselves up in your study."

My dad's eyes narrowed, his fork hovering below his mouth. "We have a meeting with a team from New Jersey today. It was the only day they would agree to meet. They came all the way down here just to see us."

I looked over at my ma who, while she ate more daintily, was still quick to finish her own breakfast. She handled the secretarial work, and at times, the finances for my dad's business, O' Hanlon Grocery Company.

"New Jersey is the way to go," Uncle James said. "They are a growing market, more so than Maryland at this time. Where will you be opening the store if you seal the deal with them?"

"Trenton," Dad said. "It already has potential to rival their main grocery store. If we seal Trenton, we can move onto their other cities and towns."

"It'll certainly be a hot-spot for shoppers," Uncle James said.

Uncle James had been Dad's partner before he went off to war. He tried to get back into business with him when he returned after being wounded and declared missing in action but was limited in what he could do, given both his physical and mental state.

My dad looked at his watch. "We have to get going, Mary."

He got up from his chair, and my ma dabbed her mouth with her napkin, following him.

"What are you doing today, Maggie?" Dad asked.

"I don't know." I shrugged. "Maybe today will be the day I meet a rich, handsome man and run away with him and live on his yacht."

"Very funny," Dad said. His eyes were stern, however, there was a small smirk in the corner of his mouth.

My ma was already outside when he grabbed his briefcase from the bench in the foyer. He put his hat on and hurried after her, closing the door behind him.

Uncle James looked at me and crossed his fingers. "Let's hope they get this."

I nodded, all while fighting off an eye roll. "I'm sure they will."

"If they do, then they'll have Maryland to cross off. That'll be it for the Northeast. Then it's off to the Midwest or the South or wherever."

I chortled. "They're better off opening a store on Mars than the Midwest or the South. Those places are pretty much all roads with nowhere to go. If they're smart, they'll go West, like California. Now couldn't you just see me soaking up the rays there? Maybe I'll run into Cary Grant, and we can ride off into the sunset together."

"Keep dreaming, kid." Uncle James laughed. He wheeled away from the table. "Why don't you get dressed for the day, then I can beat you at Gin Rummy."

I smiled as I stood from the table. I walked over, took the handles of his chair, and wheeled him out of the kitchen, fully intending to be the one to win at Gin Rummy.

CHAPTER TWO

"A sailor?" Uncle James sat in his bed, his back straight as an arrow against the headboard. He clutched the cards close to his chest.

I sat in a chair next to him, holding my cards in one hand and a cigarette in the other.

"Yes," I said. "He looked just like Gene Kelly. Only he danced like Goofy on roller skates."

"Sounds charming." Uncle James laughed.

I rolled my eyes and placed my cigarette next to my uncle's in his ashtray.

"I couldn't take being flung around like a doll. I got away from him as fast as I could."

"What was his name?"

I pulled a face as I played around with the cards in my hands.

"Maggie," Uncle James said. "Didn't he tell you his name?"

"I don't know. I think. Maybe not. It was loud in there. You know how it is with the band and everyone laughing and dancing."

"Did you tell him yours?"

"Of course!"

"Did he ask or did you offer?"

"He asked." I continued to fiddle with the cards in my hands.

"And did you ask him?"

"Let's keep playing," I said, trying to keep my concentration on my cards. "I got a good hand."

"Maggie."

I dropped the cards down into my lap and looked at him.

"What? So, I can't remember the guy's name. It's not like I was gonna fall in love and marry him or anything."

"Well, what if you did? He very well could've been your Prince Charming."

"Oh, you can't tell me you've remembered the name of every girl that you've tried to woo."

"I have." He nodded.

"Oh, come off it. You're a bigger flirt than Cary Grant! I doubt he remembers the name of every girl he charms."

"What about your girlfriends? Did they meet anyone?"

"And how! Norma met a kid that was nuts over her, and Ellen…well, you know her. She could flirt her way through a steel box."

"Did she get lucky?"

"I'll say! She managed to snag herself a handsome guy who looked like he should be running the country."

"Looked old enough to be her Old Man?"

I nodded and leaned forward to toss another card down on my uncle's lap. Then I picked up my cigarette and took another puff, blowing smoke into the air before putting it back in the ashtray.

"Well, at least they know what they want," Uncle James said.

"I know what I want, too!" I exclaimed, slightly offended.

"All right, what do you want?"

I hesitated for a moment. Honestly, I didn't expect him to put me on the spot like that. Uncle James looked at me expectantly, which fueled my determination to get back at him with a witty answer even more.

"I want…" I paused, thinking, then stuck my chin out. "I want season tickets to the Red Sox. Front row, so I can get a good look at Charlie Wagner."

Uncle James let out a scoff and shook his head. He played with a card in his hands.

"I love ya, kid. You know that. But sometimes, I just don't get you."

My parents returned home later that day with bottles of champagne. They had sealed the deal with New Jersey and invited their team to the house for a celebration and to go over immediate business on how to get O'Hanlon's up and running in Trenton.

They invited the teams from all four Boston locations. It was going to be a real soiree. This wasn't new, though; they held a big shindig every time they made a deal with a new location. It was one of the few times I saw them smile.

However, as fun as these little parties could be, it was always strictly business. Once they got their new collaborators filled with champagne, they'd whisk them into their study to sign all the contracts and get the poor suckers into giving them full creative control. Even during a party, my parents couldn't relax and enjoy themselves.

Siobhan was sweating in her gray uniform as she scurried around to make multiple plates of hors d'oeuvres and spiffy up the house before everybody arrived at seven o'clock. Uncle James, being the darling he was, wheeled back and forth dusting the tables for her before he had to change into his suit.

"Maggie, you want to help out?" Uncle James held out the feather duster.

"I can't," I said as Siobhan zoomed back and forth in between us. "I have to go get ready. It'll take me at least an hour."

"Ah, of course. Get moving, kid. You don't want everyone seeing you in a linen blouse and trousers."

After I got dressed and put on more perfume than needed, I made my way downstairs to find Siobhan wheeling Uncle James into the foyer.

"I'll take him from here, Siobhan," I said. "Why don't you finish getting everything ready?"

"Yes, Miss," she said before hurrying off to the kitchen.

"Well, look at you," Uncle James said to me. "Look out, Barbara Stanwyck!"

I twirled around, the skirt of my black velvet dress swaying beautifully.

Uncle James smiled as I hammed it up for him. He looked handsome with his dark brown hair slicked back. He wore a spiffy, black tux. From afar, anyone would think they were staring at Jimmy Stewart.

"You don't look so bad yourself," I quipped.

I wheeled him into the living room and sat down on the couch, letting out a sigh. My hands fiddled with the silver, oval locket Uncle James had given to me before he went off to war. He put his photo in it, telling me to look at it whenever I missed him. Although he was home safe and sound now, so many years later, I still couldn't help looking at his photo, even if he was sitting five feet away from me.

"What's eating you, kid?" Uncle James said.

"Nothing." I let go of the locket and brought my eyes to the ground.

"Come on, spill it. I know something is going on in that head of yours."

An amused smirk curled at the corner of my lips. He always knew how to tickle my funny bone.

"Another party, that's all," I said. "Another party where I have to be on my best and most respectful behavior. Dad and Ma will introduce me as their 'lovely daughter' while I have to stand there and act the part."

"They're not wrong. You are their lovely daughter."

I scoffed. "They only call me that so they don't have to remember my name."

Uncle James shook his head. "You know that isn't true."

"It is! How much you wanna make a bet that's how they'll introduce me? They won't even say my name, just 'our lovely daughter'."

"You're on," Uncle James said, giving my hand a firm shake.

"What's this?" Dad said, walking into the room with Ma close behind him.

They both spared no expense with their outfits. Dad wore a similar tux to Uncle James', and Ma wore a dark, emerald green satin dress with a silver brooch on the lapel.

Dad stared at us expectantly.

"What's on?" he said, his voice always in business mode.

"Nothing." I stood up, smoothing out my dress. "Just a little inside joke."

Dad adjusted his suit coat. "Everyone should be here soon. Be ready."

He walked out of the room.

Ma lingered for a minute, keeping her eyes on me.

"This is a very important night for your father," she said.

"I know," I said, as if this were news to me.

When she was finished giving me her signature glare, she turned her attention to Uncle James.

"James, be sure you're beside Richard when Mr. Fulton and his team from New Jersey arrive."

"Yes, Mary," Uncle James said.

Ma went into the kitchen to make sure Siobhan had everything prepared.

I brought Uncle James into the parlor, where he and I played a game of chess to kill time before everyone arrived.

The champagne flowed freely as Siobhan brought trays of deviled eggs, stuffed celery, and caviar around. I stood beside my ma as people from different O' Hanlon stores around Boston and the team from New Jersey came in. Dad introduced us to Mr. Fulton, who would be running the Trenton location, and his team.

"You remember my wife, Mary," Dad said, pointing to my Ma. "And this is our lovely daughter, Margaret."

"Maggie," I corrected.

I held out my hand, giving Mr. Fulton a full toothed smile, silently cursing that I lost the bet with Uncle James. Why did Dad introduce me as Margaret? He knew how much I hated that name.

As Dad and Ma whisked Mr. Fulton and his team away to have some champagne, Uncle James wheeled himself over to me, grinning like a cat.

"Looks like you'll be having crow while I have the caviar," he teased.

I shook my head. "You only half-won. He called me Margaret."

"That is your name," Uncle James said. "You just don't want to admit you lost."

"Very funny. Come on, let's go get some champagne."

I mingled about, sipping on champagne and popping deviled eggs in my mouth. I was able to bum one of Uncle James' cigarettes off him.

Even though many of Dad's employees from the Boston locations knew me well, I still told them everything I had been up to. Some of the wives admired my black dress, and I couldn't help but sway the skirt of it when they did. I was by far the youngest person there. The only other person closer to my age was a young man who worked behind the meat counter at the North End location. He was twenty-nine, a whole six years older than me.

Uncle James had been staying by my side until my dad called him into the study, where he and a few of the men from the Trenton team swapped war stories.

Siobhan was getting quite the workout between bringing glasses of champagne and brandy to the guests and handing out all the hors d'oeuvres.

I was savoring my fourth glass of champagne when someone from the New Jersey location came up to chat with me.

"What a nice picture of your family," he said, gesturing to the large portrait hanging over our oak mantle.

I was probably around ten years old or so in the picture. My parents stood beside one another, unsmiling, while I sat on an ottoman in front of them, my curls emulating Shirley Temple's and my dress ruffled and frilly. Uncle James stood next to the ottoman, the only person in the picture with any expression on his face, a tight grin curled at the edge of his lips.

"Thanks," I said. "I know we look pretty dour. Contrary to popular belief, we know how to smile."

He chortled, taking a sip of his brandy, which caused a small spritz of it to leap out of the glass.

I felt just as bubbly as the champagne inside me, satisfied that I made him nearly spill his drink from laughing. I mirrored his guffaw and took another sip.

"Of course, in order to make my parents smile, they need to have dollar signs in their eyes first," I continued.

"Your father is a remarkable businessman," he said after another bout of laughter. "We are really looking forward to bringing O'Hanlon's to Trenton and hope to expand to other towns eventually. You must be very proud of everything he's accomplished."

My good spirits sobered, and I did everything I could to keep my expression neutral. No matter what, Dad always got the full credit for O'Hanlon's success. Even when Uncle James was his business partner, Dad was the first one people would congratulate on something momentous. I couldn't count how many times a conversation focusing on me would end up being all about him, and I would have to act as if he were as perfect a father as he was a businessman.

I raised my eyebrows and forced a smile on my face.

"Of course, I am," I said, my voice stiff. "Why wouldn't I be?"

"And your mother," he added, "it's not often we see a husband-and-wife team. We mostly see the husband, but your mother is a fine businesswoman. She's quite progressive. I suspect we'll be seeing more women in this field. What about you? Do you have plans on taking part in the family business?"

I nearly snorted. "Oh, no. I don't have a business bone in my body. I'm more into modeling. There's a store downtown, Jordan Marsh? Sometimes I model for the sketches in their catalogs—"

"Mr. Shaw, there you are." Dad walked over to us, interrupting my conversation, with Uncle James right next to him. "Would you mind stepping into the study with Mary and me? We would like to go over some blueprint ideas for the store."

"Absolutely," he said, then turned to me. "It was a pleasure chatting with you, my dear."

Dad gave me a quick glare as he whisked Mr. Shaw away.

I got my and Uncle James' drinks refilled, downing mine within seconds. I stood up to get another.

"How many have you had?" Uncle James asked.

"Going on number six," I said, fighting off a hiccup. "You want me to top you off as well?"

"No, I'm good." He gestured at his glass that still had brandy in it. "You might want to take it easy, though."

"I'm fine."

"Kid, you've been drinking champagne like it's water. Give it a break."

"I'm enjoying myself," I said, walking off to find Siobhan so she could refill my glass.

I couldn't help but relish the attention I had brought onto myself when I played music on the Victrola. I snapped my fingers, all while taking large sips of champagne. I found Mr. Fulton, who had sat down on an armchair to enjoy some caviar and a brandy.

"You're quite the dancer, Margaret," he said.

"Please, Mr. Fulton, call me Maggie."

Even though it annoyed me that I had to remind him to not use my full name, I still swayed with levity—and the occasional stumble that six glasses of champagne brought.

I put my empty champagne glass on the ornamental piano beside me and held my hands out to him. "Want to dance?"

"Oh." He shook his head and smoothed out his tie. "No, thank you. I'm fine."

"Oh, come on, Mr. Fulton!" I yanked him up, barely giving him time to place his plate and glass down on the side table next to him.

I tried guiding him in the steps of the Jitterbug. He bounced around hilariously as I channeled my inner Judy Garland.

A few people wandered over and chuckled, offering playful cheers.

I let out a loud whoop as I turned out and spun around into him, clashing into his chest. I was too busy laughing to notice that my dad had seen everything.

"Maggie!" he exclaimed.

I looked over, and for a moment, saw murder in his eyes. The small vein right under his eyebrow throbbed, and I thought it would burst out. I let go of Mr. Fulton's hands and clasped mine together.

Dad blinked, covering up his horror with a twitch of his upper lip. He rolled his shoulders in an attempt to release the tension in them.

"Maggie, I've been looking for Mr. Fulton." His voice was even, however, there was a darkness to it. There was no way he would let Mr. Fulton see him lose his temper.

Mr. Fulton cleared his throat, and his cheeks flushed. "Yes, Mr. O'Hanlon. Maggie…"

He gave me an awkward wave before walking off with my dad, who sent me a chilling glare as they went toward the kitchen.

Uncle James came over to me. His expression cemented how much trouble I was going to be in when everyone left.

I sat down in the armchair, and Uncle James had Siobhan bring me a glass of water and some crackers.

"You better hope that little dance you gave Mr. Fulton doesn't lose your parents the New Jersey deal," he said. "What were you thinking?"

"I was trying to have fun! It wasn't that bad."

"Your dad is really heated up. I think you should go to bed. Don't say goodbye to anyone. Just slink away upstairs and go to bed."

"I want to stay down here!"

"Maggie," Uncle James put a hand on my shoulder, "do yourself a favor, and do what I say. You'll need to have your wits about you when your dad gets through with you tomorrow. Trust me because it's not going to be pretty."

I sat back, hesitating in obeying my uncle. I took another bite of a cracker, the saltiness burning my throat.

Uncle James took my water glass from me and lightly grabbed my elbow, giving me a gentle push to my feet. "Go," he said softly.

I looked back at him, shuffling out the den. The party went on in the background, not one person paying any attention that I was leaving.

I didn't bother with my nightly ritual. By the time I got into my room, my head was swirling, and I was exhausted. I only had the energy to put my nightgown on before I planted face down on my bed and passed out.

CHAPTER THREE

I felt as if someone drove a truck over my head. The six glasses of champagne from the night before had won the battle.

Siobhan put a cup of black coffee in front of me. She brought the milk jug over, but I covered the cup with my hand and shook my head.

"Just black, Siobhan." It hurt to speak. My skull was pounding so bad, I fought the urge to grab the coffee pot from the stove and chug it down my throat.

The smell of the eggs and bacon that Siobhan placed on the table made my stomach churn. I pushed the plate back and returned to my position of cradling my head in my hands.

"Are you not hungry, Miss?" Siobhan asked. "Is there something else I can make for you?"

"Do we have any tomato juice and Worcestershire sauce?" I groaned.

"Pardon?" She leaned closer.

"Hair of the dog." I lifted my head as far as it would go.

"Oh. No, sorry, Miss Maggie. I can go out and get some later."

I shook my head. "I'll just have the coffee."

Siobhan left the kitchen to get Uncle James ready. She returned moments later with him wheeling in behind her.

"Morning, kid," he said to me. "How are you doing?"

"Dandy," I croaked out.

"Yeah, you look it. You better fill up on that coffee. Your parents will probably be down soon."

I let out another groan and squeezed my eyes shut. Bright spots danced around beneath the darkness of my eyelids.

"Your dad was ready to burst into your room and give you the third degree when everybody left last night, but I talked him out of it." Uncle James stirred milk and sugar in his coffee. He tapped the spoon on the rim of his cup, the clinking sound graphically ringing in my ears.

"I don't understand why he's so upset!" I wrapped my hands around my coffee cup, the heat surging through my palms and all the way up to my cheeks. "I wasn't completely out of control last night."

"Maybe not to you. You know how much these parties reflect your dad's hard work and the company."

"It's a party. You're supposed to have fun, not lock yourself up in a study and go over business."

"All I'm saying is you should have just laid low and enjoyed the party like everyone else."

"Uncle James." I put my head in my hands again. "It's too early in the morning for this type of lecture."

"Believe me, this is nothing." Uncle James took a sip of his coffee.

My parents' feet were like a herd of elephants storming into the kitchen. They sat down at the table. Their chairs scraped against the floor, sending a sharp chill down my spine.

Dad took no time tearing into me. "Maggie, what the hell got into you last night?"

"Good morning to you, too." I grunted.

"I'm serious!" Dad said. "Look at me!"

I lifted my head slowly.

The anger screamed across their tight faces.

"What were you thinking?" Dad leaned forward, barely missing Siobhan's arm as she placed his breakfast in front of him.

"I wasn't thinking anything! I was having fun! That's what you're supposed to do at parties."

"You humiliated me in front of the entire New Jersey team! Not to mention the North End!" Dad said.

"Honestly, your behavior last night was completely inappropriate," Ma said rigidly.

"You're lucky Mr. Fulton didn't renege his deal with us!" Dad pointed his finger.

"At least *I* got him to have fun," I said.

"What's that supposed to mean?" Dad narrowed his eyes.

"The man barely has a chance to sit down and enjoy his brandy before you can whisk him away to your study!"

"It's how your father conducts business!" Ma argued.

"Yeah, by plastering them up until they can't see straight so you can shove your business ideas down their throat."

"Hey!" Dad slammed his fist down on the table, giving my headache a headache.

Uncle James' shoulders tensed. His jaw tightened, and he averted his gaze away from my dad, who didn't seem to notice his brother's flinch. Loud, sudden noises still bothered him from time to time, and he would often mentally count to himself to calm his anxieties.

"You humiliated me and your mother last night!" Dad said. "Everybody saw the way you were acting. You were out of control!"

"No, I wasn't! I didn't get sick all over the place or pass out on the floor."

"The point is," Ma chimed in, "you nearly ruined a perfectly good night, and you don't seem the least bit sorry."

I ran a hand through my hair and shook my head. "That's because I'm not! I'm not sorry for having a good time."

Dad picked up his coffee cup. He chugged it back, slamming it down on the table, sending another jolt of discomfort to my head.

"Of course, you're not." He shook his head. "You never take responsibility for the things you do."

"Excuse me?" I said. "I don't need to take responsibility for doing nothing wrong!"

"Yes, you do!" Dad shouted. "You don't see that the stunts you pull can have repercussions on you, me, and my company!"

I looked over at Uncle James and pointed at him. "Well, Uncle James didn't think I was out of control!"

Uncle James' cheeks darkened. He crouched his shoulders and looked away again. I didn't mean to throw him under the train, but I needed someone on my side, as I clearly wasn't doing any favors speaking for myself.

"Don't bring your uncle into this," Dad said. "He was just as disappointed in you. He told us that he tried to get you to stop, but you wouldn't listen."

I looked over at him, slightly hurt that my greatest confidante didn't try to vouch for me. His eyes glanced over to mine.

"Sorry, kid." He shrugged. "But I told you five champagnes in that you were getting in over your head."

I sat back, my pride wounded—and a little ticked off.

Dad finished off his breakfast and stood up.

Ma did the same, no longer bothering to look me in the eyes.

Dad grabbed his coat and fedora and put them on. "You need to think the next time you do something ridiculous. You do something like this again…"

"Or what?" I challenged, squinting my eyes at him. "You're going to lock me up in my room during parties?"

"I mean it." He adjusted the collar of his coat. "This is your final warning."

He and Ma left the kitchen without so much as a second glance in my direction. The door slammed, and I returned my attention to my uncle.

"Thanks for sticking by my side!" I narrowed my eyes.

Uncle James shook his head, both from early morning exhaustion and disappointment.

"Sorry, but your dad is right. You went too far last night."

I scoffed. "Everyone is acting like I committed a murder! I had a little too much champagne and danced with Mr. Fulton. I did nothing wrong!"

"That's the thing," Uncle James said, his tone holding a bit more force. "You don't see that you did do something wrong. You should have stopped when I told you to."

"You're supposed to have my back no matter what!"

Uncle James' eyes softened, and he wheeled himself over to me. "I do. I always will. But I can't always dig you out of a hole you dug for yourself. Especially when you don't seem to feel bad getting yourself into it. You need to start taking more responsibility for actions before you do something that'll get you into an even hotter mess than you were in last night."

Uncle James squeezed my hand and backed away from the table. He then gave me one last disappointed look before leaving the kitchen.

Later that week, I met Norma at her work when she finished her shift. I was a bit early, considering she was still behind her counter. I wanted to make sure that she was still going shopping on Newbury Street, thinking we could pick up Ellen together.

I told her all about my dad's party with New Jersey, how I drank my weight in champagne and woke up the next morning with an awful headache. She tidied up her counter and helped customers as I prattled on beside her.

"It was dreadful the entire morning," I said. "Not even a strong cup of coffee helped."

"Poor you," Norma said.

"Anyway, despite that and the fact that I managed to embarrass my family, I enjoyed myself."

"That's all that matters."

"Although, I couldn't help staying mad at my uncle for the rest of the day for taking my parents' side."

"How is your uncle doing, by the way?"

"He's fine. He's had a few disturbances, but nothing too intense. Other than that, he's doing well."

"That's good," she said.

Dabney O'Brien, Norma's boss, came over.

"Norma," he said, "you're all set to go. Betty should be out any minute to take your place."

"Thank you, Dabney. Maggie, I'll be right out. Let me get my things, and we can get going."

Norma scurried off to the back room for employees only, leaving me at her little work counter.

I caught Dabney just as he was about to walk away.

"Dabney!" I waved my hand.

"Oh," he said. "Hello, Maggie. How are you?"

"I'm fine. Listen, I'm ready for when you need me to model for your wardrobe sketches for the fall catalog. I assume you'll be putting it out soon."

"Sorry, but we already did the modeling for the fall," Dabney said. "We start the sketches in two days. It should be out by the end of next month."

I blinked at him. "But...but you never informed me."

He shrugged. "You never came in to discuss when we were going to do it."

I scoffed. "How was I supposed to know? I'm not a fortune teller."

"Maggie, you know we start the modeling at the end of the previous month and begin the sketching at the beginning of the following one. We have many other girls here who are persistent in asking when they are needed. While there's only a handful of you, we take the ones that come to us right away. I'm sorry, but you missed the cut this time. Come back when we're getting ready to put out the winter catalog."

He gave my shoulder a light shake and walked off, leaving me standing there, irked that he also didn't consider telling Norma to let me know when they were ready for me.

Norma came out from the back, waving goodbye to her fellow employees for the day.

"Ready?" she said.

"How come you didn't tell Dabney to contact me when they were getting ready to model for the Fall catalog?" I asked, walking beside her as we headed out the door.

"What?" Norma looked at me. "Oh, Maggie, I honestly don't think of those things. I just come in and do my job. You can't expect everyone to come to you; you have to take some initiative as well."

"Dabney knew that I am one of the girls he goes to. He should have come to me in the first place."

"Well, he didn't," Norma said. "You're just going to have to be better at remembering next time."

We walked toward Beacon Hill, our conversation now focusing on going back to Louie's Bar later that night. Norma said that she hoped to find another man to dance with who had the same smooth moves as her partner from last time. We picked Ellen up at her home, where I offered for her to drive. I figured since we were all planning on buying something, it would be silly to lug everything home, despite the walking distance being less than thirty minutes.

We strolled down Newbury Street, gazing in windows and admiring all the dresses and jewelry the stores had to offer. We went into one of our favorite department stores.

The hostess stood in the entrance way and greeted us warmly.

We split up momentarily as we each eyed something we wanted.

I went up to a gorgeous royal blue taffeta dress with a square neckline. I took it and brought it to the back fitting room and tried it on. As beautiful as it was, it didn't look right on me. The waist was a little too loose, and the skirt didn't flow the way I thought it would. I took it off and put my own dress back on, fully intending to search for something else.

I left my fitting stall to find Ellen checking her reflection in the three-way mirror while wearing a black dress with a small, narrow split down the neckline and an embroidered, green and blue peacock on the left breast. I adored it, and to my chagrin, Ellen looked positively radiant in it.

"Oh, Maggie!" she gushed, noticing me staring at her. "What do you think? I absolutely love it. Did you enjoy the dress you tried on?"

I walked over to her, my eyes glued to the dress. I wanted to buy it so terribly, but it seemed Ellen had beaten me to the punch. I suppose I could buy it as well, but then we would both have the same dress, which would be unthinkable. I didn't want to risk being out in public together with the same thing on. I imagined what it might look like on me, which made me crave it even more.

"Well?" Ellen said, causing me to break eye contact from the dress. "Should I buy it?"

I couldn't take it. I knew I would be making a big mistake if I didn't buy that dress. I cocked my head and gave Ellen an unfortunate look.

"It's a gorgeous dress, Ellen," I said. "And of course, you look lovely, but if I'm being honest, I don't think it's right for you."

Ellen's smile fell, and her eyebrows knitted together. "What?"

"Don't get me wrong, you always look beautiful." I walked closer to her. "But it's the color. It's a little dark for your skin tone and hair."

"It is?" Ellen turned her attention back to her reflection. "I thought it looked fine."

"I'm only telling you what I think." I shrugged. "It's up to you. But the color does drown you out a bit."

"I suppose it does make me look paler than I am," Ellen said, disappointment laced throughout her voice. "I didn't think it would matter much."

She stepped away from the mirror and gave a sad smile as she brushed past me, going back into her fitting stall.

After putting our dresses back, we met up with Norma, who had already bought herself a new hat.

"You two didn't find anything?" she asked us.

I shook my head. "No luck."

"I tried a very nice dress on," Ellen said, causing me to go white in the face, "Maggie, however, told me it made me look too pale."

"Do you want to continue shopping until you find something?" Norma asked.

"I think I'll just wear something I already have," Ellen said, discouragement still plaguing her. "What about you, Maggie?"

"I'm ready to go if you are," I said.

We each went back to our own homes, agreeing to meet outside of my house at nine to head over to Louie's Bar together, which was perfect because it would give me enough time to head back out and buy myself that gorgeous, black dress.

I waited an hour after getting back home to go back to the store and buy the dress. I took my dad's car, poking my head into his study to let him know. Without even looking up, he gave a quick nod of his head and waved me off.

When I went up to the dress, I could barely contain the smile that spread across my face. I gripped the dress gently, running my hands up and down the smooth and light fabric which felt wonderful beneath my fingertips.

As I took the dress off its hanger, the image of Ellen's heartbroken face flashed in my mind. If only she hadn't looked so amazing in it. I had second thoughts about buying it, but I figured the least I could do was try it on and go from there.

When I saw what I looked like in the dress, I knew that I had to buy it. I turned about as I admired my reflection in the three-way mirror. I swayed in place. The skirt had the perfect swing to it, and the silhouette was extremely flattering. Did this dress look good on everyone?

After dinner, I got ready for Louie's Bar, putting on my black swing shoes to match. I carefully did my makeup in the mirror, choosing a deep red for my lips. I applied white eyeliner to make my light blue eyes appear larger than they were and slapped on enough concealer and rouge to cover my pesky freckles. For my hair, I swiped up one side, putting in a small tortoise shell bobby pin in my dark auburn locks.

Ellen and Norma were making their way towards me as I stepped out the front door. As they approached, Ellen's eyes grew wide, and her jaw nearly hit the pavement.

"Maggie!" She traced me up and down, her mouth sputtering for words.

"What's the matter?" Norma said, somewhat alarmed.

Ellen pointed at me. "That—that's the dress I tried on!"

Norma narrowed her eyes. "Are you serious?"

"What—?" Ellen stuttered, and her eyes flamed up at me. "Is this why you talked me out of buying it? So you could have it?"

"Listen, Ellen—" I started.

"That was real crummy of you, Maggie!" Norma interjected. "You know, if you really wanted it too, both of you could've bought it."

"And be seen together with the same dress on?" I asked, appalled.

"It wouldn't have been such a big issue," Norma said.

"How could you do something like this?" Ellen accused. "You knew how much I wanted it!"

"What, did you sneak back to the store to buy it?" Norma added. "That's really nasty."

"You're not letting me finish what I was saying—" I said.

"Why should we?" Ellen shouted. "You don't have any regard for me or anyone!"

"Do you want me to change? Do you want me to put something else on?"

Ellen puckered her lips, screwing her mouth up. Her face reddened, making her bouncy blonde curls lighten against her inflamed cheeks.

"I'm not going anywhere with you!"

"Oh, Ellen," I said. "Don't be like that. It's just a dress."

"You really don't understand, do you?" she said. "It's not the dress. It's the fact that you had to be so incredibly selfish. You can't even see why I'm upset! You've always been like that, and frankly, I can't take it anymore!"

Ellen turned on her heels and spun around, walking back toward Acorn Street. Norma glared at me, shaking her head slowly.

"I hope you're happy with yourself. I don't want to go anywhere with you either. Have fun at Louie's."

Her tone was acidic. She gave one last hardened glare before going after Ellen.

I stood on my front steps, angered that they got so hot and bothered over a dress.

"Fine," I said. "I don't need them anyway. I'll enjoy a night out by myself."

I walked down the steps and headed toward Scollay Square, determined to have the most fun I could ever have.

The band was in full swing tonight as they played with great gusto. I found a few men to dance with, one of them whose Boston accent was thicker than his eyebrows.

As I danced with him, I kept glancing over at a man across the bar whom I had been locking eyes with throughout the night. Every time I looked over, I'd see him watching me, his eyes peering over the rim of his drink. I raised my eyebrows at him and offered a flirtatious wink. He seemed to have enjoyed that because he smiled, showing off his dimples from across the room. When the song ended, I thanked the guy I was dancing with and moseyed over to the bar.

I tapped my nails against the counter top, humming lightly to myself.

An arm stretched out in front of me and put an empty glass down, remnants of an amber liquid staining the bottom.

I felt someone sit down on the barstool next to me.

"What are you drinking?" a voice asked.

I screwed my mouth into a satisfied smile and turned, looking at the dimpled man in the eyes. He was even more handsome up close. His eyes were dark brown, and his face was smooth and chiseled.

"Ward Eight," I said.

The man got Rudy's attention and ordered my drink and himself another scotch.

"What do they call you?" he asked me.

"Maggie," I said coolly.

"I'm Harold. Harold Broderick."

"Nice to meet you," I said, offering a hand shake.

"You taking a break from your man?" He nodded his head toward my recent dance partner who had moved on to another girl.

"Oh, no." I leaned against the bar top. "I'm not with him."

"Are you rationed?" He took a sip of his scotch.

"Nope," I said, giving off a modest look, then let out a sigh. "I'm completely single."

"What's a pretty dish like yourself doing single?" He smiled.

I returned the smile, then put my aloof persona back on.

"Just never found the right guy, I guess." I traced the rim of my cocktail glass with my finger. "So, Harvey—"

"Harold," he said quickly.

"I'm sorry?" I fluttered my eye lashes.

"Harold. My name is Harold. Harold Broderick."

I let out a fake, embarrassed exhale. "Oh, I'm sorry. I just can't—"

"Listen, don't pull that with me." A grittiness consumed his deep, suave voice.

"Huh?" I said, confused for real this time.

"Don't pretend like you forgot my name. I hate it when dames do that. They act all cute and innocent about it. It may work with other guys, but it isn't gonna work for me."

I blinked at him, temporarily stunned. "Okay," I said slowly. "Sorry…Harold."

"That's more like it," he muttered to himself.

His eyes broke away from mine, and he took a generous gulp of his scotch.

"Look, I'm sorry if I offended you," I said, trying to get in his good graces again. "I was only ragging you, that's all."

He returned his gaze, his expression still somewhat irritated. He eventually softened and offered me a light grin.

"Hey, it's nothing. I just don't like being played with that way. Let's start again. You wanna dance?"

I smiled and held out my hand.

He guided me towards the dance floor, and when he wasn't looking, I curled my lip up into a tight sneer. What was this guy's deal? He swung me toward him, and I plastered the smile back on my face.

We made it out onto the dance floor in time for a slow song. He put his hand on my lower back and brought me closer to him. I put my arms around his neck and let him guide me across the dance floor. It was hard forcing myself not to lead, but I didn't want to do anything else that might set him off.

We looked into each other's eyes, and before I knew it, our lips were touching. He was a good kisser—and dancer. He knew exactly how to move along with the music. Our lips let go, and we went back to staring at each other again.

"I still can't believe a guy hasn't snagged you up," he said, making me blush and offer another smile. "You could be a model, you know?"

"I actually do model," I told him. "Well, for Jordan Marsh. It's a department store in Downtown Crossing. I model their clothing for the sketches in their catalogs."

He shook his head. "You're too good for that. With that hair? You could give Katharine Hepburn a run for her money."

I smiled, giving my hair a shake. "You know, I always thought I kind of looked like her."

"She's got nothing on you." He twirled me around as the song came to an end. "What do you say we have some real fun? I know just the place. It's not too far from here."

I smiled and shrugged. "Sure. What the hell?"

We locked arms, and he guided me out of the bar as we pushed our way past all the dancing couples.

CHAPTER FOUR

I was disappointed to discover that Harold's idea of fun was a bowling alley; much less the one I'd been to with Uncle James many times as a kid. I tried to hide it, but the shifting glances I was displaying must've given my hesitation away.

"I know what you're thinking," he said.

"Do you?" I looked around: teenage boys and their dates in bobby socks jumped around as they sipped sodas and bowled strikes.

He clasped his hand into mine and guided me toward the back, walking in the direction of the Employees Only room. He knocked twice, and the door opened. We walked in and were greeted by two guys in short sleeved collared shirts, both smoking a cigarette. They nodded at Harold, who nodded back to them.

"Do you work here?" I asked him.

He let out a laugh, cementing that my question was silly.

"Come on," he said as he continued to walk me through the room and towards the back. There was another door that said "John" on it.

I furrowed my brows in confusion. So, *this* was his idea of fun?

When he opened the door, I discovered that it wasn't a bathroom but a small back hallway with a set of stairs. As we climbed down them, laughter and overlapping chatter came from the bottom.

When we reached the last step, I was surprised to see that it was some kind of a casino, as people stood around drinking and playing various card games. There were even a few roulette and craps tables near the back.

Everybody looked up and greeted Harold. He was clearly a regular here. All this time I had been to the bowling alley, and I never knew what lied beneath it. I began to wonder if this had been here when I used to come with Uncle James. I looked around in awe, keeping my arm linked in Harold's as he walked me through the drab, smoky room.

"Want a drink?" he asked me.

I nodded, and he ordered me my Ward Eight and himself a scotch.

"How did you know this place was down here?" I asked. "I mean, I used to come here as a kid all the time and never knew about it."

"That's cause you weren't looking hard enough." Harold handed me my drink that the bartender had brought over and clinked his glass to mine. "Here's to having fun."

I smiled and raised my glass before taking a sip. I puckered my lips and widened my eyes at the strength of it. This place certainly wasn't playing around with their cocktails.

"So, what first?" Harold said. "A little roulette? Some craps?"

"Uh…" I looked around again. "You know, maybe I'll watch you first."

"Don't tell me you're chicken." He offered a teasing smile.

"No, I just…have never been to an underground casino before."

"That's certain. Let's try craps."

He led me over to the table and drained his drink, motioning for another one.

A bulging man lumbered over and slapped Harold on the shoulder.

"Harry!" he said, clearly three sheets to the wind. "Good to see ya!"

"Hi, Don, how are the wife and kids?" Harold asked.

"Fine, fine. I see you got a lady friend." Don turned his attention to me and sauntered over. "Well, hello there, sugar."

"Hi," I said, trying to hide my disgust.

"You a craps player? You'll never win with this bum around you." He motioned to Harold, then let out an obnoxious laugh.

"You're just cheesed because I practically grabbed the money from your pocket last time," Harold said, a joshing smile on his face.

Don smacked Harold on the shoulder again, letting out another beastly howl.

"You're a real card, Harry! Don't let the little lady steal all your money!" He laughed again and walked away, hollering for another whiskey.

"Sorry about that," Harold said.

"No, he seemed like a real sweetheart."

"So, what do you say?" He picked up the dice and held them out to me. "You wanna roll first?"

He cracked a smile, his dimple shining through. I looked at him, then back down at the dice. He shook them temptingly in his hands.

I brought my drink to my mouth, tilted my head back, and sucked it down. I locked eyes with Harold and snatched the dice from him.

"Let's play," I said.

I was already into my third drink when I rolled a seven—Harold was on his fourth. He let out a whoop, and I shrugged as if I rolled sevens every day.

Even though I had really only played craps a few times with Uncle James as a kid, I never played it enough to become proficient at it. I sucked on a cigarette that Harold had offered to me. There seemed to be something men liked about watching a young woman roll dice and smoke at the same time. Harold became especially close as he stood right beside me and put his arm around my waist while I played, often stealing kisses on my neck after I rolled good numbers.

"All right, all right," I said with the cigarette between my lips, fully into the game now. I had acquired twenty bucks and wasn't ready to stop.

I had forgotten that we were underneath the bowling alley until the sounds of bowling balls crashing against the pins from above reminded me. The sounds became more frequent, along with loud stomping. I began to wonder what time it was, as I couldn't remember what time the bowling alley closed for the night. I heard shouts and hollering coming from above. The people upstairs must've been having as much fun as we were down here. If only they knew.

I made Harold blow on the dice for good luck, something he was more than compliant to do. Just as I was shaking the dice and ready to throw it again, the door at the top of the stairs banged open. The shouts from above that I thought were gleeful turned out to be panic as I looked toward the stairway and saw a bunch of cops storming down them.

"This is a raid!" one of them shouted as he came barricading down with his fellow cops behind him.

The cigarette dropped out of my mouth, and my eyes widened as the cops tried to catch the people that were now grabbing their money and scrambling to get upstairs to blow out of the place.

Harold grabbed my arm, which made me drop the dice—and forget my money. He pushed a police officer out of the way to get up the stairs, shoving and practically pushing through other people as he dodged us up towards the bowling alley.

My eyes darted around madly, and my racing heart nearly burst through my chest with pure fear running through my veins that I hadn't felt since my uncle went missing.

I followed Harold through the crowd of both bowlers and people from the casino who were all chaotically trying to get out. Some ducked under the tally tables, and one person even went so far as to run and slide down one of the alleys on his stomach, crashing into bowling pins and disappearing under the pit. It was unlike anything I had ever seen before.

Harold was now twisting my wrist so hard, I thought he was going to break it right off.

Once we got outside, the muggy July night heat was almost as suffocating as the casino room. People were scrambling everywhere, more police officers began to give chase, and I could no longer feel Harold's grip on my wrist. My head whipped around as I searched for him until I saw his back, running in the opposite direction.

"Harold!" I called out.

Someone shouted something close by, and I looked back toward the wild scene where I was nearly blinded by a photographer's bright camera flash. I slammed my arm over my eyes, letting out a groan.

There were at least four photographers staking out the sidewalk, snapping as many photographs as they could.

I swung my head back and forth, noticing that Harold was now completely gone.

Scumbag.

Slowly, I backed away from the photographers who were harassing anyone who ran by. My heart raced as I witnessed police men practically throw people to the ground.

When I thought I was in the clear, I darted off, not knowing if the shouting was now directed at me or the people outside of the bowling alley. Running faster than I ever had in my entire life, I didn't bother to look back, fearing that someone would be right on my tail.

Once I reached Beacon Hill and could no longer hear shouting and screaming, I slowed down, breathing heavily. My feet hurt, and I could tell they would be blistered by morning.

I wasn't sure how I could let myself get into a scene like that. I should have just dodged Harold when he got all hot and bothered over me forgetting his name. It didn't matter, though. I would probably never see him again anyway. If I did, I would ignore him, act like I had never met him before. It wouldn't be the first time I did that.

My thoughts wandered away from Harold and was now occupied with the twenty bucks I had won that I didn't get to take with me, which made me angry at him all over again.

I dragged my feet up toward my neighborhood. If anyone asked where I was, I would just tell them the usual. No one had to know about tonight's little adventure.

I stopped in my tracks abruptly. To my horror, my mind brought back the memory of the photographer's blinding light. Did they get a picture of me? Is it even recognizable? The whole raid would be in the paper tomorrow morning for sure. What if my picture is in it? My mind swirled with endless outcomes. I would have to make sure I got to it before anyone else did. More importantly, I would have to make sure I snagged it before my dad had a chance to read it.

CHAPTER FIVE

I barely slept that night. Not only from thinking of schemes as to how I could get to the paper before my dad read it, but Uncle James had another one of his night terrors again. I gripped the sheets against my chin as my thoughts flopped from the newspaper to my uncle's tormented screams.

It wasn't until nearly two o' clock in the morning that his wails stopped and my eyes grew heavy, my mind at ease that he had fallen back into a steady sleep.

The next morning, I put my bathrobe on and bounded down the stairs, skidding into the kitchen where Siobhan was making breakfast.

"Siobhan, did the morning paper come yet?" I asked hurriedly.

"Hm?" She looked up. "Not that I've seen, Miss."

I breathed a sigh of relief and slumped into a chair at the breakfast table. Siobhan handed me a cup of coffee, which I drank slowly.

"Are you all right, Miss?" Siobhan asked, her eyebrows furrowed with concern. "You look like you've had a rough night."

I swallowed my coffee and looked up at her. "Hm? Oh, yeah. I'm fine. Just had a little trouble sleeping, that's all."

"Aye, did your uncle have one of his spells again?"

I nodded, his screams still echoing in my ears. For some reason, they sounded worse this time, as he continued to shout "no" and some of the names of his fellow soldiers over and over.

She brushed her hands against her apron and went back to the stove to resume cooking.

"The poor fellow." She sighed.

My thoughts traced back to the newspaper, wondering why it hadn't come yet. After I had had my coffee, I tiptoed upstairs and listened to my parents outside their bedroom door, trying to find out if they had yet to see the paper. They were—once again—discussing expanding

O'Hanlon's Grocery Company. When I heard them approaching the door, I scurried away and ran into my bedroom before they could find out I was eavesdropping.

I came downstairs to see my uncle already at the breakfast table, still in his pajamas. He looked completely burnt out. His hair was tousled, and he stared at nothing in particular with exhausted, dark-circled eyes. His cup of coffee sat on the table in front of him, the steam wasting away into the air. I gave his shoulder a comforting squeeze and knelt down beside him.

"Uncle James," I said, my voice soft.

He looked at me, his eyes still scared and vacant.

I smoothed his hair out a bit and gave him a light grin, rubbing his hand gently.

His expression softened, and the corner of his mouth twitched up, his version of trying to smile for me.

I sat down at the table in time for Siobhan to serve me breakfast.

My parents came in. They sat down and began vigorously eating, not bothering to even acknowledge my uncle's latest middle of the night spell. Not to say I didn't blame them. Uncle James didn't like discussing or dwelling on it, and it had become so custom since he came back to live with us, it was as if his nightmares were a part of an everyday schedule by now. Still, I couldn't help but feel a bit of annoyance towards my parents.

Within minutes, they had sucked their coffees down and let their silverware clang onto their plates as they headed out for another work day.

"Nice talking to you," I called out after the door slammed behind them.

It wasn't until I heard my dad's car engine start and roar down the street that I allowed myself to relax. I sat back in my chair and let out a sigh. I had dodged a bullet with the newspaper. I just had to make sure I kept checking for it before my parents came home in the afternoon to tend to business for the rest of the day in my dad's study.

A little later in the day, I knocked on my uncle's bedroom door, hoping he was in a healthier mood.

"Uncle James? Are you decent?"

"Come on in."

I entered the room and stood in the doorway, biting my lip and twisting my locket in my hand.

"What's on your mind, kid?" he said.

"There's something I need to tell you."

I spilled my guts telling him about Harold, the casino, and the police raiding the place. At first, he didn't believe me, thinking I was joshing around with him. When I told him my picture could very well be in the paper, he finally joined my side and tried to ease my senses.

"Look," he said as I paced around the room, wringing my hands. "Maybe your photo is not in the paper. You know, photographers take loads of pictures and only a handful of them actually end up printed. Just tell your parents what happened."

"Are you crazy? I'm not telling them anything! If my photo doesn't appear in it, then there's no use in telling them."

"Did anyone recognize you?"

"I don't think so."

"You better hope not."

That's the small price I had to pay for being the daughter of a well-respected businessman. I grew up going to some of the openings of his stores throughout New England. The reporters and photographers acknowledged my presence more than my own parents did. There are photos of my parents standing stoically in front of stores, and my Uncle James either holding me or his hand on my shoulder.

Uncle James offered for us to play chess to ease my senses. Although the gesture was thoughtful, I still couldn't stop thinking about the newspaper, resulting in Uncle James dominating me in the game.

When we finished, Uncle James had grown tired, and I could tell he was ready for some rest.

"I don't mean to pester you further. I know you're tired." I wheeled Uncle James into his bedroom. "But what am I going to do if my photo is in the paper? Dad reads it every single day without fail. Ma couldn't care less, but Dad—he reads the paper as if it were going out of print."

"I don't know," Uncle James said. "I wish I could help you, but you're just going to have to deal with it as it comes."

"I was afraid you'd say that." I parked his wheelchair next to his bed.

"Look, whatever happens, happens. You can't go back in time and fix everything."

"I know." I sighed.

Uncle James gripped the seat handles on his chair and hoisted himself up onto his bed.

I covered him and shut the lamp off.

"Have a good rest, Uncle James," I said, smoothing out his dark gray blanket.

"Thanks, kid. Good luck. I hope your head isn't bitten off when I wake up."

I laughed, my anxiety at ease for the first time since last night. I gave Uncle James' hair a playful tousle and crept out of his room. I hoped my parents wouldn't come home while Uncle James was still resting. If they did, then I was on my own to fight for myself against them.

As I made my way down the hallway, the front door slammed and angry footsteps entered the foyer, making me stop in my tracks.

"Maggie!" Dad's voice hollered. "Maggie! Where are you?"

The front door opened and slammed again, and my ma's heels clicked on the floor.

"Where is she?" she asked.

I hurried toward them.

My dad caught sight of me and went into the den, with my ma not far behind. He paced around the room, then threw the newspaper down on the glass table.

I stood in the entryway.

"Well?" Dad said. When I didn't answer, he pointed his finger like he was calling a disobedient dog. "Come here!"

I moseyed over. My dad picked up the newspaper, gripping it in his hands.

"What is this?" He shook it in my face.

I looked down and saw my picture staring back at me. I thought for a moment maybe I could fake it out. I could pretend it wasn't me, just someone who looked shockingly similar. I knew, however, that even I couldn't pull that off. The photo was me, plain and simple. I was appalled at the photo, however. It was terribly unflattering. My eyes were bulged out, and my mouth hung open.

"Sit down!" Dad said.

I plopped down in a leather armchair, clasping my hands in my lap.

My dad held out the paper, placing it directly under my nose.

"An underground casino? Don't you know those are illegal? What the hell were you doing there?"

He threw the paper down on my lap, forcing me to stare at my face that was front and center.

Then, I read the text that was beneath it.

```
LATE NIGHT RAID: Police caught people
illegally gambling at an underground
casino located in Strikes Bowling Alley
down near the end of Scollay Square in
Downtown Boston. Some fled the scene, in-
cluding grocery store princess, Margaret
O'Hanlon, 23 (Pictured above). Margaret
is the daughter of Richard O'Hanlon, 46,
and niece of James O'Hanlon, 39, founders
of O'Hanlon Grocery Company.
```

My eyes grazed the text. So, they called me a princess? When I looked back at my picture, I noticed something in the background. It was the faint imprint of a man running, his back to the camera. I gripped the newspaper in my hands when I realized who it was. I shot up out of my chair and walked toward my dad, pointing at the picture.

"This!" I said. "This man right here!"

"What?" Dad glanced down at the paper, equally confused and agitated.

"This is the man that brought me to the casino. His name is Harold. Harold Broderick."

I found myself feeling a bit of pride for remembering that crumb's name.

My dad squinted his eyes at the photo, then shook his head. "I don't care who that man is! You never should have gone in the first place! You could've been arrested! You could've been hurt!"

"I didn't know he was going to take me to an underground casino!" I shot back. "For all I knew, he was taking me to another nightclub across town!"

"Don't shout at your father," my ma said.

I looked over at her sitting on the sofa, her hands placed rigidly on her lap. I had forgotten she was even in the room.

"Look," I brought my attention back to my dad, "he said we were going to go somewhere fun—"

"I don't care what he said to you! Your picture is in the paper! Your name is in the paper! *My* name and company are in the paper!" He tossed it down on the table. "Do you have any idea what this could do for my business?"

"Well, I'm sorry for wanting to have some fun!" I yelled.

"Don't give me that!" Dad shook his head. "You've done things like this more than enough times. This is the final straw."

"Final straw? What are you talking about?"

"You are going to learn to take some responsibility for yourself."

"Or what? You're gonna ship me off somewhere?" I provoked.

My dad's eyes drilled into mine.

The muscles in his jaw clenched. I stood my ground against him, folding my arms tightly across my chest.

"You might want to get your luggage out," he finally said.

"Why? Where am I going?"

"I don't know." His voice was strained and tight. "But get them out and start packing."

I probably shouldn't have barged into my uncle's room the minute I heard him stir from his rest, but I couldn't help it. I needed his advice. I had startled him when I opened the door.

Thankfully, however, his rest was undisturbed, and he was able to calm himself quickly when he saw that it was only me.

When I told him everything, I was appalled to discover that he was more on my dad's side.

"How can you agree with him?" I stood next to his bed.

"Maggie," Uncle James said, "you did kind of mess up."

I paced around the room, repeatedly shaking my head in disbelief. My uncle was supposed to be my confidante, my partner in crime, my friend.

"How was I supposed to know where Harold was taking me? Sure, maybe I should have scrammed when I realized it was a casino, but I didn't think of it at the time."

"The fact is that you did stay! You didn't leave. If you had left right away, you wouldn't be in this situation. I'm sorry, but..."

"But what?"

He paused, and I could tell he was dreading to say his next words. "Maybe it's for the best."

I sat back in my chair and folded my arms, shocked and hurt over the words my uncle had just uttered.

His face held a mixture of empathy and remorse. He let out a discouraged sigh, his mouth curving downward.

"I hate telling you this. You know I always will give you the benefit of the doubt but—this time—I can't. You need to grow up, kid." Before I could rebuttal him, he continued, "Do what your dad says. Don't give him a hard time over this."

"Where do you think they're going to send me?" I asked softly, embarrassed to hear the worry in my voice.

"I don't know." Uncle James sighed.

"What if I got a job? What if I found a place to work around here? Then he wouldn't have to send me anywhere, right?"

"Did you not hear what I just said?"

"Yes, I did! But what if I could show my responsibility by finding a job here? There are tons of places in the city! I'm sure I could find something."

Uncle James shook his head, disappointed he couldn't get through to me.

"Uncle James." I leaned forward, my eyes desperate. "I can't let him send me away. I can't."

Uncle James shook his head again, this time in total defeat. "Look. All I want is for you to do the right thing. I don't want you to leave, either! Who's going to make me laugh during the day? If you think that finding a job around here can stop him from sending you to God knows where, then…what the hell? What else is there to lose?"

I barely gave my dad time to answer when I told him I was going to look for a job so I could stay in Boston.

After my talk with Uncle James, I was more determined than ever to find work. Although I had very limited experience apart from my few modeling gigs at Jordan Marsh, I decided that would be the first place I would go. Plus, I had an in with Norma working there. She for sure could get me a job despite the chewing out she gave me the other night. Even if I had to be a sales girl, I would take whatever she gave me.

"What do you mean you won't recommend me for a job?" I exclaimed to Norma after explaining everything.

I had staked her out and found her after asking Dabney about any upcoming modeling gigs, which proved unsuccessful. I stood at her counter as she folded a sweater.

"You're kidding!" she said. "After what you did to Ellen? What a rotten thing! I still can't believe you pulled something like that. Then you end up on the front page of *Boston Today*! And not for discovering a cure for pneumonia."

I let out a haughty scoff. "How do you know it was me?"

"I'd know your mug anywhere," she sneered.

My eyes widened, and I scowled. "That's a nice thing to say to your friend."

"Some friend! First, you knew that Ellen loved that dress. And you still discouraged her from buying it, only to get it for yourself and have the audacity to wear it in front of her! Second, you end up on the front page of the newspaper outside a police raid—which you don't even seem the least bit sorry about—and third, you come in here after all that and expect me to get you a job? All so your father doesn't send you away?"

I let out an exasperated sigh. "Look, I'm sorry, all right? Is that what you want to hear?"

"Yes!" Norma said. "But I want you to mean it! Which you don't! You don't want a job so you can take responsibility, you want a job so you can get out of being sent away. You're selfish, Maggie. I just never said anything before. I put up with it because I thought it was just a small part of you. But it's who you are. I hope you learn from this. Because if you don't, you're gonna be real lonely for the rest of your life."

I didn't even bother to answer her. I turned around to leave, but she walked over from her counter and faced me.

She folded her arms in front of chest as if she were a schoolteacher.

"And don't you dare think about begging Ellen for a job. If you have any decency in you, you'll stay away from her."

"Decency? What's that supposed to mean?"

"If you go to Ellen for a job after what you did to her, then you truly have no heart. She wouldn't even want to see you anyway. Good luck wherever your father sends you. You're going to need it."

Norma strode away from me, going back to her counter.

I glared at her, a look which she returned, only her dark brown eyes made it look more menacing than mine. I left the store and walked down the street, contemplating going to Ellen despite Norma's warning.

I stood outside the hospital; however, I couldn't bring myself to go in. My anger at Norma returned. She should have kept her mouth shut about going to see Ellen. I wanted to go in just to spite her. I took a step toward the entrance, stopping at the door. The image of an angry Ellen drifted into my mind, and I let out an exasperated groan. I thought better of it and turned around to head home and start circling jobs in the newspaper.

CHAPTER SIX

I continued my relentless pursuit for a job, looking through the ads in the newspaper and circling every possible job that looked fitting. I circled everything from a telephone operator to a secretary in a dentist's office.

It had been over two weeks, and Dad was being ominously quiet about any follow ups on where he was sending me. I was beginning to believe my suspicions were true that he had been bluffing the whole time. However, I didn't want to be the one to mention it in the event he told me his plan was still on.

One morning, I sat at the breakfast table with the newspaper out in front of me, in an attempt to show how determined I was being.

When he came into the kitchen, he barely gave me or the paper a second look as he and my ma sat down.

"What if I came to work with you?" I asked.

He nearly choked on his coffee and looked up at me. "Absolutely not."

"Why? It can't be that hard. I can do what Ma does. I could be her assistant."

I almost laughed at the sight of my ma's eyes bulging out of her head at the thought of me working side by side with her. Although I had no intention to work for my dad, I still couldn't help but suggest it. The looks on their faces was too priceless to pass up.

"Absolutely not," Ma repeated, her expression still horrified.

I ran some of the job ideas by Uncle James, telling him I was going to answer the telephone operator ad in person. That way they had to give me a chance after I went out of my way to meet with them.

"First," Uncle James said, "don't act like you're gracing them with your presence. Remember, you want to make a good impression. Be thankful they give you the time of day at all. They may very well send you right out the door."

"I know," I said, waving off his lecture.

"Do you? I want to make sure you understand how important this is. If they end up giving you the job, you have to work to keep it. Don't slack off. If you do, you'll end right back where you started."

"I know," I said again. "You're supposed to be cheering me on, not making me nervous."

"I am cheering you on. I want you to get this job more than you do, but it's not easy. You have to have discipline and keep up with it."

I sighed. "I'm not going to go anywhere if you keep harping on me."

Uncle James held his hands up. "All right. I obviously can't stop you."

"Wish me luck?" A mixture of hope and anxiety passed through my voice.

"Good luck." Uncle James gave me a crooked smile.

"Thanks," I said, returning the gesture.

I backed out of his room and got dressed, deciding to wear a navy-blue tea dress with matching pumps. Not exactly the most business looking outfit, but it made me feel stylish and put together.

As I prepared to leave, my parents came out of the study and headed toward me.

"Maggie," Dad said, "come with us. We want to talk to you."

I took my hand off the door knob and followed them into the parlor, walking in cautiously.

I sat down in a chair, holding my clutch purse and the newspaper on my lap.

My ma sat in the dark brown leather couch across from me.

My dad stood, his hands in his pockets. His expression was serious, although I had a feeling about what he was going to tell me. I knew he had seen how hard I was trying to pursue a job, and he was going to tell me he wasn't sending me anywhere.

He circled in place, his silence unnerving me.

I fought off an eye roll as I mutely urged him to speed it up.

My ma remained seated, stoic as ever. I wondered why she even had to be here for this in the first place. I highly doubt she had anything to do with his verdict.

"We've come to a decision," Dad said.

I nodded, even though I knew exactly where this was going. I tried to keep my expression neutral, however, I couldn't help but let a faint smirk curl up at the corner of my lips.

"We're still figuring things out," he said. "But it's pretty much set into action."

"All right," I said. "Shoot."

My dad paused for a moment, and a look passed through his stern eyes that I couldn't decipher. His brows creased together, as if he were uncomfortable. He looked over at my ma and rubbed his hand on his chin. His stern expression returned, and he cleared his throat.

I leaned forward and raised my eyebrows expectantly. Was he waiting for a written invitation or something? It was like listening to *Suspense* on the radio. I was ready to tell him to spit it out when he opened his mouth to speak.

"You're going to Georgia."

"Georgia!" I echoed after a few moments of blinking in silent shock.

I mustn't have heard him correctly. Why, of all the places on Earth, would he send me there?

"Georgia," I said again in disbelief. "But that's…"

"The South," Ma said. *Now* she decides to pipe up.

"The Sou—you're sending me to the South?"

Dad nodded. "Savannah," he said, his tone matter of fact.

"Savannah?" I shot back. "Why? There's nothing there!"

"Actually, there's a lot there," Dad said. "We've been looking to start expanding there soon, once we've reached the entire Northeastern region—"

"Oh, I see." I nodded. "You're sending me out there to scope it out. See if it's a good place to run a business and not full of tumbleweeds."

"No," Dad said quickly. "We're sending you there to learn responsibility."

"What do you call this?" I waved the newspaper in my hand. "My wrist nearly fell off from all the circling I did in this thing."

"We told you this would be happening," Dad said. "It didn't matter how many jobs you circled in the paper. You're still going."

"But…but Savannah? At least send me somewhere I'd enjoy! Like California or Paris."

"That's not the point here," Dad said. "This isn't a vacation."

"So, what am I to do in Georgia?"

"There is an older woman there who is looking to rent out a room in her home in exchange for work. She needs help tending to her house and farm since her husband passed away over a year ago and she can't keep up with it herself anymore."

"How did you even find this lady?" I asked. "How did you even know about her?"

"That doesn't matter." Dad said, shaking off my question. "You are going to go and live with her—"

"For how long?" I interjected.

"As long as it takes," Dad said. "You are going to learn responsibility and maybe even pick up a little work ethic."

I fumed in my seat and looked over at my ma, who continued to sit quietly, irking me even more.

"And you're fine with this?" I said to her.

Ma closed her eyes and shook her head passively.

"Yes," she said. "Your father thinks this is best for you, and I agree with him."

I screwed my mouth up, shot out of my seat, and marched towards my dad.

"Dad, you can't do this!"

"Don't tell me what to do!" he scolded. "You're my child, and I will do with you what I think is necessary."

"But I'm not a child; I'm twenty-three!"

"Then start acting like it! You will go and stay with this woman, you will help her out around the house and her farm—"

"What kind of farm?" I demanded.

"I don't care. Whatever it is, you'll help her out with it. You will listen to her and do what she tells you to do. You have no say in this, Maggie. You lost that privilege when you decided to get caught up at an underground casino. Don't mess this up. This is your last chance." He turned, walking away from me.

"When do I leave?" I asked.

"July thirty-first," he said over his shoulder.

I added up the numbers in my head. "That's in three days!"

Dad stopped and stood in between the parlor and the foyer. He looked at me. His eyes held anger, and that strange flash of discomfort passed through again before he hardened his glare.

"Then you better get packing," he said before walking out of the room.

Uncle James let me bring a bunch of my stuff into his room so he could help me pack. Or—more so it was—Uncle James watched as I threw things into the two giant trunks that I was taking.

I had—yet again—refused to pack until the night before I was supposed to leave.

In a way, I was still in denial. But when my dad handed me my train ticket, one way stop to New York City where I would have to board another train to Georgia, it finally sunk in.

"How many shoes do you have?" Uncle James asked as I tried to decide whether to bring my black and white swing shoes or just the plain black ones.

"I'm going to be miserable there," I huffed. "I might as well look nice doing it."

"I don't think you're gonna do a lot of dancing there. Remember, you're there to help out that old lady. The black ones." He pointed to the shoes in my right hand.

I chucked them in and added a pair of penny loafers and my favorite pair of wedge sandals. Apparently, it was twice as hot in the South as it was here. I held out my bathing suit, a blue and white striped one piece with a square neckline.

"Axe the suit." Uncle James made a cutting motion across his throat.

I threw it on his bed.

"I still can't believe they're making me do this." I threw another dress into one trunk, and then a pair of trousers and a linen blouse into the other. I slammed them shut, struggling to close the one that contained my dresses and shoes. I plopped down on his bed which was now covered in my clothing.

"Hey," Uncle James said lightly. "It's not for forever. Who knows, maybe you'll only be there a week."

I grimaced. "A week? You're off your rocker if you think I'm going to be there a week. Dad is thrilled to have me gone."

"No, he isn't." Uncle James shook his head.

"Oh yeah? This is the first time he's acknowledged my existence in a long time. Mostly it's just 'hi, how are you? That's great, bye.'" I deepened my voice which made Uncle James chuckle. "And Ma! She just…goes along with whatever he says. The only time she ever has a mind of her own is when it comes to their work."

"That's not true."

I shook my head. "They can't wait to get me out of here. They'll probably forget they even have a daughter."

"They won't," Uncle James said. "If they do, I'll knock some sense into them."

This caused me to laugh for the first time in days, the feeling making the back of my throat tickle.

"You gonna miss me?" I said, giving him a side eyed glance.

"Of course, I am! You're the best Gin Rummy partner! You make me laugh, even at times when I don't think laughing is possible. It's gonna get real lonely without you here, kid."

I let my smile fall for a moment. I looked at my uncle, thinking about how this was probably the last time I would see him for I didn't even know how long. I took every last bit of him in. His brown eyes, his lopsided smile that the girls had always seemed to go wild for, and his hair that used to be slicked back but now always had one stray piece hanging over his left eye. I even thought about the wounds underneath his clothes that were slowly but surely healing over time. I hoped that he wouldn't have any spells while I was gone, or at least have any severe ones.

"You gonna miss me?" Uncle James finally said.

I pulled a face. "Not one bit," I said, adding a teasing smile.

Uncle James smiled back. He put his hands on his wheels. "Go get some sleep. Don't forget to say goodbye in the morning."

I walked over to him and bent over, wrapping my arms around his broad shoulders.

He returned the gesture, which made me hold onto him tighter.

"I'll write to you as much as I can." I let go of him and sighed. "Let's hope they have a post office down in Georgia."

Uncle James nodded and gave my arm a squeeze. "Goodnight, kid."

I placed my trunks in the foyer and cleaned up the remaining things on his bed I had brought down. I took one last peek at him. Something hitched in my chest, and I forced myself to smile.

"Goodnight, Uncle James."

CHAPTER SEVEN

I had to be up at seven o' clock in the morning to make the nine o' clock train. It would take me nearly an entire day to get all the way to Georgia, including the additional train I had to hop on when I got to New York. It didn't help that I had one of the worst night's sleep I've ever experienced. I tossed and turned relentlessly. Nothing helped. Not even the chug of whiskey I tiptoed down the stairs to ease my senses. If anything, it made my nerves even worse.

I choked down a quick breakfast of strawberries and oatmeal, washing it down with a cup of coffee. It was the only thing I could stomach. My insides twisted and turned, making anything I consumed taste sour and acidic.

I barely acknowledged my parents when they entered the kitchen.

Dad sat down across from me, taking his coffee from Siobhan.

"Maggie, I'll drive you down to the station," he said. "Are you all ready?"

I stuck my nose in the air. "No, thanks. I'll take a cab."

"You'd rather pay for a cab than have me drive you?"

"Yes." I kept my eyes off him.

"Fine," he muttered under his breath and took a sip of coffee.

Before heading out, I peeked into Uncle James' room where he was still asleep. I was torn between waking him up to tell him I was leaving or letting him sleep. I took a piece of paper from a notepad on my dad's desk, scribbled a quick goodbye, and placed it on the table next to his bed. I gave him a soft kiss on the forehead before backing out of his room.

I hailed a cab, sitting in between my two giant trunks and placing my makeup and hat box on my lap. When I finally made it to the train station, I was surprised to see how busy it was for being so early in the morning. I looked around, struggling to keep a grip on my luggage.

I stood on the platform, glancing around at my fellow travelers.

Men in business suits were already reading from a paper, and mothers tried to calm down their excited young children, one of which was whizzing a toy airplane around in circles over his head.

I rolled my eyes making a mental note to not sit near that kid. The train whistled in the distance, and my heart smashed inside my chest as it got closer. This was really happening. The train came to a complete stop, the steam wisping out at the top.

A rounded man with spectacles stepped out and began to punch people's tickets. I staggered forward. After he punched my ticket, he helped me with my luggage and placed it to the side.

"Is there any way you could put my things with the conductor or something?" I asked.

"The conductor?" he said, his voice gruff with early morning annoyance.

"I don't want my things getting mixed up with other luggage," I said, my own tone holding irritation.

"They won't," he argued swiftly.

"How can you be sure? There are at least four people with brown trunks like mine."

"You got your name on them?"

"Yes." I nodded.

"Then they'll be fine. Come on, girlie, you're holding everybody up."

I screwed my mouth up, now equally peeved as he was.

"Thanks a lot." I stepped onto the train and shuffled down the narrow aisle.

I looked around and found two empty seats, choosing the one next to the window.

A large man in a gray tweed suit sat next to me, folding his trench coat over his arm and placing a newspaper on his lap.

"Good morning," he acknowledged with a pleasant nod.

This guy better not chat away the whole train ride. I pursed my lips, gave him a quick nod, and turned my head toward the window.

The sound of the train whistle made my skin prickle. I felt a rumble, and before I knew it, the platform to South Station was getting farther away.

I bit the inside of my lip, angry and heated. I thought of my parents who were probably already at work and not even thinking about me. Then I thought of my Uncle James who would be sitting at the breakfast table by now. Although he'd be sitting by himself. He'd be doing a lot of that from now on.

I crossed my arms as I looked out at the sights of Boston that I normally loved. Now, I couldn't even bring myself to see the beauty my beloved city held.

I sat for another hour wallowing until I was told that there was a dining car on board. I brushed past my travel partner, who was nose deep into his newspaper, and headed toward the dining car, ordering a glass of champagne and a tuna sandwich. Not exactly the greatest meal, but it was all I could take at the moment.

When the train finally arrived in New York, I had the quick thought of skipping out on the next train and staying here. I would put aside that my hometown had a long historic beef with this city and find a hotel to stay at.

My dad had given me some money for a cab to pick me up at the Savannah train station. I also had some extra cash in my purse that I always kept stashed just in case. I for sure could afford at least one night here.

I then remembered that my dad had told me to write to him as soon as I got settled in Savannah, and that he would be expecting a follow up letter from the woman who I was to be living with to prove that I had indeed showed up safely.

My shoulders slumped as I realized my plan of staying behind in New York wouldn't work. I walked toward the platform to wait for the next train. This one would take me all the way to Georgia. A whopping total of seventeen hours. I was not prepared to sleep on a train full of people I didn't even know. My plan was to drink as much coffee as my body would allow in hopes that it would keep me awake.

The urge not to fall asleep was fighting me tooth and nail. I was shown to a sleeper car where the beds were practically on top of one another. I was able to find a place to put my luggage close by without worrying someone would take them in the middle of the night. Despite it not being the most comfortable of accommodations, I passed out the minute my head hit the pillow.

When I awoke the next morning, my neck was stiff, and my back ached. I hopped off the top bed and got dressed right away. I was served coffee and a hard-boiled egg with toast for breakfast. Even though I still struggled with my appetite, I ate it anyway.

We pulled into Savannah Station at eleven o'clock in the morning. When I got off the train, I was chagrined to see that it was raining. I didn't even bring my umbrella and realized with dread that the hat I brought would not hold up to the rain.

A stray newspaper sat on a bench across the way.

I trotted over to it, gripping onto my luggage, and grabbed the paper, holding it over my head. Now, I needed to find a way to get a cab.

"Need help, Miss?" a voice said.

I turned around to see a skinny young man with white-blond hair.

"I need a cab," I said, not caring that I didn't sound very polite.

"A Yankee." The thin man smiled.

"Excuse me?" I narrowed my eyes at him in irritation, still holding the paper over my head.

"Your accent. It's funny." He pointed at me. "You from up North?"

"Yes."

I didn't know why he thought my accent was funny. He sure as hell shouldn't have been talking.

"New York?" he said, still smiling.

I stared back at him in shock. "Boston," I said, not hiding the extreme offense I was feeling.

"What'cha doin' all the way out here?" he asked.

"I asked you where I can get a cab."

"You have to call for one," he said. "I can get one for you if you want."

"Thanks," I said, struggling to hold onto the newspaper that I still had over my head.

"Here." He picked up my two giant trunks. "I'll take these. Follow me."

"Thanks." I grabbed up my hat box and make up trunk and followed him toward a phone booth.

He set the trunks down and picked up the phone, turning the dial.

"Yeah," he said into the speaker. "I need a cab. It's not for me. It's for—" He looked at me. "Name?"

I exhaled. "Maggie O'Hanlon," I said, trying to save what was left of the dry parts of my hair.

"*May-ggie O'Hahn-lyn,*" he drawled.

I looked at him, completely put off at his butchering of my name.

He chatted for a few more moments, then hung up.

"Should be here any minute. Need me to wait here with you?" He put his smile back on.

I gave him an aggravated look. "I think I'll be fine. Thanks."

"Sure thing, Maggie," he said before walking away.

I gritted my teeth and cringed at the sound of my name coming out of his mouth. I walked over to the exit from the station and waited for the cab, the newspaper now sopping. I threw it to the ground seeing as there was no use for it anymore.

The rain didn't seem to be letting up any time soon, grating me even more. Not that we didn't have our fair share of rainy days in Boston, but something about the rain in Georgia seemed different. As if it was almost mocking me for being here.

The cab finally came after waiting for what felt like an eternity. The cab driver ran out and tipped his hat, smiling broadly. He looked like he could be no more than a year or so older than me.

"Morning, Miss," he said. "Are you Maggie O'Hanlon?"

"Yeah, hi," I said, struggling to pick my belongings up.

"I'll take care of those for you," he said.

He lifted up my luggage as if they were no heavier than a feather and put them in his trunk. After a moment of struggle, he closed the trunk shut and opened the back door, gesturing for me to get in.

"Miss?" he said.

"Thanks." I climbed in.

He slammed the door shut and jogged back to the driver's seat, trying his best to avoid getting too wet.

"Where you going, Miss?" he asked.

I handed him the piece of paper with the address written down. I had only just discovered that the lady who I was going to stay with was named Flora Alcott. I couldn't remember, though, if my dad had even told me her name in the first place. I was too angry at that moment to care otherwise.

"I know that place," he said. "You ain't never seen a house as nice as that."

I fought off an eye roll and snort. *Sure.*

He started up the engine, and we were off.

I sat uncomfortably, my dress still damp. I looked at the endless greenery that was out the window. Giant oak trees with leaves that hung down as if they were ready to snatch anyone up if they got too close. I craned my neck and gawked at the sheer size of them.

"Where are you from?" the cab driver asked.

I rolled my eyes, annoyed that he was nothing like the cab drivers in Boston where they let you be and don't bother with small talk.

"Boston," I said quickly.

"I figured you were from up North. Your Yankee accent gave it away."

"Well, you don't exactly sound like Clark Gable," I quipped.

The cab driver laughed. "You got me there. My name is Clark, though. So, what are you doing all the way down here in Savannah? Is Flora your relative or something?"

"No," I said curtly. "Why would I have a family member all the way out here?"

"I don't know," he said, keeping his eyes on the road. "A lot of folks have families that's all over the place. I figured maybe you knew her, that's all."

I shook my head and crossed my arms. I wasn't going to dignify this guy with why I was here. I hadn't been in Savannah for an hour, and people were already butting in and asking questions that were none of their concern.

"Flora's a real nice lady," he said. "Everybody loves her. She'd give you the coat off her back in the middle of a hurricane. She's a sweetheart to everybody she comes across. And she's one of the best cooks you'll ever meet. Do you like macaroni salad?"

"Huh?" I forgot he was even talking to me. He had been blabbing on for so long, I thought he was just filling the air. "Macaroni salad?"

"She makes the best macaroni salad. And you know what she puts in it? Pecans. It sounds strange, I know, but it's the best macaroni salad you'll ever taste. That woman puts pecans in pretty much anything. She owns a whole pecan farm."

I looked over at him. "A pecan farm?" I echoed.

"Mhm." He nodded. "Well, it was her husband's. He passed away, though. They would plant and harvest the pecans, then when the pecans were ready, he would send them over to Farmer's Food Company to have them shipped out all over Georgia. Acres and acres of pecan trees that go on forever. Maybe she'll show you around sometime. Probably not today though, it's kind of crummy out."

He slowed down and stopped for a moment to point out the windshield and turned towards me.

"See? Just beyond those trees, is her house."

I leaned forward. There were two rows of giant oak trees with the threatening leaves standing across from each other. We drove on the dirt path, and I looked up as the leaves hung above. Off in the distance was a little white speck. As we got closer, the speck turned into a large, white farmhouse. The front porch was gigantic and wrapped around the entire house. There must've been at least ten steps leading up to it. There was even a small balcony on the second story. I wondered how an old lady could live in such a big house by herself. Why didn't she just sell it after her husband died?

Finally, he stopped the car.

I looked out the window, and the front door to the house opened.

An older woman in a drab house dress with a light blue smocked pinafore over it stepped out onto the front porch. She must've been Flora. She wore a huge smile on her face that I could see from the back seat.

Clark jogged his way over to my door and opened it for me.

I couldn't stop looking at Flora. When I stepped out of the cab, she gave me an enthusiastic wave, which I didn't return.

Clark quickly opened his trunk, took out my luggage, and promptly brought it up to the front porch.

I scurried up the steps, thankful that Flora's front porch was completely dry.

Flora and Clark shared a quick, friendly conversation.

I handed him his money, and he tipped his hat.

"Welcome to Savannah, Maggie," he said, my name coming out smoother with his drawl than the other guy. He smiled and darted off towards his cab.

Flora smiled and clasped her hands together. "Well, hello, Margaret."

Her twang was bright and clear. She sounded as if she were happy all the time.

"Maggie," I said bluntly.

"Oh, I'm sorry, hon. Maggie. I'm Flora."

"Pleased to meet you," I forced myself to say.

"Oh, come here, honey!" She wrapped her arms around me, nearly squeezing me to death.

I stood frozen, my arms limp at my sides, as she smothered me with her hug. I got a whiff of her perfume. Or at least I thought it was perfume. She smelled sweet like honey, with a small hint of something floral.

She let go and held my arms, looking directly at me, her smile never faltering.

"I'm sorry," she said. "I'm just so glad you're finally here! And look at you! Aren't you pretty? But my goodness, honey, have you eaten today? You look starved. Oh, where are my manners? I'm so sorry, hon, come on in. Listen to me chattering away while you're still drenched from the rain. I'll let you change, of course. That's such a pretty dress you have on. Come on in, don't be shy!"

Flora finally took a moment to breathe while she led the way into her home, taking one of my trunks and my hat box in her hands. The foyer was bright and warm. Even though the skies were gray outside, it still looked as if the sun was shining through the windows. Flora set my things down and wiped her hands on her apron.

I surveyed the foyer. There was a little bench that sat across from the door and next to the main staircase. The plain white wall was accented by a large painting of numerous rows of trees.

"I'm awful sorry I didn't come and get you myself." Flora's voice broke through my thoughts. "I wanted to make sure the house looked nice and spiffy for you. I did your room up and everything. Had I known it was gonna rain, I would've come and picked you up."

I shook my head, completely drained from the day so far. "It's nothing."

"I should've had a feeling it was going to rain. August is usually one downpour after another for us."

I nodded dully and shivered, running my hand across my arm.

"Oh, dear." Flora rubbed my arm. "I'm sorry. You must be terribly chilled. Why don't you go change? Are you hungry? I'll whip you up something nice and make you some tea. First, let me help you bring your things up. My goodness, what lovely traveling bags! It's got your name on 'em and everything!"

I followed Flora up the stairs.

She struggled a bit with bringing my trunk and hat box up, having to grab on to the newel post for support once she reached the top step. She let out a few quick, heavy breaths before soldering on.

Flora opened the door to the room that I would be staying in. "Take your time, honey. Come on down when you're all settled."

She left the room and went back downstairs.

I was disappointed to see how ordinary the room was. The head and foot-board of the bed were plain white bars, and the bedsheets were white with a quilted sage green blanket on top. I threw my trunks on the bed and sat down, not caring that I was getting the blanket damp.

I fiddled with my thumbs and looked around the boring room. There wasn't even a radio in here. Besides the bed, there was a small door, which I assumed was the closet, a bureau with a vanity mirror, a small, slanted writing desk with a chair, and a little bedside table with a drawer. I opened the drawer to find a Bible placed inside. I closed the drawer, rolling my eyes. I hoped she didn't expect me to attend church with her.

I couldn't believe that this would be where I was staying. It was so bland, the only bit of color coming from the blanket. Even the walls were horribly white. A person could go crazy in here. I got up from the bed and walked toward the window, looking out at the dreary day. I wished I had gotten the room with the balcony; that way, I could jump off it.

CHAPTER EIGHT

When I had finally dressed and applied fresh makeup, I went downstairs and walked into Flora's kitchen, which was just as bright as the foyer. It had a yellow and white color scheme with pale blue accents thrown in. Flora was pouring boiling water into a tea cup when I entered.

"Oh, there you are," she said. "You get all settled in?"

I nodded, standing awkwardly in the middle of the room.

"Sit down." She motioned to the table with her oven mitt clad hand. "Be right over."

I sat at the table, and Flora placed down the steaming cup of tea, which I didn't even like in the first place. I was a coffee drinker. Tea tasted like wet socks to me.

Flora came back over and placed a hunk of what looked like coffee cake in front of me.

Cinnamon instantly drifted into my nose, and my mouth watered.

I inspected the coffee cake. A cinnamon and sugar mixture sat on top with what looked like some kind of nut. It wasn't until I put two and two together that I realized it was the pecans the cab driver said she put in everything. Flora sat down across from me, a cup of tea in her hands.

"Well, don't be shy, honey. Dig in!" she said.

I picked up the fork that Flora had given me with the plate of coffee cake and took a bite. If there was one thing this lady had going for her, it was her cooking. I had to admit that this was probably the best coffee cake I ever had, even the strange addition of the pecans were tasty.

Flora watched me, smiling as I ate, which made me uncomfortable.

I stopped mid bite and glared up at her.

"Oh, I'm sorry, hon." She picked up her cup of tea and stood. "I'll let you eat. I have some cleaning up to do anyway. Take your time. Did you get to unpack everything?"

I shook my head, my mouth still full.

"Well, when you're finished eating, you can unpack. I'm going to be starting up dinner in a little while. We eat at five. Chicken and dumplings and string beans."

I barely had time to swallow, and she was already telling me about dinner. I shifted my eyes awkwardly, then realized that the reason she wasn't leaving is because she was waiting for my answer. I chewed what was in my mouth and swallowed deeply.

I put on a smile. "Sounds lovely," I said dryly.

Flora smiled and walked out of the kitchen, finally giving me a moment's peace to eat.

I wanted to take my time with the coffee cake, but since Flora was going to start dinner soon, I shoveled it into my mouth and choked down the tea which was much sweeter than I had expected.

I ran into Flora on the way upstairs.

"How was it?" she asked.

"It was good. I didn't know you could put pecans in coffee cake." I began to climb up the stairs.

"Oh, it's pecan bread," Flora said, causing me to stop. "It's my special recipe. I put pecans in practically everything."

I nodded. "Well, it was very good. Oh, and I just kept my plate and cup on the table."

"Oh..." Flora hesitated for a moment. "All right. I'll clean it up for you."

"Thanks," I said.

"You take your time unpacking. I'll let you know when dinner is ready."

I nodded again. "All right." I charged up the stairs so I wouldn't have to engage in further conversation with her.

After dinner, Flora insisted we go out and sit on the back porch to chat since we didn't get to during the day.

I was exhausted, and sitting on the porch chatting was the last thing I wanted to do. But when she handed me a large glass of iced tea, I dragged myself out and sat on the porch swing next to her.

At least it wasn't raining anymore. It was slightly muggy, with a warm breeze billowing through every now and then. The smell of the air was clean and fresh. Crickets chirped one after another, and Flora's wind chimes next to her screen door sang out behind us.

"So," Flora said after a contemplative moment of silence and rocking the swing back and forth, "tell me about yourself. You're from Boston?"

I nodded. "Yeah." I took a sip of the iced tea which was even sweeter than the hot one.

"That's nice. It's such a beautiful city. I've never been, but I've seen pictures. What part do you live in?"

"Beacon Hill," I said flatly. "It's in the North End."

"Oh, right." She nodded. "That's a fancy area. Lots of important folks have lived there."

I took another sip of my drink, staring straight ahead. The crickets that I couldn't see kept chirping away. I didn't know how people could live out here and not go insane with all the sounds.

"Now, your daddy," Flora said, her voice intruding on my thoughts once again, "he runs that big grocery store. That must be nice."

I sighed deeply. "Yes. It is."

"And he owns multiple of them, is that right? All over the Northeast?"

I wanted Flora to stop talking and leave me alone. I would have even gone up to my bedroom if it meant not having to listen to her chatter away. I nodded and let out an intentional and dramatic yawn.

"Oh, I'm sorry, honey!" Flora said. "There I go, again. You must be exhausted. Here I am chatting your ear off. I'm terribly sorry. Why don't you go on up to bed? We can talk tomorrow, when you're more bright eyed and bushy tailed."

Bright eyed and *what*? I didn't care, though. I was too tired to think about her strange phrases. I lifted myself up from the porch swing.

"Yeah," I said. "I am kind of tired. Um, I guess I should give you this?"

I handed my still half full glass out to her, which she took after a moment of hesitation.

"Well, good night." She put on her smile again. "Go on up to bed now, and I'll see you in the morning. I'll have a big breakfast ready for you."

I nodded, then hauled myself off the porch and ran upstairs. I got ready for bed, glad that I had decided to bring along my hair rollers and night cream. I opened the window before crawling into bed. I laid flat on my back and closed my eyes.

Despite my exhaustion, I couldn't fall asleep. This wasn't my room. This wasn't my bed. The sheets were itchy, and the pillow was too fluffy.

My mind wandered to Uncle James who was probably in bed now as well, but lucky for him, sound asleep. I wondered if he thought of me at all that day. I refused to let my mind think about my parents. They were the reason I was here in the first place. I shook my head as I silently cursed them for making me come here. If my dad hadn't blown his top so dramatically, I could be lying in my own bed right now instead of hundreds of miles away in Georgia.

I closed my eyes again, deciding to keep my mind on my uncle, hoping it would help me fall asleep. My breathing slowed, and a small bit of peacefulness rushed over me until I heard the loudest croak outside my window. I opened my eyes slowly; the sound of a bullfrog going off made me want to throw a pillow at it. I got out of bed and slammed the window shut.

I lay back down, trying to get myself back into my sleeping position. I closed my eyes when the damn frog croaked again. I turned my head toward the window, giving it a look of scorn. How was it possible that I could still hear it? I lay on my back for the rest of the night, my eye twitching each time the frog croaked. It wasn't until what felt like several hours later that I finally drifted off to sleep.

The sound of knuckles rapping against a door made me flinch. I had managed to turn over in the middle of the night. My face that was slathered in night cream was pressed into the sheets, and I could also feel a small spot of drool beneath my lips as well. I opened one eye, then closed it when the rapping came again. I cringed, letting out a groggy groan. The door creaked open, and the soft sound of shuffling feet entered the room.

"Rise and shine!" a bright, springy voice said.

It wasn't until I heard Flora's voice that I remembered I was in Savannah and not my own bed. For some reason, I hoped that everything within the past two days had been a bad dream. I squinted my eyes open and rolled over a bit. The sun wasn't even shining yet.

"What time is it?" I croaked.

"Five o'clock!"

"In the morning?"

"That's right! Time to get up!"

"Ugh!" I pressed my face back into the sheets. "I barely slept! Come back around eight."

I buried myself under the blanket. The sound of Flora's footsteps walking closer to the bed made me cringe.

"Well," she said, "I suppose I could let you do that. But I got a great big breakfast waiting for you, and there's lots of work that needs to be done before lunch."

I groaned again and threw the covers off my face.

Flora's hands flew to her cheeks. "Oh, my!"

"What?" I grumbled.

"Oh, honey, your face!"

My eyes widened, and I shot up, leaning on my elbows for support. "What? What's wrong with it?"

"You've got gunk all over it." She made a circling motion around her face.

I exhaled and rolled my eyes, lying back down. "It's not gunk. It's my night cream. I wear it so it doesn't dry my skin out during the night."

"Oh," Flora said, untensing a little and placing her hand on her heart. "Well, that's good to hear. Looks like your hair had quite the night too."

I reached up and touched my hair. At least one side was completely out of its rollers. I sighed in exasperation.

"I'll let you get ready," Flora said. "Take your time, but please don't be too long. Don't want your breakfast getting cold."

Once I managed to roll myself out of bed after several minutes of lying, splayed out on my back and staring at the ceiling, I took my night cream—or what was left of it—off my face and took my rollers out and brushed my hair. I put on my pink robe and slipped into a pair of my morning slippers before trotting down the stairs, letting out a giant yawn.

As I made my way around the bottom of the stairs, the front door swung open, and I nearly skidded across the floor.

An older woman with short, fluffy gray hair stepped into the foyer and stood before me. Her drooped shoulders straightened, and she gave me an immediate glare of disapproval. Her narrow blue eyes were accompanied by a slight unibrow just above them.

"You must be Margaret." Her harsh accent was a stark contrast to Flora's lilt and cheerful one.

Who the hell was this woman, and how did she know my name? I couldn't help but gape at her. My brain was too fuzzy for this early morning nonsense.

Flora patted into the hallway and smiled. "Maggie, I see you met my good friend, Clarabelle Barnett. Good morning, Clarabelle."

"Morning, Flora," Clarabelle said, giving her a quick glance before turning her attention back to me.

She traced me up and down with her gaze. This lady looked like she never smiled a day in her life. Her thin lips curled up as she continued to stare me down. I didn't like her already.

"So, you're Margaret," she said to me.

"Maggie," I corrected, my voice tight.

Clarabelle shook her head. "Margaret's the name your daddy and mama blessed you with?"

"What?" I said, not caring that my tone was coming across disrespectful. I wasn't in the mood for an early morning lecture. From what I've seen so far, Flora didn't have one bean of coffee in this place, something I was horribly desperate for.

"Margaret. It's your birth name?" Clarabelle said.

"Nobody calls me Margaret," I said. "Not even my parents. I like to be called Maggie."

Clarabelle shook her head again. "I don't believe in nicknames. You go by the name your daddy and mama blessed you with."

Flora's eyes darted back and forth between me and Clarabelle as if we were about to square off in a duel.

"Why don't we go have some breakfast; it's just about ready." Flora said, attempting to break the tension. "I'll make everyone some tea."

We followed Flora into the kitchen. I slowly sat down at the table, my eyes still matched with Clarabelle's, who was watching every small move I made.

"You always make an entrance in your bathrobe?" Clarabelle asked.

"What? You don't?" I said haughtily.

"Nope," Clarabelle said pointedly. "I get up at four-thirty AM every day and get dressed. First thing I do."

"Well, some of us like to wait a bit before getting ready for the day," I said as Flora placed a cup of tea and a plate in front of me.

I aggressively unfolded my napkin and placed it on my lap. I looked down at my plate to see a glob of white stuff with gray chunks in it. It was on top of what looked like some kind of biscuit peeking out from the bottom. I tilted my head. The biscuit was completely covered.

Flora placed two other large plates on the table, one with scrambled eggs and the other with bacon.

"Um, what's this?" I pointed at my plate.

"Biscuits and gravy," Flora said.

"*That's* gravy?" I asked.

Flora nodded. "It's a Southern specialty."

"What's the gray stuff in it?"

"Ground up sausage."

Clarabelle watched us, sipping her tea slowly as I looked down at my plate. I shot a glance up at her.

"Is anything wrong, honey?" Flora asked, concern in her voice.

"You know, I think I'll stick with the eggs and bacon." I gave my plate a light push away from me. "And do you have coffee instead of tea?"

"Ha!" Clarabelle squawked.

I locked eyes with her and folded my arms against my chest, giving off my best challenging look.

"Yes?" I said.

"Why don't you just eat the darn biscuits and gravy and drink the darn tea, and appreciate it?"

Clarabelle echoed my arm crossing. Her upper lip curled slightly. She must've made that face so many times, it was probably stuck that way.

"Oh," Flora said. "That's all right. Maggie just isn't used to this kind of food, that's all. I should have just made regular biscuits with the eggs and bacon."

Clarabelle puckered her lips and shook her head. "Uh-uh. When we were growing up, we were raised to eat what was put in front of us or go hungry. Didn't matter if you liked it or not, you appreciated what was given to you."

"It's fine, Clarabelle, really," Flora pleaded. "We have a lot to get done, and I'd like to get on it as soon as possible. Maggie, just eat what you like here and then get dressed for the day."

"What are we doing today?" I asked.

"Well, there is lots of house work that has to be done," Flora said. "This morning, we need to go out to the farm and see if the rain and wind did any damage to the pecan trees."

"Isn't rain good for trees, though?" I asked.

"Well, if the wind is coming at ungodly speeds, then it can make the pecans fall off the trees and onto the soiled ground," Clarabelle said. "If the pecans are on the ground too long, they can go bad or get snatched up by critters."

"Are uh…are you staying with us today?" I asked Clarabelle.

She gave a curt nod. "Yes, indeed." She matched my eye contact once again. "And I sure hope you brought a pair of pants with you. You won't get a lot of work done in a dress."

I choked back a snort as I took a sip of the now cold tea. I did bring a few pairs of my favorite trousers with me. But Clarabelle was bonkers if she thought I'd wear them to get work done in. This was my first full day here anyway. I wasn't planning on doing too much. I don't think Flora would mind if I was more of a bystander today, seeing as I knew next to nothing about housework let alone working on a pecan farm.

"I did bring trousers, actually," I said coolly.

"All right, then," Flora said, smiling once again. "Finish up your breakfast and get dressed. We'll get to work right away."

CHAPTER NINE

I took my time getting ready.

After Flora knocked on my bedroom door to check on me a few times, Clarabelle brought it upon herself to barge upstairs and bang on my door like she was an army officer during wake-up calls.

When I stubbornly refused to answer, she opened the door, walking in on me mid-change. I gasped and covered my breasts that were nearly spilling out of my bra.

"What's the big idea?" I said, throwing myself behind the bed.

"The early bird catches the worm, little missy. You're slower than a snail in molasses!"

"Do you mind? I'll be right down!"

"Move it, Margaret!" she said, slamming the door behind her.

"Maggie!" I shouted.

After getting dressed, I put on my straw wide-brimmed hat and round white sunglasses and wedge sandals. I made my way downstairs and outside, where I was bombarded by the sweltering heat.

Flora and Clarabelle were already waiting for me at the bottom of the front steps.

"Oh, good Lord," Clarabelle groaned as I approached them. "How do you expect to do any work in that?"

Both her and Flora wore cotton blouses with gray overalls and work boots. They each wore a small straw hat.

"What?" I said. "They're trousers. You said to wear pants."

"Yeah, but not ones that look like you stole them from Katharine Hepburn! And what's with the hat? You late getting back to your plantation at Tara?"

"She didn't know," Flora said. "Let's not give Maggie too much trouble. I'll buy her a pair of overalls and a more appropriate hat."

Clarabelle let out a grunt. "Well, thanks to your dawdling, we're an hour behind schedule."

"I made it, didn't I?"

"Yes," Clarabelle sniped. "One hour later. Come on, Scarlett O'Hara." She walked toward an old truck alongside Flora.

I rolled my eyes and followed them, trekking down the long pathway.

Flora got in the driver's seat, and Clarabelle climbed in right next to her.

I walked up to the truck, noticing there was only one long seat, and that the bed of the truck was filled by rakes, shovels, and buckets.

"What am I supposed to do, ride on the top?" I asked.

"No," Flora said, "you sit next to Clarabelle."

Clarabelle scooted into the middle part of the seat and let out an irritated huff.

"An hour and five minutes," she squawked.

I gave her a salty look all while hoisting myself up into the truck, nearly losing my hat in the process. I slammed the door, and Flora backed out of the driveway and drove through the awning of trees. I stared out the window, watching everything pass by.

Clarabelle kept letting out grunts, and it wasn't until I realized that every time I moved my head, the brim of my hat would whack her in the face. I whipped my head forward, which caused Clarabelle to let out a louder grunt than usual and me to grin with satisfaction.

After a few minutes of bumpy driving, we finally arrived at our destination. I held on to my hat as I hopped out of the truck. When I closed the door, I stopped in my tracks, letting my hand fall to my side as I stared out at the endless rows of pecan trees. There must've been hundreds of them. There were so many, I couldn't tell where the farm ended and began.

"Holy smokes," I said.

"Pretty, isn't it?" Flora said, a huge smile of pride on her face. She stood next to me, carrying a rake and a bucket.

"It's…impressive," I said, still shocked that there could be this many trees in one place.

My brows furrowed, and I realized that the pecan farm looked exactly like the painting that hung in Flora's foyer.

Clarabelle sauntered over carrying two buckets.

"Well, you're not gonna get much done by staring at it." She shoved a bucket into my hands. "Here. We need to make sure the pecans didn't get damaged."

Clarabelle led the way toward the first tree.

I trudged through, immediately regretting my shoe choice. The ground was still a bit wet from the rainstorm the day before, and I could feel my wedges digging into the wet dirt and grass. I stood holding the bucket that Clarabelle had given me and watched as Flora lifted the rake above her head and shook the leaves of the tree with it. After a moment's struggle, a few pecans came tumbling to the ground. Flora picked one up and inspected it.

"Not too bad." She threw it into her bucket and picked up a few more pecans. "Maggie, come here."

I unsteadily walked over to Flora, my arms stretched out like I was walking a tightrope. I caught a glimpse of Clarabelle rolling her eyes as I shuffled past her. When I made it over to Flora, she held out her hand, showing me the pecans in her palm.

"See that?" she said. "The shells are green now because they still have some time to grow. Notice how most of 'em are completely closed up? By October, they should be fully ready to harvest."

"October?" I asked. "You mean, they're not even ready to use yet?"

"Well, fall is the best time for harvesting. Some pecans aren't even ready until November."

November? My heart dropped at the thought of being stuck in Savannah until November. I didn't think I could last that long.

I shook my head. "That's three whole months! Is there a chance they could be ready, I don't know, in September or something?"

"Well, we have had instances where the pecans were ready early, but most of the time, October is our best month. That's when the pecans are fully matured and are easier to cook with and distribute to the public. You don't want to be putting out unripe pecans that aren't ready for use."

"In other words," Clarabelle piped in, "no."

I gave her a side-eyed glance through my sunglasses. Why was she even here? It's not like she was part of Flora's business. Her presence was not required.

"Here, honey. You try," Flora held the rake out to me.

"Uh, no thanks." I waved my hand at her. "I believe you. You look like you got most of them anyway."

"Oh, there's more where that came from!" Flora smiled.

"Plus, that's just the first tree," Clarabelle said, clearly enjoying my discomfort.

I shot Clarabelle a look and snatched the rake from Flora. I took a few more steps and lifted the rake up, slowly swatting at the tree, the tip of the rake barely touching any leaves.

"You actually gotta touch the tree, Scarlett O'Hara," Clarabelle said.

"Get right up in there," Flora said encouragingly.

I nudged forward and lifted the rake higher into the tree and rustled it around, I felt a branch and tugged at it. To my surprise, a bunch of pecans came down, hitting me on the head before dropping to the ground.

"Ow!" I clamped my hand onto my head.

"Wonderful!" Flora exclaimed. "See? That wasn't so bad, was it?"

I handed her back the rake. "Yeah, that was a blast," I said dryly. "Now what?"

"Now, we move on to the rest," Flora said, marching forward.

Clarabelle followed close behind her, offering me a pompous side eye and callous snort as she walked by.

After a long morning at the pecan farm, we stopped in Downtown Savannah to buy food and other goods at Minton's Market, which was incredibly smaller than O'Hanlon's or any other grocery store in Boston. Right next to it stood Minton's Butchery, where the board and posters outside advertised beef for fifteen cents—a complete steal.

I stayed in the truck while Flora and Clarabelle went inside. I was surprised to see that there was actually civilization out here. Although it wasn't nearly as hustling as Downtown Boston, it was still quite active. I noticed that there was a place called a honky tonk that looked to be some sort of bar. It didn't seem to be open at this time, though.

When we finally got back to the house, I immediately planted myself in the first armchair that I encountered. After being out in the hot Savannah sun and working on the pecan farm for so many hours, I thought I would knock right out in the chair and sleep for days. I was chagrined however, when Flora told me that we would take a small break for lunch and then do some cleaning around the house.

I took my hat off, fanning myself with it. I could not wrap my head around how these old ladies didn't get tired after so much work. There must've been more than sugar in their tea.

"How are you not beat?" I asked. "Why don't we do it tomorrow?"

"Because tomorrow I have something special planned for us. You're going to love it!"

Flora walked into the kitchen with Clarabelle following close behind.

"Nice hair," she said as she passed by.

I touched my hair and groaned. The top of my head was completely flat—and sweaty. One of the reasons I had taken my sweet time this morning was mainly because of my hair. I huffed as I hoisted myself from the chair and followed them into the kitchen.

After lunch, which was macaroni salad, pimento cheese sandwiches, and iced tea, Flora and I did work around the house.

Clarabelle had weaseled her way out of that by going home for the day.

Flora cleaned the upstairs, while she tasked me with cleaning the downstairs.

Even though we had opened every window and door in the house, it still felt like the heat was coming from Death Valley, prompting me to do something I had never done—or would ever have the audacity to do: I rolled up my trousers, letting out a disgruntled whimper thinking about how wrinkled they would be by the end of the day. I took off my sandals in exchange for my bare feet, which Flora seemed to be concerned with but didn't say anything.

I was to sweep the entire downstairs and porch, as well as dust the furniture and the decor. I sneezed my way through dusting, hoping that I could plead allergies so Flora wouldn't make me do it again. I took my time, working on the inside before moving to the outside. As I swept and dusted, I became unsure of why Flora wanted us to clean the house in the first place. It wasn't dirty. If anything, it was almost as well kept as my house.

When I moved to the outside, I could barely stand the tediousness anymore. I cleaned quickly, sweeping the so-called dirt off the porch. After I finished, I plopped myself on one of the wicker rocking chairs and let out a deep breath. I didn't know how much more of this I could take.

The day had seemed to drag on. Finally, dinner time came, which meant I could relax until it was time to go to bed. Since we had a long, packed day, dinner was a bit later than it was the night before. Flora made fried pork chops with mashed potatoes and something she called collard greens. I had to admit, it was quite good. The collard greens, however, I could do without.

After Flora cleaned up everything, I excused myself, pleading exhaustion—which I was—but it was more of a tact to avoid small talk for the rest of the night.

I took a bath, closing my eyes and letting the hot water soothe my aching body. I heard Flora come up the stairs and shut her bedroom door. She seemed to go to sleep early; it was barely even eight thirty. I didn't know how she did it.

Although I was tired and my muscles were sore, there was still a part of me that wanted to do something. If I were still at home, I'd be getting ready to go out to Louie's Bar right about now. My eyes shot open, and I suddenly remembered the honky tonk downtown. My mind spun as I thought of how I could get out of here and go out and have some fun. Flora did have a truck. Although I've really only driven my dad's Alfa Romero, I figured a truck couldn't be too difficult. I just hoped I could remember where this honky tonk was.

I wondered what the guys around here were like. I didn't count the two I had met when I first got here; the first one was too goofy, and the cab driver chatted more than I had cared to. I decided not to fret over it. I needed to get out of here and be amongst people my own age. I might go crazy if I'm only talking to two old ladies day in and day out; one of whom was too nice bordering on irritating, and the other who drove me up a wall just by looking at her.

When I finished my bath, I redid my hair properly, slapped on my makeup, and put on my navy tea dress. As I made my way out of my room, I glanced down the dark hallway. Flora had to be knocked out by now. I carefully climbed down the stairs and made my way out to the front porch, practically tiptoeing down it as well. The sound of the bullfrog's croak made my head snap up.

"Oh, shut up!" I hissed at it in a hushed voice.

I took one glance behind me, then hightailed it toward the truck and climbed in the driver's seat. I grabbed the keys that Flora kept on the dashboard, shaking my head at her simple-mindedness. She clearly has never lived in a big city. I searched around, letting myself become acquainted with the truck. I revved up the noisy engine, put my foot on the gas pedal, and backed out of the long pathway, driving toward the honky tonk for a few hours of freedom.

CHAPTER TEN

I ended up getting lost for a few minutes, however, I was able to eventually find the honky tonk. This time, the outdoor lights were all lit up, and music blasted from the inside. I walked in, the smell of smoke smacking me in the face. Despite that, it was cleaner than I had expected. In a way, it was a bit like Louie's with its hard wood floors and live band.

The music was certainly different from back home. I didn't like it very much. There were too many string sounds going on. I thought of busting out of here and seeing if I could find another place but didn't want to risk getting lost again, so I searched for the bar area. I made my way through the people dancing, finally finding the bar lined up with stools. I sat on one and glided my hand across the wooden bar top. Even the bar area was as well kept up as Louie's.

The bartender walked over and offered a polite smile.

"What can I get you, Miss?" he asked.

"Ward Eight," I said, taking my surroundings in.

"Come again?" he asked, leaning his head towards me.

"Ward Eight," I said again, a little louder.

"Ward Eight?" He furrowed his brows. "Sorry, Miss. I never heard of that. What's in it?"

I clasped my hands together, trying and failing to hide my irritation.

"Rye whiskey, grenadine, lemon juice, orange juice, and maraschino cherries."

"Oh, all right." He nodded. "I'm sorry, but I don't have grenadine."

I sighed. "I'll take a martini. Extra dry."

"Coming right up!" he said.

Within twenty seconds, he placed my drink in front of me. I took a sip. It burned like hell. I loved it.

I turned around in my stool and leaned my back against the bar top, crossing one leg over the other and swinging it back and forth. I scanned the honky tonk, listening to the loud country music that was wailing from the band. I took another sip of the martini, extending my leg like Claudette Colbert in *It Happened One Night*.

"Miss," one guy greeted while walking past me.

After a few more guys had walked past me with so much as a nod of greeting, I craned my neck to see a guy making his way over to this area. Once he was close enough, I hopped off the stool, pretending to trip.

"Oh!" I gasped. He caught me, holding onto my elbows.

"Are you all right?" he asked, checking to make sure I didn't hurt anything.

"I'm sorry," I said. "I'm so clumsy."

"You better be careful," he said. "These floors can get real slippery. Many folks just go flying across and twist their ankles or something. Are you sure you're okay?"

"Yes, thank you." I offered him a smile and extended my hand. "I'm Maggie."

"I'm Beau." He took my hand in his and shook it.

"Bow? Like bow and arrow?"

He let out a soft chuckle. "No, like Beauregard. Everybody calls me Beau."

"Oh," I said, giving him a ditsy laugh. "Of course."

"Beau!" a woman's voice called out.

I turned my head to see a young woman about my age walking over toward us.

She wore a green and brown plaid dress, and her curly hair was in a low ponytail.

"Beau, what're you doing?" she said. "You're supposed to be getting our drinks."

"I'm sorry, Essie. I was just helping Maggie here. She fell off her stool as I walked by. Maggie, this is my wife, Essie."

"How do you do?" I said flatly.

"Fine, thanks. Are you all right? You didn't sprain nothing, did you?"

Essie's face and voice expressed genuine concern. I was surprised that she seemed to care for someone she barely knew.

"No," I said. "Just being clumsy."

"Well, these stools can be tricky. I'm glad you're all right, though. It was nice meeting you. Come on, Beau. Let's get our drinks." She locked her arm in his.

"Nice meeting you, too," I said unenthusiastically, as they walked away to the other end of the bar.

I stood awkwardly, holding my martini. I turned to sit back in my seat, but someone had taken it while my flirting attempts were being thwarted by Essie.

I took another sip.

"Maggie?" someone said.

I looked over to where the voice was coming from and saw the cab driver walking toward me.

Great.

"Maggie, what are you doing here?"

"Hi, um…"

"Clark," he prompted.

"Clark. I just wanted to get out for a little."

"Flora work you real hard?"

"You have no idea. I got blisters from using the rake."

"She took you to her pecan farm, then? Isn't it something else?"

"Yeah, sure is," I said dryly.

"Sometimes she spends her whole day there working with Clarabelle."

I let out a snort. "Yeah, Clarabelle. She's another one."

"Real piece of work, that lady. But her heart's in the right place."

"She has a heart?"

Clark laughed. "Yeah. Real deep, deep down."

I didn't realize how much Clark resembled Mickey Rooney. Without his cab driver hat, I saw that he had strawberry blond hair and light hazel eyes. His face was full and youthful, a slight contrast to his scrawny figure.

"I help them out at the farm sometimes," he said. "You know, if they really need it."

"Why does she need me, then? Why don't you work with her?" I asked. "She obviously knows you."

"I have my cab driving job too. I only help out when I can, and if she wants it."

I rifled through my clutch to give the bartender money for my drink. To my delight, I found a stray cigarette and match at the bottom as well. I lit the cigarette and took a puff.

"Well, I—" I stopped short, my attention now fixated on the entrance. "Oh, great."

I kept my eyes straight ahead where I saw Clarabelle, her head looking around for something. She waltzed in, sticking out like a sore thumb amongst the herds of young people here. Clark must've seen my reaction because he looked in the same direction I was.

"Is that Clarabelle?" he said.

Clarabelle scoured the place until her gaze came upon me. She twisted her mouth up and charged over, her arm swinging like a pendulum. Her eyes never faltered from mine. She appeared as if she had just rolled out of her bed. Her hair was all mussed up, and she was wearing a light green house dress that looked like it had been thrown on.

"Margaret," she sniped.

"Hello, Clarabelle," Clark said.

"Not now, boy," she shot at him.

"What are you doing here?" I asked through gritted teeth.

"I should be asking you the same thing. There I am in my bed, sleeping peacefully, then the next thing I know, I'm woken up by the ungodly sound of a truck. I get out of bed to see Flora's truck passing by my house. I knew it couldn't be her because she goes to bed at the same time I do, so I had only one guess."

"You followed me here?" I narrowed my eyes.

Without answering me, she snatched my martini out of my hand and slammed it down on the bar top.

"Were you just sitting out there waiting for me to come out or something?" I asked.

Again, she didn't answer. She wrenched the cigarette out of my other hand, threw it on the floor, and ground it out with her foot.

"Disgusting, despicable things!" She grabbed my wrist and tried to pull me toward her.

"Let go!" I dragged my feet against the floor, struggling to pull my wrist out of her tight grasp.

"Clarabelle, she wasn't doing anything wrong," Clark pleaded.

"Hush!" Clarabelle snapped at him. "You stay out of this, Clark. Let's go, Margaret."

She pulled my arm and dragged me towards the door.

I looked back at Clark, who stood back with an equally confused and stunned expression.

Once we were outside, I was able to yank my wrist out of her grip. I breathed heavily as anger surged through me.

"What's the big idea?" I said, my eyes fuming.

"Why did you take Flora's truck and sneak out?" Clarabelle countered.

"I just wanted to get out for the night! I wanted to have fun! Back home, I always—"

"Well, you're not back home, Margaret." Clarabelle said.

"First of all, my name is Maggie!" I said tersely. "And don't remind me."

"What's that supposed to mean?" Clarabelle narrowed her eyes.

"I've only been here for two days, and I already can't stand it. Everything is different! The food, the people. I want to go home."

"Well, you're here," she said. "Like it or not, you need to get it through your head that this is where you'll be for Lord knows how long. I'm not fond of you either. But I have to accept that you won't be leaving anytime soon, and you have to as well. Now get in that truck and go back to Flora's where you belong. I'm gonna follow you the whole way so I can make sure you don't try to drive off again."

I stood my ground and folded my arms tightly across my chest. Clarabelle sauntered over to me, stopping until we were practically nose to nose with one another.

"Get in the truck," she said, her voice clipped through gritted teeth.

I wanted nothing more than to tell Clarabelle to pound sand. Her eyes narrowed, and she took another step towards me.

I instinctively backed away, then slammed my arms to my sides and stomped toward Flora's truck.

"And another thing," Clarabelle said, "I won't tell Flora about this. Although, you better hope the sound of her truck didn't wake her up, too. I won't say anything so long as you stop acting like the sun rises and sets just for you and start showing Flora some respect, you understand?"

I kept my hand on the door handle, giving her a hard glare.

"You hear me, Scarlett O'Hara?" she barked.

"Yes," I spat.

"Then get in that truck. Remember, I'll be following you all the way to Flora's, so no funny business. Get in."

I yanked the door open and climbed in, slamming it with more force than I had intended. I put my hands on the steering wheel, stewing there for a moment. Bright headlights beamed up, and a horn honked. Clarabelle was parked next to me, waiting for me to leave. I glowered at her and revved up the engine, pulling away from the honky tonk and making my way back to Flora's.

I got lucky sneaking back in. Flora must've been some heavy sleeper because when I entered the house, it was still as quiet as it was when I had left it. Clarabelle had been annoyingly firm on her word about following me back to the house. She drove so close to me that if I had tried to turn quickly, we would've gone right into each other. She even stayed in her truck, watching me go inside and didn't leave until my bedroom light went on.

The next morning, Flora was as chipper as ever. She made boiled eggs, sausage patties, and homemade biscuits for breakfast. She trilled and hummed tunes as she made her way around the kitchen, cleaning up everything.

"I need to plant some flowers and vegetables out in my garden today. Did you write that letter to your daddy saying you got here all right?"

I closed my eyes and sighed. After the long train ride that took pretty much a whole day and a half, being too exhausted to function, and yesterday's long day and night, I had completely forgotten. I shook my head.

"No. I forgot. Everything these past few days happened so fast."

"Well, when you're finished breakfast, get dressed for the day and write to him, letting him know that you got here safe and sound. I need to send my follow up letter that he requested. I'm sure he's wondering if you got here all right. Your mama must be too."

I fought off a light snort as I threw a piece of biscuit into my mouth. Sure, they are. My Uncle James on the other hand, I bet he missed me. I thought about him and how he would still be sleeping as it was almost six in the morning. I let my mind stay on him, unaware that I was staring into space and picking pieces off my biscuit and flicking them onto my plate.

"Maggie? Maggie?" Flora's voice took me out of my trance.

I looked at her.

Her eyes were etched with concern. She put a gentle hand on my arm. "Everything all right?"

I glanced down at her hand and quickly moved my arm. I put the rest of the biscuit on the plate and gathered myself together.

"Yes," I said hastily, standing up so I could go upstairs as quickly as possible. "I'll make sure I write to my parents."

"I'll be out in the garden if you need me," Flora said as I made my way out of the kitchen. "And remember, I have something special planned for us this afternoon!"

After I got dressed, I found some paper and a fountain pen in the drawer of my desk. I sat down and wrote a letter to my dad. I made it short and sweet, informing him that I got to Georgia fine and had settled into Flora's house, adding the biting remark that I hoped he and Ma were happy with themselves.

At the end of the letter, I told him I was also including a separate letter to Uncle James and if he could give it to him. I hesitated for a moment before spilling my guts to him.

Dear Uncle James,

Can you die from misery? Because that's what I think is happening to me. I absolutely hate it here. First, it was raining when I arrived in Georgia. Not just normal rain, but an honest to goodness downpour. Everyone here is friendly. Too friendly. They're always asking questions that are none of their concern. All these people think my accent is funny—as if they had never heard themselves talk. I can hardly understand a word some of these people are saying most of the time!

And then there's Flora, the woman I'm staying with. She's nice, but she is always so damn happy! All the time! I don't think I've ever seen anyone that is always so happy and friendly and nice. It's quite irritating. Nothing bugs this woman! Even if I do or say something that looks like she disagrees with, she doesn't say anything! She just smiles away like some sort of Pollyanna character. And then there's Clarabelle. Oh, Uncle James, I can't begin to tell you how much I despise this old bat. She counters everything I say! She is the most insufferable person I have ever met! She has a comment for every little thing, and she seems to enjoy seeing me uncomfortable. Now, she's blackmailing me.

I took Flora's truck out last night. I just wanted to get out and have some fun! I found a honky tonk in Downtown Savannah, and Clarabelle followed me there! She told me she wouldn't say anything as long as I started acting respectful toward Flora. Which is a load of crock, I've been nothing but respectful! By the way, don't tell Dad and Ma about my little escape. They—Dad—would never let me live it down and probably send me some place where there's no civilization whatsoever.

I started working on Flora's pecan farm, too. You would've surely gotten a real kick out of seeing me trying to use a rake! I must say though, the farm is quite impressive. There are rows and rows of pecan trees. There must be about a hundred of them! Working on it, however, I cannot say the same. It's hotter than hell out there! I don't understand how these two women—who are practically old enough to be grandmothers—can work out in the blistering heat every day! I was only out there for a few hours and almost died from sweat and dehydration.

Anyway, I should go. Flora has a special surprise planned for this afternoon, and I am dreading it. Uncle James, I want to come home so badly, it makes me want to scream. I don't know how much more I can take of this. I—

I stopped for a moment, the pen hovering above my words. I was about to tell him how much I missed him, but for some reason, I couldn't bring myself to write the words. I thought about him reading this letter and getting all sappy. The image of him gripping my letter in his hands and hanging his head in melancholy ached me. I snapped myself out of my thoughts and shook my head, bringing the pen back to the paper.

—I can only imagine how much you miss seeing me around the house and playing games of Gin Rummy and Chess. Take care of yourself, Uncle James. I will write back again as soon as I can.

Your Favorite Niece,

Maggie

I folded up the letter and put it in the envelope, licking the seal and shutting it. After writing my dad's name and address, I put the envelope and pen down on the desk.

I slid the chair back and walked over to the window, watching Flora plant things in her garden. She was still wearing her house dress and smocked pinafore with a straw hat. She stopped for a moment. From where I was standing, it looked as if she were breathing heavily. I could only see her from the back. Her shoulders drooped forward, moving up and down quickly. She straightened up and wiped her arm against her forehead before getting back to work.

I stepped away from the window and moseyed down the upstairs hallway. I meandered around, opening doors, seeing what was behind them. I came across a bedroom that was similar to mine. The only difference was a cross hanging above the bed on the wall. This must've been Flora's room. So, this was the room with the balcony. I entered it and looked around. She had a small white bottle of perfume on her vanity. I picked it up and sniffed it. It smelled just like her, however, I still couldn't place what the scent was.

After nosing around, I moved out of the room and to another one that was at the end of the hallway. I opened the door to find that it was another bedroom. I furrowed my brows in puzzlement. How many bedrooms were in this place? What, was she renting it out as a hotel or something? I walked further into the room.

The bedspread was a dark navy blue with a plaid print. The sheets and pillows were light blue. It looked as if it had been untouched for years.

Above the bed on the wall, was unsurprisingly a cross. I walked over to the bureau and opened up the drawers to find men's clothing. They must've been her husband's. I picked up one of the shirts. It was a button down, something similar to what Uncle James wore when he was in the war. Only this was a light blue instead of khaki. I folded the shirt over my arm and took another one out of the drawer. This one, however, was a dark navy-blue sailor's shirt. Was her husband in the Navy? She never mentioned anything about that, just mostly about his farming work. I glided my thumb against the fabric, tilting my head to the side as I inspected it.

The front door closed downstairs, and my head snapped up. My eyes widened, hoping Flora wouldn't come up here. I didn't want her to know I've been snooping around her dead husband's stuff.

"Maggie?" she called out; her footsteps padded about at the bottom of the stairs.

I gulped. "I'll be right down!"

I hastily folded the shirts back up and put them back in the drawer. I tiptoed softly towards the door and closed it behind me, making my way downstairs to see what surprise Flora had in store for the afternoon.

CHAPTER ELEVEN

The kitchen counter was cluttered with mixing bowls, baking pans, and baking goods. Flora was humming the same tune for the past few days. She looked up and smiled as she saw me come in.

"There you are," she said. "Did you write your letter?"

"Yes," I said. "It's on the desk in my room."

"Well, when we're finished with this, we can take a ride to the post office and drop it off. Here." She handed an apron to me, similar to the one she always wore.

I shook my head. "Oh, no thanks. I'm not much of an apron girl."

"You're gonna get that pretty dress you're wearing all ruined. It can get quite messy in here."

"All right." I took the apron from her and put it on. "What are we doing?"

She slammed a giant canister of flour down on the counter. It looked and sounded as if it weighed fifty pounds.

"Well, first we're gonna make cinnamon pecan cake for our dessert tonight. Then, we're gonna make pecan bread for some of the folks in town, and then we're gonna make fudge with—"

"Let me guess," I said. "Lobster."

Flora let out a loud, hearty laugh. She threw her head back and shook her head.

"Oh, honey, you are too much! No, silly. Pecans." She was still giggling as she measured the flour.

"Oh, okay." I grinned, giving a light hearted nod.

"I just find your accent so fascinating, Maggie. The way you say things like *lobstah* and *cah*. It's amazing how this country has so many different people, and while we're all brothers and sisters in some way, everyone has their own way of talking. You know what I mean?"

I shrugged. "I suppose. I never really found anything fascinating about the way I talk."

"Well, it's different when you're with people you've been around all your life." She added cinnamon to the bowl of sugar and flour. "I'm sure that when you're with your mama and daddy, everything sounds the same." Flora handed me a measuring cup full of pecans. "Here. Throw these in."

I hesitantly took the measuring cup from her and dumped the pecans in the bowl with the flour mixture. Flora handed me a spoon and told me to mix everything up while she got the cake pan ready.

"What's your favorite thing to make at home, Maggie?" Flora asked.

"I don't really cook." I shook my head, mixing up the ingredients as small bits of flour flicked out of the bowl. "We have a housekeeper, Siobhan, who does all of that."

"Oh," she said lightly. "Well, that must be nice. Now, you don't have any brothers or sisters?"

"No. Just me."

"Just you and your mama and daddy? And the housekeeper?"

"And my uncle," I said before realizing I had told her more information than I had ever intended to.

"Oh, you have an uncle who lives with you?"

I closed my eyes, internally scolding myself for my stupidity at letting something slip out of me. I went back to mixing.

"Yes," I said.

"What's his name?" Flora asked.

"James. He's my dad's brother."

"That's nice! Now, what does he do?"

I shook my head, fully prepared to tell her it wasn't any of her business asking me such personal questions until I heard Clarabelle's voice squawking in my head about being respectful. I couldn't risk telling Flora to mind her own business when Clarabelle was holding that she knew about my little escape last night over my head. I subtly rolled my eyes and let out a sigh.

"He used to be my dad's partner at O'Hanlon Grocery Company," I said. "Then he got called off to war."

Flora paused for a moment, her hand frozen on the measuring cup, then she began throwing more flour into her bowl.

"Oh, honey," she said. "Your uncle was in the war? Where did he serve?"

"Germany," I said. "Hürtgen Forest is how you pronounce it, I think. Anyway, while fighting, he went missing. They couldn't find him for weeks. A lot of other men that went missing had died, so that's what we thought happened to him until we got a telegram saying he had been found alive but was severely wounded. He was shell-shocked and parched. They kept him in a German hospital until he was able to come back to a hospital in the states, where he stayed for a few months before returning back home. He can't walk anymore, so he has to use a wheelchair. Sometimes he has nightmares where he thinks he's back in Germany—"

I stopped for a moment, realizing I had revealed too much. I had let myself open up about something in my life—probably the most important thing in my life—and ramble on. I was irritated with myself for going against what I had initially intended, and that was to not connect with anyone here.

It didn't help that Flora was listening and looking at me with so much sincerity in her eyes. She was so engrossed in everything that she was bound to ask more questions, and I couldn't let that happen. I cleared my throat and gave a flippant shrug of my shoulders.

"Other than that, he's a good guy. Very funny and handsome."

"You must be very close with him," Flora said.

I nodded. "Yes, I am. Uh, what do I do with this?" I said hastily, indicating to the bowl of cake mix, hoping that this would be an opportunity for a change of subject.

"Oh, here let me take that." She took the bowl from my hands and mixed it up a bit more before putting it in the cake pan and into the oven. "Now, onto the bread!"

For the next few hours, Flora showed me how to make her pecan bread and pecan fudge. This time, it was her turn to be the storyteller. She mostly talked about her husband and how he was practically born into the pecan farming business. This farmhouse apparently had been in his family since the Civil War. Flora told me that by some miracle, his business survived The Great Depression by distributing pecans and pecan-based foods to people who were struggling. Flora said she would pickle vegetables from her garden as well, giving people something a little extra during that period of hardship. Since I was only a child during The Great Depression, and the fact that our family wasn't affected by it, I really didn't remember it all that much, so I couldn't chime in with any personal stories on it. I just nodded along with whatever Flora said. When she began telling me about her pecan bread, she beamed with pride.

"I guess you could say I'm a bit famous for it around here," she said, her rosy cheeks deepening into a bashful blush. "At least that's what folks tell me. I just like to make it and give it out to everyone. It makes me happy. It makes them happy too. That's all I care about, making others feel good. It makes my days brighter."

When we finally finished, Flora cleaned up the kitchen while I changed into a new dress to go out and help her deliver pecan bread to the people in town.

Before we left the house, Flora quickly wrote her follow up letter to my dad vouching that I got to her house safely. She even went on to say how I am such a pleasure to have, and that I make her laugh.

We brought the bread to the local post office, police station, and hospital, where Flora proudly introduced me to the folks in town. I forced myself to smile through the handshakes and pestering questions about where I was from and how I knew Flora, to which she saintly answered for me, saying I was only around to help out with her pecan farm.

After our errands, we went to a small clothing store Downtown. Flora advised me to wait in the truck while she went in.

I sat by myself in her husband's old truck, yet again, gazing out the window and watching the people stroll by on this hot summer day. Everyone seemed to be so at ease with this slower pace of life. In Boston, life was always one step ahead of itself. Looking out at Downtown Savannah made me want to jump out of this truck and run home without looking back. Flora finally came back to the truck, holding a large brown bag and a round hat box asking me to hold them on my lap.

"No peeking!" she said with a teasing smile.

We drove back to her house, and when we got inside, Flora could barely contain her excitement.

"Open 'em, honey!" she said, clasping her hands together.

I opened the bag to find a pair of dark blue overalls and a short sleeve blue and white gingham blouse.

"They're for when you work out on the farm!" Flora said. "I told you I would get you something more appropriate to wear!"

I held them out at arm's length, my lip curled up and my nose wrinkled. I took the top off of the hat box and stared into it. It was a straw hat exactly like the one Flora always wore. She took it out of the box and propped it on my head.

"Oh, look at you!" she gushed, her chin resting on her clasped hands. "How cute!"

I didn't even want to see what I looked like in this thing. What was wrong with the hat I brought? The brim was much larger and would most likely protect me from the sun better than this one. I whipped it off my head as quickly as I could.

"Look, Flora," I said, "it was nice of you to—"

"Oh, go try everything on at once!" she said, practically shooing me toward the staircase. "I wanna see you in the whole outfit. Go on! Go on!"

I begrudgingly dragged myself upstairs to my room. I put the outfit on and forced myself to look at my reflection in the vanity mirror. All I needed were pigtails and a basket with a dog named Toto.

"Ugh," I grumbled. I couldn't believe I had to wear this thing. Flora clearly didn't know my taste—or my size. The overalls were too baggy and did nothing for my figure. And the shirt—well, the shirt fit fine, but it wasn't even my style. I dropped the hat on my head and looked at myself once more.

Dear God.

I went back downstairs to find Flora talking with Clarabelle in the hallway.

Oh, no. I immediately swiveled around to head back up to my room, but Flora caught sight of me.

"Oh, Maggie! Come on down and let us see you."

I clomped back down the stairs, hanging my head, my cheeks flamed, surely a shade lighter than my hair.

"Don't you look nice!" Flora said.

She flicked at the sleeves of my shirt and flattened out some of the wrinkles.

I shifted my eyes toward Clarabelle, who looked like she was struggling to fight off a smug grin. I took the hat off and scratched at my head.

"You know," I said, "maybe I'll just wear my own hat. This one is sort of itchy."

"Oh, you'll get used to it," Flora said. "Plus, your other hat is too nice. You don't want it getting all ruined by the windy days, do you? It can fly right off into the dirt. I know this hat isn't the fanciest looking one, but it gets its job done."

There was no way out of this. I would have to suffer through wearing this hideous outfit and itchy hat for as long as I was here. Thank goodness Uncle James would never see me in this. He would never let me live it down.

"And you might want to do something with your hair while you're at it," Clarabelle chimed in.

I touched my hair. "Why? What's wrong with it?"

"It'll get too mussed up under that hat. You should put it up."

"That's a wonderful idea!" Flora said.

"I didn't bring any hair clips with me," I said, offering Clarabelle a contemptuous glare.

"Oh, that's all right!" Flora said. "I have some twine in a drawer."

"*Twine?*" I grabbed at my hair protectively.

I rarely ever put my hair up—only in the rollers at night before bed, but not ever in front of other people. I hated the way my neck looked. It was awfully short, and I felt it didn't look right with an updo.

Flora waltzed into the kitchen and returned holding a piece of twine out in her hands. I instinctively backed away.

"Oh, no, no, no." I held my arm out to keep her at bay. "Don't put my hair up. You have no idea how long it took me to—"

"It's all right," she mollified. "I'm not gonna make it too tight. I just want to see how it looks."

She twirled me around, bunched up my hair into a low ponytail, and tied the twine around it.

"There ya go, darlin'. No harm done."

I touched my hair again and brushed a stray lock out of my eyes. The back of my neck felt naked. I hated it.

"You look lovely. Don't worry," Flora said, seemingly aware of my discomfort. "You look like that actress. The one with the red hair. What's her name again?"

"Katharine Hepburn," I said flatly.

Flora snapped her fingers. "Yes, that one. You look just like Katharine Hepburn with your hair like that."

She gave my shoulder a light rub and walked into the kitchen saying she would make lunch before taking a late afternoon ride to the pecan farm.

"Ha," Clarabelle snorted, following Flora toward the kitchen.

"What?" I mocked.

She stopped and turned to me. "If you think you look like Katharine Hepburn, then I must look like Greta Garbo."

After lunch, we made our way back to the pecan farm where Clarabelle grumbled about her dead husband, Dale for the entire ride. She claimed that his spirit was haunting her house as she's had two potted plants fall over in the past few days.

"The bane of my existence, that man," she squawked, sitting in between me and Flora. "Even in death, he can't let me have a moment's peace and quiet. Never could when he was alive, he's still gotta find a way to aggravate me."

"Oh, that's not true," Flora said, keeping her eyes on the road. "Those potted plants fell because you don't give enough space between them. Plus, your shelves are too short."

"Well, I never!" Clarabelle exclaimed. "That's another thing! Dale put those dang shelves in. He could fix your tractors and trucks in sleep, but the man couldn't build a shelf to save his life. Sometimes I wondered if his mama dropped him on his head at all when he was a youngin'."

"Dale was a good man," Flora said. "He loved you more than life itself."

"You mean he loved to irritate me more than life itself. Man had rocks for brains."

"Then why did you marry him?" I asked, agitated at Clarabelle's complaining.

"Because," Clarabelle said, keeping her eyes straight ahead, "I loved him. He may have been duller than dirt, but he would've moved the moon for me. And he was quite the sensitive lover."

"Oh, Clarabelle!" Flora gasped.

"Oh!" I repulsed. "Please stop talking."

A small grin cracked at the side of Clarabelle's mouth. Our eyes locked with one another's, and I grimaced again. Clarabelle suppressed a strained snort, offering me gleeful side glances the rest of the way.

When we got to the pecan farm, I hopped out of the truck, my wedged sandals digging into the grass again. I had rolled up the bottoms of my overalls at Flora's insistence.

Clarabelle handed me a bucket and rake.

I trudged after them, taking baby steps to avoid falling over. I used the rake as some sort of a walking stick, hoping it would give me an extra boost of support.

As I walked forward, my heel landed in a small divot and my left ankle twisted beneath me. I let out a yelp, taking the rake and bucket down with me as I face planted to the ground.

Flora and Clarabelle rushed over.

I lifted my head, my face now covered with dirt. I sat up, wiping it off me.

"Oh, Maggie, are you all right?" Flora asked, her face pink with concern.

"You didn't break nothin', did ya?" Clarabelle asked.

I winced at the throbbing pain my ankle was in. "No. I think I just twisted my ankle." *And a bit of my pride.*

"Here, let us help you up," Flora said, grabbing my arm.

Clarabelle made her way to the other side and put her arms around mine. They both hoisted me up back to my feet.

I shook them off of me and shifted backward a bit.

"I'm fine," I said, but when I went to take a step forward, I stumbled.

Flora and Clarabelle quickly grabbed hold of me again.

"It's those dang wedges ya got on," Clarabelle said. "They ain't good for working."

"They're fine," I said pointedly through clenched teeth. "I lost my balance, that's all."

"Sometimes you gotta put comfort before style, Scarlett O'Hara," Clarabelle said.

"It looks like you fell in some sort of a gopher hole or something," Flora said, glancing at the divot. "Thank goodness you didn't break anything. Are you still all right to work? Or do you want us to bring you back to the house?"

The pain seemed to have gone down a bit. I was more stunned than anything, but the thought of lying down on a nice sofa sounded like Heaven. I decided to play it up a little.

"Oh, yes. Ow! Ow!" I groaned, rubbing at my ankle. "Maybe I should sit this day out."

"Of course. I wouldn't want you working in pain."

"It's how you build up a good work ethic," Clarabelle croaked. "She oughta stay and tough it out."

Flora rubbed my back gently and picked up my hat off the ground. She dusted the dirt off of it and put it back on my head.

"Oh, she just needs to rest, is all," she said. "A good old hunk of ice will help. You can get back to work tomorrow."

"Swell," I said.

"Come on, hon," Flora said, linking her arm into mine. "I'll bring you back to the house and get you some iced tea and pecan bread. You just rest your ankle. Clarabelle, would you mind getting a head start? I'll be right back."

Clarabelle huffed as Flora guided me back towards her truck. I hopped on one foot, letting her hold onto me and thinking to myself that I was never happier to have a twisted ankle in my life.

CHAPTER TWELVE

Flora set me up like a queen at the house. She even brought down one of my dresses when I expressed wanting to change out the overalls. She instructed me to relax on the sofa while letting an ice pouch rest on my ankle. She gave me a glass of iced tea and a generous piece of pecan bread to tide me over for the next few hours.

"Now, don't fill up too much," she said, "I'm making fried chicken with all the fixing's for dinner."

I gave her an "A–OK" signal before she left the house. At the sound of the front door closing, I let out a long sigh. Finally, I was completely alone. Although my ankle did hurt a little, it wasn't nearly as bad as it was when I first fell. I took the iced tea and laid back, one arm resting behind my head. I drained the entire glass and put it back on the table.

Needing to stretch my legs a bit, I got up and hobbled around downstairs, striding past her gigantic painting of the pecan farm. It made me think of the portrait of my family that hung above our mantle back home, however, this was a little more pleasant to look at.

I wandered about, looking to see if Flora had any magazines lying around. Although, she probably didn't read the same things I did. She most likely read things like *Knitter's Digest* or something.

I went into her study, poking around her bookcases to see if I could find anything interesting. She had rows and rows of books nestled on the shelves. F. Scott Fitzgerald, John Steinbeck, and Jane Austen were among the many authors she had in her collection.

I opened and peered through the drawers that were attached to the bookcases. Most of the contents were either random junk, some knitting supplies, or papers regarding her husband's pecan business.

I searched around a different, more interestingly filled drawer, coming upon a piece of cream paper. I took it out and unfolded it.

The name Alfred Alcott Jr. was printed in bold lettering on the top. Underneath was a date of death, September 13, 1943. I furrowed my eyebrows. I thought my dad mentioned that Flora's husband died last year or so. Either he got the date wrong, or I had misheard him.

I shrugged, putting the paper back in its spot and closed the drawer.

I limped out of the study, grabbed the ice pouch from the sofa, and went to sit out on the front porch.

I sat down in a wicker armchair and propped my foot on the tufted ottoman, placing the ice pouch on my ankle. I relaxed my body and closed my eyes.

The sound of tires on the path made my head snap up. It was a beaten-up, red truck. I couldn't make out the driver until the door opened and Clark stepped out.

I laid my head back down. This was the last thing I needed.

He trotted up the front steps.

"Hi, Maggie," he said. "Heard you took a tumble. Are you doing all right?"

"Yes, I'm fine," I said curtly. "Wait, how did you know I fell?"

"Well, I was on my way back from town when I saw Flora's truck at the pecan farm. I stopped by to see if they needed any help. When I saw you weren't with them, they told me how you fell in a gopher hole and twisted your ankle. They asked me if I could come back and check on you since they'll still be a little bit longer. Aren't you supposed to be on the couch?"

I shook my head. Of course they had to send him to check in on me. It was probably Clarabelle's idea. I could just see her smug, wrinkly face telling him to go check on the silly girl that twisted her ankle because she was wearing the wrong shoes.

"I wanted to get some fresh air," I said pointedly. "Look, it was nice of you to check up on me and everything but, I don't need a babysitter. So, you can go."

Clark stared at me, seemingly taken aback. He shifted his eyes away then returned his gaze to me. His face looked as if I had kicked him in the gut.

"Well, okay then," he said quietly. "Sorry to bother you. Hope you feel better soon."

He put his hands in his pockets and hung his head, walking slowly down the steps, looking like a puppy that had just been scolded for having an accident on the rug.

I rolled my eyes. *Dammit.*

"Wait!" I called out. He turned back around. I propped myself up into a more comfortable position. "Sorry. I didn't mean to sound like such a crab. You can stay if you want," I added, trying to hide the reluctance in my voice.

"I don't want to impose," he said.

"No." I sighed. "Come on up."

He climbed back up the steps. "Can I get you anything?"

"No, thanks." I shook my head.

"So, how do you like it here, so far?" Clark sat down on a wicker chair across from me.

"I'm not going to lie, it's not exactly my ideal place. It's so different from Boston."

"Why did you come here? I mean, was it for a vacation, and it just didn't live up to your expectations?"

"No, it's…hard to explain," I said, not wanting to get into the whole story.

"Oh. I'm sorry. I didn't mean to pry."

I shook my head. "It's fine. It's just…I don't really want to get too attached to anyone here. I don't plan on being here very long, and…I just want to do what I came here for, and that's it. Sorry if that sounds rude, but I'm not looking for any friendships or anything like that."

Clark nodded his head. "All right. I can respect that. I won't try to impose anything on you, but I do hope we can still be friendly when we see each other."

I gave him a quick nod. "Sure."

He smiled, showing off his slightly crooked teeth. "Sounds good, Maggie."

It was then I noticed that he had a small dimple on his left cheek. I caught myself staring at him a bit too long. I blinked and averted my eyes quickly, then looked back at him coolly so as to not make it too awkward.

"Sounds good," I said.

The next day, Flora surprised me with a pair of gray work boots that she used to wear. They were terribly scuffed, and the tips still had hints of dirt on them. The laces were thick like straw with bits of mud caked into the fabric. I couldn't stop my face from expressing appall. She caught on to my disapproval right away.

"I know they're not the cleanest." She tilted her head. "I tried to spiff them up a bit, but this was the best I could do. They may be a tad big on you, but if you wear some nice thick socks and tie the laces real tight, they shouldn't give you any trouble."

"I didn't bring any socks," I said dully. "Just nylons."

"Well, not a problem." Flora smiled and patted my arm. "I can lend you a pair."

She walked off, leaving me holding the boots by the laces at an arm's length. Someone knocked on the door. I opened it and came face to face with a young boy who looked no more than twelve. His face was littered with freckles, and he wore a cap over his moppy brown hair and had a giant burlap bag slung over his shoulders.

"Yeah?" I said, still holding onto the boots.

"I got some mail for ya," he said.

"Oh, wait a minute." I turned my head. "Flora! The mail kid is here!"

Flora appeared, wearing a giant smile on her face.

"Hello, honey," she said to the boy. She handed him a dime from her coin purse. "There ya go."

The boy tipped his hat. "Thank you, Ma'am."

Flora closed the door and sifted through the mail. "Looks like you got something."

She handed me an envelope, and I dropped the boots onto the floor without thinking. It was my uncle's handwriting. Nothing from my dad or ma. I wasn't surprised, however. Not that I was expecting a follow up letter from one of them—my dad at least—but I wasn't shocked that they couldn't take five minutes to write a follow up letter to their daughter who was hundreds of miles away. Besides, Uncle James was the only person I cared to hear from, anyway.

"It's from my Uncle James!" I said, expressing excitement for the first time in ages.

"Oh, isn't that nice!" Flora beamed, nudging a little closer to me and looking over my shoulder.

I opened the letter, my eyes skimming over it. Flora was still standing, her chin perched inches away from my shoulder and smiling, making me feel extremely uncomfortable and invaded.

I shifted my eyes to her.

"Do you mind?" I said, the words coming out ruder than I had intended.

"Oh!" she said, waving her hand. "I'm sorry, honey."

She padded off back into the kitchen.

When she was completely out of sight, I began to read the letter.

Hey, kid,

Sounds like you've had quite the week. Glad to hear you got to Georgia all right. Everything is pretty much the same here. Your parents are still trying to sweet talk Maryland into opening O'Hanlon's in their state. If they agree, then your parents will have guaranteed locations all over the Northeastern region. Your dad wants to start working on the South next and told me to ask you how Savannah does in the grocery business. Don't worry, I don't expect you to answer that just yet.

It sounds like you've met some pretty interesting people out there. Yes, folks from the South are incredibly friendly. I had a guy in my division who was originally from Alabama. Nicest guy you could ever meet. Anyway, I know you are homesick, but it seems as if you are not giving these people and their town a chance. I know it's not your choice to be there, but it is your choice on how you present yourself. If you decide to be miserable, then that's how you will be. Eventually, it will make everyone else around you miserable. You don't want that, do you? Remember why your dad sent you there in the first place. This is your chance to start anew. Gain some responsibility in your life.

This Flora woman you're staying with sounds like a real nice lady. Do your favorite uncle a favor and give her a chance? She's doing you a solid by letting you stay with her. The least you can do is be grateful for that. I might have to agree with this Clarabelle woman you don't like so much. She sounds like she knows what she's talking about. She kind of sounds like you in a way. Headstrong, not afraid to say what she wants. Anyway, that's enough of me giving you the third degree. You're an adult, and you can make your own decisions. But, kid, I know you better than anyone else. And I know you can make this work. I know you got a good heart. You don't always like to show it, but it's there. Do me a favor and show them. Anyway, I hope to hear from you soon. Keep writing, kid. I always look forward to it. And remember, be good out there. I love you.

Uncle James

I folded up Uncle James' letter. I didn't expect to get such a lecture from him but couldn't help but feel glad that he wrote to me at all. Of course Dad wants me to stake out Savannah for potential business. Well, I wasn't going to, so he could board a train and do it himself.

I walked up to my room and put the letter into the small drawer next to my bed, that way I could read it again anytime. I did, however, disagree with him that I was just like Clarabelle. I nearly fell over when I read that! How could Uncle James make such a comparison when he hadn't even met her! I clearly didn't do a good enough job at describing just what that woman is like. I'm just like Clarabelle. What a bonkers idea.

Uncle James seemed to miss the entire point of my letter. I was certainly respectful toward Flora. Well, I tried to be. Sure, I got irritated easily, but I wouldn't if she wasn't so happy all the time. Even though I thought Uncle James didn't need to come down on me so hard, I didn't want to disappoint him. I guess I could try to be a little nicer towards Flora. I wasn't sure I could say the same about Clarabelle, however. But

Flora, I could. Besides, she seemed to be the only one besides Uncle James who put up with me and everything I threw at her.

I sat down at my little desk and took out some paper and the fountain pen and began to write Uncle James another letter.

It had been almost two weeks since I sent Uncle James his second letter, telling him I would try to be more well-behaved for his sake. Although I hadn't heard back from him, I figured it would take a while for his response to get to me, like his last letter did.

Somehow, I made it to the end of August. I continued to help Flora and Clarabelle on the pecan farm and had grown more accustomed to using the rake to get high into the trees. Flora even gave me a pair of gardening gloves to keep my hands from getting dirty whenever I would pick up pecans from the ground. Although I was doing better than I had when I first began, that still didn't stop Clarabelle from running her mouth at every little thing I did.

One morning, I sat at the kitchen table, sulking. It was August 30, Uncle James' birthday. I suddenly felt angry that I was here again. He was forty years old today, and I wasn't even there to celebrate with him.

"Everything all right?" Flora said, looking at me with concern. "You look a little down."

I glanced up at her and shook my head. "It's nothing."

"Are you sure?" she asked. "You're not feeling sick, are you?"

"No." I shook my head again. "Today is my uncle's birthday."

"Oh." She drew out the word sympathetically. "I'm sorry. You must miss him terribly."

I nodded. "It's just, normally Siobhan would make a big supper like Shepherd's pie or a boiled corned beef dinner."

"You're missing home extra today?" she asked.

I shook my head quickly. "It's fine. I'll just write him a quick letter wishing him a happy birthday. I'm still not sure if he got my previous one, but it wouldn't hurt."

I got up from the table and pushed my chair in.

"Listen," Flora said, putting her hands in mine, "you write your uncle that letter and take an easy day. I need to go over to the general store and butchery anyway."

I stopped short for a moment. "Are you sure?"

"It's fine." She patted my hand. "Go on, write that letter to your uncle."

"All right."

While Flora was gone, I wrote Uncle James a quick letter wishing him a happy birthday and told him that I would treat him to a toast of whiskey when I eventually came back home.

Throughout the day, Flora remained in the kitchen. She instructed me to take my lunch on the back porch. While I was enjoying this quite a bit, I still couldn't help but feel a sense of crumminess that I wasn't with Uncle James. Flora mailed my letter for me. Although he wouldn't get it for a while, I was glad I sent it to him.

Finally, dinner came. Flora called me into the kitchen to eat. When I sat down at the table, she put a hefty plate of casserole in front of me. It had ground beef, carrots, peas, and corn, and was topped with her homemade mashed potatoes. It wasn't any casserole; it was Shepherd's pie.

"Is this—?" I pointed at my plate.

Flora nodded. "Shepherd's pie! I know you're missing your uncle on his birthday, and I know you're missing home and everything. You've been here almost a whole month. I wanted to make you something that reminds you of home. I used beef instead of lamb. I hope that's okay."

I didn't know what to say. I was about to speak up when Flora began before me.

"Oh, and there's more where that came from!" she said.

She walked over to the counter and brought over a large plate with a dome over it. She set it down on the table and took the cover off to reveal a cake with chocolate frosting.

"Since you can't celebrate with your uncle, that doesn't mean you can't celebrate at all," she said. "We'll have a piece of this cake in his honor."

Again, I was speechless. My eyes went from the Shepherd's pie—which looked exactly like Siobhan's—to the cake, and back to the Shepherd's pie again. I shook my head.

"I don't—you didn't have—" I stammered out, mercilessly stumbling over the words. My breathing quickened, and my underarms began to sweat. I don't think I could recall a time anyone had ever done something this nice for me. I twirled my necklace in my hand.

"Oh, honey." Flora sat down in the chair next to me. She put a gentle hand on my arm. "It was nothin'. You just seemed so homesick. I thought this might cheer you up a bit. I know it's not the same, but it's something I wanted to do."

A tight knot gathered in my stomach, and something became lodged in my throat. I quickly swallowed and gave Flora a satisfied grin.

"Thank you," I said. "It was…real nice of you to do this."

"Well, of course! Now, let's eat dinner before it gets too cold. Then, we can slice into that cake."

The Shepherd's pie was to die for. It tasted exactly like Siobhan's. I didn't know how Flora did it. She must've had magical powers when it came to cooking. The vanilla cake was equally delicious—homemade, of course. She gave us each a large slab of it, and we toasted to Uncle James and his birthday.

The first few days of September brought a hefty amount of rain. Flora made us go to the pecan farm anyway. Although the rain wasn't as bad as it was the day I first arrived, I still wasn't too pleased being outside. The gray boots Flora had given me were starting to get a little more comfortable. Flora let me wear one of her husband's old rain slickers, which I was hesitant to put on.

Clarabelle didn't come this time; she was probably afraid she would melt or something. Flora and I spent the afternoon picking up as many pecans as we could from the ground to prevent them from getting soiled or stolen by any animals within the coming days.

After we returned to the house and changed out of our wet clothes, Flora and I dried the pecans that would be used for recipes and distribution. She then brought me down into her basement, where the largest freezer I ever saw in my life stood.

"Holy mackerel," I said. "That's where you keep all the pecans?"

"Yes!" Flora said, carrying the dried off pecans in the bucket. "Would you mind opening it for me?"

I lifted the latch, which took a bit of elbow grease, but I eventually got the thing open. I was met with a cold breeze that wafted out. I shivered and rubbed my arms with my hands.

"Jeez," I said. "You could get frostbite just by looking inside."

Flora giggled. "I don't notice much, anymore. Been using this thing for so long, my body doesn't react to it anymore."

I peered inside the freezer. It was lined with at least ten long shelves, each one holding a tray.

Flora walked over and slid one out. She moved a few pecans around, then dumped the ones that were in the bucket on the tray. She fixed them up again, slid the tray back in, and locked up the freezer.

"There we go," she said with a satisfied smile. "All in a day's work."

"Exactly how many pecans are on those trays?" I asked, as we made our way back upstairs.

"Well, each tray can hold about a few hundred or so, depending on the size of the pecans," Flora said. "I got about four and a half trays full about now. That's why I'm so concerned about this season's harvest. I would normally have all the trays filled up. They go fast. I need to start getting them ready to send to my distributor, Mr. Winston, whose company puts the pecans out in stores. My husband took care of that business stuff. While I would help, my duty was more so out on the farm and making recipes. Clark—you remember him—that cute cab driver?"

I fought off an eye roll and nodded my head. "Yes, I remember Clark."

"He's been helping me since Alfred died. He's such a sweetheart. I have a shed out back that I put the pecans that are ready to be distributed in. He comes by a few times a week and takes them to Farmer's Food Company so they can be distributed to stores."

"And what would happen if you couldn't get the pecans out in time? Why don't you just use the ones you have in the freezer and worry about it next year?"

"It's not that easy," Flora said. We stopped in the middle of the kitchen. "If I don't have enough to distribute, then the business could go bankrupt. My husband left me with enough money to live comfortably before he died, but that's not what it's about. It's about Alcott's Pecans living on and hopefully selling forever. Remember, this was his family's business. It would be a terrible betrayal to him if I just neglected it."

"Well, I mean, you could still cook with them, right? Why don't you just make your recipes for the people around town? They seem to enjoy it. If he left you enough money to keep living here, couldn't you relax for the rest of your life?"

"I suppose." Flora sighed, then she shook her head. "But I couldn't do that. This business meant everything to him. It does to me too. I get all the help I can. Clarabelle helps with the farming, and now you do, too. But you won't be here forever. I'll eventually need someone here to help full time."

"But you know the distributors, right? Wouldn't they just listen to you?"

Flora shook her head. "They do know me, but like I said, my husband Alfred took care of the business side. Since I'm female, they won't take me as seriously if I tried to handle the business."

"Well, that's a load of crock!" I placed my hands on my hips.

Flora shrugged. "That's the way it works," she said before walking off to answer a knock at the door.

Why did it matter that a woman was taking care of her husband's business? In the end, everyone was getting paid, and that's all anyone ever really cared about. Except for Flora, that is. She seemed to care more about the business itself than the money it brought in.

I thought of my parents, and how they could be ruthless when it came to running their business. While my dad was more of the leader, that certainly didn't stop Ma from adding her two cents every now and then. I'd seen her in action. It seemed she put the fear of God into potential investors more than my dad did at times. She had a way of staring people down. She would sit, still and quiet while silently judging the person in front of her, making them sweat in their suits. Flora wasn't like that. She was too nice and—no offense—too mousy to judge anyone.

CHAPTER THIRTEEN

Flora walked back into the kitchen, sifting through the mail. She handed me an envelope.

"Looks like you got something today." She handed me the envelope before walking off to make a pot of tea.

It seemed as if my Uncle James had gotten my last two letters. I was glad to see that he had taken the time to write back to me. I opened it up and sat down at the kitchen table to read it.

Hey kid,

Thanks for the birthday letter, it really made my day. Siobhan treated me like a king. She made her Irish bangers and mash for supper. Sorry it took so long for me to get back to you. I've been having a few rough nights lately. I've been sleeping a lot during the day. Don't worry, though, Siobhan is taking good care of me. On a lighter note, you'll be happy to know that the leaves are starting to change over here. I can see bits of red and orange from my window, and it looks like we're going to have a colorful autumn this year. Remember when I would take you to Boston Common when you were little during the fall, and you would collect the leaves and bring them back to the house? Siobhan flipped her wig whenever she found them in your sock drawer.

Your parents are doing fine. They're getting close to sealing the deal with Maryland. Looks like they'll be working on the South soon! Your dad asked me if you had anything to say about businesses out there. I just told him that you said they do well. I know you don't want to hear your favorite uncle rag on you some more, but I hope you're doing well out there and have taken what I said to you last time into consideration. I know you weren't too happy about me lecturing you. I'm just looking out for you. You know that. Anyway, I wanted to check back in with you, make sure you didn't run off to a honky tonk again. Be good out there. Keep doing what you're doing, and I hope to see you soon. Until next time, kid.

Love,

Uncle James

I gazed over the letter again, letting out a suppressed chuckle at the memory of when I used to bring fall leaves home. I had completely forgotten I used to do that. Although, I did have a bit of agitation over my dad still being so hung up on bringing O'Hanlon's to the South. He didn't seem to care how I was doing here, as long as he didn't get any letters that I was acting up or anything. The only thing he was after was expanding his business. I folded up the letter and set it face down on the table, just in time for Flora to walk over with a cup of tea and piece of pecan bread for each of us. She set mine down in front of me.

"Everything all right back home?" she asked, her innocent smile plastered across her face.

I looked up at her, playing with the corner of the paper.

"Yes," I said. "Just getting some updates. That's all."

I blew on my tea. Flora had finally found a way to make it somewhat tolerable for me: a squeeze of lemon instead of sugar.

Flora sat down at the table across from me, gripping the tea cup in her hands.

"That's nice. And your uncle is doing fine?"

I took a bite of the pecan bread and nodded. "He is."

However, my mind lingered on that one line about him having sleepless nights recently. Even though he told me not to worry, I couldn't help but think about it. I hoped his episodes weren't severe. I looked back up at Flora, who I realized was waiting for me to elaborate. I shrugged.

"He was happy to hear from me," I continued. "Siobhan made him bangers and mash for his birthday."

"Well, that sounds nice," Flora said. "I'm glad to hear he had a good birthday."

I nodded, bringing the teacup to my lips. "Yeah. Me, too," I said, my mind drifting back to Uncle James' recent sleeping habits.

It was after dinner when I had finally gotten a chance to sit down at my little desk to write back to Uncle James. I had changed out of my dress and into my nightgown and robe.

Dear Uncle James,

I'm happy to hear you had a good birthday and that Siobhan treated you well. Even though I wasn't there with you, I still celebrated. I told Flora that it was your birthday, and she made an entire Shepherd's pie and a cake to honor you. I have to say, I didn't expect her to do that. It was real nice of her. Maybe she's not as irritating as I thought. Clarabelle, on the other hand—I still haven't forgiven you for comparing me to her. She's a real piece of work. The leaves aren't doing much over here. Flora said that they don't normally change until October. I don't know how you remember me bringing leaves into the house! I was quite the rascal, wasn't I?

Glad to hear Dad and Ma remember that they have a daughter. I was starting to think they thought they were a childless couple. It sure is good to know that they seem so thoughtful about my well-being out here. Anyway, I don't mean to go off on you like that. You know what I mean. I know you're just looking out for me. And no more honky tonks. I promise.

Well, I should get to bed. Flora still wakes me up at the crack of dawn. And, if you can believe it, I think I'm starting to get used to it. What's happening to me? Don't wait too long to write back. I hope to see you soon.

Your favorite niece,

Maggie

I pondered whether or not to bring up his sleepless nights. I didn't want him to think I was worrying too much, so I decided that it was probably best to not mention it. I folded up the letter and put it in the envelope, addressing it. I placed it on my desk so I could give it to Flora to send to the post office tomorrow morning.

After putting my hair up in rollers and applying my night cream on my face, I slid into bed. Although the weather was still hotter than heck, the warm breeze that drifted through the window was comfortable. I let sleep wash over me as I closed my eyes and listened to that pesky bull frog croak its night time lullaby.

September spared no expenses with the heat down in Savannah. Not that Boston didn't have its warmer days during this month, but the weather was usually somewhat milder by now. Even so, I enjoyed getting to bask in summer-like weather a little bit longer than I was used to.

It was a Friday, and it was getting a lot closer to harvest season. However, Flora decided to take the day off from the pecan farm, which I found odd. Not that I was complaining or anything—I wasn't about to oppose a day off.

Although today, she seemed different. She wasn't her usual cheerful, overly happy self. She still made breakfast with a smile, but this time, it didn't reach her eyes. She pattered around the house, often seeming like she was in some sort of a daze as she busied herself with housework. At one point, she left the house saying she had an errand to run which resulted in her being gone for nearly two hours and coming back home empty-handed.

When it came to four o'clock in the evening, I found her sitting on the back porch with Clarabelle. They were having a quiet conversation when I walked up to them. Flora was normally getting ready for supper by now. I stood there, waiting for them to finish talking.

"Flora," I chimed in, "it's four o' clock. Aren't you going to start supper?"

Flora nodded quietly toward Clarabelle before bringing her attention to me. Her expression was neutral. Her eyes widened, as if she forgot supper existed. She let out a light gasp and stood up.

"Oh," she said. "Oh, yes. I'm sorry, honey. I'll get it started. Excuse me, Clarabelle."

She walked into the house, the corners of her mouth slightly drooped. I looked back at her in puzzlement.

"What's with her today?" I asked more to myself than to Clarabelle. "She seems out of touch."

"Are you serious?" Clarabelle said.

"What?" I faced her. "She's been in a crummy mood all day. She's barely talked at all, and she left the house for nearly two hours. Even when she smiles, it looks forced."

"You don't even know, do you?" Clarabelle said, her eyes narrowed.

"Know what?"

Clarabelle stood up from her seat and walked over to me. "Do you know what today is?"

"No," I snipped. "How am I supposed to know? I'm not a mind reader."

Clarabelle shook her head. "Today is the anniversary of her son, Alfred Jr.'s, death."

"Her son? Flora never told me she had a son."

"Did you ever think to ask?"

"No. Why would I? I didn't know."

"Let me guess. All this time you've been here, Flora has asked you about yourself and your family, right?"

I nodded curtly. "Yes."

"And it never occurred to you to ask her about herself? Her husband? If she had any children?"

I shook my head. "No, I mean…I never thought to…"

Clarabelle nodded. "That's right. You never thought to because all you think about is yourself. You have no consideration for anyone else."

"That's not true!" I folded my arms tightly across my chest.

"I can see right through you, Margaret." She pointed at me. "You're selfish."

"I am not!" I exclaimed. "So, I didn't think to ask Flora about her family? Is that a crime?"

"No, but it's common decency to ask others about themselves."

"Okay, so how did her son die?" I asked.

Clarabelle glowered at me, her icy blue eyes piercing through mine. Her lips were tin and tight.

"He was killed," she said. "Nineteen-forty-three. Three years ago."

My eyes widened slightly. I didn't know how to respond. I opened my mouth to say something but immediately shut it, knowing my words would be nonsense.

I suddenly remembered the death certificate I found at the bottom of her study drawer, thinking how I assumed it was her husband's at the time.

"He was a sailor in the Navy," Clarabelle continued. "He was fighting in the Atlantic Ocean when his ship was attacked. Over one hundred men in his division were killed, himself included. Apparently, he died trying to get his fellow sailors to safety. He stood in front of them, blocking them from the cannons. One week later, Flora and Alfred Sr. buried him in Bonaventure Cemetery."

I stood frozen, still unable to conjure words. My flesh prickled, and a coldness rushed through me.

I thought back to that empty bedroom with the navy plaid bedding and the drawer full of clothes. The light blue shirt that looked like my uncle's khaki one and then the sailor uniform.

She had seemingly kept his bedroom exactly as it was when he left for war, hoping he would come home to return to it, not knowing that the bed would remain empty from then on.

"I…" I started, my voice quiet for the first time in my life. "I didn't know."

Clarabelle nodded lightly. "You have an uncle that was in the war, too, correct?"

"Yes," I said.

"And he came home?"

"Yes, but he was missing for a while—"

"But they found him," Clarabelle said. "Alive."

"Yes, but—"

"Tell me something," she interjected. "What was it like? When he was missing? When you didn't know if he was dead or alive? That every knock on the door, you didn't know if it was a telegram about him or just regular mail?"

I hesitated for a moment, shifting my eyes away from Clarabelle. She took a step toward me, her glare daggering.

"What was it like, Margaret?"

"It was awful," I finally said.

"And how was it when you finally found out that he was alive? That he was coming home? What did that feel like?"

"Relief," I admitted.

"Flora never got that." Clarabelle shook her head. "Now, you may think you're different from Flora, you may even think you're better than her, but let me tell you something. You two have a lot more in common than you think, whether you like it or not. You have a connection with the war. It don't matter if your uncle was in the Navy or the Army or whatever, you two are connected with each other."

I looked at Clarabelle, the sounds of Flora pattering about in the kitchen filling the awkward silence that I so desperately wanted to escape.

"Okay, well," I said. "What do you want me to do?"

"For starters?" Clarabelle said. "You can talk to her."

I shook my head. "I'm not good with…this kind of stuff. I appreciate you telling me all this, but I'm just uncomfortable with it."

Clarabelle shrugged. "Maybe being uncomfortable is exactly what you need. To learn how to care about others. You could use some discomfort in your life."

"I wouldn't even know what to say to her. I don't want to make her sadder than she already is."

"Don't say anything, then," Clarabelle said. "Just listen. You have ears. You may not use 'em all the time, but they're there."

Flora walked up to the screen door. "Well, you two have been quite chatty," she said. "I think this is the most you've ever said to each other. Dinner's coming along. Clarabelle, would you like to stay? I'm making plenty."

"You don't have to ask me twice," Clarabelle said.

Flora walked back into the kitchen.

Clarabelle turned toward me. "I'm not gonna bug you anymore. You make the decision. You can listen and talk to Flora, or you can go about the rest of your day as if you know nothin' about what that woman has been through."

Clarabelle brushed past me and walked into the house, leaving me standing on the back porch, a chill still surging through my body.

Dinner was quiet tonight. I would often steal glances at Flora, who ate her chicken and mashed potatoes slowly. I would then look back to see Clarabelle staring at me, her previous words drilling into my head. When we finished, Flora was getting ready to clear the table.

Clarabelle shot me a look, her eyes piercing right through mine.

"Here." I got up and took the plate from her. "I'll take care of it."

"What?" Flora said. "Oh honey, don't worry. I've got it."

"No," I said. "It's all right. I can do it. Why don't you…relax?"

"It's no problem," Flora insisted.

"Flora, let the girl do the dishes," Clarabelle piped in.

Flora looked back and forth between me and Clarabelle, hesitating before handing me the dishes.

"Well, all right," she said. "Thank you. Let me know if you need any help."

"She'll be fine," Clarabelle said. "Come on, let's go sit on the back porch."

It took me longer than expected to clean up. Clarabelle came through once to make Flora some tea before she went home for the night. She didn't say anything to me, but I could feel her eyes in the back of my head as she boiled the water and poured it in Flora's cup.

When I finished, Flora was still out back, sitting on the porch swing, her hands wrapped around her cup of tea. She swung lightly back and forth.

"I'm uh…all done." I walked up to her.

She looked up at me and smiled softly. "Thank you, honey. I appreciate it."

I hesitated for a moment, watching her as she took sips from her tea and stared straight ahead, listening to the crickets and grasshoppers and that bullfrog that seemed to never go away.

"Um…" I started. "Well, I guess I'll go to bed early, then. Goodnight."

"Goodnight, honey," Flora said, continuing to stare off.

I started to turn around but stopped myself, holding onto the door frame. I tapped it with my fingers, then turned towards Flora, the back of her head facing me.

"Flora?" I said.

"Hm?"

I paused for a moment, clasping my hands together. Even though I was staring at the back of her head, I still had trouble looking at her.

"Clarabelle told me about your son. Alfred? I'm…" I rubbed my hand against my wrist, struggling to say the next words. "I'm sorry."

She let out a silent exhale, and her shoulders drooped forward. She gave a slight nod of her head.

"He was a good boy," her voice hushed out.

I pried myself away from the door and walked slowly over to her. I hesitated for a moment before carefully sitting myself down on the porch swing next to her. I fiddled with my thumbs awkwardly, unsure of what to say until I remembered the words Clarabelle had told me earlier this evening.

Just listen.

"What was he like?" I asked, my voice robotic and quiet.

At first, she did not answer. I started to wonder if it was such a good idea trying to talk to her. It seemed as if I was making it worse.

"He was the sweetest boy a mama could ask for." She stared into her teacup, tracing the rim lightly with her thumb. She lifted her chin a bit, something I couldn't decipher crossing over her face. She let out another breath through her nose and then a peaceful smile formed on her lips.

I folded my sweaty hands in my lap, waiting patiently for her to continue.

"He had volunteered to join the Navy," she said. "He was almost finished with school to become a doctor while helping my husband and I with the pecan farm and business at the same time. He said he wanted to do both." She let out a soft chuckle. "While we knew he loved working in the family business, we knew his heart belonged in the medical field. We never discouraged it. We just wanted him to be happy. And he was. Even when he enlisted in the Navy. Although I didn't want to see him go off to war with the chance that he may never return, I couldn't stop him. I had always raised him to do what he believed was right."

She let out a sigh and took a sip of her tea that I could tell might as well be iced by now. She continued to stare straight ahead, the floor of the porch supporting her heels as she rocked the swing gently back and forth.

"Unfortunately," she continued, "my worst fears came true. Although, I knew that for a second, my boy never regretted his decision. I don't like to think of how he died. But that of how he was proud to be in the Navy. How he always looked out for his fellow sailors, and how in the end, he protected them. However, I'll always remember him as the little rascal who played Cowboys with his daddy."

I let out a soft smile. My shoulders untensed, and I felt more at ease. I could just picture Flora baking something delicious in the kitchen while her young son ran around the house in a cowboy hat and spurs playing with his father. I could see her smiling as she watched them while she whipped up something in a bowl thinking how in that moment, she had the perfect life.

"Would you like to see a picture of him?" she asked me, her eyes finally settling on mine.

I nodded. "Yes."

Flora dug her hand into her apron pocket, took out a weathered, grainy photo and handed it to me. I looked at the picture of Alfred Jr., holding it gently in my hands as if it were a newborn baby. His expression was neutral, but there were hints of a muted smile in the corners of his mouth, as if he was forcing himself to stay serious for the sake of the picture. He wore his sailor suit and hat. He looked like—what I would imagine—his father would've looked like as a young man.

"He's handsome," I said.

I handed the photo back to Flora who looked down at it as well, a proud and maternal smile crossing her lips. She brushed it with her finger tips before putting it back into her pocket.

"He was," she said reflectively. She looked at me, her eyes shiny and pink rimmed. She gave me a light smile. "He would've liked you. You would've made him laugh."

"I'm sure I would've liked him as well," I said, returning the smile.

She gave my hand a soft pat. "You go on up to bed now. It's getting late."

I stood up and started walking toward the door. I turned around, seeing that Flora remained sitting on the swing.

"Aren't you coming in, too?" I asked.

She nodded. "In a bit. I want to stay out here a little longer."

I looked inside through the screen door, my bed calling to me all the way from upstairs. I turned back toward Flora. The sight of her reflectively content with a glimmer of grief made me want to continue keeping her company. I stepped back over to my seat on the swing and sat down again.

"Honey, you don't need to stay here with me," she said, her voice nurturing with concern.

"I know," I said. "I want to."

Flora smiled, her eyes crinkling at the sides. She nodded in approval. Sitting together, we didn't say much. We just listened to the sounds of the night and the slight creaking of the swing going back and forth.

CHAPTER FOURTEEN

The kitchen smelled of hearty sausage and buttermilk biscuits, and the sounds of Flora's early morning trilling told me that she was back to her cheerful self. I was glad to see a genuine smile on her face.

As much as I could tell she liked being able to talk about and remember her son, there was still such sadness in her expression. Seeing her melancholy was a hard thing to watch, however, there was a bit of gratitude that Clarabelle got me to let Flora open up.

We dropped my letter to Uncle James off at the post office downtown. Flora told me that we had quite a few errands to run for the day saying that the majority of tomorrow would be devoted to the pecan farm. Our first stop was Minton's Market.

As we perused the aisles, Flora nodded a friendly "hello" to anyone that passed by and proudly introduced me to them. Even though I had been here for well over a month, I still wasn't used to Flora introducing me to the townsfolk every chance she got.

I noticed one of the shelves had a few tin cans of Alcott's Pecans on them. I'm not sure why I was so surprised; I knew that Alcott's Pecans sold all over Georgia, but it was still sort of neat to see it out in the wild, on shelves, and to see that people really did seem to enjoy them.

"Hey," I said, pointing to it.

I picked up a can, and examined it, then turned it toward Flora as if she didn't know her last name was out in the world.

Flora smiled, and the look of pride brimming in her eyes was unmistakable.

"It must be neat seeing your name in stores," I said.

"Well, you would know," Flora said.

I tilted my head. "What do you mean?"

"Your name O'Hanlon is outside many grocery stores. And from what you've told me about it, it's a very popular and respected market."

"Yeah, but it's my dad's." I put the can of pecans back on the shelf. "Not mine."

"Your name is still O'Hanlon," she said.

I shook my head. "It's all his. And my uncle's, and I guess a bit of my ma's as well. I had nothing to do with it. I just share their last name."

"You should still be proud." Flora said.

"I am proud." I stuck my chin up slightly. "I've gotten some pretty good benefits out of it."

"Sometimes it's the pride of knowing your name belongs to something that people can depend on—like food and goods in our case—rather than the materialistic things it can bring us is what matters," she said before walking back off down the aisle.

I picked up the can of pecans again, looking at the name Alcott printed out in a bold red color. The establishment year and Alfred Sr.'s name were underneath. I turned it over and examined the back. The only thing that was there was where the pecans are grown and the name of the distribution company, Farmer's Food Company.

Aside from the bold print of "Alcott's Pecans" on the front, the can was quite bland and didn't offer much of anything else. Even though the taste of them was what people mostly cared about, the presentation of the canister was unappealing. I browsed the long shelf of nuts. Some labels were about as plain as Alcott's, making me breeze past them without so much as a second look. The others, however, were much more eye-catching, even offering a recipe on the back. I picked up a can of different pecans.

I held the two contrasting canisters in my hands. My eyes floating back and forth from one to the other. If I hadn't already known how delicious Flora's pecans were, I would've picked the competitor's canister without a second thought. It was a bit of a shame that Flora's product suffered from a lack of presentation when the pecans themselves tasted like they came straight from Heaven. I shrugged, putting the canisters back on the shelf and hurried to catch up with Flora, who was already a few aisles down.

Back at the house, I decided to peek through Flora's cupboards in her kitchen while she tended to her garden out back. I found a few cans of Alcott's Pecans and examined them. They were the same exact ones that were being sold in the store. A black background with the bold red lettering.

I set them on the counter and searched further into the cupboard, pulling out an almost empty box of cornmeal. I turned it over and looked at the back. It displayed the ingredients and where it was distributed from. Off to the side, there was a quick recipe for basic cornbread. I set it down next to the pecans on the counter and snooped further into the cupboard, pulling out a tin can of peanuts. I examined it, noticing it was pretty similar to the packaging of Alcott's Pecans, only there was a recipe on the back for roasted peanuts. I rummaged through the cupboard some more, seeing that many of the things that Flora had included a recipe on their packaging.

I put everything back in place and opened the drawer where Flora kept her grocer advertisements and magazines. I flipped through Minton's Market and Butchery's catalogs and noticed that pretty much everything except Alcott's Pecans were featured with a coupon offering a good deal. I went through a few more, losing myself in the advertisements.

"What in the heck are you doing?" Clarabelle's voice croaked from behind me.

I let out a shocked gasp and twirled around, my hand placed firmly over my thumping heart.

"Jeez! What are you trying to do, give me a heart attack?" I said, still clutching my chest and taking deep breaths.

"What in the heck are you doing?" Clarabelle asked again. She stalked over to me and pointed at the advertisements I had splayed out on the table. "What's all this?"

"I was just looking," I said. "Did you notice how plain the Alcott's Pecans canister is?"

Clarabelle shrugged. "It ain't plain. It's fine as it is."

"I mean, there's really not much on there. Look." I brought over the box of cornmeal and the can of peanuts and pecans. "The cornmeal and peanuts have recipes on them."

"So?" Clarabelle said.

"So, Alcott's Pecans just has where the pecans are grown and where they're distributed from. No recipe on what to use them in or anything."

"Margaret, this is Georgia. We're practically born with pecans coming out of our ears. We know what to do with 'em. We don't need a recipe on the back of a can."

"But what about the people that don't normally buy pecans? They wouldn't know where to start. Aren't these things sold all over Georgia?"

"Yes, but everybody knows about pecan pie. And they can eat 'em right out of the can."

I shook my head. "No, I mean, what if Flora put her pecan bread recipe on the label? We already know everybody here in Savannah loves it. That way, they can make it in their own homes. And look, Alcott's Pecans are nowhere in Minton's advertisement catalogs. No offer for a coupon or anything."

Clarabelle shook her head and screwed her mouth up. "Flora don't want to sell out."

"It's not a sellout. It's a good deal. She can advertise the pecans in catalogs so more people will want to buy them. There's some heavy competition out there."

"I say it's a sell out," Clarabelle snipped. "Now you better put all of this away before Flora comes back in. You got no right snoopin' around her kitchen like this. This is her business. She never sold out before, and she's sure as heck not gonna do it now. Now mind your own beeswax and clean this up."

Clarabelle brushed past me and charged out the back door, walking down the porch steps and toward Flora, who was finishing up in her garden.

I let out a huff as I begrudgingly put everything back, giving the occasional narrow, side-eyed glance to Clarabelle who was still speaking with Flora outside. I slammed the cupboard door, agitated that I couldn't get that miserable woman to listen to me. So much for trying to help for once.

I knew I shouldn't have dwelled over something so trivial, but I couldn't help it. I continued to replay Clarabelle's reaction to my suggestion of putting Flora's pecan bread recipe on the can of pecans over and over in my head for the next few days. She acted as if I told her I was going to steal the Mona Lisa or something.

When Flora was out of earshot later that day, Clarabelle hissed to me not to even breathe my idea to Flora. I nearly told her to pound sand but held my tongue. Just because Clarabelle helped Flora at the pecan farm sometimes didn't give her the right to make business decisions.

One afternoon, after I helped Flora bring more maturing pecans to the freezer, she taught me how to make candied pecans, telling me that it was her go-to table snack for Thanksgiving and Christmas.

"I know Thanksgiving is still a while away," Flora said, "but the foliage is going to start showing soon. I got such a hankering for these."

"And you make these every year?" I asked, using a metal nutcracker to shell the pecans.

My hands had turned red from squeezing the two tongs together. The first time Flora tasked me to do this, the pecan went flying across the kitchen, and the shell nearly hit Flora in the face, causing her to let out one of her boisterous laughs. Once I got the hang of it, I used some kind of a metal pointy thing—that Flora later told me was called a picker—to dig the pecan out from the shell.

"Sure do," she said, mixing together warm butter, cinnamon, and sugar. "They're addicting. Once you've had just one, you're liable to eat the entire bowl!"

"So, I guess people like them as much as your pecan bread," I said, more as a statement than a question.

"People do like them very much. But my pecan bread is what I'm known for around here, even more than the pecans themselves. I've been making it for a very long time."

"I bet everyone wishes they could make it, too."

Flora gave a modest smile. "Oh, I'm sure they could. Why, it's easy. Anyone can make it."

"But there seems to be something about the way you make it," I said. "It's like when Siobhan makes corned beef and cabbage for dinner; I've had it at many restaurants and other people's houses, and they've all been good, but there's something about the way Siobhan cooks it that makes it better than everyone else's."

"Well, that's cause you're used to her recipe. It sounds pretty standard. My mama used to make the best canned peaches you've ever had. There ain't much to 'em. When we tried them from the store, they weren't the same. It's another reason I dogged her for the recipe growing up.

She finally gave it to me before she died. I make them now, same exact ingredients and way she used to, but they're not as good as hers. It's just the way she made them."

I winced as I squeezed the nutcracker, the shells cracking loudly beneath the tongs.

"No. I mean, it would be nice for everyone if they could make your specific recipe," I said.

"What are you getting at, honey?" Flora smiled.

I placed the nutcracker down on the counter and breathed in deeply through my nose. I didn't care what Clarabelle said. She was just a wacky old lady who didn't know what she was talking about anyway. She only wanted to annoy me. I turned toward Flora.

"I'm saying that you should put your pecan bread recipe on your labels," I said.

Flora slowed down her mixing. Her movements became stiff and rigid. Her smile faded a bit as she looked down at her bowl. She let out a light scoff and began mixing normally again.

"Oh," she said, "why would I do that? I enjoy making my pecan bread for everyone. Plus, if everybody made it for themselves, they wouldn't need me to do it for them anymore. I like doing it. It makes me feel good."

"It's something to think about, though. If you sold your pecans with a recipe on the package, it might make people want to buy them more. Not that they don't already, but it could help."

"Maggie," Flora said, her smile gone again, "it's real nice of you to be offering this idea. I know you're just trying to help, but I don't think it would work. I have to meet with Mr. Winston in a few days, and I don't think it would go over well."

"Why not?" I asked, not bothering to hide my irritation. "A lot of other products have recipes on their packaging, and they do really well. You've got a can of peanuts in the cupboard that tells you how to roast them. It sounds like a cinch!"

"Look," Flora said, her voice gentle, "it's just not how I—my husband used to do it. I'm not looking to change anything. I just want to keep selling the pecans the way he and his family did. I appreciate your ideas, but it's best if you keep them to yourself. I know you mean well, but it's really not your place to say how I should market my pecans. Do you understand?"

I hesitated, the disappointment rushing through my body from my head and down to my toes. What was so wrong with switching up the packaging a little? It would certainly bring her more sales. If she was so worried about how she would do this season, why couldn't she take my suggestion into consideration? She could at least take the time to think about it for a day or so. However, I was too annoyed to argue with her. I nodded stiffly.

"Fine." I turned back towards the counter and began feverishly cracking the pecans from their shells again.

CHAPTER FIFTEEN

I had to admit that I was a bit embarrassed over how snippy I got over Flora rejecting my pecan recipe idea. It was her recipe—and business now—after all. Still, I didn't expect her to basically tell me to stick my ideas where the sun didn't shine. Even if it was in her own, kind way.

On the day she was supposed to meet with Mr. Winston at Farmer's Food Company, she was a bundle of nerves, despite the fact that Clark would be tagging along.

"I always get like this whenever I have to meet with Mr. Winston," she said to me. "Ever since my husband died, I just get a little more nervous than usual."

"Why? Is he a boor?"

"Heavens, no!" Flora chuckled. "He's a very nice man, but he oversees everything that happens with my business. As you can imagine, it's a daunting feeling."

All of this business talk made my mind drift to my dad, which instantly gave me a headache. I shook him out of my head.

Flora spent the morning getting ready for her meeting and making sure she had everything she needed. I had the pleasure of spending the day with Clarabelle on the pecan farm, which I was not looking forward to in the slightest.

Flora was getting ready upstairs when a knock came at the front door. I opened it to see Clark. He looked like a kid that was dressed up in his dad's clothes.

"Hi, Maggie," he said entering the foyer. "You look cute."

I looked: I was wearing my farming outfit. I wasn't sure if he was being serious or making fun of me.

"Thanks," I said. "You look…grown up."

Clark let out a laugh. "Thanks. I know I probably look like I'm playing dress up. I don't wear a suit very much."

"Really? I would never have known." I gestured for him to come into the house further.

"So, you get the pleasure of spending the day with Clarabelle." A teasing smile crossed his lips.

I rolled my eyes. "Don't remind me. I want to get this over as quickly as possible. I'll go and harvest and store pecans with her, and when it's over, I'm going to settle myself into a warm bath because God knows I'll need it."

"Well, hello, Clark!" Flora came down the stairs and gave him a big kiss on the cheek.

Flora had traded in her homely house dress for a slightly upscale looking one. This one had a small floral print with a ruffled collar and fluttered sleeves that came up to her elbows. She even wore a nicer looking hat and a small string of pearls, which I had no idea she even owned. She grabbed her purse and papers.

"Oh, Maggie, remember, Clarabelle will be picking you up at about eleven." Flora said, standing in the threshold.

"Yes, I know." My tone was already filled with dread.

"Have a good day. I'll be back in the afternoon."

I nodded. "Well, knock them dead, or whatever it is you do there."

Flora smiled. "Thank you, honey. I hope to return with positive news."

"See ya, Maggie." Clark gave me a lopsided smile as he closed the door behind them.

I have never argued with a person more than I have with Clarabelle. Everything I said, she countered. We bickered the entire ride to the pecan farm—which was not even five minutes away from Flora's house.

I offered to drive Flora's truck, but she squawked about how she insisted on driving. It didn't help that Clarabelle was one of the worst drivers ever. The only time my life flashed before my eyes is when she came to a complete, halting stop when we finally arrived at the pecan farm. I thought I was going to shoot right through the windshield.

Clarabelle barked orders at me the entire time, constantly telling me what buckets to put the mature pecans in as if I were born yesterday, making me take mental notes of how many matured pecans there were versus the ones that were of no use.

It took everything in me not to lash out at her. She walked around the farm as if she owned the place, watching me do my tasks as she stood there with her arms folded.

"You can move faster than that, slow poke!" she said as I bent over on my hands and knees, picking pecans off the ground and putting them into a bucket.

I sucked in a deep breath and closed my eyes. "Don't kill her, Maggie. Don't kill her," I muttered to myself.

When we finally finished, and Clarabelle had run out of orders to give, we packed up the pecans in the back of her truck and headed back toward Flora's.

Clarabelle stopped in front of her house and shut the truck off, putting the keys on the dashboard. I really needed to tell these ladies a thing or two about car theft.

"Aren't we going to bring the pecans to Flora's?" I asked.

"We are." Clarabelle hopped out of the truck. "We're gonna have a little snack first."

"Oh." I shook my head. "I'm not hungry. Let's just take the pecans back. I'm tired and want to get out of these clothes."

"You'll be fine, Scarlett O'Hara. Get out of the truck and come in."

I begrudgingly obliged, following Clarabelle into her home. While I'd seen her house many times, this was the first time I'd ever been inside. It was a lot smaller than Flora's but equally bright and clean. She had just as many bibles and crosses, if not more.

I followed her into the kitchen, where a small, rounded wooden table sat in the center, holding the room together.

"You can sit." Clarabelle pointed and opened a cupboard.

She placed two short crystal glasses on the table, then walked into another room where she rustled things about. She came back holding a bottle in her hands.

I nearly fell out of my seat when I saw that she was pouring us each a generous glass of whiskey.

She sat down across from me, putting the bottle of whiskey in the center of the table.

"You drink whiskey?" I couldn't take my eyes off the bottle.

"Every now and then." She took a sip. "Burns something fierce, but I can't help but loving the stuff."

"I cannot believe you drink whiskey." I shook my head.

"You don't?" Clarabelle said, holding the glass to her lips.

"No, I do." I took the glass in my hand. "I mean…I'm more of a martini and Ward Eight kind of girl, but I've had whiskey before."

"Bottoms up, Margaret." Clarabelle raised her glass to me and took another sip.

I did the same, gulping deeply as the fiery taste careened down my throat. I let out an involuntary belch.

"Excuse me." I clenched my hand into a fist and held it against my mouth.

"It ain't for the light headed, I'll tell you that."

"Does Flora know you drink whiskey?" I asked.

"No. Why should she?"

"No offense, you don't seem like the whiskey type. Neither of you do. You seem like the type of person that would turn their nose up at the mere thought of consuming any kind of alcohol."

"They serve red wine in church, Margaret."

"I know, but that's different."

"I like to indulge myself in a glass of whiskey every now and then. Flora doesn't need to know about it. And I don't need to know what she does in her own home when I'm not there. I'm sure she has her own vices."

I shook my head. "She really doesn't. She's kind of saintly. I guess you could call indulging in all the treats she makes a vice, but other than that, it's all tea and cookies with her."

"Flora is a saintly woman." Clarabelle nodded.

"Why whiskey?" I took another sip.

"My husband Dale enjoyed it when he was alive. Sometimes I use it in my cooking—don't tell anyone that—and my daddy used to make it."

"Did he sell it?"

"Not in stores. He had these big ol' empty jugs that he used to put the whiskey in, then he'd give 'em to people in our town."

I never in my wildest thoughts would think that Clarabelle Barnett, who seemed to go out of her way to irritate me, would be a whiskey drinker. She tossed her sips back like she was drinking water. I thought I could hold my liquor quite well, but Clarabelle had certainly beaten me to the finish line in that department.

"Now don't you go telling Flora about this," Clarabelle said. "You might want to brush your teeth and wash your mouth out when you get back."

"She wouldn't approve?"

"She wouldn't be happy with it. Best to just cover it up so she doesn't know you were drinking."

"You really know Flora well."

"We're best friends."

"How long have you known each other?" I took another sip of whiskey.

"Since we were young girls. We were in the same cotillion class. I was twelve, and Flora was eleven. Turns out, we lived in the same town not too far from one another and never knew. We were inseparable from then on. We went to high school together, and she even introduced me to my husband, Dale—which was both a blessing and a curse. I was her son's Godmother. Loved that little boy as if he were my own."

"Really? No offense, I can't picture you being around kids. Or quite frankly, tolerating them."

"I loved Alfred Jr.," Clarabelle said, her tone somewhat defensive.

"Why didn't you and Dale have children?"

Clarabelle became quiet for a moment. Her gaze floated down to her glass of whiskey, and her shoulders drooped slightly.

"I was supposed to be a mama."

"Did you just never get the chance?"

When her eyes drifted back up to mine, there was a sadness etched through them. "She didn't make it home from the hospital."

It took me a moment to realize what Clarabelle was telling me. When I understood, my heart dropped, and a pain twisted in its place.

"Oh. I'm sorry."

"Thank you," Clarabelle said, her voice soft. She blinked, reassuming her rigid position. "It was a long time ago. It still hurts to think about every now and then, but I'm glad I still got to be part of a wonderful, young child's life, even if he didn't belong to me."

I was still at a somewhat loss for words. However, I could tell that Clarabelle wanted to get off the subject. I did, too, not because I was uncomfortable, but because I saw how much pain it still brought her.

Clarabelle crinkled her nose and screwed up her mouth. "Come on." She took one last swig of whiskey. "Let's get those pecans back to Flora's before she gets home."

I went upstairs to take a bath and get dressed the minute I arrived back at Flora's. I did as Clarabelle advised and brushed my teeth to wash the whiskey smell off my breath. I was reading a magazine in the den when Flora returned.

"Hi, honey," she said lightly and plopped down on the sofa.

"Hi." I straightened up and placed my magazine down on the table next to me. "How did it go?"

"It went fine," Flora said. Judging by her tone, however, I didn't buy a word of it.

"Are you sure? You seem kind of down."

Flora expelled a deep sigh. "I guess the sales in my pecans have decreased a bit more since our last meeting. They haven't been performing as well as Mr. Winston would like."

"Oh," I said. "Well, I'm sure you'll get them back up."

She gave me an empty smile. "Thank you, hon. I'm gonna make some tea. Would you like some?"

"Sure."

I followed her into the kitchen where we sat at the table with our tea and some pecan bread. Flora nibbled at hers in silence. I felt sort of bad for her. She let out a deep breath as she popped a pecan in her mouth.

I took a sip of my tea. "Hey, it'll be fine. I mean, I'm sure this isn't the first time your sales have dipped…no offense."

Flora shook her head gently. "No, you're right. It's not like my pecans have been hot sellers since day one. Even when my husband and his family ran the business, they saw their times of hardship. It happens to the best of us. I only hope things pick up soon, especially since Thanksgiving and Christmas will be coming around the corner before you know it. I just don't like letting people down, that's all."

"Well, if sales don't pick up, what can happen?"

"For starters, Mr. Winston's company would lose money. Of course, they have other products that sell fine, but my pecans are usually the best seller for them. I know it doesn't sound like a lot, but it's important to me and Mr. Winston that my pecans have steady sales. There are a lot of other great pecans out there that give mine a run for their money."

I looked down at the crumbs of pecan bread on my plate, my rejected idea from the other day popping back into my head. I brought my eyes back up to Flora.

"Maybe this would be a good time to run the idea of putting your recipe on the labels," I said.

Flora's eyes creased, and her brows knitted together. "Maggie, I already told you, it's not happening."

I shrugged. "I know, but maybe he would go for it if the sales aren't doing as well as before."

Flora shook her head. "He wouldn't. It doesn't matter how good or bad my sales are doing, Mr. Winston would never agree."

I lowered my head, not so much from dejection but from the fact that Flora seemed to not want to consider a change that might help her out.

She reached over and grabbed my hand in hers.

"I'm sorry to sound so short, but I need you take your idea out of your head. Take it out, and don't ever think about it again because it's never going to happen. Okay?"

After some hesitation, I nodded. Although I gave her my word, I still kept the thought tucked away in the back of my mind.

It was unusually warm for the first day of October. Flora assured me that it was quite normal. Even though I had been in Savannah for nearly three months, I was still getting used to the Southern weather in contrast to Massachusetts, which would be experiencing cool and crisp days by now. The warmer weather didn't stop Flora from making pecan laced fall treats, however.

One afternoon, Flora convinced me to make an apple crisp with her. I guess she wanted to take a break from the pecans. The entire house filled with the warm smells of cinnamon, brown sugar, and apples. If I could, I would've bottled up the scent and worn it as a perfume.

Flora sang *"By the Light of the Silvery Moon"* as she peeled the apples. Her lilt voice wobbled up and down. So, maybe there was one thing she couldn't do. When she asked me to join in, I shook my head and grinned at her silly pleading for me to sing. I sang a few bars of *"Lydia, the Tattooed Lady"* to humor her.

"Oh, Maggie! You have a lovely voice!" Flora said.

"At least someone thinks so." I grinned.

Flora sang again, and before I knew it, she roped me into crooning along with her. I found myself enjoying our little kitchen concert more than I thought I would have. So much so that Flora and I didn't realize a loud knock was banging against the front door.

"That must be the mail," I said, still chuckling from our singing.

"Here." Flora took a nickel out of her apron pocket and handed it to me. "Would you mind getting it?"

I wiped my hands on my own apron and walked out to the hallway. When I opened the door, a different kid than our usual mail boy was standing on the porch. He looked around twelve-years-old and wore a more tailored outfit.

"Maggie O'Hanlon?" he said, his Southern accent squeaky with innocence.

"That's me," I said.

"Here you go." He held out an envelope to me, and I gave him the nickel in return. "Thank you, Miss." He tipped his hat.

I closed the door behind me. The words on the envelope read *Western Union Telegram* in bold caps on the top. I tore it open and began to read. I immediately dropped the envelope onto the ground. My hands cramped up and prickled as if they were made of needles. I gripped the letter so hard, I thought my nails would tear through it. My legs began to feel invisible beneath me. I reached a hand out, searching for something to support me. I slumped down onto the little bench against the wall, my head swirling as I stared at the words on the paper, which was now shaking violently beneath my grasp.

Flora appeared next to me, her presence hovering near my shoulder.

"Was that the mail?" she asked.

I shook my head. Or at least I think I did. My entire body felt paralyzed.

"What is it, honey?" Flora asked, stepping into my view.

"My uncle." The only words I could muster from my mouth as my hand searched for the locket around my neck. I gripped it tightly.

"Oh. What does he have to say?"

I forced my head to shake slowly back and forth, the gesture physically aching me. Everything in that moment felt paused, as if all life around me had stopped moving. The Earth had come to a screeching halt. All I could hear was the sound of my own hollow, constricted breathing.

I swallowed hard. "He's dead."

CHAPTER SIXTEEN

Flora's voice sounded like it was coming from a tunnel. It took me a second to realize that I was still in Savannah, and that she was sitting right next to me.

"Oh, my goodness!" she exclaimed. "Oh no! How did it happen?"

"His nightmares. Couldn't breathe." My words came out in fragmented, confusing sentences.

I stared ahead, my eyes fixating on the painting of the pecan farm, its muted brown and green colors blurring together.

"May I?" Flora asked.

I let her take the letter from me, not moving a muscle. I didn't have to turn my head to look at her. I knew her mouth was moving along to the words on the paper, something I had come to learn she did when reading.

She let out a shuddered breath. "Your daddy wants you on the first train out of here tomorrow morning."

I still didn't move. I continued to sit on the bench, staring at the wall. It hurt to breathe, as if someone punched me right in the stomach.

"I'm so sorry." Flora's voice warbled with sympathy.

I had to be on the morning train home tomorrow. I tried to move my legs to stand up, but nothing happened. Flora must've read my mind because she linked her arm into mine and helped me to my feet. I forced myself to turn my head and look at her. Her lashes were wet, and there were small streaks of tears at the corners of her eyes.

"I know you don't like hugging very much," she said. "So, I don't want to make you uncomfortable. Why don't you go pack your things and get ready to head home for tomorrow? Do you need any help?"

I shook my head slowly.

Flora held my hand in hers and squeezed it gently.

"Go on, honey," she said, guiding me towards the staircase and patting my hand. "Go get ready to go home."

I managed to walk upstairs to my room. I took out all my luggage from under the bed and packed them tediously, forgetting how much I had actually brought with me. My body was numb as I packed. Even the tiniest movement felt as if I were dragging thousand-pound weights.

Flora made an early dinner so I could go to bed and be up in time to catch the morning train. I barely ate anything, picking at my meatloaf and potatoes as I stared blindly at the salt and pepper shakers in front of me.

"I know it's hard," Flora lulled. "But you must try to eat a little something. Grief isn't kind to an empty stomach."

I mustered enough energy to lift the fork and bring it to my mouth, taking a bite. Even Flora's delicious food had no taste. It was as if my senses were shut off.

After dinner, Flora sent me upstairs to get some sleep. I lay on my back, not bothering to apply my night cream to my face or put my hair up into rollers. I couldn't even bring myself to close my eyes. It was as if they had been glued open. It was still light out, and even though I had pulled the shades down as far as they could go, I could see slivers of late evening sunlight trying to creep its way through my window.

My entire body was still numb the next morning. The muscles in my face ceased to show any flicker of expression. Even my eyes, which were exhausted and dark rimmed from a lack of night's sleep, were unable to produce a single tear of grief.

Flora, on the other hand, couldn't stop herself from welling up every time she looked at me. She made me breakfast, asking every five minutes how I was doing. I could only bring myself to nod my head stiffly; speaking still feeling like an insurmountable obstacle.

Flora drove me to the train station. I sat still as a statue next to her, staring out at the road ahead.

"I don't expect you to come back." Her voice trembled. "I would understand if you didn't. If you can, would you write a letter to me, to let me know how you and your folks are doing? If you think of it. If you don't, I understand."

Flora helped with my luggage and walked over to the platform with me. We stood waiting as the train whistle sounded off in the distance.

"Well…" Flora said, her voice one tremble away from a full on sob.

She was trying to keep it together, however, the tears that escaped from her eyes didn't help. She bit the bottom of her lip and wiped her nose with a handkerchief.

"It's been a pleasure getting to know you, Maggie." She began to cry. "I can't tell you how much joy you brought to me these past few months. You made my life a little less lonely."

I nodded. "Thanks." It was all I could bring myself to say.

"Again, I am so very sorry about your uncle. I know how much he meant to you."

"Thanks," I said again.

The train chugged closer.

Flora looked at me, her eyes continuing to produce fresh tears.

"Goodbye, Maggie," she said.

I swallowed. "Bye."

I let her give me a small hug. Unlike her others, this one was light and quick.

The conductor came out and helped me board my ridiculous amount of luggage into the undercarriage. I was able to turn my head and look out the window. Flora waved to me from the platform, a gesture I couldn't bring myself to return.

As I sat on the train, I read my dad's telegram obsessively but had to stop myself when I couldn't tear my eyes away from his opening sentence:

MAGGIE,

UNCLE JAMES HAS DIED.

I must've read that line one hundred times. Every time I tried to read the rest, my eyes would drift back to that sentence. I couldn't stop reading it. I even saw it flash in my mind when I stuffed the telegram into my coat pocket. No matter how many times I tried to digress my thoughts, it kept coming back and haunting me the entire ride home.

My dad stood on the train platform of South Station amongst the swarm of people waiting for their own family or friends to get off with me. He was wearing his dark gray trench coat and fedora, and his hands were stuffed into his pockets. Judging by the expression on his face, the train station looked like the last place on Earth he wanted to be. I could see from my window that his knees were shaking back and forth. Not because he was cold; it was something he usually did when he wanted to get a move on.

I barely had time to step off the train when he motioned for me to hurry up. I grabbed my luggage from the undercarriage and walked over to him. He promptly grabbed two of my trunks out of my hands and walked swiftly.

"Nice to see you, too," I said, trying to catch up with him.

"I'm in a rush, Maggie." He swung his arm back and forth, pushing his way through everyone on the platform. "We have to get back home. I'm in the middle of finishing some stuff up for the funeral. My whole day is thrown off. Your mother and I had to postpone a meeting with a potential new location."

"Oh, well, sorry Uncle James' death is so inconvenient for you."

Dad stopped in his tracks and turned to me, pointing his finger. "That's enough. I'm not in the mood for your wisecrack comments. Now let's go."

The car ride home was silent. Dad sped his way through town. I looked at the trees outside my window. They were bursting with vibrant colors of red, orange, and yellow. They stood out particularly on this dreary, gray afternoon.

We finally made it home. I looked up at my house as I entered it, gliding my hand over the black wrought iron rail, which was cold beneath my skin.

When we entered the house, I could smell Siobhan's corned beef and cabbage from the door. Although the scent was comforting and familiar, it brought no sense of pleasure to me.

I placed my makeup trunk and hat box in the foyer, and Dad dropped my other two trunks that he was holding to the ground.

"Siobhan!" he called out, taking his coat and hat off. "We're back!"

Within seconds, Siobhan scurried out of the kitchen and took my dad's things out of his hands.

"Miss Maggie!" she said, her green eyes lighting up. "I'm so sorry about your unc—"

"Siobhan, is everything almost ready?" Dad cut her off.

"Oh yes, sir." Siobhan nodded, still holding onto my dad's hat and coat in her hands. "Miss Maggie, may I take your things for you?"

"No thanks," I said. "I'll take everything up to my room and unpack myself."

"Oh, but you have so much with you." Siobhan opened the closet door and put my dad's hat and coat inside. "At least let me help you bring them up."

"All right." I nodded. "Thank you."

Once alone in my bedroom, I looked around. At one point, I thought I may never see it again. I sat down on my pink bedspread and swept my hand against it, feeling the soft, cozy fabric beneath my fingertips. I lay down on my bed, remembering how much I missed the feel of its mattress beneath me.

After I finished putting my stuff away, I went back downstairs and saw my ma reading something in the study. I walked in and stood in the doorway, waiting for her to look up and notice me. When she didn't, I made my presence known.

"I'm back," I said dully.

She looked up, her face void of any expression. "Yes, your father told me he brought you home before he went back out."

"Where did he go?" I walked further into the room.

"He had to go to the store to pick up some extra potatoes for Siobhan. She put the corned beef on a little while ago and wants to keep an eye on it."

"That was nice of him," I said, not caring to cover up my sarcasm.

My ma shot me a glare. "Did you put your things away?"

I stared at her. Not even a simple 'hello.' No expression over how much she missed her only child who was gone for nearly three months. Nothing. It was as if I never left.

"Yes," I said, my voice curt and dry.

"Good." She nodded. "You know Uncle James' funeral is in two days. I advise you to find something suitable to wear. Put it on your bed. I'll make sure Siobhan irons it."

I didn't bother to answer her, not that she would care in the first place. I just turned around and left the room.

I walked down the hallway and stopped outside of Uncle James' bedroom. The door was closed. I put my hand on the knob, freezing for a moment. I closed my eyes and turned the knob slowly, the door letting out an eerie creak.

It was dark inside his room. I walked in, not even bothering to turn the light on. His bed was all made, as if Siobhan thought it would be indecent to keep it unkempt despite the fact that he would never lie in it again. I glided my hand across his soft blanket.

His wheelchair sat next to his bed. I gripped the handles, as I had done so many times whenever I would wheel him around the house or take him for a walk outside. I bent over and placed my hand on the seat where his imprint still sat. The cushion was cold, giving me the cruel reminder that it hadn't been occupied for a long time.

In my dad's telegram, he had mentioned how Uncle James' night terrors got worse, and how he would have episodes during the day, even when he was awake. It got to the point where he refused to leave his bed, no longer wanting to sit in his chair. I couldn't help picturing him, lying in his bed, his tortured screams reverberating throughout the house as Siobhan helplessly tried to calm him down. I shuddered and took my hand off of his seat.

I slowly lowered myself into the armchair where I used to sit every day, talking to Uncle James about things that seemed so trivial now.

Siobhan was hard at work, doing double duty in the kitchen. In between cutting potatoes and chopping carrots, and keeping an eye on the corned beef, I'd never seen her look so unglued before.

"Need any help?" I walked up beside her.

She looked over at me, continuing to chop carrots. A lock of her blonde hair had fallen out of its updo. Small beads of sweat had formed beneath her hairline.

"No, Miss Maggie," she said hastily. "I've got it. Thank you."

"Are you sure? I don't mind."

She furrowed her brows. I couldn't tell if she was confused or annoyed that I was offering to help. She cocked her head.

"You can cut the potatoes in half." She brought her concentration back to the carrots.

I took the knife beside her and began to work.

We were silent for a moment. While Siobhan was always friendly and kind, she was not one for small talk. My dad had instilled that in her when she first began working for us when I was a kid. Even though she lived with us, she still left very little time for getting to know her.

"I'm very sorry about your uncle, Miss Maggie," she said, not breaking her concentration from her work. "I know how close you both were."

I slowed down my cutting. This was the first time Siobhan had ever tried to have a real conversation with me. Not that I ever tried to in the past either, but it was something in that moment that made me appreciate her more than I ever had—or should have.

"Thanks," I said.

"That poor fellow." She shook her head. "At least he's finally at peace, thank the Lord."

I bit the inside of my lip. The thought that the last year of my uncle's life was spent in emotional and psychological torment made a horrible feeling burn in the pit of my stomach.

"Do you want to talk about it, Miss?"

I shook my head. "No, thanks."

"Are you glad to be home, at least?"

I hesitated. For the longest time, I had wanted nothing more than to come home, than to be in my own bed, kitchen, to be with Uncle James. Now that he was gone, I felt like a visitor in my own house. As if I didn't have any business being here. While I was glad to be back in my own environment, it still felt uneventful. I had missed my city so much and would've given my left arm to come back, but not under these circumstances. Not like this.

"I am," I finally said. "I just wish it was for a different reason."

"Aye. Me, too."

After Siobhan and I finished with the vegetables and put them in a pot with the cabbage, we set up the dining table. Deciding to lighten the mood, I told her everything about Savannah. I told her about Flora and her pecan farm and how she made the best pecan bread I'd ever tasted. I told her how Flora and her late husband are household names down in Georgia, akin to how O'Hanlon's is known throughout the entire North East. I told her about Clark and how he looked like Mickey Rooney to the point where the resemblance was eerie. I even talked about Clarabelle and how much she irritated me and couldn't help but laugh when I mentioned her little secret about being a whiskey drinker.

"She would absolutely murder me if she knew I told you," I chuckled.

"Do you miss it already?" Siobhan asked.

I didn't answer for a moment. I stopped, thinking about everything I had left back in Georgia and how my real life was now back before me, even if the most important piece was no longer here. I let out a scoff and shook my head.

"No. I learned a lot there, but I'm happy to finally be home."

"Don't seem that way, Miss." Siobhan placed down a fork and knife at my dad's place on the table.

I turned around and looked at her, my eyebrows furrowing. "What?"

"Pardon me," Siobhan said, "but the way you talk about this Flora, and what's her name, Clarabelle? And this fellow, Clark? I've never heard you talk about a boy this much before. The way you talk about this pecan farm, forgive me, but it sounds like you miss it quite a bit."

"Well, I don't." My voice took on a slightly defensive tone. "Sure, I ended up thinking Georgia wasn't as bad as I was expecting it to be, and maybe Flora is one of the nicest—if not the kindest person I've ever met. And Clarabelle—while terribly irritating—is not afraid to back down to anyone. I mean, I knew my time there wouldn't last. I knew not to get attached to anything or anyone."

"If you say so, Miss."

I would sneak a glance at her every now and then as we finished setting up the table. While I hated admitting defeat or being wrong, there was no way on Earth I was going to tell Siobhan that there was a part of me that knew that she was right.

CHAPTER SEVENTEEN

Despite having my favorite meal in front of me, I had no appetite. I moved the potatoes and cabbage around on my plate with my fork and took small nibbles of the corned beef. My dad worked and ate simultaneously. He shoveled the food into his mouth, all while looking over paperwork. My ma, on the other hand, ate her dinner meticulously. I had been home for nearly three hours and barely had a full conversation with either of them. Siobhan came in and refilled our water glasses.

"Thank you." I glanced up at her.

She nodded in return.

I looked at my parents who didn't even bother to say a word to her. Siobhan and I met eyes again, and she gave me a light, melancholy smile before heading back towards the kitchen. I took my fork and stabbed a few pieces of corned beef with it, shoveling it into my mouth.

I looked back at my dad, who continued to keep his attention on his paperwork. I don't know why I couldn't stop watching him; this wasn't the first time he had brought his work to the dinner table. In fact, I couldn't recall a lot of instances when he didn't have some form of work with him while he was eating. The times he didn't, he ate like he hadn't had food in months, taking large forkfuls, barely having any time to enjoy or appreciate the taste of it.

"It's amazing how you don't miss your mouth," I said.

Dad stopped for a moment, his face a mixture of confusion and frustration that he had been disrupted. He went back to eating.

"I have a lot to get done," he said.

"Still," I said. "It's quite impressive, I must say."

Dad looked back up at me, this time his eyes furrowed with annoyance. His mouth was full of corned beef and cabbage. He took a giant swallow.

"Are you finished?" he said.

I took a sip of my water, my eyes watching him over the rim as he shook his head and went back to work.

"Hey, listen." I put my glass back down on the table. "Can I ask you something?"

"What?" Dad said.

"Do a lot of the products in your stores have recipes on the labels? You know, like nuts and corn meal and stuff?"

Dad looked up at me and screwed his mouth. "I don't know, Maggie. Why does it matter?"

"I'm only wondering. The label for Flora's pecans is pretty drab and—"

"Who is Flora?" Dad interjected.

I stared at him, my mouth almost hanging open. Was he being serious?

"Flora?" I said. "Flora Alcott? The woman you sent me to stay with? I've been gone for nearly three months."

"Oh," Dad said, the light bulb finally going off in his brain. "Yes, what about her?"

"You seriously forgot the name of the woman I was staying with?"

Dad took a sip of his water and slammed it down on the table. "I've been kind of preoccupied. It slipped my mind. Now what about her?"

I hesitated before speaking as an attempt to wash away my bewilderment. "Well, she makes this pecan bread that'll knock your socks off, and everyone over in Savannah loves it, so I—"

"What are you getting at?" Dad's tone held agitation. "Why are you going on about pecan bread? Why would I care about that?"

I furrowed my eyebrows and shook my head. "If you would listen to me and let me finish my sentence, I could tell you!"

"Don't yell at your father," Ma said.

"I'm not yelling! He's not letting me get a word in edgewise! All I'm trying to do is ask if it's common for products to have recipes on their labels."

"I don't know, Maggie," Dad said. "I don't pay attention to those things. All I care about is if the product is good and if it will sell."

"But wouldn't having a recipe on the label be an extra boost? You sell pecans at your store, right? Well, don't you think people would like to have an idea on what to do with them? I'm talking other than roasting them or making a pie. Anyone can do that."

"Then let them!" Dad said. "If that's what they want to do with the pecans, let them make the damn pie!"

"But that isn't the point." I placed my clenched fist on the table. "I've been trying to convince Flora to put her pecan bread recipe on her labels. I think it could help her sales!"

"You don't know the first thing about sales," Dad said. "How do you know it would help? What if she went along with your idea and it ruined everything? Don't be telling people how to run their business."

"Your father is right," Ma said. "Best to stay out of it."

I looked at my parents back and forth. I took my napkin off my lap, wiped the corners of my mouth with it, chucked it onto the table, and stood up. I picked up my plate.

"What are you doing?" Dad asked.

I looked at him, my chin raised and my eyes narrowed. "I'm going to eat with Siobhan in the kitchen."

"Why?" he asked. "Sit back down, and finish your supper."

"I'm going to eat with her," I said defiantly, before heading out of the dining room and into the kitchen.

The fact that it rained on the day of Uncle James' funeral was another punch to the gut. While we were inside during the sermon, the gray clouding outside the stained-glass windows made the inside of the church seem darker than it actually was. I sat stoically in between my parents, who were just as emotionless and expressionless. We listened to the priest give his sermon as he stood next to Uncle James' casket with a large American flag draped over it. Although I kept my Bible open during the hymns, I never once opened my mouth to sing along. My parents, surprisingly, were a little more compliant as they mouthed the words in a tight-lipped murmur to themselves.

The congregation was nearly full. All around us sat neighbors, workers from O'Hanlon's, as well as friends and investors that my Uncle James knew through working with my dad. Siobhan was right next to my father, a handkerchief gripped in her gloved hand.

In the pew across from us sat Ellen and Norma. I was surprised to see them here, given our last meetings were disastrous. Guilt stabbed at me as I thought of how much I hurt Ellen when I bought the dress she loved, my selfish act feeling like a lifetime ago. I wouldn't have blamed her if she never forgave me and didn't come. Still, I couldn't help but be grateful and appreciative that either of them showed up at all.

After the sermon, we moved to the cemetery to lay Uncle James to rest. I stood next to Siobhan, who held an umbrella over our heads. My dad and ma stood next to the priest, their eyes not leaving the ground the entire time. The priest said one final prayer, and everyone took turns throwing a rock on the casket one by one as "Taps" played.

The Army Lieutenant meticulously folded the flag on Uncle James' casket. He stood for a second before taking it in his hands and walking over to us. I thought he was going to present it to my dad when he came over to me and held it out.

My stomach dropped, and my entire body shivered. With shaking hands, I took the flag from him.

He stood tall and gave me a cordial salute.

My chin trembled, and I immediately bit the inside of my mouth. I swallowed as I felt the cool fabric of the flag beneath my fingers. I gave him a muted nod, my words lost.

Just like that, it was over. Once the priest closed his Bible, everyone dispersed out, giving my parents and me one more hug or silent shoulder rub.

My dad motioned us to hurry along.

I followed them slowly toward the car, clutching the flag close to my chest, the last piece of my uncle that I would ever get to hold.

Ellen and Norma walked over to me, both huddling together under the same umbrella. They were shivering from the cold October air, and their cheeks were stained with a mixture of rain and tears.

"Oh, Maggie," Ellen said, her voice thick with sympathy. "We're both so terribly sorry about your uncle."

"We know how much he meant to you," Norma said.

"He was such a good man," Ellen countered.

"Thank you," I said, my voice sounding foreign to my own ears. "I...uh...really appreciate that you came."

"Of course, we would!" Norma said.

"Listen." I brought my eyes to the ground, belated shame coloring my cheeks. "I owe you both an apology. Especially Ellen." I looked up at them. "I'm sorry I bought that dress when I knew you wanted it so much. It was very selfish of me. If you want...you can have it. I can bring it over to you—"

Ellen shook her head. "It's all right, Maggie." Her voice was soft. "I shouldn't have let myself get so upset over a silly dress."

"No," I said. "You had every right to. I was an awful friend, and I'm sorry."

"Well, thank you." Ellen took hesitant pauses in between her words. "Your apology means a lot."

"And, Norma," I turned to her, "I'm sorry to you as well. I tried to use you to find me a job and still treated you like scum while doing it."

Norma paused before nodding, her expression neutral. "I forgive you, Maggie."

A lump lodged in my throat. I didn't deserve friends as kind as them. If someone had done to me what I did to Ellen and Norma, I would've told them where to stick it and never give them the time of day again. Ellen and Norma were better friends than I could ever be. I only wished I could go back and be the kind of friend they deserved. However, despite their forgiveness, I knew our friendship would forever be tainted.

"Well," I said, struggling to hide the strain in my voice. "Thank you again for coming."

"Wait," Ellen said, putting a gentle hand on my arm. "Now that you're back home for good, won't you come with us for a drink or something? It'll be just like old times."

I hesitated for a moment, taking their offer in. However, I shook my head and met my eyes with theirs.

"You know what?" I said. "Thank you for the offer, but no."

"Oh, well, we understand," Ellen said after exchanging a glance with Norma. "I guess it was sort of indecent of us to ask right after the funeral."

"Some other time, then?" Norma asked.

Again, I didn't answer right way, knowing very well what it would be. But to appease them, and to get myself out of this cemetery and into the warm car, I nodded.

"Sure. Some other time."

Ellen and Norma each took a turn giving me a small hug and a quick kiss on each cheek.

I watched them walk off, their black stockings peeking out from the bottom of the umbrella. I watched until I could no longer see them, then I walked back to the car by myself.

We scurried back into the house, shaking off the rain from our umbrellas.

Siobhan put our coats and hats in the closet while my parents and I went into the parlor. Siobhan took the flag from me and brushed it gently with her hand.

"I promise I'll put it somewhere good and safe, Miss," she said after I expressed hesitation with letting it go.

I sat in the large, tufted, leather chair while my dad nursed a brandy that Siobhan had brought him.

My ma sat on the leather sofa across from me, silent as always.

My dad tossed back the last of his brandy and set it down on the table. He stood, fingers interlaced through his belt loops. I watched him as he stared out of the rain-streaked window, unsure of what to say.

"That was a nice sermon," I finally spoke up.

My dad nodded. "It was," he said, his voice even.

"It was nice seeing everyone again." I gave an absent-minded shrug and looked down. "Despite the circumstances."

Dad continued to stare out the window. His features were hard and chiseled, almost as if he were made of stone. My eyes focused on the chess set in front of me. A melancholic grin twitched at the edge of my lips, and I let out a pensive chuckle.

"I used to play so many games with him. He used to let me win as a kid, but—"

I was interrupted by Dad's loud sigh as he swiftly walked away from the window. "I need to start getting things in order."

I furrowed my eyebrows. "In order? What do you mean?"

"I have to go down to the North Shore location today. I need to do one last run through before we leave."

"Leave?" I said. "Where are we going?"

My dad looked at me as if I were the craziest person on Earth. "Your mother and I are going down to Tennessee. We want to see if we can open a new location there."

"Wait a minute." I put my hand up, trying desperately to wrap my head around what my dad just told me. "You're going to Tennessee? When?"

"We're scheduled to leave tomorrow morning," Dad said.

"Tomorrow?" I exclaimed. "When did you decide this?"

"While you were gone," Dad said.

"We wanted to go to Savannah," Ma said. "But you never got back to us."

Now it was my turn to look at them as if they were the craziest people on Earth.

I shook my head. "I'm sorry. I don't understand. You're going to Tennessee the day after Uncle James' funeral?"

"Yes," Dad said. "Our jobs can't stop just because he passed away."

"But a day after?"

"Yes! I had to take a lot of time away from my work to plan his funeral."

"Oh, how terrible for you," I shot.

"Hey!" Dad pointed his finger at me, his eyebrows knitted together and his lips sucked in. "Watch your mouth. This is important for our business. I had no choice."

"You had no choice?" I said, animosity surging through my voice. "It's your business! Of course you had a choice. You just decided to take the wrong one!"

"That's enough, Maggie!" Dad shouted, a slight crack in his voice. "I don't need to hear this right now."

"Dad." I stood up from my chair and walked toward him. "I know you're upset, but Uncle James was your brother and business partner. You're allowed to take a few days off to grieve for him."

Dad looked away, the temple in his jaw pulsing.

"Dad. Dad, look at me."

He continued to keep his gaze averted.

Hesitantly, I held his hand in my own.

The vein in his forehead throbbed, and his body stiffened. His eyes shifted, finally meeting mine, and I gave his hand a gentle squeeze.

He turned his head again, a small quiver hitching in his chin. With a swift move, he wrenched his hand out of mine.

"I'll be back, Mary," he muttered, walking past me. "Make sure Siobhan has dinner ready for when I return."

I clenched my fists at my sides and glowered at him.

"What is wrong with you?"

Dad stopped. He turned slowly and faced me. Right then, he looked much older than his forty-six years. His face was gray, and dark stubble had formed around his usually clean-shaven mouth and chin. His eyes possessed dark circles underneath, and he had acquired small wrinkles around the corners of them.

"What did you say to me?" he said, his voice low.

"You heard me. What is wrong with you?"

Dad walked slowly toward me, his arms dangling at his sides. He stopped, staring me down.

"Don't talk to me that way, Maggie," he warned.

"Why? You obviously don't care that Uncle James is gone. Siobhan and I seem to be the only ones that do."

"Of course, I care!" Dad said.

"Oh, sure. You just couldn't wait to get the funeral over with so you could get back to your precious store."

Dad pointed his finger in my face. "Now, listen. I worked damn hard to make this business what I wanted it to be. I've been working since I was ten years old, and I'm not stopping anytime soon. Stopping gets you nowhere. You have to keep going no matter what. I've worked my rear end off to give this family a good life. All of this is the reason for my hard work, your uncle's hard work, and your mother's. We wouldn't be living here if it weren't for my business. You wouldn't be able to wear your dresses and go wherever you want to go if it wasn't for my business. You have absolutely no respect for this family or responsibility. I thought sending you away for a few months would shape you up, but it just made everything worse. It was a huge mistake. What did this Florence lady teach you anyway? To bake a pie? She obviously did nothing for you."

My nostrils flared. I balled my fists up at my sides. My breathing quickened, and my heart thumped madly in my chest.

"Her name is Flora," I said, my teeth clenched. "Flora Alcott. And she is the nicest, kindest person I've ever known. She didn't care how I was when I got there. I showed no appreciation toward her, and she still treated me with kindness. She showed me how to work hard, even on the days when you don't want to lift a finger. She showed me how to bake with pecans and how to tell if they're ready to harvest or not. She showed me how to care about other people for a change.

"When it was Uncle James' birthday, she saw how much I missed him and made a Shepherd's pie and a cake to cheer me up. She didn't have to do that for me, but she did. She did it because she cares. She's done more for me in the past three months than you have in twenty-three years!"

"Don't you raise your voice at your father!" Ma piped in.

"And you're no better!" I turned, jabbing my finger in her direction. "You just followed whatever he did! You were never there! You were either at the stores with him or holed up in the study counting your money! Flora's a better mother to me than you'll ever be!"

My ma sat back, aghast. Her eyes widened, and she looked at me as if I had clobbered her across the face.

"Hey!" Dad screamed. "Don't you dare disrespect your mother. Apologize!"

"No," I growled.

"Dammit, Margaret! Apologize to your mother."

"No," I said again, my lip curled up into a sneer. I stared at my dad with cold eyes. "I'm going back." I started to walk away.

"Like hell you're going back," Dad said. "You're staying here."

I stopped and turned around to face him. I shook my head.

"No, I'm not," I said, my voice carrying a small hitch. "I wish you had a son like you always wanted. That way, he could've turned out just like you. A selfish, heartless money grubber."

I gave my dad one last icy glare before turning back around and storming upstairs to repack my things.

CHAPTER EIGHTEEN

I packed my things immediately, this time opting for one large trunk and fitting in as many things as I could into it. Siobhan had put the flag from Uncle James' casket at the top of my closet. I brought it down and sat on my bed, gliding my hand over it. I put it on top of everything in my trunk and closed it shut.

I telephoned Western Union and asked them to send a telegram to Flora, letting her know that I was coming back right away, and to not worry about meeting me at the station. I would take a cab to her house. I didn't mention anything about the events at home, just that I was coming back and was planning on staying for as long as I could.

I felt a little guilty giving Flora such short notice about my return. However, knowing the kind of woman she was, I had a feeling she would greet me with open arms and that kind, warm smile of hers.

My parents left for Tennessee as planned the next morning. Not once did either of them come up to my room and try to talk to me about our argument. I was no better, either, blatantly ignoring them and coming down for breakfast after they had left. I honestly didn't know if I would ever see them again, and in that moment, I didn't care. They certainly didn't, so I figured why should I?

I did, however, feel bad saying goodbye to Siobhan. All those years she helped take care of me, and I never took the time to thank her for everything. Until now.

"Thank you for everything, Siobhan. You practically raised me along with Uncle James. I'm sorry I never showed you appreciation."

"Oh, Miss Maggie," she said. "I do wish you were staying."

"I can't." I shook my head. "You can tell my parents I went back to Flora's. They won't care. I'm sure they'll find something else to occupy their minds."

"That isn't true," she said.

I gave Siobhan a sad smile. "No, it is."

"Be good, Miss Maggie." She rustled in her apron pocket and clamped her hand over mine.

When she let go, I saw that she had given me ten dollars. I shook my head.

"Oh, Siobhan, no," I said, holding the money out to her. "I can't take this."

Siobhan folded my fingers over my palm. "Take it," she said, her tone hushed. "I won't tell your ma and dad if you won't."

"Thank you." I reluctantly stuffed the money in my coat pocket. "Goodbye, Siobhan."

"Goodbye, Miss Maggie."

"Call me Maggie," I said. "Just Maggie."

Siobhan let out a sharp gasp, and her bottom lip hitched. "Maggie," she breathed, although I could tell she felt awkward saying it.

She gave me a quick hug, hastily running off after so I wouldn't see the tears in her eyes.

After taking a cab to South Station, I was able to buy a one-way ticket to New York.

I sat in my same seat, looking out the window on the train, getting nudged lightly every so often by the large man sitting next to me whenever he turned the page on his newspaper. I leaned my head on the window and watched the red, orange, and yellow leaves on the trees glide by as the train took me out of Massachusetts once again.

It was a bit after four o'clock in the afternoon by the time I got off the train to Savannah Station. I used the telephone booth to call for a cab. I stood on the platform, waiting as hundreds of people walked by me, going on about their day. As I watched everyone in their own little worlds, I began to wonder what was going on in their lives. Did they recently lose someone important to them too? Or were they living out their best days, feeling as if nothing in the world could come between them and their happiness?

Finally, the cab pulled up, and Clark got out. I wasn't sure why, but there was a small part of me that was relieved to see him. He jogged over to me and held out his hand to take my trunk.

"I can hold on to it in the back," I said, gripping it tighter in my hands.

"Are you sure?" He furrowed his eyebrows, slight concern flashing in his eyes.

"Yes. I'll be fine, thank you."

Clark shrugged. "All right, then." he opened the back door, allowing me to slide in and place my suitcase next to me.

He shut the door and got into the driver's seat. As we drove out of the station, something inside my stomach fluttered about. I knew it wasn't hunger, as I had a scone on the train for breakfast and a tuna sandwich at lunch. Still, I placed my hand on my stomach thinking it would mollify it somehow. My entire body felt strange. Something in my throat kept tightening, making my skin prickle whenever it happened. I let out a low, quiet breath to ease myself.

"I'm glad you're back." Clark's voice broke into my thoughts.

"Hm? Oh, yes. So am I." I gave a short, polite nod.

"Listen." Clark paused. His voice was soft and gentle. "Flora told me about your uncle. I'm very sorry."

My throat tightened again, making it difficult for me to answer Clark right away.

"Thank you," I finally managed to say.

"I hope it's all right," he said, his eyes giving me a quick glance through the rear-view mirror. "I mean, I was worried that you left so suddenly. I asked Flora if everything was okay, and when she told me, I felt so awful. I just wanted you to know that I was thinking about you the whole time."

I let out another breath; it was ragged this time. I looked out my window, hoping he had broken his eye contact with me. I closed my eyes for a second. When I opened them again, I nodded, forcing myself to look back at him.

"It's all right," I said, my throat raw and dry. "Thank you."

We stayed silent for the remainder of the ride, aside from the occasional observations about how pretty the Georgia foliage was starting to become. I was grateful for the digression, but still felt something gnawing at me inside. I was afraid what would happen if I let it overcome me, so I continued to swallow the knot that kept forming in the base of my throat and forced a smile on my lips.

Finally, we reached the large awning of trees that led the pathway to Flora's home. I looked up at them, wonder struck by the Spanish moss leaves that hung above. I craned my neck to get every last leaf of them in my mind. This was the first time I had noticed how incredibly beautiful they were.

As we drove closer to Flora's home, the fluttering and knotting inside of me went bananas. I had to grip the door handle just to calm my nerves. I looked out the windshield, and as if she had been watching from her window, Flora appeared on the front porch. She wore her usual blue plaid smock apron over her house dress. And her smile, that could be seen from the moon, was spread wide across her rosy cheeks.

My bottom lip twitched and my eyes began to sting. I fumbled around for the money to give Clark, switching my gaze from my coin purse and back to Flora, whose smile never left her face. I handed him the money and thanked him, gripping my suitcase in my hand. I stepped out of the cab and closed the door, hearing him drive off as I walked toward the house.

I climbed up the front porch steps quickly, bounding toward Flora as everything inside of me went haywire. When I reached the top, I dropped my trunk to the ground and rushed into her arms, breaking down into tears. I wrapped my arms tightly around Flora, my body slumping against hers. I buried my head into her shoulder as she put her hand on my back and held me close.

The sky was pink, and the sun was slowly disappearing behind the trees. Flora and I sat on the back porch, swinging back and forth on the porch swing. An empty cup of tea sat on the little table next to me. I had taken off my shoes and curled my feet beneath me, letting my dress flutter against my skin. Flora, despite her dislike of bare feet, had also taken her shoes off, her heels supporting her as she rocked the swing.

I hadn't said much since I arrived. All I knew was that when I saw Flora standing on her front porch, I'd never felt so much care for anyone since Uncle James. She looked so happy to see me, despite the last-minute telegram and recent circumstances. I couldn't remember the last time I let someone hold me. When I saw her face smiling back at me, I knew from the inside that I was going to fall apart, and that there was no one's comforting arms I would rather be in than hers.

"What made you decide to come back?" Flora asked softly.

I stared ahead at Flora's luscious backyard. The light breeze that billowed through almost felt as if a ghost were brushing past my face. The back of my eyes burned, and I cast them downward.

"I couldn't stay there."

"Too many memories of your uncle?"

I shook my head. "My parents. They were so…unfeeling. I mean, Uncle James was my dad's brother, his business partner for years, and my dad acted as if his death was a burden in his life. And my ma…she just goes along with whatever my dad does."

"I'm sorry, honey," Flora said.

"I went into his room, and his bed was all made up as if no one had ever slept in it. It was so empty. And his chair—" Tears welled up in my eyes and slipped down my cheeks. "The seat was cold. It was as if he never existed. It was almost as if my dad wanted to get rid of any evidence that my uncle had been there. He was just erasing him away."

"Or maybe, it was his way of grieving," Flora said. "Grief makes us do strange things. It's almost as if we become an alternate version of ourselves. As if we're watching us do these things from behind a wall of glass and can't stop ourselves from doing it because it's how we cope. It's how we heal."

"Did you ever act as if your son or husband never existed after they died?" I asked.

Flora hesitated for a moment, as if taking my question in. Then she shook her head.

"No. But I'm telling you I wasn't myself for the longest time."

"But you're so brave. You stay so strong every single day."

"Oh, honey, no." Flora shook her head lightly. "What I am is human. Believe me, I've had days where I felt like I couldn't go on. When I found out my son died, I stopped moving. I felt as if the ground had been pulled from beneath me, and I was falling down this large pit that I couldn't get out of. And when my husband died, I felt the exact same way. But I never forget them. I keep my son's picture with me at all times." She patted her apron pocket. "And my husband, I never take my wedding ring off. It's a constant reminder that we are bound together for eternity. I will always remain true to him, right up until the day I meet with him again."

"Does it get any easier?" I asked. "Does it always feel this awful?"

"There will be days when you feel as if their spirit is beside you, guiding you through life, giving you all the love in the world. And then there are days like this, where you feel as if nothing is worth it. As if you're staring back at the world feeling empty. But you always wake up the next day and feel grateful knowing that you're alive to keep their memories living on. That's how I see it."

"I always thought my uncle was invincible. He went to war, and even when he went missing, even though I was terrified, there was some part of me that knew he was all right. As if I could see him, hiding and waiting to be found. When he came home, I knew he wasn't the same person anymore. Although, he tried to be for me. And even though he got a little better as time went on, there would be moments where I was afraid I would lose him to his memories. But he always came back. He would become my Uncle James again and find some way to make me laugh and smile. He went through so much, but he always made sure he was there for me." My eyes welled up again, and my face crumpled. "I never thought to tell him how proud I was of him."

I hung my head and covered my face with my hand, weeping.

Flora took my other hand in hers and squeezed it gently.

Grief slammed itself down in my chest, and I cried harder. This was the first time since Uncle James had died that I didn't feel so alone. I felt the warmth from her weathered skin surge through mine. I leaned over and cradled myself in her arms, letting her stroke my cheek. She kissed the top of my head and rubbed my shoulder.

I shot up and hastily wiped my eyes, turning my head away from her.

"I hate crying," I said, attempting to wipe my tears away. "I can't—" I broke off again, gulping at the lump in my throat that wouldn't go away. My cheeks warmed, and I couldn't help the embarrassment I felt as I continued to sob.

"You cry your heart out, honey." Flora put her hand on my back. "You have every right to sit there and cry until every last tear inside of you is gone. You cry until you can't anymore, until it feels as if your body will explode. You cry all you want. There is no shame in it. It doesn't make you any less of a strong person."

I hesitated for a moment, collecting myself. I sniffled and wiped my eyes. I took a few shaky breaths before turning back around and looking at Flora. She kept her hand on me the entire time. I rubbed the bottom of my nose.

"I remember one time," I sniffled, "when I was seven, Uncle James had bought me a pair of roller skates. He strapped them on over my shoes and took me outside to try them out. He watched as I wobbled around the sidewalk trying to hold myself steady. We both couldn't stop laughing. Then, I lost my balance and fell, scraping my knee and getting dirt on my favorite pink dress. I started to cry. Uncle James ran over to me and picked me up and brought me into the house. He sat me on the kitchen counter as he cleaned up my knee. My dad walked in and barely noticed that I got a scrape or that I was still crying. In three seconds flat, he walked in and out. Uncle James, though, even though he knew I would be all right and that a scraped knee is nothing to fuss over, he kept checking in on me all day. Almost playing doctor."

I smiled lightly as this memory came back into my mind.

"He could've just slapped a bandage on my knee and called it a day, but he didn't. He went out of his way to make sure I was feeling better for the rest of the day." I looked over at Flora. "You're a lot like him in that way."

Flora smiled softly, her eyes beaming with thoughtfulness. She held my hands in hers, protectively shielding them with maternal warmth. I looked down at the ground for a moment. Then I brought my eyes up to her.

"Your son was very lucky," I said, my voice tight. "I wish I had a mother like you. I wish you were my mother."

Flora's eyebrows knitted, and her green eyes shined. She tilted her head, her lips inches apart from one another. She shook her head.

"Oh, honey," she whispered. "Don't ever wish that. Your mama loves you."

"She doesn't," I choked out.

"She does." Flora nodded knowingly. "Same as your daddy. They both love you. They may not show it, but trust me, they love you."

"But, why? Why don't they show it?" My voice shook with desperation.

Flora shrugged. "People have a way of doing things we'll never know why they do them. Did you ever show that you loved them?"

I thought for a moment, remembering all those times my parents and I would barely say a word to each other. How business always came first. It was never like that with Uncle James. Even though he wasn't exactly an overly-affectionate person either, he showed love just by being there. By letting me know that he would always be there.

"No." I shook my head. "I knew that if I did, they wouldn't have cared much. But with Uncle James, even though we never really said 'I love you' a whole lot, we didn't need to. Because we knew how much we loved each other. We didn't have to say anything, we just knew."

I gripped onto my locket, twirling it in my fingers. I looked down at it and grinned lightly.

"Uncle James got me this before he went off to war. He put his picture in it so I could look at him whenever I missed him, or as he put it—if I needed a reminder on how handsome he was."

I let out a sad laugh, my memories bringing me back to that day. I opened the locket, and my uncle stared back at me. This was my first time seeing him since the morning I left for Georgia for the first time. My breath caught in my throat as I took his image in. Tears welled in my eyes again, and my chin trembled. The fact that I was never going to see his face in person anymore destroyed me. I broke down again, the oval locket still in my hands. I didn't think I would ever let it go.

Flora leaned closer to me, her gaze over my shoulder.

"Oh, honey," she said, her voice strained. "He was a handsome fella. He looks like such a kind man."

I nodded, the words lost in my throat. I willed myself to look at the photo again. I wished that I could stare at it forever. I brushed my thumb against it before clasping the locket shut and letting it dangle around my neck.

Flora interlaced her fingers through mine and squeezed my hand, stroking the back of it with her thumb. I scooted closer to her, feeling another tear slip down my cheek as I rested my head on her shoulder. We looked out at the darkening Savannah sky ahead of us. The relaxing sound of the crickets and far off wind chimes made me smile, something I never thought would happen. Suddenly, the bullfrog let out it's loud and vibrating croak, the sound of its echo floating into the sky. I couldn't help but laugh through my tears, as did Flora. We sat there, laughing as we listened to the sounds of the night.

CHAPTER NINETEEN

Something inside of me opened up that night. After I had let myself weep for the first time in forever, I felt as if an entire weight had been lifted off me, allowing me to breathe after feeling so closed up for so long. Flora sat next to me, listening as I let everything out, baring every last thing I had in me.

The next day, we sat out in the garden, planting violas and pansies. Yet again, the October weather was balmier than I was used to. I decided to wear my farming outfit as I didn't want to get any of the dresses that I had brought with me dirty. I wrapped my hair up in a headscarf to keep my neck from sweating bullets. I listened as Flora told me what each flower symbolized, saying that violas stood for innocence and modesty, and pansies of admiration.

"Well, isn't this chummy?" Clarabelle's voice said from behind, startling the both of us.

"Oh!" Flora said, her hand clasped against her heart. "Clarabelle! What are you doing here?"

"Did you forget that we have to go to the farm today?" Clarabelle crossed her arms against her chest.

"Oh, dear!" Flora put her hand on her cheek. "Yes, I did. I'm sorry! Maggie came back yesterday, and I completely forgot. We're done here anyway."

Flora got to her feet in a wobbly fashion. She brushed the dirt off of her knees and took her gardening gloves off.

"Do we have time for a cup of tea?" she asked.

"Of course!" Clarabelle said, as if Flora's question was rhetorical.

"Maggie, would you like some?" Flora asked, starting to walk off.

"Sure," I said.

"Do you want to come to the pecan farm with us? I understand if you don't."

"No." I shook my head. "I'll come, too."

Flora smiled before heading back towards the house, taking her time to climb up the steps and walk through the back door.

"So, you're back," Clarabelle said.

I turned toward her. "Yes. I wanted to come back."

Clarabelle gave a curt nod. "Flora told me about your uncle."

I averted my eyes away from her, staring down at my scuffed-up work boots. I nodded.

"I'm very sorry about that, Margaret," she said.

I lifted my head, my eyes meeting with hers again. "Thank you," I said quietly.

"From what Flora told me about him, he sounded like a good man."

"He was." My voice hitched.

"How are you doing?"

"I'm fine. I talked to Flora yesterday, and she made me feel a lot better."

Clarabelle gave another stiff nod. "You've got good company here. You know that, Margaret. Not just Flora."

I nodded lightly. "I know. Thank you."

"Well now that you're back, we can put you to work harder."

I let out a small laugh. "All right."

I saw the tiniest of smiles curl at the edge of Clarabelle's lips and a glimmer of jest flash in her eyes.

"Come on, Scarlett O'Hara," she said. "Let's get you back to work."

Flora, Clarabelle, and I shelled the pecans we had gathered from the farm in the basement. The end of the harvesting season was on the horizon. Flora had said that since this year brought such great pecans, November was going to be a hot selling month, saying that despite the heavy rain this summer, somehow, the pecans held up.

"Thank goodness no critters got to them this year," Clarabelle said. "Do you remember back in '42 when we weren't sure if you'd even sell that year?"

"Poor Alfred was so mad." Flora shook her head. "He spent day in and day out at the farm. Barely slept a wink."

"Did animals get to the pecans?" I asked.

"Huh!" Clarabelle touted. "Did they ever! Gophers! Nasty little rascals. They were out in full swing that year."

"We never did catch them," Flora said. "Alfred couldn't bring himself to shoot at them anyway."

Flora put a bunch of the shelled pecans in the freezer and kept some out to cook with later. I was shocked by the amount she still had left. Her pecans sold year-round, but they made a killing in the autumn and during Christmastime. With Thanksgiving over a month away, she had to shell out twice as many batches, since everyone in Savannah seemed to have their own take on pecan pie.

"I'll also need to save some up for the Harvest Festival," Flora said, shutting the freezer door and latching it.

"Harvest Festival?" I said. "What's that?"

"Oh, it's this event we have every year," Flora said.

"It's in November," Clarabelle said. "About two weeks before Thanksgiving. Everyone gathers at a lovely little park in the center of town. There's food, music, dancing…"

"A Harvest Queen is crowned," Flora added.

"Harvest Queen?" I raised my eyebrows.

"Yes," Flora said. "A young woman is crowned the Harvest Queen. There's at least four young ladies in the running for the title."

"How does she get crowned Harvest Queen?" I asked.

"Oh, it's just a fun little thing," Flora said. "It's usually a young woman who's lived here her entire life. But she's had to make an impact on our town."

"We once had a girl win three years in a row," Clarabelle said.

"It's a way for everyone to come together and eat and have a good time!" Flora added.

"What kind of food do you have?"

"Well, almost everyone brings something. Martha Jessop from down the road makes her famous blueberry pie."

"And Hank Tucker makes a cornbread that would knock you off your feet," Clarabelle said.

"Do either of you make anything?" I asked.

"I bring my pecan bread," Flora said, "and Clarabelle makes her peach cobbler."

I turned to Clarabelle. "You make a peach cobbler? How come I've never had it?"

"Because I ain't never had you over for it," Clarabelle said, her lips a tight line.

"It's delicious!" Flora put her hand on Clarabelle's shoulder. "She has a secret ingredient in it that she won't tell anyone about. Not even me!"

"A secret ingredient, huh?" I said, giving Clarabelle a wry smile. "Gee, I wonder what it is?"

"Ain't never going to tell you," Clarabelle said, her eyes narrowing. "Over my dead body."

"She's so stubborn about it!" Flora laughed. "I've pestered her so many times, but she just won't budge!"

"I'll have to try it sometime," I said, still giving Clarabelle a teasing grin.

"You can; at the Harvest Festival," Flora said. "That is, if you're still here."

For a moment, Flora's eyes softened, and a flash of melancholy flickered in them. She wiped her hands on her apron. I hadn't really decided how long I would be staying this time. All I knew was that I wanted to be out of my house. But I knew I couldn't let Flora down about the Harvest Festival. It seemed too interesting to pass up. Plus, I just had to try Clarabelle's peach cobbler with her not-so-secret ingredient. I lifted my chin and smiled at Flora.

"Of course, I'll be here. I wouldn't miss it for anything."

Flora and I stopped at Minton's Market after Clarabelle went home that afternoon. As she perused the aisles, I made a quick detour for the nuts section. I saw that they had stocked new canisters of Alcott's Pecans. I picked one up and turned it over, staring at the bland packaging. I shook my head. It was such a shame that Flora wouldn't consider re-branding and put her pecan bread recipe on the label. It for sure would make them sell like hot cakes even more.

A woman with dark brown hair and a well-tailored dress fit for the First Lady came up next to me and picked up a canister, turning it upside down, as if inspecting it.

She turned her head slowly, noticing that I was staring at her.

I smiled awkwardly and shook the canister in my own hand.

"Can't get them any better than this, can you?" I said.

"I prefer Golden Hills pecans," she drawled.

"Oh, these are far superior," I said.

"How so?"

"Well, for starters, they're grown right here in Savannah."

"So are Golden Hills," she said flatly.

"Yes, but the owner really knows her stuff. She works hard on the pecan farm every day to make sure that she's only distributing the best pecans so that you can bring them home and make the greatest treats you've ever tasted."

"You sound like a radio ad," the woman said, her tone haughty.

"Is it working?" I asked. "Flora Alcott is the best pecan grower you'll ever know. And she makes a pecan bread to kill for."

"What's in it?"

"What?"

"The pecan bread. I don't see a recipe for it or anything."

My stomach dropped to my knees. I hadn't thought about being asked to list the ingredients. I wasn't sure if Flora would be too happy with me giving her recipe out considering how hesitant she was to put it on the label. The woman was still staring at me expectantly, her eyebrows raised with impatience.

"Oh, well, that's coming!" I said before I could stop the words from tumbling out of my mouth.

"There's going to be a recipe included on these things?" She motioned to the canister in her hand.

"Yes," I said slowly.

There was no turning back now, I figured. I had to just keep going with my fib and hope it would eventually come true.

I lifted my chin and held my gaze in an attempt to appear confident. "She's in the process of it. We're going to be meeting with her distributor to discuss how to do it soon."

The woman looked down at the canister, then back at the shelf full of other pecan companies, including her beloved Golden Hills. She let out a small sigh and shrugged.

"You won't be disappointed," I said, giving her my best winning smile.

"I hope not," she said before walking off with Alcott's Pecans in her hand.

I exhaled deeply, the smile now frozen onto my face. "I am in so much trouble," I muttered to myself when the woman was finally out of sight.

CHAPTER TWENTY

I didn't tell Flora about my little sales pitch at the market. Although I've never seen her mad before, and couldn't even picture it, I had a feeling she wouldn't have appreciated me telling that woman that the pecan bread recipe would be put on the label. Guilt washed over me every time I looked at her.

I considered telling Clarabelle, but thought better of it as she would probably tear my head off and most definitely go to Flora and blab about it. I was afraid to speak at all—which was a first—at the risk of running my mouth off and digging myself into a deeper hole than I already was in. Flora seemed to notice one afternoon out in the pecan farm.

"Maggie, you've been awful quiet lately," she said, her eyes furrowing with concern. "Are you feeling all right?"

"Oh," I said, putting on a smile. "I'm fine, thanks."

"Are you sure? You haven't said much the past two days."

"Flora, don't jinx it!" Clarabelle called from across the pecan tree where Flora and I stood.

I gave another forced smile. "I'm fine, really. It's just…the heat. You know how I get. I thought I'd be used to it by now, but I guess it still bothers me."

"Oh. Well, why don't you go to the truck and put your hat on?" she said. "Maybe that'll help."

"Sure." I nodded. "Thanks."

I walked over to Flora's truck and opened the door, reaching across the seat for my hat.

"Hi, Maggie!" Clark's voice nearly made me leap out of my skin.

I felt as if I jumped three feet into the air. I twirled around, clutching my chest, my hat in my hand.

"Jeez! Are you trying to give me a heart attack?"

"I'm sorry," Clark said. Although, I could hear a slight chuckle in the back of his voice. "I didn't mean to frighten you."

I took a few deep breaths before taking my hand off my chest. "It's all right. What are you doing here, anyway?"

"Just wanted to check in." He shoved his hands into his pockets. "How have you been?"

"I'm fine, thanks…" I paused, biting my bottom lip. I was unsure if I should tell him about the other day. "But, um, I'm sort of in a jam."

"What is it? Anything I can help with?"

"Uh…" I looked off at Flora and Clarabelle, who were busy gathering pecans and chatting quietly. I grabbed Clark by the elbow and brought him closer toward me. I spoke in a low voice just in case Flora or Clarabelle wandered over, keeping watch out of the corner of my eye. "I sort of did something I shouldn't have."

"What?" Clark asked, his expression a mix of concern and patience.

"Okay, if I tell you, you have to promise me that you won't tell Flora or Clarabelle. Promise?"

"Sure. I mean, how bad can it be?"

"Huh." I scoffed. "The other day, Flora and I went to the general store. I saw a lady pick up a canister of Alcott's Pecans, and I sort of became a walking advertisement. She said that she preferred a different brand, and I just kept going on and on about how great Alcott's were."

"Did she end up buying them?"

"Yes."

"So, what's the problem? Flora would be happy about that."

I let out a sigh. "Well, there was a moment where I was afraid I wasn't convincing her, so I told her about the pecan bread." I twisted my fingers around my locket. "I raved about how delicious it was, and how Flora makes the best one anyone's ever tasted. So, she asked what was in it, and I may have told her that Flora is going to be putting the recipe on her labels so everyone can make it."

I winced, unsure of how Clark would react. For a moment, he didn't say anything, then suddenly his eyes nearly bulged out of their sockets.

"What?" he said. "Maggie, why did you—?"

"I know!" I groaned, putting my hands on my face. "I know, I never should have done it! But I couldn't help myself. The lady was going to buy Golden Nuts or whatever it's called! I just thought I was doing something nice! I couldn't stop myself by the time I was saying it. And this lady was a real piece of work, all right? She was looking at me with hoity-toity eyes, like her opinion on pecans was the only one that mattered!"

"Maggie!" Clark said.

"Sorry," I said, pacing in place. "I…I really wanted to help Flora out."

Clark sighed and put his hand on my shoulder. "Look, your heart was in the right place. But Flora has no intention of putting her recipe on the labels. What if this lady comes back and expects to see that? She may never want to buy Alcott's again. Then, she may tell everyone she knows about it."

"Maybe she won't," I said. "Maybe she'll forget."

Clark shook his head. "Forgetting about things isn't exactly people's strong suit around here."

I dropped my shoulders. "So, what do I do now?"

"I think you know," Clark said. "You need to tell Flora."

"Tell Flora?" I shook my head. "No, I can't. I don't want her to be upset with me. Does she even get upset?"

"Maggie, you don't know who this lady was. She could've told anybody about this."

"Well, what if the next time you and Flora meet with what's his name—Mr. Winston, you can run the idea of putting her recipe on the labels by him? Maybe he'll listen to you, then convince Flora to do it."

Clark shook his head again. "You know that won't work. You need to tell her."

I let out a dramatic exhale. He was right. As much as I didn't want to admit it, he was right. I looked up at him, his knowing hazel eyes and boyish face stared at me expectantly.

"Hey, Bergen and McCarthy!" Clarabelle called out. "What have you been yammering about?"

"Nothing!" I called back.

"Well, let's get a move on! These pecans ain't gonna pick themselves!"

"Be right over, Clarabelle!" Clark said. He turned back toward me and patted me on the shoulder. He raised his brows, and a flash of warning glimmered through his eyes. "Tell her."

Clark's words kept repeating in my head. I tried many times to tell Flora what I had done, and each time, I chickened out. I would open my mouth to tell her, then slam it shut and lamely comment on something about the nice weather or how pretty the foliage was coming along.

One morning, I got dressed for the pecan farm and when I came downstairs, I saw Flora was in one of her house dresses, this time with no apron. She wore a light sweater over it and a hat with a little flower sticking out.

"Are we not going to the farm today?" I asked.

"No, we are not." Flora smiled.

"But…but I thought this was your busiest season?"

Flora swatted the air. "We can take a day off."

"What about Clarabelle?" I asked.

"Oh, I let her know. We're going someplace special today."

"Where are we going?"

"You'll see." She made a shooing motion with her hand. "Now, go upstairs and change into one of your pretty dresses. We leave in five minutes. Go on!"

"All right," I said warily before slowly ascending back upstairs.

Within five minutes, I had styled my hair back to normal and was wearing a ruby colored dress with a belt attached to the waist. I hoped it was appropriate enough for wherever we were going. While Flora drove in silence, she never lost the smile on her face. I smiled to myself—for the first time in days—wondering what exactly she was up to.

"You're really not going to tell me?" I asked at one point.

"Nope." Flora shook her head, her green eyes sparkling with excitement and slight mischief.

Flora finally turned into a large dirt area. Ahead, were numerous pathways and people idling by, enjoying the beautiful day.

I furrowed my eyebrows. "What is this place?"

"Forsyth Park." Flora beamed. She shut off the truck and put the keys on the dashboard.

"Oh," I said, taking them in my hands and putting them into my clutch. "You might not want to do that."

"Why?" Flora said. "They'll be fine."

"Just let me hold onto them." I snapped my bag shut. "I'll give them back to you when we're leaving."

Flora shrugged. "Suit yourself." She hopped out of the truck.

"So, what are we doing here?" I stood next to her.

"This," Flora said, her eyes starry and proud, "is my favorite place on Earth."

"Oh, really?" I said, my voice teasing. "Not the pecan farm?"

"This is where I come when I want to get away for a little while."

"What's so great about it?"

Flora took my hand and smiled at me. She looked younger than her sixty-something years. It was almost as if she became a young woman again. I could see for a second what she might have looked like at my age, care-free and full of wonder.

"Come on," she said softly. "Let me show you."

We walked down one of the many pathways the park had to offer. The oak trees above were similar to the ones that led toward Flora's house, only these ones were larger and the leaves hung low enough that I could nearly touch them. Between the sun shining down and the foliage, the leaves gave off golden hues that I had never seen before. It was almost as if I was in another dimension—a beautiful one.

"Wow," I said, gazing all around me. "This is incredible."

The smile on Flora's face was more than enough to tell me how much this place meant to her. She didn't need to say anything. She closed her eyes and drew in a deep breath, slowly letting it escape from her lips. She opened her eyes again and looked ahead. I wondered what she was thinking about in that moment. She looked so serene and peaceful, as if she had the entire world at the fingertips.

Flora linked her arm into mine and began leading the way down the path.

I was curious to see if there was anything else to this place. It was certainly beautiful by itself, but I wondered if there was something that was at the end of the path. We walked in silence for a bit.

Flora hummed that little tune that I always heard her humming throughout the house and at the pecan farm.

"I used to come here with my husband and son," she said. "We would come here and walk our troubles away."

I thought for a moment, then came to a sudden realization. I turned toward her.

"Is this where you came on Alfred Jr.'s death anniversary? You were gone for quite some time."

Flora nodded. "Yes. Like I said, I come here when I want to get away for a bit. I've told you that I've had my bad days. I didn't want to look rude or anything. I was quiet, as you know. So, I came here. I talked to Alfred Jr. and told him how much I missed him. It's a nice place to come to talk to your loved ones who have passed on. A lot of people around here do it."

"That sounds nice," I said. "We have a park sort of like this in Boston. It has beautiful pathways, and there's even a little pond with geese and ducks. I used to go there with my uncle when I was a kid. It's simple, but that's what makes it so pretty. It forces you to stop and look around at its beauty."

"That's a wonderful way of putting it," Flora said. "You're a lovely girl, Maggie. I'm glad you decided to come back."

My eyes knitted together as sudden guilt ripped through me again. I wanted so badly to tell her about my flapping lips at the general store. I opened my mouth to say something, however, the words got blocked in my throat.

"Me, too," I replied instead, immediately feeling regret.

We continued to walk arm in arm through Forsyth, the chirps of small birds breaking through the silence between us. My obsession with the incredible oak trees never faltered. I felt like *Alice in Wonderland*, believing how magical this place was.

We stopped at a grand water fountain at the end of the pathway and sat down on the edge. The sound of the water brought an additional peacefulness to this lovely day.

"Alfred Jr. used to splash his little hands in the water," Flora told me, a nostalgic smile curling at her lips. "It drove me positively mad. I knew he was only doing it to push my buttons. At the same time, it brought him so much joy."

We stood up and headed back for the truck. After a while, Flora began to grow tired, and it was my turn to lead her. She had been sniffling on and off since we left the house, letting out a cough every now and then. I noticed that her eyes had become watery. She blamed it on allergies, saying sometimes the pollen in the air bothered her. I nodded, humoring her even though I knew they were tears of nostalgia and memories.

I wrapped my arm around hers as we made our way back through the park. It was such a long trek that I too began to feel a bit winded—and hungry. When we finally got back to the truck, I could see that she was visibly panting, and I could feel her hand shaking slightly in mine.

"Do you want me to drive?" I put a gentle hand on her shoulder.

"Oh no," Flora swatted the air. "I'm used to it."

"Are you sure?" I reached into my clutch for the keys.

"Yes, dear. I'm fine."

I gave Flora the keys, and we both hopped in, sitting for a moment to let her catch her breath.

"Whew!" Flora smiled. "Well, that was nice. What do you say we go home and have a nice piece of pecan bread and some tea?"

"Sounds lovely." I smiled.

Flora looked at me, the sides of her eyes crinkled as she let out one of her thousand-watt smiles.

"Oh, I'm so glad we came here," she said. "I am so happy I got to show you this place."

"I am, too. Thank you for bringing me here."

Flora patted my hand and smiled, her nose crinkling with innocence. My stomach twisted into another guilt-ridden knot. It gnawed at me, and I couldn't take the feeling anymore. I gulped as the truck engine revved up.

"Flora?" I said, my voice sounding hollow in my ears.

"Yes?"

I shut my eyes tightly and bit my lip, the words so close to being uttered. "I have to tell you something."

I opened my eyes again and willed them to meet hers.

Flora took her hands off the steering wheel and turned her body to face mine.

"Yes, honey. What is it?"

I let out a deep exhale and looked away again, not wanting to see the look on her face.

"Remember when we went to the market a few days ago?" I asked.

"Yes."

"While you were shopping, I wandered off and went into the nuts section." I looked up at her.

Flora looked back at me calmly. Her eyes were relaxed, and her mouth was a straight line as she listened to me with such focus and care.

"All right," she said.

I looked back down. "Well, I picked up a canister of Alcott's Pecans and was still disappointed to see that there's no recipe on the label—"

I heard the tiniest of sighs escape from Flora. She didn't interrupt me, however. Even though her unapproved sigh was evident, she never lost her calm demeanor or changed her facial expression in any way.

"I know how you feel about that," I continued, "but a woman walked over and picked up a canister of your pecans. I couldn't help it. I began flapping my gums about how great Alcott's is and how wonderful of a pecan grower you are, that I sort of lost the ability to shut my mouth."

Flora cocked her head slightly, her eyes creasing together. "That's all?"

I shook my head. "No. It looked like she was going to put them back on the shelf and grab the kind she prefers—Golden something or other—"

"Golden Hills?"

I nodded.

Flora sighed. "They're our biggest competitor."

I let out a disheartened groan. "Well, when she told me she preferred Golden Hills, I went into advertising mode. I kept saying how great you were and how you make pecan bread that's to die for. She wanted to know what was in it, and I told her that you would be putting the recipe on the labels, and she went off and bought it! It wasn't until she walked away that I realized what I had done. I was so worried that she would put your pecans back that I just kept running my mouth and said anything that would get her to buy them."

I took a deep breath, continuing to keep my gaze on Flora. My rapid-fire confession made my heartbeat elevate and my cheeks warm up.

Flora's expression remained the same. I wondered if she even caught what I had said given that I talked so fast, I sounded like a Humphrey Bogart film. She looked away from me, keeping her gaze on the steering wheel.

"I'm sorry, Flora," I said.

She nodded lightly. "Thank you for telling me," she finally said, her voice calm as ever.

This woman really was a saint. I knew that I didn't deserve such kindness from her. Yet, no matter what, she still showed it. Flora was the definition of kindness. If there was a medal out there for it, she for sure would have hundreds of them.

"However," her calm tone was laced with firmness, sending a chill through my body, "I am disappointed that you lied. You know I have no intention of putting my recipe on the labels. I understand that you were trying to help, but sometimes you gotta learn when to stop talking."

My shoulders drooped, and I sat back in my seat, hugging my arms close to my body. Although I felt as if a weight had been lifted off of me, my cheeks still burned, and the acidic churn of shame lingered in my stomach. As much as I couldn't bear to know that Flora was upset with me, I knew that I had done the right thing by telling her, even if it meant putting a wrench in our lovely day.

"Let's go home," she said. "We'll have some pecan bread and tea."

I didn't answer, my appetite no longer a priority.

Flora backed out of Forsyth, and we spent the entire ride back to her house in silence.

CHAPTER TWENTY-ONE

I continued to carry my guilt with me over the next few days. Although Flora had moved on, I still couldn't help but dwell on it. I've disappointed people so many times in my life, but this was the first time I felt absolutely rotten over it.

I knew in my head that the amount of guilt I consumed was a little extreme. My heart, however, had never experienced such a feeling, and I let it overwhelm me.

Flora's sniffles and cough from our day at Forsyth had accumulated.

I came downstairs one morning to find her sluggishly moving around the kitchen in her robe. The tip of her nose was red, and her eyes were watery. When she walked up to me with my breakfast, I saw that her entire face was flushed.

"Good morning, honey." It was as if she swallowed a frog.

"Are you all right?" I asked.

"Oh." She blew her nose with a rumpled tissue from her robe pocket. "Just feeling a little puny, that's all."

"Puny?" I raised my eyebrows.

"Not feeling well," she translated. "It's nothing to worry about."

"Are you sure? You look like death."

Flora let out a strained chuckle which aggravated into a cough and then a double sneeze. She blew her nose with the tissue again.

"*Gesundheit*," I said.

"Oh, excuse me." She put the tissue back in her robe pocket.

"Are your allergies still bothering you?"

"It's just a little cold. Happens to me every time during this time of the year."

"Still," I said. "Doesn't sound so great."

"It's fine. I'll have some tea, then get dressed and we'll get to work."

I put my biscuit down. "Work? You're actually going to work when you're sick?"

"I have to! It's only a cold. Clark and I are meeting with Mr. Winston tomorrow, and he wouldn't be very pleased with me if I canceled at the last minute. Besides, I don't feel nauseous or anything."

"Well, you might if you're in the hot sun all morning."

"Honey, I've worked in worse conditions. I'll be fine. I'll wear a hat if it makes you feel any better."

"You shouldn't be working when you're sick. My dad did it all the time, and it made him more miserable of a person than he already was."

"I appreciate your concern. But sometimes you just gotta work through it."

"Well, if you're handling the pecans while sick, that might not be good for the people who buy them later."

"I'll wash them," Flora said.

I sighed. As much as I admired Flora, she was one hell of a stubborn lady. I wasn't sure of how I was going to convince her to take it easy for the day.

Flora continued to roam about the kitchen. She stood at the sink, her back facing me. She unsuccessfully suppressed a nasty cough.

I took my napkin off my lap, put it on the table, and stood up, unable to take it any longer.

"Sit down," I said.

Flora turned around and looked at me, her eyebrows furrowing. "What?"

"Sit down."

"Oh, honey, I'm fi—"

"No, you're not." I walked over to her and guided her to the table, pushing her down gently into her chair. "Sit. I'll get you your tea."

"Oh, now really." Flora went to stand up, but I pointed my finger at her, causing her to freeze in place. I pointed to the chair. Like an obedient child, she sat back down.

"You took care of me when I twisted my ankle at the pecan farm and when my uncle died. Now, I'll take care of you."

"Oh, Maggie. That's very kind of you, but—"

"Do you want Clarabelle coming over and taking care of you?" I sat down in the chair across from her.

"Oh, no!" She shook her head feverishly.

"Then at least let me do it. And if you feel better later, we can go to the farm."

Flora sighed. "I hate not being able to take care of things myself."

"It's okay to ask for help every now and then."

Flora looked down, shaking her head lightly. "It would be nice to sit down for a while."

I smiled at her and stood up from my chair. I went over to the stove and poured her a hot cup of tea.

"Thank you," she said as I set it down in front of her.

"Would you like a biscuit and eggs?"

"Yes, please." She took a sip of her tea and let out a satisfied exhale as I handed her a biscuit and already cooked scrambled eggs.

After breakfast, Flora went to lie down on the sofa while I cleaned up the kitchen. When I finished, I went out to her garden and watered the flowers, making sure that they were blooming all right. I could hear Flora coughing from the backyard. For such a dainty woman, she sure had a cough the size of a bull.

I spent the rest of the morning tending to Flora. Although I could tell she quite enjoyed being waited on, I could see in her eyes that she felt a small twinge of guilt, offering to get her own tea every now and then. By the time afternoon came, I noticed that her face wasn't as flushed, but she was still quite stuffy and had that gut-wrenching cough.

After giving her what felt like her twelfth cup of tea, I came back into the den to discover that she had fallen asleep.

Flora continued to nap on the couch. She had been passed out for forty-five minutes and was lightly snoring. I sat in the armchair across from her and curled up, dozing off.

The knob to the front door rattled, wrenching me from my sleepy haze. I bolted up and leapt out of my seat. I stumbled warily towards the door, picking up an umbrella from a bin right outside the den. I held it up, ready to swing at any moment, taking a quick look at Flora to make sure she hadn't woken up; she was still out cold.

The knob turned, and the door slowly opened.

I raised the umbrella over my head. Clarabelle sauntered in, and I dropped the umbrella to my side. Clarabelle's eyes darted from me to the umbrella as I regained control of my breath.

"What's with the umbrella?" she asked. "You expecting a storm?"

"Jeez!" I slammed my hand over my chest. "What's with you always trying to give me a heart attack? You're like Creeping Jesus!"

Clarabelle shut the door behind her, shaking her head. "I don't like you using the Lord's name like that, Margaret. Where's Flora?"

"She's sleeping," I said.

"Sleeping? It's two-thirty in the afternoon! We were supposed to go to the farm!" She walked into the foyer further.

"She isn't feeling well." I stepped in front of her.

"Not feeling well? She sick or something?"

I nodded. "Cough, sneeze. The works. She feels crummy."

"Well, that ain't no reason to stop working." Clarabelle shook her head and tried to get past me, however, I stepped in front of her again.

"She needs a day off," I said.

"No, she don't. Flora's a tough bird. She can handle it."

"She needs rest."

"And since when did you become a doctor?"

"I'm not. I have enough sense to notice when someone isn't feeling well."

"You saying I don't have any sense?" Clarabelle put her hands on her hips.

"No, I'm saying Flora needs to take a break."

"You know what? Flora never needed to take a break before you came along. She worked day in and day out, even in the off seasons. Ever since you got here, she's been taking a day off here, a day off there. You—who's never worked a day in your life—wouldn't know the importance of hard work. Flora and her husband kept this business running, then when he died, she worked extra hard to make sure it didn't fail. You're not going to take this away from her."

"I'm not trying to take anything away from her, I only want her to get better! I've been taking care of her."

"You? You've been taking care of Flora?" Her eyes widened. She sized me up and down, as if this were the first time she ever saw me.

"Yes. I've been giving her tea and making sure she's comfortable. She's taking a nap and seems to be doing fine."

Clarabelle poked her head past my shoulder and looked at Flora sleeping peacefully. She screwed her mouth up and clicked her tongue.

"You better hope she don't fall behind with her work. She's got another meeting with Mr. Winston tomorrow. The sales in her pecans have been dipping, and if she falls behind Golden Hills, it'll absolutely kill her."

"I'll make sure that doesn't happen," I said, my voice even and confident.

"It's your behind in the line of fire if she does."

"I'll take the blame for it." I nodded.

"I don't like this, Margaret. But I also don't want Flora feeling terrible. You come by and let me know when she's feeling better. Understood?"

"Yes, Ma'am," I said.

Clarabelle moseyed to the front door and opened it giving me one last disapproving look for good measure before walking out.

I didn't tell Flora about Clarabelle's little visit when she woke up from her nap nearly an hour later. She got up from the sofa, immediately concerned about the kitchen. When I told her I had cleaned up everything, a mixture of relief and gratitude flooded her face.

"How are you feeling?" I asked.

"Oh, much better!" she said, her voice still croaky. "Thank you, Maggie."

Her cheeks were still hectic, and she was sweating bullets. However, the smile on her face offset those two factors.

"Are you sure?" I said. "You still look a bit flushed."

"Oh, it's just from being in my robe all day and cuddled up under that blanket. It can get quite hot in this house. I should go change."

"It's already late in the afternoon. You'll just end up back in your nightgown and robe in a few hours."

"I know, but it will make me feel better knowing I at least got dressed. I'm going to take a bath, get dressed, then we can have some tea and pecan bread. I'm famished!"

"Would you like me to draw your bath for you?" I walked over to her.

"No, thank you. You could get the tea and pecan bread ready, though. I'll be down in a jiff."

By the time Flora came back downstairs dressed in one of her house dresses and smelling like roses again, I had placed two teacups and plates on the table with a good hunk of pecan bread in the center. I kept a watchful eye on Flora as she nibbled on her pecan bread and sipped her tea, using both hands to hold the cup. She put it back down on the saucer, her hand trembling slightly.

"Are you sure you're all right?" I asked.

"What?" She looked up at me. "Oh yes, I'm fine."

"You look a little shaky."

"I'm always like this after a cold. It takes a little longer for me to get back to normal. I'm no spring chicken, you know!" She smiled.

I gave her a side eyed glance over the rim of my teacup. Despite her shakiness and flushed face, she didn't seem like it was bothering her. I took a sip of my tea, and she gave me another smile as if she was attempting to reassure me she was fine. When we finished, I stood up to take our cups and plates to the sink, but Flora swatted my hand away and offered to do it herself.

"Won't help anything if I'm sitting on my behind all day." She got unsteadily up to her feet. "I need to move around."

Flora took our cups and plates and shuffled over to the sink. Suddenly, she paused, the teacups shaking beneath her limp grip. Her knees buckled, and she nearly collapsed against the counter, sending the plates and cups crashing into the sink.

"Flora!" I shot out of my chair and hurried over to her.

I wrapped my arms around her waist for support and led her back to the table, sitting her down in the chair. I knelt before her, keeping my hand on her shoulder.

Her eyes wandered, and her face was as pale as a ghost. She wobbled in the chair, panting furiously to catch her breath.

I tightened my grip on her shoulder, hoping she wouldn't fall over again.

"Flora? Are you all right?" I tried desperately to hide the panic in my voice.

Flora reached for my other hand, missing it a few times. When she eventually grabbed a hold of it, she squeezed it tightly and looked into my eyes.

"Bring me upstairs." Her voice was straining to take deep breaths. "Call the doctor."

I lifted Flora off her chair and guided her up the stairs in a mix of haste and gentleness. I helped her into her bed and put the covers over her, then bounded down the stairs. I sped into the study and picked up the phone, however, I realized I had no idea what the number for the operator was around here. I slammed the phone back down and ran out the front door, sprinting down the porch steps.

I had never been the fastest runner, but in this moment, I felt like I could outrun a cheetah. I flew out of the pathway to Flora's house and charged toward Clarabelle's cottage, running up her front steps. Like a hurricane, I threw the door open and skidded into her foyer, searching madly for her. I found her knitting in a chair in her den.

When she saw me, she nearly jumped out of her skin. Clarabelle threw her knitting into her lap and looked at me with narrowed eyes and tight, thin lips.

"What in the name of Sam Hill?" she said. "What in the heck are you trying to do, give me a heart attack?"

I panted heavily, my eyes wide and desperate. I stood, my shoulders rigid, and my hands clenched at my sides.

"What's gotten into you? What's the matter?" she squawked.

"Something is wrong with Flora."

CHAPTER TWENTY-TWO

Never in my life had I ever seen an older lady move so fast as Clarabelle did at that moment. She shot out of her chair like a bat out of Hell and jumped into her truck, hollering at me to get in as she turned on the engine. We roared out of her driveway and fled down the dirt road and around the corner to Flora's house. I held on to the door handle for dear life as Clarabelle came to a screeching halt. She flew her door open and dashed into the house with me trailing not far behind her.

When we got into Flora's room, she was so drenched with sweat, it was as if someone had dumped a bucket of water on her face. Her skin was pale and had lost its rosy hue, and the light that normally sparkled in her green eyes was dimmed out by exhaustion and defeat.

Clarabelle placed her palm on Flora's head.

"Dear Lord, she's burnin' up," she said. "Margaret, go call the doctor."

I stood there, trembling slightly as I watched Flora struggle to keep her eyes open, trying to comprehend what was happening around her. My fists were knotted into each other as I continued to keep my helpless gaze on her.

Clarabelle snapped her head toward me.

"Do you have rocks in your ears?" she chastised. "Go call the doctor!"

I shook my head. "I don't know the number," I said, trying to keep my voice even.

Clarabelle sighed and stepped away from Flora's side. "You stay with her, I'll go call."

She gave me a gentle push toward Flora and left the room.

I walked over to Flora, unsure of what to do. She looked so tired, helpless, and run-down. It was awful seeing her like this. I thought of my uncle and what he may have looked like during his last moments of life. The image of him lying alone in his bed with no one to comfort or hold his hand was too much for me to bear. Flora raised her eyes up at me.

"Maggie." Her voice was barely above a whisper.

I could tell that it took all the energy she had to utter that single word. I couldn't believe that this was the same woman who was insisting she was fine not more than half an hour ago.

Her hand twitched slightly.

I took it in mine, grasping it with a gentle tightness to reassure her I wouldn't leave her side. Her hand was just as sweaty as her face, and the heat coming from it was enough to fry an egg. I knelt beside her bed.

"It's all right, Flora," I said, still attempting to keep away the pesky tremble that was trying to invade my voice. "Clarabelle's going to call the doctor."

I rubbed the back of her leathery hand with mine, relief surging through me when Clarabelle entered the room again. She appeared to have calmed down a bit, yet there was still a hint of agitation that dwindled in her eyes. She drew out a breath and swiped her fluffy gray bangs aside.

"Margaret, can I see you in the hallway for a minute? Flora, dear, we'll only be a moment."

Flora gave a slight nod of her head. I didn't want to let go of her hand, but I didn't want to keep Clarabelle waiting, so I forced myself to pry my hand out of Flora's and stood up, backing out of the room, not taking my eyes off of her.

"I'll be right back," I said, my voice soft.

When Clarabelle and I went into the hallway, I turned to her. "What's going on?"

"I called the doctor, and he should be here within an hour," Clarabelle said.

"An hour?" I exclaimed. "What happens if she gets worse by then?"

Clarabelle shook her head. "I'll make sure she doesn't. What I need you to do is go run a cloth under cold water, we'll put it on her head until the doctor comes. When he gets here, you may wait downstairs, and I'll let you know—"

"No," I said. "I am not waiting downstairs. Are you crazy? I'm going to be in there with you."

"Don't say no to me, Margaret. I know what's best—"

"No, you don't!" I said, trying to keep my voice hushed so Flora wouldn't hear. "You don't know what's best for me or for Flora. I wasn't there when my uncle died. I had to find out through a damn telegram from my dad. It was awful knowing I wasn't there with him when he was suffering. I'm not leaving this room. I am going to be in there. I don't care if I catch whatever Flora has, I am not leaving her side."

Clarabelle screwed her mouth up, her hands resting on her hips. "Fine. I'm too tired and ruffled up to fight you. You will sit in a chair, keeping your distance—"

"I will hold her hand if she wants me to."

"You will not speak." Clarabelle pointed her finger at me, ignoring my words. "You'll let me do the talking. Do you understand?"

I hesitated, biting the inside of my lip before nodding in compliance. I didn't intend to keep my mouth shut if I could help it. I just wanted to appease Clarabelle so we could get back in the room with Flora.

"Now, go get the cold cloth and bring it back up here," Clarabelle said before opening the door and disappearing into Flora's bedroom.

I brought a chair over to Flora's bed, gently patting her forehead with the cold cloth, which seemed to soothe her.

Clarabelle had gone downstairs to wait for the doctor to come.

I had unbuttoned the top of Flora's nightgown to let her skin breathe and to bring her body temperature down, pressing her chest gently with the cloth every so often. A bowl of cold water that I had brought up, sat on the table beside her bed. I soaked the cloth in it and wrung it out before bringing it back to her chest and forehead.

Flora seemed to have relaxed a bit. I didn't speak much. Partly because I didn't quite know what to say, but also because I didn't want my voice to give away how worried I was, and I certainly didn't want to upset Flora.

Clarabelle walked back in with the doctor behind her.

He was an older man who looked as if he could be my grandfather. He wore a dark business suit and rounded glasses. He instantly commanded the room, putting his bag at the foot of Flora's bed and opening it.

When he looked back up, he smiled, and I could see a small dimple in the crook of his left cheek.

"Hello," he said, his Savannah drawl warm and nurturing. "I'm Dr. Meadows. This must be Flora." He stepped over to her and offered a gentle smile. He looked over at me. "And I'm guessing you're her daughter?"

I shook my head. "No. I'm Maggie. I…I'm her friend."

"Oh," he said, giving me a kind smile and a chivalrous nod of his head. "Nice to meet you, Maggie."

Clarabelle gave me a quick glance out of the side of her eyes while Dr. Meadows returned his attention back to Flora.

He bent down and put his stethoscope around his neck and placed it on her chest and listened to her heart beat.

From where I stood, I could tell Flora's breathing was hollow and rattled.

Dr. Meadows stood back up and turned to us, taking the stethoscope out of his ears and letting it hang around his neck. He gave us a gentle smile.

"Would you two ladies mind waiting outside for a little?"

Clarabelle and I exchanged concerned looks.

"Why?" I said, looking back at Dr. Meadows.

"I want to diagnose Flora in private. Don't worry, I'll let you know how everything goes. This way, it's easier for me to keep my entire focus on her."

"Private?" I said, my voice raising slightly. "Why? What do you think is wrong with her?"

"I just think it would be best if you two ladies would wait outside," he said, his tone never losing its patience. "I will let you know when you can come back in."

Clarabelle put her hands on my shoulders. "Come along, Margaret," she said, pulling me with her. "The doctor knows what's best. Come on, hon. Let's go have a cup of tea while Dr. Meadows takes care of Flora."

I walked backward out of the room as Clarabelle kept her hands on my shoulders.

Dr. Meadows closed the door behind us.

"Come on," Clarabelle said, gesturing for me to follow. "I'll put a pot of tea on."

"I want to stay here."

"Margaret, Dr. Meadows needs his privacy with Flora. He'll let us know when he's ready for us to come back in."

"Why aren't you worried? What if something is really wrong with her? You're not even worried in the least!"

"Of course, I'm worried!" Clarabelle snapped. "Flora is my greatest friend in the world, and it absolutely tears me seeing her like this! For her to go from such a hard-working woman to someone who can barely keep their eyes open is…"

Clarabelle's voice trailed off. She placed her hands on her hips, averting her eyes away from me. I could tell that she was biting the insides of her cheeks as she let out ragged breaths through her nose. She puckered her lips, twisting her mouth about. She shook her head.

"She's the only true friend I really got," she said, her voice uncharacteristically thick. "I know I may seem like I know about everybody in town and everything but…Flora's been the only constant in my life.

"Even after my husband, Dale, passed away, she was there. We've picked up each other's hearts when they were shattered on the floor, we've been there for each other no matter what. That woman is made of pure steel, and I'll be darned if I'm the one that doesn't go first because she's supposed to outlive us all. So, yes, Margaret. I'm worried. I'm worried as hell."

I swallowed the lump that was lodged in my throat. Seeing Clarabelle so unraveled and vulnerable made me see the woman that she truly was. She may have been irritating as all else, but there was no denying that she was a good and loyal friend to Flora. The corner of my mouth turned up in a gentle grin. I nodded slowly, trying to gather myself to speak so I wouldn't sound as broken as Clarabelle.

"Let's go have some tea," I finally said.

Clarabelle nodded back and led the way down the staircase.

CHAPTER TWENTY-THREE

Clarabelle and I sat across from each other drinking tea and sharing a canister of butter mints that we found in the back of Flora's pantry. We filled the silence with humdrum talk.

"The Harvest Festival is approaching quickly," Clarabelle said. "Only a few more weeks now."

"I'm looking forward to attending," I said.

"I'm hoping it's a good turn out this year. Lord knows the food will be the most popular attraction as it always is."

"So, exactly how much whiskey do you put in your peach cobbler?" I popped another mint into my mouth.

Clarabelle shook her head. "Flora never should have mentioned I put a secret ingredient in it. It's nobody's business."

"But you told me yourself that you put whiskey in some of your recipes. That wasn't Flora's doing. I just put two and two together."

"Leave it alone, Margaret." Clarabelle took a sip of her tea.

The creaking on the stairs signified that Dr. Meadows was on his way down. We stood up from the table and met him in the foyer. His expression was neutral, giving nothing good nor bad away.

"Well?" Clarabelle said.

"Well," Dr. Meadows replied, "Flora has quite the case of pneumonia. Her lungs are terribly inflamed. I gave her some medicine to help her for now, but you're going to have to go to the drug store to buy some more. She should stay in bed until her fever breaks, and then, if her pneumonia is cured, she may start moving about again."

"*If* her pneumonia is cured?" I echoed.

Dr. Meadows titled his head, his eyes apologetic. "I'm afraid that it's very difficult for a woman Flora's age to recover."

My heart dropped to my knees. I thought they would buckle beneath me. I swallowed hard and tried my best to form a coherent sentence.

"But…but there is a possibility she could get better," I said, forming my words as a statement in the hopes it would bring me a sliver of comfort.

"Yes," Dr. Meadows said, although his tone was cautious. "The only thing you can do is exactly what you've been doing, such as keeping her body temperature as normal as possible. As well as the medicine I want you to administer to her. It's up to her body to decide whether to fight off the virus or let it spread through her."

The horrid image of Flora's body losing the fight against her illness possessed my mind. I pictured her becoming more and more frail by the minute. I quickly closed my eyes to shake it out of my head. I couldn't be thinking these terrible things.

"What's her temperature at now?" Clarabelle asked.

"She currently has a fever of one-oh-one-point-five," Dr. Meadows declared. "She needs to be at least ninety-seven, no higher than ninety-eight-point-seven. Oh, and I advise that she lay off any strenuous work if she does recover. If Flora's condition gets any worse, I'm afraid she will need to be administered to the hospital immediately."

I was getting tired of Dr. Meadow's usage of the word "if." I knew he couldn't promise a recovery and had to be realistic, but at the same time, I needed him to have some spark of positivity, even if there was a small chance of it.

"When she does recover," I said, "how long can she not work for? I mean, the pecan farm is her entire life. She's worked so hard to keep it running."

Dr. Meadows sucked in his cheeks and bit his bottom lip. His eyes creased together, and I could tell that he was trying to find a gentle way to express his next words.

"It would probably be best if she doesn't work. The weather will be getting cooler, and it would be too much of a risk for her to be outside all the time lifting heavy buckets and everything. Trust me, I understand how much this means to her, but she needs to seriously consider slowing down. She's not going to be here forever, you know."

Although Dr. Meadows' words were a stab to the gut, he was gentle with his approach, which told me that he's had to do this numerous times. It made me think of the doctor that told us Uncle James would never walk again. How he said it to us in a way as if we should have expected it. As if telling us was wasting his time, when he could be tending to other patients who had the chance of using their legs again.

Dr. Meadows was the complete opposite. There was no shortage of Southern hospitality and gentleman-like charm. The way he chose his words and looked Clarabelle and me in the eyes, said how much he knew Flora meant to us and that he cherished her as a patient as well.

"Can I at least go see her?" I asked.

"You may." Dr. Meadows nodded. "But please remember that she must rest. We mustn't excite her too much."

"Thank you, Dr. Meadows," I said, ascending the stairs.

"Margaret, I'll be up in a minute," Clarabelle said. "I'm gonna see Dr. Meadows out."

I gave Clarabelle a quick nod before hurrying up the steps. I carefully opened the door to Flora's bedroom, the sound making a slight creak.

Flora's eyelids fluttered, and she turned her head toward the door.

"I'm sorry." I walked up to her. "I didn't mean to disturb you."

Flora shook her head slowly. "It's all right." Her voice was nearly shot. "I'm having trouble resting. Dr. Meadows…medicine…" She was straining to form a full sentence, so she stuck her tongue out and made a repulsive sound.

I expelled a giggle and pressed my hand over my mouth, not wanting to be so loud that Clarabelle could hear me from downstairs, resulting in another one of her lectures that I didn't need to hear.

"It'll make you feel better." I kept my voice above a whisper.

Clarabelle walked in the room. "Dr. Meadows gave me the name of the medicine he wants Flora to have. Margaret and I will go to the pharmacy to pick it up, and I'll get some things to make soup. I'll make it here in case you need me."

"I can stay with her," I said.

"Margaret," Clarabelle said, "it's best if I'm here, too. Dr. Meadows told me to call him if Flora gets worse or we need anything from him."

Flora nodded. Her eyelids became hooded, and she nuzzled her chin in the crook of her shoulder.

"Come on, Margaret." Clarabelle grabbed my arm. "Let's go get the stuff we need. Let Flora rest; we can check on her a bit later."

Clarabelle tasked me with getting the medicine at the pharmacy, while she gathered the ingredients for the soup at the general store that was across the road.

When we arrived back at Flora's house, Clarabelle asked me to help her make the soup. She nagged and henpecked every little move I made as

I chopped the carrots and celery. My blood was boiling faster than the chicken in the pot.

"You're cutting them too big, Margaret," Clarabelle squawked. "Smaller pieces. Flora can barely open her mouth as it is. We don't need her straining to eat a piece of celery."

I slammed the knife and my fists down on the counter. "Then you cut them." I untied my apron and took it off, chucking it onto the floor. "If I'm doing such a lousy job at cutting a damn vegetable, then why don't you do it? Stop belittling every single thing I do and do it yourself."

I stalked off with Clarabelle hot on my trail. "Don't you talk to me that way, Margaret! I'm trying my darnedest to keep Flora comfortable and make her feel better. This isn't the time for you to have one of your little tantrums."

"Tantrums?" I echoed. "If you weren't so patronizing to everything I do, I wouldn't have to have my little tantrums! I'm trying to help Flora, too! But it's not good enough for you. Nothing I do ever is. I can't even walk into a room without you telling me I'm doing it wrong."

"That isn't true." Clarabelle grunted.

"Of course, it is. Everything has to be done your way. God help anyone who disagrees with you. I'm trying my best as well! You're not the only one who wants Flora to get better. I hate seeing her like this! I hate…" My voice hitched. I put my hands on my hips and averted my eyes from Clarabelle.

She walked in front of me, forcing my eyes to meet hers again. Her lips were a straight line, and her eyes had relaxed.

"Margaret," she said softly.

"I hate knowing there isn't a lot that I can do. I don't know the first thing about helping someone who's sick. But I'm trying. I'm really trying."

"I know you are," Clarabelle said, her voice a mixture of comfort and defeat. "Come here, Margaret."

I looked at her, my lip curling up slightly, unsure of what she was going to do.

"What?" I said.

"Come here," she said again, stepping closer to me.

She opened her arms and pulled me into her, giving me her version of a hug. I hesitated, a little put off and honestly frightened by her action. However, I wrapped my arms around her and squeezed my eyes shut, accepting her thoughtful yet awkward gesture. We held each other for a moment longer before finally letting go. When I looked at her again, I saw that she too was trying to keep her own eyes dry.

"I wish...I wish there was more I could do." I sighed. "This doesn't seem like enough."

"Why don't you try praying?" Clarabelle said.

"Praying?" I raised my eyebrows. "No offense, I'm really not the praying type."

"You must've prayed before, Margaret. Everybody does it. It's helped me. And it sure as heck has helped Flora."

"I don't think it would work. Thanks for the suggestion, but it wouldn't do much."

I turned, making my way back towards the kitchen again.

"Why don't you believe in God, Margaret?" Clarabelle said.

I faced Clarabelle again who was looking at me with judgment in her eyes.

"What did you say?" I asked, narrowing my eyes

"I know you heard me. Why don't you believe in God?"

I lifted my chin, matching my eye contact with hers. "Why do you?" I countered.

"Because He's always been there for me. You know I've had my fair share of heartache. He's kept me going, even on days when I didn't want to move out of bed. Now I know you turn your nose up at everything that has to do with Him—"

"There you go again." I charged over to her. "Assuming you know everything about me, when you don't. I've prayed. When my uncle went missing in action, I got down on my knees every single night and prayed that he would be found. And when he came home, I prayed even harder for him to heal and get better. When he didn't, I stopped. Because I realized it was useless to wish for something that was never going to happen. I was wasting my time with empty prayers that I knew would just leave me disappointed and my uncle still broken."

I fought at the tremble in my voice as I tried to stand my ground against Clarabelle. I couldn't crumble in front of her. I didn't want to risk her hugging me again, for the fear that if she did, I would fall apart in her arms.

Although there was still a trace of judgment in Clarabelle's eyes, they had softened a bit, and her mouth relaxed. Her gaze flickered away from me.

"I can't force you to pray," she said, her voice soft. "But it can be a nice relief. You make the decision yourself. Now, let's finish making that soup. Flora must be starving."

I managed to convince Clarabelle to finally go back home at seven o' clock at night. She was exhausted after making Flora soup, cleaning up after it, and cleaning up the house in general. I told her to go home and that if I needed her, I would let her know.

Before going to bed, I made a quick check on Flora, who was knocked out by the medicine that Clarabelle had given her. I walked up to her bedside and watched as she slept, the dimmed light next to her bed gave off a warm glow, making her features appear softer. I forced myself to tear my eyes away from her, silently repeating that I would check on her again in the morning and that everything would be fine.

I didn't realize how tired I was until I climbed into bed. I switched off the lamp next to me and cozied myself under the covers, laying there in the darkness as the silver moon peeked through the curtains, and the nighttime sounds of the crickets and grasshoppers that I had grown accustomed to keeping me awake, lost in thought.

I drummed my interlaced fingers on my stomach, trying to find a way to get my mind focused on sleep. However, every method eluded me as I continued to stare up at the ceiling, thinking about Flora just a few doors down. I continued to reassure myself that she would be all right and that we did everything we could to take care of her today.

I thought of Clarabelle's suggestion about praying, which I still believed to be useless, however, I sat up and clasped my hands in my lap, hesitating for a moment and brushing my thumbs against one another before finally raising them up under my chin. I sat awkwardly, unsure of how to begin.

"Um…I'm not sure how to do this. It's been a while. As you know, Flora isn't doing well right now. And I'm not sure if she's going to get any better. And I just wanted to tell you that…if you could help her…"

I slammed my hands down in frustration. I couldn't do this; I sounded like a greeting card. It was a ridiculous idea in the first place. I shook my head, thinking how silly I sounded. But when I looked back up at my door, thinking again about Flora sleeping across the hall and wondered if she would be better or worse tomorrow, I rubbed my hand across my forehead and sat up straighter. I clasped my hands again and closed my eyes.

"I know I haven't exactly been the greatest person, and I know I gave up on you a long time ago, but I don't know what else to do. Clarabelle told me to give you another chance, so…here it goes. Flora is the greatest person I've ever known. You probably know that, too. And…she needs to get better. She has to. She's the only person who never judged me, even when I was a real creep to her. She's too strong to lose like this. There's so much she still needs to do. She needs to be here, smiling and making everyone else happy with her pecan bread and…just being the way she is. You have to help her. She needs to get better. I…I need her. Please. Please help her get better."

I unclasped my hands and laid back down, snuggling up under the covers again. I felt relieved and a bit exposed. As I lay on my back, I let out a deep sigh, which allowed me to finally close my eyes and fall asleep.

CHAPTER TWENTY-FOUR

The next three days went by like a snail trying to move through honey. Although it seemed as if Flora's fever had gone down one day, it spiked back up in the afternoon, forcing Clarabelle to phone Dr. Meadows again, who administered a stronger medicine. She decided to stay at the house, opting to sleep in Alfred Jr.'s old bedroom.

One morning, which was supposed to be a quick check up on the pecan farm, ended up being a two hour clean up fest when we discovered that critters had gotten to the pecans before we did.

"Don't tell Flora about this," Clarabelle said, throwing gnawed on pecans into her bucket. "She's going through enough right now. Best if we don't even mention we came here at all."

When we arrived back at the house a little after noon, we realized that we hadn't eaten since breakfast, so we helped ourselves to some tea and leftover pecan bread, which had been sitting under a dome for more than a week. It must've been absolutely killing Flora not being able to work out in the pecan farm and make her recipes. I asked Clarabelle if she knew how to make Flora's pecan bread.

"I would never even try to do it in the first place," she said.

"How come?" I asked.

"Because it's her recipe. She should be the only one making it."

"Well, if she ever decided to put her recipe on her labels, then everyone would be making it."

"Which is exactly why she shouldn't do it. It's her recipe, and her recipe only."

After our snack, we sat in the den, completely bushed. I looked over at the side table near me, wanting to read my latest issue of *Modern Screen* Magazine that I picked up at the drug store. However, I didn't have the strength to reach out for it. Clarabelle was knocked out cold on the sofa. Her chin dipped down, touching the top of her chest as she let out little whistling noises, her lips flapping as a puff of sleepy air escaped from them.

A light knock came at the door.

I rolled my eyes and hoisted myself up, tiptoeing past Clarabelle. When I opened the door, I was surprised to see Clark standing in front of me.

"Hi, Maggie." He smiled.

"What are you doing here?" I asked, my tone unintentionally ill-mannered.

"I'm here to bring Flora to Mr. Winston's office. She has another meeting today."

"Oh." I stepped out onto the porch with him and shut the door behind me. "Actually, Flora's not feeling well."

Clark's eyes widened. "Is she all right?"

"She's been sick in bed with pneumonia for the past few days."

"Oh, gosh." Clark rubbed the back of his neck. "I wish I had known. Does she need anything?"

I shook my head. "I think we're all set. Clarabelle and I have been taking care of her. Her temperature has been a little wacky, but it's gone down a bit since yesterday."

"Well, that's a relief." Clark let out a sigh.

"Sorry we didn't tell you. Honestly, I didn't even think of it."

"It's all right." He shrugged. "I guess I'll just go myself and tell Mr. Winston that Flora's sick. Maybe we can reschedule."

"Wait," I said, touching his arm as he began to turn away. "I'll go with you."

"Oh, you don't need to do that. You should stay here with Flora."

"She's asleep, and probably will be for quite a while. That medicine knocks her out pretty well. Besides, Clarabelle is in there; she'll be fine."

"It's really not necessary." Clark shook his head. "It won't take too long. Plus, I don't want it to be an inconvenience to you."

"It won't be. I want to get a good look at this Mr. Winston guy anyway. Just let me go change, and I'll be down in jiff."

Clark let out a suppressed chuckle. "A jiff? Sounds like Flora's been rubbing off on you."

It took me a moment to realize what I had said, and a light smile curled at my lips. "Yes. I guess she is."

After changing out of my farming clothes and into something more presentable, I scribbled out a quick note to the still sleeping Clarabelle and placed it gently on her chest before rushing back out of the house. I got into Clark's truck, who was already waiting for me in the driver's seat. It was strange sitting next to him, instead of in the back like in his cab. I would often peer over at him, watching as he kept his eyes focused on the road. He was unusually quiet. Normally, he chatted up a storm while driving.

As we drove out of rural Savannah and into downtown, my stomach fluttered, and my palms began to sweat. I thought of what I might say to this Mr. Winston who seemed to be almost an enigma at this point. Flora only mentioned him a few times, which piqued my curiosity even more. This was the man that was responsible for putting Alcott's Pecans out into stores. I smoothed out my navy-blue skirt and made sure the top button to my cream-colored blouse was secure.

When we arrived at Farmer's Food Company, I was surprised to see how small the building was. Although it wasn't tiny by any means, I was expecting something a lot grander. Clark parked right in front of the building and turned his truck off.

"Ready?" he said.

"Yes." I nodded.

"Oh," Clark said as I was getting ready to open my door, "this probably shouldn't take long. So, don't feel like you have to participate in the conversation."

"Excuse me?" I took my hand off the door handle and narrowed my eyes at him. "You wanna repeat that?"

Clark swallowed hard. His eyes registered panic and fear for a quick moment. He licked his lips and nodded, as if he were trying to save what he had just said.

"I-I mean, Mr. Winston will probably just be updating me on recent sales," he stammered out, "and how many more shipments of pecans I need to bring to him, so…I'm sorry. I didn't mean to say it like that. What I meant was, you don't need really to do much talking."

"Come again?" I raised my eyebrows at him.

"Well…you know what I mean." He gave me an innocent lopsided smile.

"If I want to talk, I will." I opened the door.

Clark nodded, choosing the appropriate option to stop digging himself into a deeper grave.

We walked toward the building, and Clark held the door open for me. The inside was clean and warm. In a way, it reminded me of O'Hanlon's office building. This place, however, had a much more inviting feel to it. I looked around at all the offices we passed by; each one had its door closed.

We took the elevator to the second floor. Clark gave the attendant a courteous thank you before walking off. Mr. Winston's office was the first door on the right. Clark knocked, and a muffled voice advised us to come in.

"Afternoon, Mr. Winston," Clark said, taking his hat off.

Mr. Winston looked up from the paperwork on his desk. His dark brown hair had the beginnings of gray at his sideburns, and he had a clean-shaven face, revealing a small cleft in his chin.

"Ah, Clark! How are you, son?" He stood up from behind his desk and walked over.

"Very well, sir," Clark took Mr. Winston's hand in his and gave it a firm shake. "How about yourself?"

"Oh, can't complain," Mr. Winston said. His eyes focused on me, and he offered a charming smile. "And who is this?"

"Maggie." I held my hand out for him to shake. "Pleased to meet you, Mr. Winston."

"Well, aren't you a pretty little thing?" He took my hand gently in his and turned it over, giving it a small kiss. "Very pleased to meet you as well, young lady."

I took my hand out of his and discreetly wiped it on the back of my skirt, all while hoping the smile I was presenting him with appeared polite and not uncomfortable. He gestured to the two seats in front of his desk. Clark and I sat down, while Mr. Winston took a cigar out of a wooden box and lit it, puffing away like a dragon as he sat behind his desk.

"So, what brings you here with Clark, Maggie?" Mr. Winston asked. He squinted his eyes, his glance pacing the room as if he just realized something. "Where's Flora?"

"Oh, well…I'm a friend of Flora's," I said. "She's not feeling very well, Mr. Winston."

Mr. Winston's eyes crinkled with concern. "Oh, the poor thing. What's the matter with her?"

"She's got pneumonia," I said. "She's been in bed for about five days. So, I'm here in her place today. She's not as bad off as she was—"

"That is quite the interesting accent you got there," Mr. Winston interjected, catching me off guard. "Are you from up North?"

"Yes, sir." I nodded. "Boston. Anyway, she's—"

"Boston. That's quite a ways away. What are you doing all the way down here in Savannah?"

I blinked, fighting the urge to twist my mouth up and tell him to zip his lips and let me speak. However, I shook my head slowly.

"Oh, it's a long story, Mr. Winston."

"Well, glad you're here anyway." Mr. Winston offered me a large grin, showing off the gap in between his two upper teeth. "Now, Flora has pneumonia? My goodness. The poor thing. She's one of the hardest working people I know. Always out in that pecan farm. For a woman, that's quite impressive."

I nodded but stopped short when I realized the sentence he ended his statement with. I tilted my head, giving him a glare as I leaned forward slightly in my seat.

"Excuse me?"

"Uh!" Clark cleared his throat, holding his pointer finger up and jumping in before I could give Mr. Winston a piece of my mind. "How are sales, Mr. Winston?"

"Oh, yes!" Mr. Winston turned his attention to Clark. "Well, as you know, we hit a rough patch a few weeks back, but the sales have picked up again, although slightly. Those Golden Hills are coming in hot. However, I expect to see a boost closer to Thanksgiving. People sure do like putting Flora's pecans in their pies."

Mr. Winston's eyes gravitated to me, and he gave me a small wink before looking back at Clark. This time, I couldn't hide my discomfort. I curled my lip up into a sneer as he continued to talk to Clark about the sales and when to bring another batch of pecans to their factory.

I looked at Mr. Winston's sausage-like fingers that sat interlaced on his desk and noticed a gold band around his ring finger. This man was quite the package, and not the kind you wanted to receive in the mail.

When Clark and Mr. Winston were finally finished, we all got up from our seats. Mr. Winston and Clark bid a cordial goodbye.

"And, nice to meet you, sweetie," Mr. Winston said to me, taking his hand in mine.

"Likewise." I forced myself to sound sincere and offer a polite smile.

"You tell Flora to feel better, and I hope to see her again soon." He bent down and gave the back of my hand another kiss.

I let out an awkward chuckle as I slipped my hand out of his. "Sure thing," I said before scurrying out of the office as quickly as I could.

Clark put his hat back on his head. "That went well, huh?" He grinned, walking up to the elevator.

"You're joking," I said.

"I'm sorry?"

"That guy was such a heel! He couldn't stop taking a peek at me every chance he got! And the way he talked about Flora?"

Clark tilted his head. "I didn't hear him say anything bad about her."

"*For a woman*," I said, mimicking Mr. Winston's deep, southern drawl. "Like he's surprised that a woman can be hard working."

"Oh, I don't think he meant anything like that. Most of his suppliers are male-owned businesses. I mean, I know her husband used to be the owner, but now that he's gone, Flora's taken on a lot of the business, all while continuing to work on the farm. I saw it more as a sign of respect."

I shook my head. "I didn't get a good feeling from him."

"Look, Maggie, he's a business owner. Of course, he's used to working with men more than women. But Mr. Winston is a good man. He's done a lot for Alcott's Pecans over the years."

The elevator doors opened, and we stepped in.

"Ground floor, please," Clark said to the attendant, putting his hands in his trench coat pockets.

I stood with my arms crossed and shook my head again. "There was just something about him."

"I think you're just imagining things," Clark said. The elevator doors opened, and we stepped out.

"I would like to start coming with you and Flora," I said once we got back in his truck.

"Oh, I don't think that's really necessary."

"Yes, it is," I said. "I want to start accompanying you two."

"Maggie…"

I shot him a look. "You can't talk me out of it, Clark. From now on, I tag along."

Clark gave a defeated shrug. "Suit yourself."

"What in the name of Sam Hill, Margaret?" Clarabelle grumbled to me when I got back to the house.

"Well, if it isn't Sleeping Beauty!" I said, taking my hat off.

"None of your smarty remarks," Clarabelle said. "How dare you leave without telling me!"

"I left you a note. Didn't you get it?"

"Yes, but it fell off of me when I went to stand up. Then I kicked it under the sofa when I bent over to pick it up, so I had to get down on my hands and knees and search for the darn thing. By the time I stood back up, I needed to sit down again."

"Goodness," I said. "Good thing you didn't pull a muscle."

"That's enough, Margaret," Clarabelle warned. "What made you think you had the right to visit Mr. Winston? Sometimes I wonder if your head is screwed on at all."

"I went with Clark. I explained everything in the note. I don't understand why you're so upset."

"I'm upset because you left a dang note instead of waking me up to tell me."

"If I had done that, you wouldn't have let me go."

"Exactly! You had no business going to see Mr. Winston with Clark."

"He just showed up. I felt bad because he had no idea Flora's been sick! I figured I wasn't hurting anyone by going. I was only trying to help out. And you know, that Winston guy is a real piece of work."

"I don't care!" Clarabelle said. "You shouldn't have gone! You didn't say anything, did you?"

"What do you mean?" I asked, tilting my head to the side.

"Oh, don't give me the innocent Mary Pickford act. You know what I mean. You didn't mention her pecan bread recipe, did you?"

"No, I didn't." I crossed my arms. "And honestly, I'm a little offended that you would think I would do that without Flora's permission."

"Well, you've proven time and again, Margaret, that you have a tendency to say and do whatever you want, without taking any consideration of others."

"Guess what? I went, and I don't regret going. I can't go back in time and change that. So, you're just going to have to understand that." I shook my head, wanting to change the subject so Clarabelle would get off my back. "How's Flora doing?"

"The same," Clarabelle said, her prickled tone smoothed out just a touch.

"You didn't tell her I went, did you?" I asked.

"No." Clarabelle shook her head. "I didn't want to upset her while she's up there hacking her brains out."

I rolled my eyes. Clarabelle seemed like she was going to be milking the guilt card as much as she could. I didn't want to argue anymore though. I was tired and hungry. It was three o'clock in the afternoon, and I was ready to eat my own arm off.

"I'm going to make us some chicken and dumplings for dinner," Clarabelle said, "and another batch of chicken and rice soup for Flora. Her appetite seems a little stronger today. I may see if she would like some of our dinner as well."

I helped Clarabelle clean up after dinner. Flora ate the soup in her room, but the minute Clarabelle mentioned chicken and dumplings, Flora's face turned greener than a shamrock. Although her fever had gone down again, she still suffered from the chills and hot sweats.

I kept her company after dinner by reading an article from my *Modern Screen* magazine to her. Her voice was still weak, and it was physically draining for her to talk, but I could tell she was getting lonely while in her room all by herself, so I figured I would sit with her while giving Clarabelle a break.

Later that night, I crept out into the hallway to check on Flora one last time before bed. I opened the door a crack and peeked my head in. It was dark in her room, and the only source of light was coming from the hallway. From where I was standing, she seemed to be asleep. I began to close the door gently.

"Maggie?" Flora's voice whispered.

"Yes?" I stepped into the entryway of her room, opening the door further so I could see her better.

Flora continued to lay there flat on her back, her arms rigidly at her sides. She was so still, almost like a painting. Did she even say my name at all? A jolt of concern coursed through me, and I took another gentle step toward her bed, not wanting to startle her.

"Flora?" I said, keeping my voice low.

Again, Flora remained unmoving. I waited for a moment watching her, the light from the hallway barely helping. She made a light whistling sound, making me realize that it was the cruelty of my imagination conjuring up her being awake. I chalked it up to wishful thinking, hoping that I would've been able to at least say goodnight to her.

I lowered my head, casting my eyes downward to the floor. Although I was filled with defeat, the sound of her soft snoring brought a glimmer of comfort to me, knowing she was still breathing. I raised my head, giving her one last look before backing out of her room and going to bed.

CHAPTER TWENTY-FIVE

The lovely colors of autumn were slowly but surely beginning to show on the leaves. Despite the temperature still being quite warm, it made me want to cozy up in a sweater. Since I didn't bring any of my cardigans with me the last time I left home, I went to the local store where Flora had bought my farming outfit and got myself a caramel-colored sweater with a matching pleated skirt with some of the money Siobhan had given me.

I figured that since Flora's fever and symptoms were beginning to go down significantly, and since Clarabelle was still staying with us, I could take Flora's truck and leave for a little while. While at the store, I got Flora a little present and even bought Clarabelle something as well.

I returned back to the house with my bags, and Clarabelle gave me a disapproving head shake.

"What?" I said, setting the bags down on the table.

"You never fail to astound me, Margaret," she said, her upper lip curled.

I gave her a smile. "Thank you." I took off my coat.

"That wasn't a compliment!" Clarabelle called out.

"I know!" I crooned, moseying into the hallway to hang my coat up.

When I walked back into the kitchen, I caught Clarabelle peering into my bags. I cleared my throat in a loud and dramatic fashion, startling her. A gleeful smile tickled my lips as I walked over to her.

"Don't you have enough clothes?" Clarabelle grumbled.

"Not for the autumn. All my other clothes are back home."

"When I was your age, I waited until I had run my clothes into the ground before buying new ones. None of this fashion nonsense you're getting from them stars on the screen. It was all about comfort and practicality."

"I'll write that down," I said, making a check mark gesture with my hand. "Anyway, I didn't only shop for myself."

Clarabelle arched an eyebrow up at me, a quizzical expression crossing her disapproving pout.

I offered a minx-like grin.

"What did you do?" she sighed.

"Take a look." I gestured to the bag.

She reached in and pulled out two small boxes and opened them, revealing two brooches. One cream-colored and another with an amber hue. She opened her palm and looked at them, speechless—a first for her.

"Margaret..." she said.

"I figured Flora could have the cream-colored one, and you could have the other," I said. "Or whichever either of you prefer."

"Margaret," she said again. "You shouldn't have done this."

"Why? I wanted to. I thought since Flora is finally starting to get better, it would be a nice surprise. And, you've done a lot helping me take care of her. I just wanted to show my appreciation."

"Do you know how much these cost?" Clarabelle said.

"Yes, I bought them."

"Margaret, this is too much." Clarabelle shook her head. "Flora most definitely deserves it, but—"

"So do you," I said. "I know we don't always see eye to eye, and we may have wanted to rip each other's hair out during all of this, but I couldn't have taken care of Flora without you."

Clarabelle let out a sigh and looked down at the amber colored brooch. She picked it up in her other hand and brushed her thumb over it.

"This is my favorite color," she said, more to herself. Her eyes flickered up at me. "Thank you."

I smiled at her. "Put it on!"

Clarabelle handed me Flora's brooch and put hers on the lapel of her house dress.

I adjusted it, making sure it was straight. I reached into my clutch on the table, pulled out my compact mirror, and handed it to Clarabelle.

She looked at her reflection, and I could tell she was trying not to show too much pride in how good she thought she looked. A small curl at the side of her mouth turned up as she admired the brooch in the little mirror.

A knock came at the front door.

Clarabelle handed me my mirror, and I put it back in my clutch before following her toward the hallway. Clarabelle opened the door to reveal

Dr. Meadows standing on the porch, holding his doctor's bag. He tipped his hat at us and offered his usual charming and polite smile.

"Afternoon, ladies!" He walked in and took his hat off. "Just checking in on my star patient. May I go up and see Flora?"

"Yes, you may," Clarabelle said, pointing to the stairs. "She's doing much better, Doctor. I think if her temperature stays where it is, she can be nearly fine by the end of the week."

"Well, that's good to hear!" Dr. Meadows smiled. "Let me just check on her, and I'll let you know if Flora can start getting back into the swing of things. She's been up in that room for so long, she needs to be stretching her legs."

"Does that mean she can go back to work on the farm when she's all better?" I asked.

Dr. Meadows shook his head. "I'm afraid I'm still concerned about that. I'm sure she can go back to baking her treats, though. You said she makes a darn good pecan bread."

"She does," I answered.

"I hope to try it sometime," Dr. Meadows said. "When she's ready to, of course."

"I'll bring you up to Flora, Dr. Meadows," Clarabelle said.

"Thank you, Clarabelle." Dr. Meadows gave a gallant nod. "Say, that's a nice brooch there."

"Oh." Clarabelle touched it with the tips of her fingers, the hint of a flattered smile crossed her lips. "Margaret got it for me."

"Well, that was nice of her," he said, giving me a smile before climbing the stairs to Flora's bedroom.

"Well, your breathing certainly sounds better." Dr. Meadows took the stethoscope out of his ears and draped it around his neck. He patted Flora on the shoulder. "Your fever has gone down significantly. How do you feel?"

"Much better than before, Doctor. Thank you," Flora said.

Although her voice was still a little weak, she looked much better physically. She sat straight up in bed with no sign of fatigue. Her eyes were more alert, and her nose no longer sounded like she had a truck rammed up it. She gave Dr. Meadows a light smile, her first one in an achingly long time.

"You are most welcome, my dear." He grinned. "It wasn't all my doing, though. You had two great little nurses helping out right over there." He pointed at Clarabelle and me, causing us to blush a little.

Flora looked over at us and smiled. "I do have the two best friends."

Her words made something flutter inside my stomach. I'm sure Clarabelle wasn't surprised by what Flora said, but for me, it was such a lovely thing to hear. I had been referring to Flora as my friend to get out of explaining why I was here in the first place, but to hear her say it, made me feel more special than anyone could since my Uncle James.

"That you do." Dr. Meadows put his hand on Flora's shoulder and gave it a gentle rub. "You're very lucky to have Clarabelle and Maggie at your side."

"Yes, I am," Flora said.

"Now, I still would like you to take the medicine," Dr. Meadows said. "You don't need to be taking as much as before, but just until the rest of your symptoms go away. I would also like you to start getting up and stretching your legs a bit. You've been in this bed for a long time, only getting up to go to the bathroom."

"Yes, Doctor." Flora nodded.

"I believe there is a light at the end of the tunnel," Dr. Meadows took off his stethoscope and put it in his bag. "It may take a little longer to get there, but it's definitely on the horizon."

"Thank you so much again," Flora said, followed by a raspy cough.

"You are welcome again," Dr. Meadows snapped his bag shut and turned toward Clarabelle and me. "Well, I'm off. Maybe try getting her downstairs a little later today. And as always, if you need anything, just ring me up."

"Thank you," I said.

"Thank you, again Dr, Meadows," Clarabelle said. "I'll see you out."

They left the room, and I walked over to Flora's bed. "Would you like to go downstairs?"

"Oh, I would love that," Flora said, letting out another raspy cough. "I just hope I remember how to use my legs."

I took the covers off of her and held my arms out. She held onto them with as much strength as she could muster and wobbled out of bed, losing her footing slightly.

"You good?" I said.

"Oh, yes. Just a little shaky."

"Take your time," I said, still holding onto her arms.

Clarabelle walked back into the room. "What are you doing?"

"Flora wants to go downstairs," I said, glancing quickly at Clarabelle before bringing my attention back to Flora.

"Here, let me help," she said, walking over. "You two look like you're about to start doing the Waltz."

Clarabelle stood on the other side of Flora, and we both grabbed an arm, guiding her towards the door. That was the easy part. Getting Flora down the stairs, however, was another story. We looked like something out of *The Three Stooges,* causing Flora to burst into fits of giggles, which sent off a chain reaction. I began laughing so hard, I was afraid we would all tumble down the stairs. Even Clarabelle was cackling and gasping for breath.

When we got to the sofa, we all collapsed on it, laughing with tears streaming down our cheeks. Clarabelle let out a snort, which was the final thing that destroyed us as we melted into the couch, laughing for the first time in what felt like forever.

With Flora finally settled on the sofa, I was able to convince Clarabelle to go home. She took Flora's bedsheets and the sheets she slept on with her, saying she would wash them at her house and bring them back before the end of the day.

It took Flora a little bit to adjust to the brightness of the den after being in her bedroom for so long with the shades down and a bedside lamp as her only source of light. She still looked quite pale, and her lips were dry as a bone.

I made her some tea, and she insisted that she drink it at the kitchen table. I handed her the teacup, and she drank it with shaky hands. She licked her lips, letting the tea linger on them.

"Are you hungry?" I asked.

She nodded. "Yes, but none of that soup or broth. I practically got it coming out of my nose! I need to start eating more solid foods again. Is there any pecan bread left?"

I shook my head. "No. Clarabelle and I ate as much as we could, but it ended up going stale, so we had to throw it away. There wasn't a lot left, though. So not too much went to waste." I walked over to the pantry and brought back the tin of butter mints.

"I guess I should start making some more, then."

"Don't force yourself to, really." I sat down across from her. "Take your time feeling better. I mean, you've been in bed for over a week. Don't put too much stress on yourself."

"I know, but I want to. It makes me happy. You have no idea how much I missed being in the kitchen and the farm. I can't wait to get back to it."

My gaze fell. I forgot that Flora still didn't know that Dr. Meadows instructed that she no longer work on the pecan farm. I looked back up at her, my eyes apologetic.

"Well, that's the other thing," I said.

"What?" Flora tilted her head, her eyes filled with concern.

I sighed, pausing to find a gentle way of telling her. "Dr. Meadows said that it would be best if you don't work on the farm anymore."

Flora's eyes rounded, and her mouth hung open, as if she were trying to register what I had just said. Then her eyebrows knitted in indifference. She swatted her hand in the air.

"Oh, I'll be fine. I've been sick before and always healed enough to start working again. I appreciate his concern, but I don't think he needs to be jumping the gun on this one."

"He seemed like he knew what he was talking about. You don't want to go against the doctor's orders. I know you want to continue working, but maybe at least for now, you can ease off on the farm. He said you can still bake, just take it easy on yourself."

Flora sighed, her face colored with defeat. "It's going to be hard not working on the farm. I'm going to need extra help."

"Well, I'm here. And so is Clarabelle."

"Yes, but Clarabelle isn't as spry as she once was, either. She can still do work, but I don't know for how much longer. This past week has made me see just how old I am. I didn't want to believe it. I was planning on working out in that pecan farm until the day I died. That's how I always thought I'd go, picking pecans on the farm. It's an awful thing to realize you're getting too old. I thought I could convince myself that I was forever twenty-five. That if I kept convincing myself, I would feel twenty-five, and maybe I could keep doing what I love forever."

Flora traced the rim of her teacup with her finger. Her eyes stared into the cup, as if she wished it were the Fountain of Youth, and that drinking the tea inside would grant her desire to be young again. The wrinkles on the sides of her eyes creased as she squinted, holding on to the memories of her youthful years. She lifted the cup and took a sip.

"Well, you've worked on that farm for so many years," I said, raising my voice to a positive tone. "You should be proud of it. And you can still run the farm, just not work on it. Plus, you can go back to making your pecan bread. Dr. Meadows said he would love to try it sometime."

I gave Flora a smile, and she chuckled, although there was still a melancholy tone to it.

"That Dr. Meadows was a doll," she said.

"He was very nice." I nodded.

"Was Clarabelle really here the whole time?" Flora asked.

"Oh, yes." I drew the words out. "The whole entire time."

Flora laughed, which caused her to let out another cough. She patted her chest and took another sip of her tea.

"I was in and out of it so much," she said. "I thought I heard her say she was going to be staying here, but I guess I didn't quite know what she was saying."

"She did stay. She slept in Alfred Jr.'s old room."

"Oh," Flora said, her expression caught off guard. Her eyes floated away from mine, and she began staring off into space again.

"She didn't change anything," I said. "She brought a carpet bag with a few clothes in it. She didn't use any of the drawers or move his things around. She just wanted to be close to your room in case you needed something."

Flora looked back at me, then smiled, the trace of sadness crossing her lips. "That's fine. Of course, I wouldn't expect her to sleep on the sofa."

I felt bad that Flora's first day feeling better kept making her sad. I wanted to make her smile like she used to again. Then I remembered the cream-colored brooch I had bought her. I turned to her, a mischievous smile on my face.

"I'll be right back," I said.

I got up from my chair, went upstairs, grabbed the brooch and my hand-held mirror from my bureau. I brought them back down and handed Flora the small box with the brooch in it.

"What's this?" she said.

"Open it." I smiled. I brought a chair next to her and sat down.

Flora opened the box and pulled out the brooch. She held it in the palm of her hand, inspecting every inch of it.

"Oh, Maggie," she said, her green eyes wide. She kept turning the brooch over in her hand, unable to take her eyes off of it. "Where did you get this?"

"That store where you bought my farming outfit. I bought myself a sweater and skirt for the autumn. All my cold weather clothes are still in Boston. But I saw this brooch and knew I had to get it for you. I got Clarabelle one as well."

Flora looked back up at me. "Honey, you didn't have to do this."

"I wanted to. After being in bed and feeling crummy for so long, I thought I would get it for you. You know, to make you feel better."

"And you got Clarabelle one, too?" she asked.

I nodded. "I couldn't leave her out. If it wasn't for her, I would've lost my head. She was a great help." I chuckled at the image of Clarabelle admiring herself in my mirror. "Even though she didn't say it, I think she thought she looked like quite the catch."

Flora smiled, her eyes crinkling as they welled up. "Thank you."

"You're welcome. Let me put it on you."

I pinned the brooch to her nightgown and gave her my mirror. I watched as she smiled at her reflection. She touched the brooch gently with her fingertips, rubbing the cream-colored opal in the middle.

My chest grew heavy as I watched her smile widen. The bottom of my lip hitched, and I bit the inside of it. Seeing Flora happy again and knowing that she was going to be okay—that she was here, right in front of me and not wasting away up in her bed anymore—sent an overwhelming surge of gratitude through me. There were moments during this past week when I didn't know if she would get better or worse. How there were days when she could barely open her eyes or even speak. My eyes welled up, and I thought the heaviness in my chest would burst. I couldn't resist as I put my arms around her neck and squeezed her gently, my head resting next to hers.

"Oh!" She placed the mirror on the table and put her hand on my arm as I continued to hug her.

I finally let go and looked at her, my lips trembling as I smiled. "Sorry," I said sheepishly.

"It's all right. Oh, sweetheart!" She put her hands on my cheeks and brushed her thumbs across my eyes, wiping under them. "Why are you crying?"

"I'm just…I'm really happy you're feeling better," I sniffled, wiping my eyes.

"I am, too." Flora smiled. "And I want to thank you for taking such good care of me."

"Don't mention it." I shook my head.

"Oh, you know I'm never gonna forget it."

Flora opened her arms and brought me in for another hug, holding me tight as I nuzzled my head on her shoulder, giving a silent prayer of thanks that she was better again.

CHAPTER TWENTY-SIX

After Clark dropped off a batch of pecans to Mr. Winston one afternoon, he came back to the house to check on Flora before heading off to his cab driving job. Flora was thrilled to see him. She squished his cheeks with her flour covered hands. Since she was back to baking her treats again, she was more chipper than ever. Even the smallest thing delighted her. Her eyes would light up, turning as big as saucers. Flora was back, and I couldn't have been happier as well.

"I'm glad you're feeling better, Flora," Clark said, walking to the front door.

"Thank you, Clark." Flora smiled and handed him a freshly-made loaf of pecan bread. "I'm so glad you stopped by."

"Anytime, you know that." Clark smiled and put his hat on.

"And thank you so much for taking such good care of my business while I was sick. I really appreciate it."

"Not a problem. Like I said, everything is hunky dory. Mr. Winston is pleased the sales increased a bit and is optimistic for the upcoming ones as well."

"Well, that's good to hear."

"Besides, I had Maggie to help me."

"Oh?" Flora turned to me. "Maggie, you went to see Mr. Winston with Clark?"

"Yes," I said. "But only once."

"She wanted to come along, figuring she could step in for you," Clark said. "Mr. Winston took quite a liking to her."

I rolled my eyes, his kiss on my hand still lingering on my skin. I must've washed my hands five times that day.

"That's nice!" Flora said. "Mr. Winston is such a gentleman."

I snorted, causing Flora and Clark to turn towards me. "Oh yeah. A real gentleman."

"Well, I need to get going," Clark said, heading out the front door. "Glad you're feeling better, Flora. Thanks for the pecan bread."

"That was nice of him to visit," Flora said after Clark had gone.

"Yeah," I said. "I felt bad that I had forgotten to tell him you weren't feeling well when he came by last week."

"Oh, don't worry about it." Flora waved her hand. "He's a busy young man, anyway."

We walked back into the kitchen, and I helped Flora clean everything up. She made us each a cup of tea and cut two pieces of pecan bread and brought them out to the front porch where we sat in the white wicker chairs. I took my shoes off and curled my feet beneath me. I took a bite of my pecan bread. How much I missed the taste of it! Flora's baking skills were still as magical as ever. It was as if she had never left the kitchen.

"So, that's good that Mr. Winston liked you," Flora said after taking a sip of her tea.

I picked at my pecan bread, grabbing at the morsels of pecans and popping them in my mouth. I honestly didn't understand what Flora saw in that guy. He seemed like a pompous crumb to me, and I was there only ten minutes. I wondered if he gave Flora his faux compliments to her face. She was such a nice person, I wasn't sure if she would realize how thinly veiled his words were.

"To be honest," I said, "I didn't really like him. Actually, let me rephrase that; I couldn't stand him."

"How come?" Flora asked, genuine curiosity and puzzlement crossing her face.

"He was such a heel! He makes it sound like he's complimenting you, but it's just his way of being a cad."

"Oh, that's not true!"

"He said you were a hard worker for a woman. That doesn't bother you?"

"Well, I would rather my hard-working skills be seen just like everyone else's, but you can't help how other people view it."

"Has he ever talked that way to you, though?"

"I've never really noticed." Flora shrugged. "He's always been very polite to me. My husband was more of the talker when he was alive, anyway."

"He kept leering over at me while he was talking to Clark, too," I continued, unable to stop my tattling. "And he kissed my hand…twice!"

"He kisses my hand all the time. It's just his way of being friendly and charming. I know it's not the most solicited of gestures, but he's only trying to be nice. Besides, he's a married man! Him and his wife have been happily married for twenty-five years."

"I told Clark that I would like to continue to accompany you two whenever you go see Mr. Winston."

"Oh, that's not necessary." Flora shook her head. "I appreciate you wanting to help, but it's really not needed. Besides, you've already done so much to help me out. Just by working on the pecan farm alone. That's all I could ask for."

"And all I could ask for is that you let me come with you and Clark from now on. Who knows, I may have some neat business ideas up my sleeve. And I think you already know what one of them is."

"Yes, I know," Flora said, dragging out the words. "But I've already told you, I'm not putting my pecan bread recipe on the label. For all I know, no one would make it themselves. They would probably just bake them in a pie."

"Are you kidding? Everyone loves it! I truly believe that everyone in Savannah and probably wherever else your pecans are sold, people would be making your bread all the time."

"I don't know." Flora shook her head, her eyes downcast and her lips set in a tight, thin line.

"At least think about it. I hate to bug you so much about this, especially since you're starting to feel like yourself again. And I'm sure you're sick of hearing me ramble on about it, but—will you at least think about it? I promise, I won't say anything to Mr. Winston. Trust me, I don't want to bring any attention to myself in front of him."

Flora twisted her mouth as if she were deep in thought. She took a sip of her tea, taking another moment to ponder her decision. It certainly wasn't helping that I was staring her down like a Rottweiler waiting for her to answer. Finally, she sighed.

"Fine. I'll think about it." She shot a glance toward me. "But I don't want to hear about it again until I've made my decision. Understand?"

I nodded, failing to hide the satisfied smile that spread across my face. "Understood."

Clark set up a meeting with Mr. Winston at Flora's request. She wanted to discuss recent sales and inform him about Dr. Meadows orders.

"I hope he's not too upset," Flora said.

"Why would he be?" I asked. "Your health is the most important. I'm sure you'll be able to work on the farm again. Besides, if he gives you any lip, I'll nail him in the teeth."

When we got up to Mr. Winston's office, Flora knocked on the door and opened it.

Mr. Winston sat behind his desk smoking a cigar and sorting through papers. He looked up and gave a huge smile when he saw us enter the room. He stubbed out his cigar and walked over.

"There's my favorite girl!" He gave Flora a hug and a kiss on the hand. "How are you feeling, Flora? I heard you were quite under the weather."

"Much better, Mr. Winston. Thank you," Flora said.

Mr. Winston moved on to Clark, exchanging a civil handshake and greeting with him.

"And there's my other favorite girl!" Mr. Winston pointed his finger at me. He took my hand in his and kissed it. "Maggie, correct?"

"Yes, Mr. Winston," I said, suppressing the urge to let out an exasperated sigh.

"It has been too long, little lady." He smiled.

"About a week." I gave him a biting smirk.

"You are a hoot, missy!" he howled. "Sit down, everyone! Sit down."

Clark let me and Flora sit in the chairs while he stood behind us.

Mr. Winston sat behind his desk and lit up another cigar. He leaned back in his chair, his smile looking as if he had just won a million dollars.

"What's new, Flora?" he said.

Flora removed her hat and set it on the chair next to her. She fluffed her hair out.

"Well, Clark informed me that sales have picked up since the last few weak ones," she said.

"Oh, yes!" Mr. Winston grinned. "Although not as much as I would like. We're still in heavy competition with Golden Hills. They are, at the moment, a bit ahead of us. Now, I understand you've been ill lately, so I don't fault you at all for the slow boost, given how the sales were decreased well before you got sick. However, I am optimistic that the sales can increase more since Thanksgiving is approaching soon."

Flora nodded. "I am pleased to hear that they've picked up a bit. It's better than staying where they were or dipping further."

"I quite agree," Mr. Winston said. "And now that you're better, you can get right back out on that farm again!"

Flora's cheeks flushed a bit. "Well, that's the other thing, Mr. Winston. Dr. Meadows thinks I should ease off working on the farm."

Mr. Winston cocked his head. "Oh?"

"I can still run it!" Flora said. "He just thinks that given how sick I was and my age, I shouldn't be working on it so much anymore. I'm still able to foresee everything that goes on with it, though. I lost over a week of work and am determined to get right back to it. Maggie was a wonderful help, too. She was out there with Clarabelle picking pecans and working her little rear end off."

Flora put a gentle, appreciative hand on mine. She turned and gave me a light smile, which I mirrored.

"Dr. Meadows is concerned Flora would work herself too hard," I informed. "However, I believe she could still work on the farm. She just needs a little break. Flora's tough. I have no doubts that she can get right back into it."

Mr. Winston stroked his chin and shrugged. "Well, Flora, I wouldn't want you to overwork yourself."

"I wouldn't be," Flora said. "I'm still fully capable of running everything."

Mr. Winston looked down at his desk and cleared his throat, interlacing his fingers together. I couldn't decipher his expression. He didn't seem upset nor pleased. There was something in his eyes, however, that I couldn't pinpoint. I knew one thing though; I didn't like the feeling it was giving me.

I watched him cautiously. He was being surprisingly likable, which immediately made me wonder what he was thinking. There were definitely wheels turning in his head.

"Let's take everything slow for now," he said. "We'll start by getting more pecans ready to distribute. Clark, I'm going to need you to bring more shipments in by the end of next week."

"Yes, sir," Clark said.

We stood up, and Mr. Winston bade us goodbye, giving me yet another unwanted kiss on the hand before we left. As we headed out the door to the parking lot, Flora stopped short.

"I left my hat in Mr. Winston's office," she said.

"I'll go get it," I said.

When I reached Mr. Winston's office, I raised my fist to knock on the door but stopped when I heard him talking to someone. He seemed to be in the middle of a serious conversation. I put my hand on the door knob and opened it a crack, not wanting him to know I was there. I turned my ear so I could hear what he was saying. He must've been on the phone because I couldn't hear anyone else.

"That's right," he said. "Well, she said she can't work on the pecan farm anymore. Who? The boy just delivers the pecans to me. He works as a cabbie during the day. Yes. Yes, sir, I agree. Well, I like her, too. She's a very lovely woman, but she just can't do it anymore. Let's face it, I saw this coming when her husband died."

My eyes widened in disgust, and my upper lip twitched as it took everything in me not to march into his office and give him a piece of my mind. I could just picture his balding little head nodding up and down as he spoke to his mysterious caller. I leaned in closer, straining to hear.

"Yes, well, if that's what it takes," he continued. "All right, then. We're gonna have to find someone else to take over Alcott's Pecans."

CHAPTER TWENTY-SEVEN

When Mr. Winston ended his call, I straightened up and gave the door a forceful knock. I walked in, not giving Mr. Winston the satisfaction of allowing permission for me to enter.

"Maggie!" He beamed. "Long time no see!"

He let out an obnoxious chuckle.

I forced myself to stay cool, offering a muted smile. I knew that if I raked him over the coals for what I just overheard, he may turn a sour mood onto Flora, and I couldn't do that to her.

"What brings you back here?" he asked.

"I'm just grabbing Flora's hat." I walked over to the chair where her hat was placed and picked it up. "I'll be out of your hair in a second."

"You're not bothering me," he said. "I was going over everything I spoke to Flora about."

He needed a shovel the size of Flora's pecan farm for the amount of manure he was offering.

I glared at him, my smile now acidic. "Really? Well, I'm glad I wasn't a disturbance."

"Never!" He smiled.

"I must go, now." I backed away toward the door. "Flora and Clark are waiting for me out in the truck."

"Good to see you again, sweetie."

I fought the urge to throw up all over his rug. I tightened my smile and held my hands behind my back to avoid another kiss on them.

"Yes," I said. "And thank you for being so understanding toward Flora. She's been through a lot lately, and it's nice to know that you are so incredibly supportive of her. She loves this job more than anything. It's why she gets up in the morning."

If I hadn't known, I thought I detected a glint of anxiety in Mr. Winston's eyes, which is exactly what I was going for. However, it was either fleeting or he was one hell of an actor because he covered it up with a Cheshire like smile.

"She's a wonderful lady, you know that," he said.

"I do." I nodded. "I'm glad you know that as well."

I offered another thin-lipped smile and backed slowly out of his office.

The minute I closed the door behind me, my animosity turned to devastation. I felt awful for Flora and didn't know how I would tell her. This was going to break her heart. She had already been through so much—not just from the past week, but over the years. I wanted to tell Clark what I had heard, but since he was just as busy as he usually was, I didn't want to pester him any further.

Clarabelle, well, it was understandable why I didn't want to tell her. She would probably get all worked up and tell me to stay out of it. It was too late for that. I was knee deep in this situation, as well as Flora's life. I had come to truly care for and appreciate her, and to see all her hard work and dedication to keeping her husband's business going be in jeopardy, broke my heart as well. I couldn't let this happen. I had to find a way to make everything right.

After mulling over Mr. Winston's phone call in my head the next day, I decided I had no choice but to do the right thing and tell Flora. I only hoped I wouldn't work myself up and become hot headed like I was known to do whenever I would become anxious. I found Flora sitting on the porch swing out back, lost in her needle point and calmly listening to the insects of the late morning.

"Flora?" I said softly, as to not startle her. "Can I tell you something?"

Flora put down her needle point and took off her glasses. She turned to me. "Sure, honey. What is it?"

I took in a deep breath and sat down next to her. "When I went back to Mr. Winston's office to get your hat yesterday, I heard him talking on the phone."

"Oh?" Flora said.

"I went to knock on the door and heard him speaking, so I opened the door and listened."

"Oh, Maggie, eavesdropping isn't very polite." She shook her head.

"I know, but I couldn't help it. I honestly wasn't trying to. I just sort of stumbled into it."

"All right." Flora gave an accepting nod. "Go on."

"Well, I wasn't sure who he was talking to. He was talking about you and Clark. So naturally, I leaned my ear closer to the door to hear better."

Flora dipped her head and gave me a disapproving look. "I thought you didn't mean to eavesdrop."

"Okay, so maybe I meant to a little; but you know how I feel about that guy!"

"Yes, I know." Flora nodded. "Mr. Winston was having a private conversation. I don't feel comfortable with you telling me about it."

"But it was about you and your business. You have every right to know what he was saying."

"I don't think it's decent—"

"He wants to sell your business to somebody else!" I blurted. So much for trying to maintain my cool.

Flora's eyebrows furrowed and her head tilted slightly. She blinked, and for a second, I thought I saw a glimmer of sadness pass her face. Her eyes floated down to her needle point. She picked carelessly at the small threads. I wanted to know what she was thinking. Her silence was puzzling. I couldn't tell if she was shocked or if I had told her something she wasn't surprised to hear.

"Flora?" I said, my voice interrupting the cool, hushed air.

Flora remained silent. She continued to stare down at her needle point, the *Home Sweet Home* and bird stitchings looking back at her. She put her glasses back on and looped another stitch through, remaining unsettlingly quiet. Whether she was choosing to ignore me or not, I had no clue.

"Flora," I repeated. "Did you hear what I said?"

Flora put the needle down and sighed. "I knew this was going to happen," she muttered, shaking her head. "I knew. It was only a matter of time."

"Well, he can't do that without your permission." I paused. "Can he?"

Flora shook her head. I could feel the defeat radiating off her body. "Technically, no. But like I said, I figured this would be coming soon."

"You can't let him do that, though. It's still your business."

Flora shrugged. "I don't know." The tremble in her crestfallen voice ached me. "Maybe he's right. Maybe I shouldn't be doing this anymore."

I couldn't believe I heard those words come out of Flora's mouth. I stared back at her, flabbergasted, wondering what on Earth possessed her to say such a thing. I understood that she wasn't surprised by Mr. Winston's decision, but I couldn't fathom that she was willing to let go of so many hard-earned years of work and success. She was throwing away something not just she, but her husband and his family worked so hard for.

"Are you serious?" I said. "You told him yourself yesterday that you could still run everything. You were so determined! Why are you going back on your word now?"

Flora shrugged. "What else can I do? I got sick and lost over a week of harvesting to accomplish. Apparently, I can't work on the farm anymore. What's going to happen next? I can't prevent whatever new obstacle comes my way."

"No, but you can go to that heel's office and tell him where to put his cigar."

"Maggie!" Flora exclaimed, her expression a mixture of horror and amusement.

"I know these past few weeks have been crazy. But that's no reason to give up on your business altogether. When my dad and uncle opened their first grocery store, they had a lot of mishaps. Their first year was unsuccessful. Uncle James wanted to quit, but my dad knew that their grocery store was destined to become something bigger, something no one's ever seen before. Now, O'Hanlon's is all over the East Coast and is growing more and more each day."

"Yes, but that was when they first started out. It's easy to get both discouraged and determined during your first years of business."

"But that's the thing," I protested. "You've been at this much longer than my dad has. You've seen all the good and the bad that comes with having your own business. Mr. Winston has, too. I'm sure he's had his share of failures over the years."

Flora shook her head. "It's not that easy. Of course I don't want to give up the business. It's been a part of my life for over forty years. I love it as if it were my own child. But I can't do this by myself anymore."

"You don't have to. You've got Clark, and Clarabelle…and me."

Flora patted my hand. "Yes. And I'm very grateful for you all. But Clark has his own life. He helps me whenever he can, but he has a job of his own. And Clarabelle is a year older than me. She may have a bit more spring in her step than I do, but she too won't be able to do this for long. And you; you're a lovely girl, Maggie. You've been so much help to me, you have no idea. But you don't know the first thing about business, much less running one."

"Well, I can learn," I said, sticking my chin out.

"I'm sure you could, honey," Flora said, giving my hand another mollifying pat. "But there's just so much to it."

I was becoming aggravated that I wasn't getting through to her. I folded my arms across my chest.

"Maybe this would be the time to bring up your pecan bread recipe," I said, my eyes challenging hers.

A look of disapproval flashed across her face. "Maggie. I told you, I didn't want to discuss that matter. It's not worth it anymore."

"What do you mean it's not worth it?" I said, not bothering to hide the ire in my voice. "He didn't slap the cuffs on you just yet. Maybe it's the thing that can help you keep your business."

"I think we should stop discussing this," Flora said, her voice even but warning.

"And I think that medicine Dr. Meadows gave you is still swimming around in your head!"

Flora's jaw dropped. She looked at me as if I had smacked her across the face. Her rosy cheeks whitened, and a mixture of hurt and devastation filled her eyes.

"Maggie!" Her breath caught in her throat.

I could tell that I struck a nerve I shouldn't have, but I couldn't help what tumbled out of my mouth. Even though I didn't mean to say it, I didn't exactly regret it. I looked back at Flora, my defiant stare not wavering. Her mouth trembled as she fumbled around for words.

"How dare you say that to me!" she said, finally finding her voice. "You're being very disrespectful."

"And you're being very unreasonable!" I shot back.

Flora got up from the porch swing. She walked into the house, holding onto her needle point. I followed, hot on her trail. I wasn't going to let her back away from the conversation. Not this time. I marched after her, fully intending on standing my ground no matter what.

Flora put her needle point down on the counter and fumbled around the kitchen.

"What is so wrong with at least running the idea by Mr. Winston?" I said. "The worst thing he can do is say no, then you would have your answer. But nothing is going to happen if you don't at least try."

"Maggie, you need to understand. This is my business now, and I decide what is best to do with it. It's my choice."

"This is ridiculous!" I threw my hands up in the air. "Why can't you just do this? You know, I bet that if your husband and son were still alive, they would think you were being unreasonable as well!"

Flora's face dropped. Her eyes creased and began to fill up. This time, I knew what I said had gone too far. She swallowed, her eyes flickering away from me. She wavered back and forth, her face one hair away from crumpling as she brushed past me and stormed out of the house.

CHAPTER TWENTY-EIGHT

I never knew where Flora went. When she left the house, I followed her, stopping at the front door. She got into her truck and sped off. She was gone for nearly two hours and didn't mention anything about her whereabouts.

Although she was still ticked when she returned, she seemed to have eased a little. She addressed me cordially, however, her tone was bitter, which remained throughout the rest of the day. She made dinner and cleaned up after without a word. After, she went straight to bed instead of her usual late-night lounge on the back porch.

I had never seen her so upset before. I knew that I should never have mentioned her husband and son, but at the time, it's what tumbled out of my mouth. I wanted to apologize, but at the same time, I didn't. I didn't want to be the first one to crumble.

The next day, Flora was still visibly agitated.

I entered the kitchen to find her setting three teacups down on the table. She placed the milk and sugar down and put out a loaf of pecan bread. I crossed my arms.

"Three teacups?" I said.

Her eyes flickered up at me. "Yes. Clarabelle is joining us this afternoon."

Oh, great.

The last thing I needed was to have Clarabelle here poking her nose in our business. She for sure would notice the hostility between Flora and me and would most definitely call us out on it.

"You still want to have me at your table?" I said.

"Yes," Flora said coolly. "You're my guest, too. Unless you don't want to join us…"

"No, no." I shook my head, desperately hiding the hurt that plagued me at being referred to as her guest. "I'll join you."

"Very well, then." She walked off.

I gripped my hands on the back of the chair, leaning on it. I hoped that Flora was cordial enough to not let any of her sourness show. Since she was normally happier than Shirley Temple skipping rope, her current mood would be glaringly obvious. I just had to make sure that I acted as well-mannered as I ever could.

Flora and I gave the performance of our lives in front of Clarabelle. I could tell that she was suspicious, however. She sipped her tea slowly, her piercing glare leering at us over the rim as Flora made small talk about her garden. Clarabelle put her teacup down, her eyes darting back and forth.

"What's going on?" she asked.

Flora tilted her head. "Pardon?"

"There's something going on with you two." She continued to stare us down.

"I don't know what you mean," Flora said, putting on a smile. "Maggie and I are perfectly fine. Aren't we?"

I nodded, shoveling a forkful of pecan bread into my mouth to avoid speaking.

"The air is thick with something. I can sense it." Clarabelle squinted her eyes.

"Nonsense," Flora said, adding in a stale chuckle. "Clarabelle, would you like some more tea?"

Flora got up and grabbed Clarabelle's teacup before waiting for an answer, trotting to the other side of the kitchen.

Clarabelle leaned in close to me. "All right. Spill it."

"Spill what?" I whispered back.

"I know something is up with you two."

"I don't know what you mean," I said, mimicking Flora's incredulous tone.

"Come off it, Margaret. You've barely said a word since I got here."

"I'm just being polite."

"That's exactly why I'm worried. You're not polite! What did you do this time?"

"Clarabelle," I whispered, glancing up to make sure Flora was still out of earshot. "Everything is fine. There's nothing to worry about. And I'm offended that you would think I did something wrong."

I sat back in my chair, noticing that Flora was turning around to come back to the table. I picked up my teacup and took a long, slow sip hoping to hide the sweat that had formed on my upper lip.

"I'm onto you," Clarabelle mouthed before leaning back in her chair and accepting her next cup of tea from Flora.

Clarabelle eased off and kept her mouth shut for the remainder of her visit. Although I could sense the side glances she was throwing at me, she didn't mention the awkward tension again. That is, until she was leaving.

She was able to poke her head back into the door once Flora had gone into the kitchen to clean up. She gestured for me to come out on the front porch.

I hesitated before taking a look back to make sure Flora didn't hear Clarabelle come back in. I walked out onto the front porch and shut the door gently behind me.

"All right, Margaret," Clarabelle said. "Now do you mind telling me what the heck is going on?"

"Holy smokes! You're like a dog with a bone, aren't you? There is nothing going on."

"You're full of malarkey!" She pointed her finger at me. "I can tell something is bugging Flora. She has a lot of wonderful qualities about her, but acting isn't exactly her strongest suit."

"What acting? She's fine. Everything is perfectly normal."

"It is not! I've known Flora since we were young girls. That woman wears her heart on her sleeve. I can tell when something is bothering her. She pretends to be happy. She always has a smile that could light up the entire city. That woman in there is not the Flora I know!"

I held my hands up. Not so much in surrender, but to ward off Clarabelle's agitation. She was getting way too ahead of herself. I understood that Flora was her best friend, but the way she initiated herself into Flora's life to the point of bordering on meddlesome unnerved me quite a bit. I didn't know how a person could be so intrusive and observant about every little thing.

"You really need to calm down," I said. "Maybe Flora is just tired."

"Tired my foot! I saw her speeding out in her truck like she was on a mission from God yesterday."

"Clarabelle, Flora is fine. If there was something going on, I'm sure she would tell you. And if she didn't, well, that's her choice."

"She tells me everything!" Clarabelle shook her fist.

"I understand that. But as I've told you before," I said, stressing my words, "nothing is going on. You're overreacting."

Clarabelle let out a huff. "I'm gonna find out. Somehow, I'm gonna find out what you aren't telling me."

"That's wonderful." I crossed my arms. "We have nothing to hide."

Clarabelle gave me one of her sneers and turned around, stomping down the front steps.

I went to open the door.

"Margaret!" Clarabelle said, causing me to turn and face her. She pointed her finger at me. "Flora is my best friend. She may be made of steel, but she can wilt like a tulip. And if you did something to upset her…"

She trailed off, her finger still pointing at me. She curled her lip up, her blue eyes narrowed. She was fighting herself to get the next words out. She didn't have to say them though. I already knew what they were. I took my hand off the door and walked to the edge of the steps. I stood before Clarabelle and nodded.

"Believe me, Clarabelle," I said, "I wouldn't be able to forgive myself, either."

After Flora and I finished supper, I offered to clean up in hopes that my gesture would help a little. Flora couldn't have accepted fast enough. Normally, she told me not to worry about it, eventually letting me when I persisted, or she would offer that we clean up together. Tonight, she gave me a quick thank you before striding off into her den to knit.

I offered her a quiet goodnight before heading upstairs.

She replied curtly, not taking her eyes off of her knitting.

I couldn't sleep. The number of times I tossed and turned was ridiculous. All I could think about was how upset Flora still was. While we put on a good enough show for Clarabelle—who was onto us like a mosquito on a hot summer night—Flora went back to being generally quiet for the rest of the day. Although she was still polite, the smiles she graced me with didn't reach her eyes. If anything, they were biting. No teeth, just a long, thin line that wasn't genuine. I was beginning to succumb, my guilt at breaking her heart gnawing at my bones.

As I lay in bed, my mind replaying our quarrel, I began to think that I should have apologized immediately after hurting her. Although I didn't regret putting up a fight, I did regret my choice of words. It was a lousy feeling knowing I hurt someone I cared about. I didn't even know what she did during the time she was gone. Where did she go? Did she cry? That thought made me feel even worse. I brought up something so personal and still so freshly painful and dug it into her like a knife.

I turned my head, facing the window. Even with it closed, I could still hear that bullfrog croaking away. Did that thing ever sleep? I let out a groan and threw off my covers. I staggered out of bed and tip-toed downstairs to get a glass of water.

As I made my way toward the kitchen, a sound rustled in the den. I craned my neck, noticing that there was a lamp on in there. I walked into the den and discovered Flora in her nightgown and robe sitting on the sofa, a cup of tea on the table in front of her. She looked like something out of a painting, seemingly lost in her own world. I shuffled into the room, not wanting to startle her.

"Flora?" I said.

She brought her eyes up to me, her expression neutral. She didn't seem mad or upset that I was here, just aloof. I felt as if I were intruding on her, even though she wasn't doing anything. I stood there awkwardly, not knowing whether to stay with her or go back upstairs and try falling asleep again.

"Oh," she finally spoke, "hello, Maggie." She looked away, her fingers resting on her cheek.

"Are you all right?" I asked.

I walked over to the sofa and sat down beside her.

Flora didn't say anything.

I was beginning to think that it was a bad idea to have come and sit next to her. I was obviously being a bother. I looked down at my fidgeting hand. The thumping inside my chest was beating quicker than it should have. I couldn't stand the awkward tension anymore.

"Flora," I said, pausing a beat before speaking again. "I'm sorry. I didn't mean to hurt your feelings. I wish I could take back what I said. I mean,

I don't regret speaking my mind, but I do regret hurting you. I was just so upset that you wouldn't listen to what I was saying, I went over the line. I know I can get riled up easily. If you haven't noticed, I have a hard time admitting when I've done something wrong. It's something everyone has called me out on, and I was always too proud to accept it. But I was wrong to hurt you. I don't blame you for staying mad at me. I'm honestly surprised you're still letting me stay with you. I was afraid I would be on the first train back to Boston. I just…I'm sorry, Flora. I really am."

Flora remained silent, keeping her gaze ahead.

I figured she still wouldn't forgive me. I didn't blame her. Although, I was terribly heartbroken that she wouldn't answer me. I deserved it, anyway. I let out a quiet, defeated sigh before standing back up, deciding to go back to bed.

"Maggie?" Flora said. She took a moment before turning her head and looking at me. "I'm sorry as well."

"What?" I sat back down. "You did nothing wrong. I was the one who—"

"No." Flora shook her head. "I shouldn't have been so cold toward you. I should have just talked to you and told you how bothered I was."

"But I deserved it! I could see how upset you were. I didn't say anything after because I was trying to be stubborn and didn't want to be the first one to come crawling for forgiveness. Which is…exactly what I just did."

"Maggie, you said a lot of things—while hurtful—that were true. I didn't want to believe you about Mr. Winston. I thought I still had a few years left. He's been making thinly veiled comments about giving the business to someone else since Alfred died. I just thought that he was talking about if there were an unfortunate turn of events, but now I know that it's been something he's been planning all along. It makes me feel as if all he ever saw me as was the wife who bakes and helps pick a pecan or two. Even though I would sometimes be present for meetings, it was as if he would talk to me like I was a small child."

"So, you did see him for the skunk that he was."

Flora nodded. "I thought that if I did everything he said and learned as much about the business side as I could, he would be fine with me. And now, what with being sick for a while and told I can't work anymore, I think he has a good reason to go in another direction."

"But none of that is your fault! You couldn't help being sick. Do you really want to give up on everything because of this?"

"Of course not!"

"Then show him!" I couldn't help the desperation that shook in my voice. "I don't want to see you lose this, either."

"Oh, honey." Flora held my chin in her hand. "I know how much you care."

"That's just the thing." I looked down. "I haven't cared so much about something in my life. I always put myself before others. The only thing I ever did care about besides myself was my uncle. Now he's gone. And then when you got sick…"

I broke off, and my eyes welled up.

Flora grabbed my hand in hers and gave it a comforting squeeze, instantly easing me.

I let out a sharp exhale and looked up, finding the strength to meet her gaze again.

"When you got sick, I was afraid to lose you as well. I had never felt that about another person before. I thought about how even though I've only known you for a few months, you treated me as if you had known me your entire life. You treated me like a daughter. My own mother never did that. So, yes. I do care. And I know you do, too. I realize it's silly to continue harping on this, but let's show Mr. Winston that you are not stopping anytime soon. Let's show him what ideas we have for Alcott's Pecans. You have to fight for this, Flora. Please!"

Flora squeezed my hand harder, rubbing the back of it, her maternal gesture sending warmth through me. She smiled, a real one this time, and nodded. I smiled back and threw my arms around her, relief surging through my heart at being embraced by her again.

CHAPTER TWENTY-NINE

I opened the front door to find Clark standing on the front porch. A smile instantly hit my lips.

It had been a few days since Flora agreed to put my idea into action. I gestured for him to follow me to the kitchen, aching to tell him.

"So, we have some news," I said.

Clark grinned. "Swell! What is it?"

"I convinced Flora to put her recipe on the back of her labels."

Clark paused, and his brows knitted together. "Really?"

Flora and I nodded.

His hazel eyes widened, and his mouth hung open as if I had just pulled a rabbit out of my hat. To be honest, I was quite amused by his reaction.

"This is great!" he said.

"We would like your help convincing Mr. Winston and getting any information we need on how to advertise my pecans and recipe, as well as how much it would cost to add extra space on the label," Flora said.

"I'll try to help as much as I can, but I don't know too much about advertising or where to begin with packaging."

"That's fine," I assured him. "It's new to us as well. And it's not like you'll be handling the manufacturing work."

Clark told us that he would find out as much as he could and get back to us. He also had the task of setting up a new meeting with Mr. Winston, and to advise him it was urgent that we meet with him as soon as possible.

After Clark had left, Flora wanted to take a ride to the pecan farm, assuring me that she would try to restrain herself from doing any heavy-duty work. I got my farming outfit on in the event that I would end up picking some pecans for the day. Since the harvesting season was nearing to an end, I wanted to make sure I got enough pecans for Clark to bring to Farmer's, for Flora to use in her recipes, and for the Harvest Festival, which was approaching quicker than I realized.

I couldn't stop inhaling the air as I threw shelled pecans into my bucket. The mixture of warm autumn air and fresh pecans was heaven to my senses; I could practically taste them. Flora only lasted two minutes before trotting over to help me.

"I can't take it anymore." She bent over, holding onto her knee for support, and tossed a few pecans in the bucket. "It's like telling me I'm not allowed to breathe."

"I won't tell Dr. Meadows if you don't." I smiled at her.

Flora bent down, inspecting the pecans. She threw the rotten or disfigured ones into the other bucket that we brought along. I didn't have the heart to stop her. She was so joyful digging her hands into the soil and holding the pecans in her palm. She ran her fingers over their rough exterior and closed her eyes, blissful peace spreading across her face. I wasn't going to take this away from her, no matter what Dr. Meadows said. The pure delight that radiated from her was incomparable. Flora was in her element here. This was her happy place—her heart and soul.

When we got back to Flora's house to dry and store the pecans, we were surprised to see Clarabelle there. She was standing with her arms crossed, wearing a worn cardigan over her house dress.

"Clarabelle," Flora said, hopping out of the truck. "What on Earth are you doing here?"

"I came to visit." Clarabelle walked over. "I figured we could catch up on some tea and pecan bread."

"You saw us just a few days ago," Flora said. "What could possibly change since then?"

"You've been to the pecan farm?" Clarabelle acknowledged the buckets in my hands.

"Yes!" Flora said. "It was so nice to be back there. I missed it terribly."

"You didn't do any work there, did you?" Clarabelle put her fists on her hips.

"A little," Flora said. "Oh, you know me, Clarabelle! I couldn't help myself! I was itching to pick pecans. Maggie made sure I didn't overdo it."

Clarabelle sighed, her eyes darting over to me.

"It's all right," I assured her. "Flora only did a little bit. I couldn't stop her. She was so happy!"

I walked through the house and down into the basement, put the buckets on the counter, and began to dry the shelled pecans.

Flora and Clarabelle followed me, both of them taking a rag and drying pecans as well.

"Besides," I said, "we weren't there for long. Just doing a little check-up."

"I only hope you don't get sick again, Flora," Clarabelle said. "You can't afford it."

"Don't worry," Flora said. "I'll be fine. By the way, Maggie and I have something to tell you."

"Oh?" Clarabelle turned to Flora, her eyes officiously intent. "And what exactly is it?"

"Flora is going to ask Mr. Winston if she can put her pecan bread recipe on her labels." I peered at Clarabelle, giving her a triumphant grin.

At first, it didn't seem like my news registered to her. She looked perplexed, her eyebrows knitted together, and her lips separated as if she were pondering everything I had just told her. She came out of her uncertain trance and licked her lips, her eyes floating over my head and directing themselves at Flora.

"Are you serious?" she said.

"Yes." Flora nodded. "I asked Clark to set up a meeting with Mr. Winston for us. I'm hoping he can meet with us sometime over the next few days."

Clarabelle jutted her hip out, placing her hand on it. She twisted her mouth, giving us a curt nod of her head.

"You should have said something to me first."

Flora and I exchanged puzzled glances as Clarabelle glowered back at us.

Flora blinked and shook her head. "I'm sorry?"

"You should have told me you were going through with this," Clarabelle said, "so I could've talked you right out of it."

"Why?" Flora asked. "It was a decision Maggie and I made together."

"I knew Margaret must've had something to do with it." Clarabelle focused her glare on me and took a step closer. "You just couldn't leave it alone, could ya? You had to go poking your nose into something that wasn't any of your business."

"Clarabelle!" Flora exclaimed.

"Excuse me?" I narrowed my eyes at Clarabelle. "You're telling me *I* was the one nosing around in other people's business?"

"Yes! You should have left it alone!"

"If anyone is the nosy one around here, it's you!" I pointed my finger at her and charged towards her until we were nose to nose with one another.

"Oh!" Clarabelle gasped.

"This is something that could really help Flora's business, and you want to take that away from her?"

"I'm not taking anything away from her! I'm concerned that this is all a silly pipe dream. Her pecans were selling perfectly fine before you came along and put the idea into her head!"

"Stop it, you two!" Flora scolded, holding her hands up. "That's enough bickering. Yes, Clarabelle. Maggie was the one who thought of the idea in the first place. She's been asking me for so long, and I didn't want to go along with it because I was afraid I was selling out something my husband and his family worked so hard for. I didn't want to change anything, thinking that I could just live off of what I had for the rest of my life. It's not like I have a lot of time left anyway. Maggie overheard Mr. Winston say that he wanted to sell the business to someone else."

Clarabelle's eyes shot toward me, her mouth gaped open. "You never told me this!"

"Because I knew you would be just as upset!" I said.

"After everything within the last few weeks," Flora continued, "I really thought that this was going to be the end for me. I had accepted the fact that Mr. Winston didn't need me anymore. I was ready to give everything away to him. Maggie was able to talk me out of it—not long after having a little tiff of our own."

"A tiff?" Clarabelle said. "Is that why you two were acting so strange a few days ago?"

Flora nodded. "She said some things that—while upset me greatly—were true. If I'm going to continue running this business, I have to make some changes. And maybe putting my pecan bread recipe on the label is a start. I don't know if it'll do much, but nothing will happen if I don't at least try. Believe me, I have thought long and hard about this. Maggie is going to help me, and Clark said he will, too. It's something I want to do, and I would love your help as well."

Clarabelle's eyes softened, and she loosened her posture. Although her mouth still looked like a corkscrew, her lips were relaxed. She looked over at me for a second, then returned her attention back to Flora.

"You're my greatest friend in the world, Flora. You know that," she said.

Flora nodded, a light smile touching her lips. "And you're mine."

"I still wish you had told me first." Clarabelle shook her head lightly. "But if it's something that you really think will help your business and will make you happy, then consider me your first customer when your new pecans are out."

"Oh, Clarabelle!" Flora threw her arms around Clarabelle's neck.

"I know my words don't mean much to you," Clarabelle said, hugging Flora back.

"Of course, they do!" Flora let go of Clarabelle. "You're my greatest friend. Of course I care what you think. I know that this may seem like a crazy idea, but I want to do it. Besides, if it sells outside of Georgia, other people around the country can try my pecan bread. It's something I'm proud of and happy to share."

Clarabelle looked at me. "You're a crazy girl, Margaret. You really believe this will help Flora?"

"That's what I'm hoping," I said.

"Are you prepared for this?" Clarabelle asked. "You don't know the first thing about running a business."

"I am," I said, my voice confident. "I may not know exactly what I'm doing, but I want to help Flora. I care about her just as much as you do."

"That is something even I can see," Clarabelle said. She gave me the tiniest of smiles, the corner of her mouth turning upward. However, it dropped quicker than a sack of potatoes. "You do know that if this fails miserably, it's on you."

"Yes." I nodded. "I will take full responsibility."

"Well, then," Clarabelle said, raising her chin. "What's the first step?"

Flora brought me to the store to buy a new outfit for our meeting with Mr. Winston, which Clark managed to schedule for the next day. I wanted to look as professional as possible. If there was one thing I inherited from my ma, it was her sense of style. I chose a navy-blue victory suit and a white blouse to go underneath.

Flora chose a neutral gray dress with a matching suit coat to go over it. I told her that if we wanted to look our most professional in front of

Mr. Winston, we had to look the part of serious business women who knew what they were doing.

Flora let me do her hair the night before, allowing rollers in it for the first time. She couldn't stop touching them with her hands, making me have to take them out and start all over again.

"I don't know how you can sleep with these things in your hair, Maggie," she said.

"You get used to it after a while. I don't even notice them anymore."

"I just don't want to have to wear that gunk you put on your face."

"Don't worry." I giggled. "You don't need that stuff anyway."

I finished up, making sure the rollers were secure enough in her hair. I didn't put too many in, just enough to add a little something extra for tomorrow.

"That should do it," I said.

"Thank you, Maggie." Flora took a sip of her tea and set it back on the kitchen table.

I sat down across from her. There was something that had been bothering me for the last couple days. I still didn't know where Flora went for those few hours the day we had our fight. I had been wanting to ask but didn't want to open up another can of worms and have Flora go back on her word. Tonight, however, I decided I couldn't take not knowing any longer.

"Flora, can I ask you something? That day you left the house when we had our fight? Where did you end up going? You were gone for so long."

A little exhale escaped from Flora's nose. She rubbed her thumb against the rim of her teacup and picked it up, taking another sip. She swallowed slowly before placing the cup back on the table.

"I went to Forsyth," she said softly.

Of course! The one place besides the pecan farm that held her heart. The place that would always bring her back to peace and calming. I scolded myself for having to even guess her whereabouts.

"I should have known that's where you went." I sighed.

"It's all right. We were both pretty ruffled up. I went there to clear my mind. As you know, that's where I go when I want to get away. I went there and sat on the edge of the fountain. I closed my eyes, and I talked to Alfred, and to my son as well. I asked them to give me a sign about what I should do. I knew that they were lookin' down on me, but I needed to know if going through with changing up the labels was a good idea. I know it seems like such a small, insignificant thing, but our packaging hasn't changed since the beginning. I needed to know if this was something I could do. I needed their blessing."

"What did they tell you?" I asked.

Flora sighed. "Well, when I was leaving to come back home, a cardinal flew by me. That was Alfred's favorite. It was then I knew that I had their blessing."

"But why were you still so upset when you came home?"

"I was very much hurt by what you said," Flora admitted. "I guess I wanted to continue being a little stubborn. It wasn't very polite of me, I know that. And even though I knew that my husband and son were fine with the decision, I was still struggling with it. I had to look into myself to decide once and for all if this was the right thing to do. And when you came downstairs the other night, you were so upset; it broke my heart. I knew that you didn't mean any harm over your words."

"I truly never meant to hurt you." I shook my head.

"I know." Flora put her hand on mine. "It's very difficult to change something that has been in your life for so long, even if it may be for the best."

I smiled at Flora. "I'm so happy we're doing this together."

"So am I." Flora smiled back. "Now, let's go to bed. We have a big day ahead of us tomorrow."

CHAPTER THIRTY

Clarabelle came over to see us off before visiting Mr. Winston the next morning. She wanted to stay at the house while we were gone; that way, we could tell her all the details right away when we returned.

Flora could barely keep anything down; she was so nervous. She nibbled on a biscuit with peach jam, unable to finish the rest. She kept wasting cups of tea, taking small sips then throwing it out when it got cold. I offered to run to the general store and pick up some coffee, saying that could help with her jitters.

"I never liked that stuff," she said. "Too strong for me."

"How about a shot of whiskey, then?" I teased, adding under my breath, "I know where we can get some."

Clarabelle shot me a look, her eyes widened and her mouth screwed up tight, warning me to keep my mouth shut.

"What?" Flora said, furrowing her eyebrows.

"Nothing!" Clarabelle said quickly.

"Oh, I'm so nervous!" Flora wrung her hands.

"It'll be fine," I said. "The worst thing he can say is no. I'll be right there with you if he gives you any trouble."

"Just don't ramble on too much," Clarabelle said. "Tell him what you're there for. Keep it short and sweet."

"I don't want him to think I'm being ungrateful," Flora said.

"Why would he think that?" I asked.

"Because he's done a lot for this business. I don't want him to think I'm trying to overtake anything."

"You're not." I put my hand on her shoulder. "You're just making some changes, that's all."

Flora exhaled. "Still, you can't blame me for being nervous."

"I know," I said. "Come on, Clark should be here soon."

"Now, remember what I said, you two," Clarabelle reminded us as we walked into the foyer, "get straight to the point. Don't ramble on, and don't show that you're nervous. You love this pecan business more than anything, Flora. Prove it to him."

"Thank you, Clarabelle," Flora said.

"And Margaret." Clarabelle turned to me. "I expect you to act professional. Don't lose your head if Mr. Winston disagrees with something you say. Do not embarrass Flora."

"It's like you don't know me at all," I said to her.

"That's just the thing," Clarabelle said. "I know exactly what you're like."

"Don't worry," I assured, walking out onto the front porch to wait for Clark to arrive. "I'll behave."

Clark said that he would accompany us for good luck, and to vouch for us if Mr. Winston disagreed with our new business idea. Even Clark looked well put together. He wore a light gray suit—complete with a pocket square—and his strawberry blond hair was combed back nicely.

When we arrived at Farmer's, Flora's jitters went up another notch. She expelled a deep breath and took a moment to stop before giving a determined nod and walking toward Mr. Winston's office.

When we entered, Mr. Winston was behind his desk, putting out a cigar. He saw us and stood up, smiling from ear to ear.

"Hello, there!" He walked over to us, his arms outstretched. "Good morning!"

"Good morning, Mr. Winston," Flora said, accepting a kiss on the hand.

"Flora, my dear, how are you?" Mr. Winston gave Flora's hand a light pat.

"Fine, thank you." She nodded.

"Maggie!" Mr. Winston pointed his finger at me, grinning like a cat. "Look at you, all dolled up!"

"Mr. Winston." I sighed. "Pleasure to see you again."

He gave me a kiss on the hand, which I immediately wiped off on my skirt.

Mr. Winston gave Clark a firm handshake, and we followed him to his desk and sat down in our chairs as he sat behind his desk and lit up another cigar.

"So, Flora, Clark said you wanted to discuss something with me," Mr. Winston said. "Shoot."

All eyes turned to Flora, who sat up straight in her chair and cleared her throat.

"Yes, Mr. Winston," she said. "I was wondering, well, I've been doing this for a long time. As you know, my husband was more of the lead business man, and I helped out on occasion."

"Yes." Mr. Winston nodded. "Alfred was a wonderful business man. One of the best we had. And your contributions of course, also did not go unnoticed."

Sure, I thought. What a load of crock this guy was dishing out. If he appreciated anything Flora did, he wouldn't be thinking about handing her business off to someone else.

"I appreciate that," Flora said. "However, there is something I would like to talk to you about."

"I'm all ears," Mr. Winston said.

Flora hesitated for a moment, taking a quiet breath before looking back up at Mr. Winston and putting on her best serious face.

"I understand that Alcott's has been with you for a very long time and that it has been a successful product."

"It has," Mr. Winston said.

"And I am very grateful for everything this business has done. Not just when my husband was alive, but even after he passed. Everyone was still so kind to me and helped me learn the business side of things."

"Well, your husband brought a wonderful product to our company," Mr. Winston said. "As did you. People down here love their pecans, and yours are certainly one of the best."

"Thank you." Flora gave a light smile before letting it fade off. "But I wanted to tell you about something that Maggie and I have been discussing. You see, there are a lot of great pecan companies out there—Golden Hills being one of them. They're still so new, and quite frankly, giving us a run for our money. We've been in business for so long that maybe it's time to make some changes."

"Changes?" Mr. Winston raised his eyebrows.

"Yes. You know about my pecan bread. Well, Maggie had the idea to put the recipe on the labels, that way people can make it for themselves at home. And maybe if we were able to start selling outside of Georgia, it could bring in more success for the company. More people would want to buy Farmer's products other than my pecans."

"Well, that all sounds very nice," Mr. Winston said. "And Maggie came up with this?"

"Yes, I did." I sat up straight and stuck my chin out. "I think it would be good for Flora—Alcott's Pecan's. I think that by adding her recipe to the label, it would bring in more sales. Her pecan bread is practically famous around here, why not share it with everyone who loves it? And like Flora said, if you could start selling Alcott's outside of Georgia, you could reach new customers to buy it."

Mr. Winston's eyes fell on Clark. "Did they run this by you?" he asked.

"Yes, sir." Clark nodded. "And I think it's a swell idea. I know I don't have much say in all of this, but I for one support Flora and Maggie."

"So, what do you think, Mr. Winston?" Flora asked. "Would it be possible to change up the labels a bit?"

Mr. Winston stroked his chin, which had the early beginnings of a light stubble. He took a puff of his cigar and placed it down in the ashtray.

"Flora." He interlaced his fingers on his equally large chest. "Of course I want Alcott's Pecans to continue to be successful. And your pecan bread is by far the best. However, I don't think I see how slapping a recipe on the label will help with sales."

"Oh." Flora's eyes rounded and downcast to her lap.

My stomach dropped, and my skin prickled with disappointment. I closed my eyes, infuriated by Mr. Winston's words.

Clark exhaled deeply behind us, his fingers gripping the back of my chair.

Flora looked back up at Mr. Winston.

"Would it be a money issue to need extra space on the label?" she asked.

"Well, yes, it would," Mr. Winston said. "And to be quite honest, I don't think adding your recipe will do much. I know it's something everybody loves, but it's only here in Savannah. It wouldn't matter much anywhere else."

"I see," Flora said, the eager brightness in her voice had dimmed out.

"Listen, if it were something I believe would work out, I would go for it. I just don't think it's necessary to be changing up a label that has stayed the same for decades."

"But it wouldn't be completely changing it up," I intervened. "Just adding a simple recipe. It's not like she wants to redo the entire thing."

"Maggie." Flora put a gentle hand over mine. "It's all right. Mr. Winston has made his decision. Thank you for your time, Mr. Winston."

Flora got out of her chair and walked over to Mr. Winston, who got up to give her a kiss on the hand goodbye.

"I'm sorry," Mr. Winston said. "But you understand don't you, Flora? It's just not a necessary change."

"Yes, Mr. Winston," Flora said, giving him a dejected smile. "Thank you."

I shot Mr. Winston a daggered stare as he shook my hand goodbye. I didn't think I could despise him anymore than I already did, but somehow, he always managed to make me dislike him even more. As we walked out of his office and down the hallway, I fumed, deciding I wasn't finished with him just yet.

When Flora and I arrived back at the house, Clarabelle was passed out, snoring on the sofa in the den. I walked right next to her and snapped my fingers loudly in her ears.

She bolted upright, her eyes wide and startled.

"Hell's bells, Margaret!" She put her hand to her head. "What the heck is wrong with you?"

"Getting your daily beauty sleep?" I said, still laughing at her reaction.

Flora was already in the kitchen making a pot of tea. I followed her with Clarabelle close behind.

"So, what happened?" Clarabelle asked, sitting down at the table. "Tell me everything."

"Well," Flora said, bringing the kettle to the table and pouring the tea into our cups, "long story short, he said no."

Clarabelle grimaced, releasing a disappointed sound from her lips. "I'm sorry, Flora. I was really hoping he would agree. Now you see, Margaret? You tried and it didn't work out. You can leave it alone."

"Don't be too hard on her," Flora said, putting her hands on my shoulders. "Maggie did a wonderful job. She really did."

"Thanks, Flora. But I'm not done yet." I took a long sip of my tea.

"Oh, yes you are." Clarabelle put her teacup down before she could drink anything. "You got your answer, now it's best to leave it alone. Let us sleep peacefully again."

"No. I think I can convince him. He's just being stubborn."

"He ain't stubborn," Clarabelle said. "He made a decision."

"It's all right, Maggie. Really." Flora sat down next to me and enveloped her hands over mine. "We tried, and that's all there is to it."

"I'm still going," I said. "I'll surprise him tomorrow, catch him off guard. That's what my parents do."

"You're like a dog with a bone, you know that?" Clarabelle said to me. "If it weren't for your accent, I'd swear you were Flora's own daughter."

"Why, Clarabelle." I smiled. "That's the nicest thing you've ever said to me."

I have never walked with such determination than I did when marching back to Mr. Winston's office the next day. I smoothed out my dress before knocking. I opened the door and entered when he told me to come in.

Mr. Winston was standing beside his desk and offered me a smile.

"Why, Maggie!" He grinned. "Back again?"

"Yes." I walked up to him and crossed arms in an attempt to evade a kiss on the hand.

"Is there something I can do for you?" he asked.

"Actually, there is. I came back to ask you to reconsider about putting Flora's recipe on her labels."

Mr. Winston let out a scoff. "Oh, Maggie. I understand you care very much about Flora. I do too—"

"Then why won't you do this for her? If she's been so loyal to your company for the past forty years, and you care so much about her, then why won't you at least consider it?"

"Maggie, sweetie, it's not that easy. You just can't up and decide you're going to change a label that has been the same for the past four decades."

"It's barely even a change! It's one measly little recipe on the back! Surely, you can find some room for that."

"No one really cares about recipes," Mr. Winston countered. "They just want the product."

"That's not true, Mr. Winston," I argued. "Look in any advertisement or magazine. Most of the products in there come with some sort of recipe to go with it. People like to know what they can do with the products."

"Yes, but that's for things like cornmeal or oats."

"Is it because you're planning on selling Flora out?" I blurted.

Mr. Winston straightened. A flash of impromptu surprise passed through his eyes, however, he covered it up quickly with a light chuckle.

"Maggie." He loosened the base of his tie and tugged at the collar of his shirt. "I don't know what you're talking about."

"I heard your phone conversation."

Mr. Winston's face darkened. His mouth drooped downward, and he swallowed, his Adam's apple visibly quavering.

"I know you're planning on giving Flora's business to someone else," I continued.

He licked his lips, shifting his eyes toward the door. When he looked back at me, his expression was threatening.

"That was a private conversation," he said, a slight gravel inhabiting the back of his low voice.

"Well, I heard it. I heard everything. And Flora knows, too."

Mr. Winston's eyes widened, and his face went from sheet white to beet red in a matter of seconds. "You told Flora?"

"Of course! She has a right to know. I think it's real crummy that you would do this to someone who has worked for you for so long. Especially if you were close with her husband while he was alive."

"What did Flora say when you told her?"

I stared Mr. Winston down, my eyes searing directly into his. I wanted to garner every last bit of guilt from him.

"She was heartbroken. She wasn't surprised, but ultimately, she was devastated."

"Look, I love Flora. I really do."

"You keep saying that, but I don't think you mean it."

"Maggie, sweetie—"

"Don't call me sweetie!" I growled. "Flora has worked hard to keep her husband's business alive since his death! She's worked day in and day out on that pecan farm until she had blisters on her hands!"

"But she can't work anymore," Mr. Winston said. "She said her doctor told her not to harvest."

"That doesn't matter! She can still run the business. She has me and Clark and Clarabelle to help on the farm."

"Clarabelle's another one. Besides, she's not even part of the business. Neither are you or Clark. He's just a fill-in until I can find someone else with actual experience."

"But it's her business now," I said. "I may have not known her husband, but I don't think he would be happy with you selling to someone else."

"He understood how business worked. These things happen."

"But not to everyone. Why can't you keep Flora with the company and at least try advertising her recipes on your labels? It may be the thing to boost sales."

"What do you know about sales?" Mr. Winston challenged. "You don't know the first thing about running a food business."

"No." I shook my head. "But my father does. Have you ever heard of O'Hanlon's Grocery Company?"

"Yes," Mr. Winston said. "I hear they're looking to build a store down here in the South. Your father is Richard O'Hanlon?"

I nodded. "His partner, James, was my uncle. He passed away recently."

I paused, a rush of sadness overcoming me. I would never get used to saying those words out loud. I shook my head and forced myself into business mode again. I couldn't let my emotions get the better of me in front of Mr. Winston.

"The point is," I continued, "I may not know anything about business, but I know what sells. And I can tell you that if Alcott's Pecans were being sold in my dad's stores, they would fly off the shelves in a heartbeat."

"Is that so?" Mr. Winston said.

"Yes." I nodded, confidence running through my veins.

"I've been trying to get our products in your father's stores since finding out he's expanding to the South."

"I'll do it for you," I said. "I can ask him if he'll consider putting Alcott's Pecans on his shelves."

"You will?" Mr. Winston raised his eyebrows.

"Yes. And if he does, and if they sell just as well as they do here, would you consider taking Flora's idea of putting her recipe on your labels?"

"I'll have to see," Mr. Winston said, a hint of challenge in his eyes. "Just contact your father first and see what he says."

I nodded and shook Mr. Winston's hand, bidding him good day. As I walked out of his office, however, my confidence slowly unraveled. I was now tasked with calling my dad and asking him to do something I knew he would have no intention of doing. To be honest, he was the last person I wanted to speak to. But for the sake of proving Mr. Winston wrong, and to help Flora, I was going to do something I've never done in my life: ask my dad for help.

CHAPTER THIRTY-ONE

I wrapped my coat tight around me as I made my way to a public phone booth downtown. Yet again, I had succumbed to my flapping gums. I dug my hands into my pockets, shaking my head at my motor mouth. I was so riled up by Mr. Winston that I couldn't help but name drop my dad. I toyed with the idea of calling at the house, however, I couldn't risk Flora listening in.

I walked up to the phone booth and opened the door. My knees knocked together, and my palms were sweating so badly, I had to wipe them on my coat. I brought a shaky hand to the phone and picked it up, dropping a coin in the slot. The operator answered and asked how she could be of service.

My mouth was bone dry, and I had to clear my throat before speaking. I licked my lips to give them moisture.

"I'd like to call the O'Hanlon residence in Boston, Massachusetts, please," I said, my voice sounding like an echo.

"One moment, please," the woman on the other side said.

I waited, my knees shaking beneath me. What if he wasn't there? What if no one was there? I didn't consider that no one would be home. If anyone was, it would be Siobhan, who would be of no help in this matter. For all I knew, my dad could be off in who knows what state trying to look for a new place to open a store. The waiting felt like an eternity. I could swear three seasons had passed outside. I tapped my nails against the window, my stomach doing somersaults inside of me. Finally, I heard a click, and I immediately straightened up.

"Hello?" My ma's voice came through the other end.

I closed my eyes slowly. She was another one who I did not care to talk to. Hearing her sharp voice made the back of my neck prickle. She had no idea who it was on the other end, and yet her business woman voice was in full use. Not that she spoke any other way, even with her own family, but there was something particularly serious about her tone. I gripped the phone in my hand.

"Hello?" she said again, this time with more force. "Yes? Who is this?"

"Hi, Ma," I finally said.

"Maggie? What on Earth are you doing? Where are you?"

"Don't worry, Ma," I said. "I'm still in Georgia."

"What's that supposed to mean?" she snipped.

I sighed. "Nothing. Look, I need to talk to Dad. Can you put him on the phone?"

"How much is this phone call costing you?"

I rolled my eyes. Of course this would be the thing she'd be concerned about. It's a good thing I wasn't calling about a broken limb or anything.

"Don't worry about it," I said. "Is he there? I need to talk to him. It's…it's sort of urgent."

"Your father's not here," she stated, her interest floating over the word urgent.

"What?" I exclaimed, panic running through my veins. "Where is he?"

"He had to go down to the North End store for a while."

I ran my fingers through my hair. So much for perfect timing. What was I going to do now? I wondered if I should call back later. However, that would require more money.

"What's this about, Maggie?" Ma's voice sounded like talking to her daughter was the last thing on Earth she wanted to be doing.

I exhaled through my nose. "All right. I need you to tell him something for me. Can you do that?"

"Sure, dear," she said, her voice bored already. "If I think of it."

"Lovely," I said sarcastically. "I need you to tell Dad that I would like him to consider selling Flora's pecans in his stores—"

"Gracious, Maggie," Ma interjected. "You're still harping over those pecans?"

I blinked. "It's not harping, Ma. It's something I really want him to consider. I'm asking you nicely, if you could please tell him for me."

"Maggie." Ma sighed. "Your father is a very busy man. He is consumed by trying to open a new store in Tennessee, which—thank you for asking—is close to sealing the deal. It's why he's out. He is certain that Tennessee is going to accept, so he's already preparing for our celebration. He hardly has time to think about putting silly pecans in his stores."

The pulse in my neck thumped. I gripped onto the phone harder, sweat forming beneath my hands. The feeling of blood rushed through my skull and to my ears. I leaned my fist on the window and thumped my head against it.

"They're not silly pecans, Ma!" I protested. "This is a woman's business we're talking about. A hard-working woman! You of all people should understand this! This pecan business is everything to her! And she's in danger of losing it. She's been through so much lately. She's been sick, and now her doctor told her she shouldn't be doing manual labor anymore. She has a new idea to add her pecan bread recipe to the labels of her packaging to help boost sales. She needs this! If Dad's stores started selling her pecans with her new packaging, that could be a big deal for her! All I need you to do is talk to him. Let him know what's going on and see if he can set up an appointment to meet with Farmer's Food Company and begin selling her product in his stores."

"Maggie, I think it's very touching that you care so much about this woman and her little pecan business," Ma said, her voice still gratingly flat. "But you know your father won't give it a second thought. You left here after your little outburst, declaring you're going back to Georgia and you call back over a month later asking for his help?"

"I've never asked you for anything in my life, Ma. You know that."

Ma chortled. "Oh, dear. That's because you had everything handed to you before you could."

"Yes," I said. "To keep me out of your hair. Now, I'm coming to you to ask this one little thing. That's all I need. This is important. Please!"

"Darling," Ma said. "You know begging isn't going to get you any-where."

I sighed. "You won't do this?" My voice was laced with disbelief.

"No. I told you, your father has other things to worry about."

I scrunched my face up, heat rising from my neck to my cheeks. My nostrils flared in and out as I tried to keep my ragged breaths steady.

"You know what?" I gritted my teeth. "Forget it. Forget I said any-thing, forget I even called you!"

"Well, now you're being dramatic. Honestly, Maggie, is this how you really want our conversation to go?"

"And while you're at it," I continued, "forget I even exist."

"Excuse me? Don't you talk that way to me, young lady."

"Why not?" I said, my voice cold. "You've been doing it to me my whole life."

I slammed the phone down before she could even respond. The inside of the phone booth was warm. The windows began to fog up as I let out sharp, ragged breaths. My hands shook with such fierceness that I had to ball them into fists. My bottom lip threatened to tremble. I retaliated by biting down on it. I shook my head. No. I wasn't going to become emotional. I couldn't. I had to think of what to do next, how I was going to tell Flora.

I opened the door to the phone booth and stepped out, the early November air whipping at my face. I wrapped my coat tightly around my body, hugging myself, feeling much smaller than I was. Hopelessness gutted my insides. Even though I battled with both disbelief and not being surprised, I still felt like a failure. I failed Flora, and I was dreading breaking the news to her.

I stared off into the distance, the morning bringing people out of their homes and into town to go about their daily routines. I dipped my chin into my coat and walked off toward Flora's truck, my mind racing with how we were going to have to do this on our own.

Flora was right there to greet me at the door when I returned. Naturally, she had a hot cup of tea and a slice of pecan bread waiting for me in the kitchen. We sat down at the table, and I let out a long, exasperated sigh and rubbed my hand over my face.

"Oh, that doesn't sound too good," Flora said, her eyebrows knitted together. "Were you at Mr. Winston's this entire time?"

"No." I wrapped my hands around my cup of tea, the steam floating into my nose as I inhaled its calming scent. I took a small sip, burning the tip of my tongue.

"Well?" Flora looked back at me expectantly. "Where were you? What happened?"

I sighed. "Well, first, I went to Mr. Winston's."

"And?" Flora said, raising her eyebrows.

"He basically said the same thing he told us yesterday. Only more irritating."

Flora's eyes flitted downward. She fiddled her thumbs together. "So, that's it, then? He made his final word on the matter?"

"Not exactly. When he declined again, I got a little riled up."

"Oh, Maggie, I hope you didn't give him a hard time." Flora shook her head.

"Don't worry," I said. "I behaved…to the best of my ability. I explained to him how well your pecans would sell if you put your recipe on the label, and I mentioned how my dad owns O'Hanlon's Grocery Company, which Mr. Winston has been trying to get his products into."

"You mentioned your daddy?"

I nodded. "I was so aggravated that he wasn't listening to anything I was saying, so I told him that I could get your pecans in my dad's stores."

"Oh, Maggie, you shouldn't have promised that."

"I know. But I was desperate for him to listen to me. I made the ultimatum that if my dad began selling Alcott's Pecans in his stores, that Mr. Winston would have to consider keeping you with his company and put your recipe on your labels."

"And what did he say?" Flora asked.

I shrugged. "He challenged me to it. That's why I took so long." I paused. "I went into the center of town to call my dad."

Flora straightened up. "You called your daddy? I thought you two had a huge fight."

"We did. But I went to call him anyway. I figured if anything, I could grovel on my hands and knees to help."

"I know you don't have a good relationship with him. You didn't have to do that."

"I wanted to. For you."

"Oh, honey." Flora's eyes softened. She rubbed my cheek with her thumb.

"He wasn't there, though," I said. "So, I had no choice but to grovel to my ma."

"And what did she say?"

My brows creased together, and my lips drooped into a frown. "They're not going to help us, Flora. I'm so sorry."

Flora rubbed her thumb against my cheek again and gave me a sad smile. "That's all right. You tried. I really appreciate how much you've done to help me and how much you care about this business. I honestly don't know how I could ever repay you. It would take a lifetime of gratitude."

"No need." I shook my head. "Because we don't need my parents. We're going to do this ourselves."

"What? Maggie, if your parents were our last hope, then that's it. Mr. Winston won't go for anything else. We tried our best. We have to accept the fact that this is how it's going to be. I can still make my pecan bread whenever I want. It's not like Mr. Winston owns that. We will be fine. *I* will be fine."

"No. I'm sorry, Flora, but I am not satisfied with this. I am going to go to Mr. Winston's office again and convince him until one of us is blue in the face."

"I don't think that's a good idea," Flora said warily.

"Flora." I held her hands in mine and looked at her directly in her eyes. "I love you. I don't want to see you lose something that you care so much about. I'm going back to Mr. Winston's office tomorrow with or without your blessing, and that's final."

CHAPTER THIRTY-TWO

Flora had breakfast on the table when I woke up bright and early the next morning.

I came downstairs, fresh faced and ready to take on Mr. Winston. I wore my favorite navy-blue dress and made my hair look especially presentable. I wasn't against making myself look attractive for Mr. Winston, even though I got the willies every time I looked at him. I was doing this for Flora. I would go in, put on my best and most elegant business voice, and not lose my head if he refused again. I found myself shockingly calm and confident, although I'd be lying if I said there wasn't a touch of anxiety inside of me.

"At least let me come with you," Flora said, sitting herself across from me at the breakfast table.

I shook my head, placing my teacup on its saucer. "No. I want to do this by myself. I will make sure I do my best to return with good news."

"You promise that if he says no, you'll lay this matter to rest?" Flora asked, a glint of hope passing through her exhausted eyes.

"Don't worry, if Mr. Winston's final word is no…" I let out an exasperated sigh at the thought of it. "I will lay off for good."

When I arrived back at Mr. Winston's office, I smoothed out my dress and knocked on his door.

"Come in!" he called out.

I entered, giving him a reluctant polite smile. "Good morning, Mr. Winston."

"Well, Maggie!" He smiled, taking my hand in his and giving it a kiss. "Don't you look lovely, as always."

"Thank you." I offered a teeth baring grin and sat down in a seat across from his desk.

"Now," Mr. Winston said, sitting behind his desk. "Did you get the chance to speak to your father?"

"Actually, I didn't," I said.

"Oh?" Mr. Winston interlaced his fingers, placing them on his desk.

"He was out for the day, you see. I spoke to my ma—my mother, though."

"Your mother?" Mr. Winston let out a chuckle. "No offense Maggie, I'm not sure your mother would be much help."

"On the contrary, Mr. Winston, my mother works very closely with my father. She mostly takes care of the secretarial and financial part of it. However, she still accompanies him to meetings and everything. If you were so set on affiliating with him, you would've known that."

Mr. Winston stiffened, and I couldn't help but crack a grin. To be honest, I was quite proud of how I was handling myself. I never sounded so elegant in my life; it was almost as if it wasn't my voice, but it was! Those drama classes I took while I was in school were certainly paying off. I sat up straighter in my seat and raised my chin.

Mr. Winston cleared his throat. "Yes, of course," he said quickly. "Of course I knew that. I was just expecting to hear from your father, that's all."

Sure, I thought.

"What did your mother say?" Mr. Winston asked.

My premature confidence shattered. My shoulders dropped, and I couldn't help but furrow my eyebrows.

"Well, I asked her if she could relay the message about putting Flora's pecans in his stores and meet with you, but she wasn't able to, saying he was very busy at the moment."

I didn't want to go into detail on how dysfunctional my relationship was with my parents. I didn't want him to know that this was the first time I had tried to contact them in a long while. I didn't want him to know how our fight ripped us further apart than we already were. I wanted to create a ruse that we were the perfect family—the hardworking patriarch, his devoted wife, and their wonderful daughter.

Mr. Winston sat back in his chair and placed his folded hands on his rounded belly. His expression spoke volumes that he didn't need to say what I knew he was thinking. *I knew it.*

"Mr. Winston, I know what you are thinking," I said.

"You do?" He cocked his eyebrows, an amused look crossing his face.

"Yes. I wasn't able to come through and reach my father for you, but it's fine. We don't need him, anyway."

Mr. Winston straightened up. "I'm sorry? That was the entire point of this. To convince your father to put Flora's pecans—and other products of ours—in his stores. You said you would be able to."

"I know, but just listen for a minute."

"Maggie, I'm sorry." Mr. Winston shook his head. "Now, unless you can reach your father again and ask him personally—"

"I am not going to call him again," I said, my voice coming out with more force than I intended.

"Why?" Mr. Winston tilted his head.

I almost let myself lose my cool, and Mr. Winston seemed to pick up on it. I sighed and shook my head, trying to regain my composure.

"I told you," I said. "He is very busy. He is focusing on opening up a new store. The point is, he cannot help us at the moment."

"Well, if that's the case, then I don't think there's much left to discuss," Mr. Winston said.

"But we don't need him!" I shot up from my seat. "If my father was the last hope to keep Flora's business around, and you can't fight for it yourself, then she doesn't mean much to you in the first place."

"Of course, she does!" Mr. Winston said. "Now, I'm not saying that Alcott's can never be in your father's stores. I could still have them and my other products selling there after someone else takes over for Flora."

My eyes widened. "You wouldn't!"

"I would," Mr. Winston stated. "Remember, I have the right to do what I want with my company, that includes Flora's business. And if I want to go to your father myself, I will. Maybe if someone else is running Alcott's, he'll be more obliged."

"I never said he wasn't obliged," I protested. "I only said I couldn't reach him directly and that my mother wouldn't speak to him for me."

"That is true, but coming from a fellow business man's perspective, he may be more inclined to cooperate if Alcott's was being run by a different person."

"You mean a man?" I challenged.

His eyes rounded, and he shook his head. "That's not what I meant. Now, I'm sorry. Believe me, I wish you were able to speak to your father as well. I love Flora, but I think it's time to go in another direction."

"Mr. Winston, you're not even giving me a chance to tell you what I have to say!" I pleaded.

"All right." He folded his arms across his chest. "What do you have to say?"

"I really think you should help Flora promote her pecan bread recipe. I understand that her pecans haven't been selling as well as they used to, given the increasing popularity of Golden Hills, but I feel like putting a little something extra on the labels will help boost your sales."

"Look, I wish your little idea would work, but I just don't see it being enough to do so."

I paced around in a circle, my mind racing with numerous thoughts. I ran my fingers through my hair, not caring that I was messing it up at this point. My brain suddenly remembered something. I turned to Mr. Winston, my eyes wide and an idea on my mind.

"The Harvest Festival," I said.

"The what?"

I stepped closer to his desk. "The Harvest Festival. You know about it, don't you? It's next week. Flora always makes her pecan bread for it. Why don't you come and see how much everyone goes crazy for it?"

"I've never really cared to go. I'm always too busy."

"Make room in your calendar, then. That way, you can see how well Flora's pecan bread does. And I'll do you one better—let her sell her pecans there as well."

"What?" Mr. Winston shot out of his chair. "Now that's ridiculous!"

"Why? Her pecan bread is already famous around here. Why not sell the pecans as well? That way, it'll spark the idea in people's heads that they can make Flora's recipe too."

"Yes, but it would never work. Alcott's Pecans are to be sold in stores only. I'm not going to have my pecans—"

"Flora's pecans," I corrected, a steely glint in my eyes.

Mr. Winston paused, caught red handed at his little hiccup. His eyebrows creased, however, and he gave a careless shrug.

"Same thing," he said.

I drew my mouth downward and shook my head. "No, I don't think it is."

"The point is, this Harvest Festival is just a little get together that the mayor holds every year. It's nothing more than a social gathering."

"But wouldn't you, a business man, want to see your product flaunted about? Wouldn't you want it selling?"

"Yes, but not at a festival that's only purpose is for mingling about. This is merely a once-a-year event."

My nerves took on an edge. I shook my head, dumbfounded over his decision to blow his chance at having his company represented at the festival.

"You can by all means mention my company," he offered, "but I will not let you sell the product itself."

"Well, why don't you come regardless? See how well Flora's pecan bread sells. If not for your product representation, then for recipe, something that means the world to her."

"I realize that everyone loves Flora's pecan bread, but I don't need to be there to see it."

"I think you do. I think if you come to the Harvest Festival and see how well Flora's pecan bread does, and how she is as a business woman, then I truly believe you would change your mind on handing her business to somebody else and allow her to put her recipe on the labels."

"You believe that?" Mr. Winston gave me a challenging glare.

I held my own, giving him a confident nod. "I do."

Mr. Winston screwed his mouth up and placed his hands on his hips. "When is the festival?"

"November sixteenth." I smiled. "It begins at noon. So? Will I see you there?"

Mr. Winston took another moment to answer. He pinched his bottom lip, then gave a shake of his head.

"I suppose."

I offered another smile and stuck my hand out. He took it in his and gave it a firm shake.

CHAPTER THIRTY-THREE

I waltzed into Flora's house, beaming like I had just returned from Cloud 9. I couldn't help feeling immense pride that I was close to finally convincing Mr. Winston. Despite his reluctance and lack of enthusiasm, I was still grinning ear to ear.

Flora and Clarabelle were out on the back porch chattering away. I decided to have a little fun with them, smirking to myself before clearing my throat and putting on my best poker face. I walked out the back door to find them sitting on the porch swing sipping tea. I stopped in front of them, keeping my lips in a thin, straight line and my shoulders slightly drooped.

"What is with your face?" Clarabelle was the first to acknowledge me. "You look like you ate a rotted apple."

"How did it go, Maggie?" Flora asked, a trace of anxiety in her hopeful tone.

Without answering right away, I moseyed over to the tufted wicker chair across from them and plopped down, crossing my legs and lowering my head as if I were dejected.

"Oh, for heaven's sake, Margaret!" Clarabelle trilled. "Stop playing games and tell us what in the heck is going on! Were you able to convince Mr. Winston or not?"

"Well…" I said.

"Oh, that doesn't sound good," Clarabelle said immediately.

"How do you know it's not good news?" I asked.

"Margaret, I've been around a very long time. I've learned not to hope for the best right away. Just cut to the chase and tell us."

Flora looked at me, her expression resembling a small child's who was desperately hoping to get the baby doll in the window. Her green eyes were wide, and the tip of her nose just as rosy as her cheeks. She seemed as if she were going to jump out of her seat if I didn't tell them soon.

I couldn't hold it in anymore, and my serious face broke into a smile.

Her shoulders relaxed, and her eyes widened even more. She nodded her head, and I reciprocated.

Flora gasped. "Oh, Maggie!" She leapt off the porch swing and wrapped her arms around me. "Did you really convince him?"

"Sort of," I said.

"What do you mean, sort of?" Clarabelle said.

Flora let go and held me by the arms. "I don't understand. Didn't he say yes?"

I sat in my seat, and Flora sat back down on the swing.

"He didn't say no, but also didn't say yes just yet."

"What the heck is that supposed to mean?" Clarabelle said.

"I had to make somewhat of a deal with him."

"What kind of a deal?" Flora asked, her tone wary.

"It's not bad," I assured them. "I told Mr. Winston about the Harvest Festival coming up next week and how you make your pecan bread every year. I invited him to come, hoping he would see how much everyone loves your bread there, and that it would finally convince him to let you put your recipe on the labels."

"That's all?" Flora said. "Why, that doesn't sound so bad. I would love it if he showed up! He never comes, always claiming to be too busy."

"He wasn't too pleased about it. He did say if something else arises, he won't be able to attend the festival."

"I suppose that's fair." Flora shrugged. "I certainly wouldn't want to get in the way if something more important came up."

"Don't worry about that." I stood up and sat in between her and Clarabelle. "The point is, he's set on coming. Once he sees how well your pecan bread does, he'll join our side for sure. We're going to make this happen, Flora."

Flora leaned forward and hugged me tightly, rubbing my back.

"You really did more than I could ever ask for," she said. "Thank you for not giving up on me."

"Don't mention it." I pulled myself away, a determined glare bouncing back and forth between Flora and Clarabelle. "Now, let's get a head start on things. Are you ready to make the best damn pecan bread you've ever made in your life?"

Flora was brimming with such euphoria that she decided to whip up a fresh loaf of pecan bread on the spot. She bustled around the kitchen, her grin up to her ears as she mixed and baked.

While ecstatic, Flora was a bit clumsy with her movements, hastily setting down her flour canisters and shakily cracking eggs in the bowl which garnered a piece or two of eggshell falling in.

"Flora, what are you so darn worried about?" Clarabelle said, sitting with me at the kitchen table. "You could make that pecan bread with your eyes closed and your hands tied behind your back. Everybody loves it. It's not like this is a competition or anything."

"I know," Flora said. "I want to make sure it's perfect for the Harvest Festival."

"It's not for another week," I said. "You don't want to start making a bunch now. They'll be stale by then."

"I know," she said again. "I can't help myself. I have to make a practice loaf."

Clarabelle snorted. "Flora, hon, you don't need practice. What you need is to take it easy."

"I'm fine." Flora waved off Clarabelle's warning.

Clarabelle got up from her chair with a grunt. "Well, I'd love to stay, but I need to get back home."

"Oh, no!" Flora exclaimed. "The bread should be ready in an hour. Stay, have some."

"I'd love to, but I have to go. I'll have Margaret bring me a piece when it's done. In fact..." Clarabelle turned to me, "Margaret, would you walk me home? Flora picked me up earlier today. I don't have my truck."

"Sure." I stood up and turned to Flora. "Will you be all right?"

"Yes, I'll be fine. Go on," Flora said, still paddling about the kitchen.

"All right," I said. "I shouldn't be longer than five minutes. Don't lose your head!"

Flora didn't seem to pick up on my teasing tone, as she was busy throwing pecans in a large bowl.

I followed Clarabelle out the front door, strolling down the pathway that led away from Flora's house.

We walked in silence, the Georgian November air whispering its melody in our ears. The vibrant red and oranges that had hung above on the trees were beginning to brown, signifying that a new season was on the horizon.

"That woman would still make pecan bread on her deathbed." Clarabelle's voice broke through the air. "She loves it more than anything, I'll tell you that."

"Well, she does it better than anyone, that's for sure," I said.

"You're the reason she's so determined about this, you know. I've never seen so much grit in her eyes since..." Clarabelle's voice trailed off.

"Since when?" I prompted.

"Since her husband and son were alive," Clarabelle said after a few moments of silence. She stopped walking and turned to me. "Let's face it, Margaret, Flora's always been a happy, sweet lady. It was almost as if the sun shined just for her. She was that joyful. While she's always been like that, a piece of it died when her son and husband did. She just didn't let it show. That's how she's always been. She wanted to be happy because she wanted others around her to be happy. She did it for everyone else, not herself."

"You're on the money with that one. When I first arrived, she was so overjoyed with every little thing. There was this pure innocence and happiness about her that I had never experienced before. At first, I was terribly irked by it. I saw it as another reason to be miserable."

"You chose to be miserable, Margaret."

I nodded. "Yes, I see that now, and I'm embarrassed by the way I behaved."

"Did you ever tell Flora that?"

"No." I shook my head, a flicker of shame warming my cheeks. "In a way, I thought she didn't notice. I thought she was so happy-go-lucky that she didn't catch on to my terrible attitude."

"She noticed." Clarabelle nodded.

I raised my eyebrows. "How do you know?"

"She confided in me the day you twisted your ankle. She was worried that she wasn't being welcoming enough to you."

"That's ridiculous! She was all that and more! I just didn't appreciate it."

"You still have a lot of learning to do, Margaret. You've certainly grown a lot since you first got here. I know that you were here for a specific reason—I don't need to know what it is—but you weren't just here because your parents sent you. You were here because you needed to be here. You needed Flora. And she needed you. Call it whatever you want, but Margaret, you coming here was the best thing that ever happened to you."

I nodded, my chin threatening to hitch. Just when I thought I couldn't appreciate Flora even more, Clarabelle of all people cemented how much she had come to mean to me.

"I know," I whispered.

Clarabelle averted her eyes away from me, her glance fleeting before returning her gaze. "I appreciate everything you've done for Flora. I may be her greatest friend in the world, but you? You're her kindred spirit. A reluctant one, maybe, but you two were meant for your lives to collide. Whether you want to believe it or not."

"I believe it." I nodded.

Clarabelle gave me the tiniest of smiles, the small corner of her mouth turning upward as her blue eyes crinkled at the sides.

"Come on, Margaret. Let's go so you can get back home to Flora."

CHAPTER THIRTY-FOUR

I let my mind wander as I strolled back toward Flora's house, once again admiring the beauty that autumn brings. However, I couldn't help but linger on Clarabelle's words to me.

"Let's go so you can get back home to Flora."

Home. This was the first time anyone had regarded Savannah as home to me—and Clarabelle of all people!

Thinking back, I had always referred to Flora's as just her house. Now, I see that while Savannah isn't the place I was born and raised for twenty-three years, it was just as much home to me as Boston, especially considering that my Uncle James was no longer with me. I was able to see it that way instead of just a place I was sent to for my silly and rotten behavior. And even though I still missed Boston with every piece of my soul, I smiled to myself, content with knowing that I had another place to call home.

When I returned, Flora was still in the kitchen, putting her loaf of pecan bread into the oven. She closed it and looked up at me, her smile beaming across her face.

"Hi, honey." The pure enthusiasm in her voice made me smile as well.

I loved the fact that she still greeted me, even though it had been only five minutes since we last saw each other.

"Did Clarabelle get home all right?" she asked.

"Yes," I said. "Although, I am afraid she'll find her way back here, despite my efforts at taking away the trail of breadcrumbs."

Flora laughed. "Oh, honey, you're too much!"

I walked over to the table and sat down. "More importantly, how does your pecan bread look?"

"Wonderful!" She clasped her hands together. "I think this may be the best one I ever made."

"Well, that certainly calls for a celebration!" I smiled.

Flora sat across from me and fiddled with the rumpled tissue she took out of her apron pocket. She pressed it against her nose and sniffled. My expression fell, concern now inhabiting my eyes.

"Everything all right?" I asked.

Flora looked up. "Oh, yes." She gave a small wave of her hand. "A little nervous, I guess. I just hope everything goes well."

I shook my head. "You shouldn't be nervous. I mean, I know that this business and your pecan bread means everything to you, but you have to have faith in yourself. Everyone else does. Why don't you?"

"Oh, Maggie," Flora said. "I know very well that my bread and pecan business has done wonderfully for the past forty years, but I can't let it show too much. It would be indecent."

"Indecent? Flora, you kept this business going after your husband died! You've been a big part of it for over four decades, and you make one hell of a pecan bread! You should be shouting your pride from the rooftops!"

"Oh, I couldn't do that." Flora shook her head.

"Well, if you don't, I will."

Flora blushed, a scoff escaping her lips. "I'm perfectly content with how everything is."

"Flora." I reached across the table and took her hands into mine. "What you've accomplished is nothing to sneeze at. You should be incredibly proud of everything you've done. You should wear it like a badge of honor. You need to have confidence in yourself."

"I am proud! I just wasn't brought up to relish in myself. I was raised to grow up to be a modest and giving woman."

"And you are! But it's okay to take pride in yourself every now and then. It's okay to look at yourself in the mirror and say, 'I'm pretty damn fantastic'!"

The pink in Flora's cheeks deepened, and she let out a chuckle.

"The point is," I continued, "you are fantastic, Flora. And you should know that. I know you've already done so much for me, but can I ask one more thing of you?"

"What?" Flora said.

I gave her hands a gentle squeeze.

"Please be kind to yourself," I said.

The smile that spread across Flora's face was delightful. The twinkle in her eyes came back, and she dipped her chin to conceal the additional flushing that had swept across her cheeks. She looked back up at me and nodded.

"I'll try," she said. "Thank you, Maggie."

She patted my hand and stood up, walking over to the oven and peeking in.

"It still has quite some time to go." She closed the door back up. "What do you say we sit out on the back porch, and have a cup of tea?"

"Sounds lovely." I stood up and walked over to her, taking the kettle out of her hands. "You go get comfortable. I'll take care of the tea."

"All right," Flora said before giving me a relaxed smile and disappearing behind the screen door.

It wasn't easy, but somehow, I convinced Flora to relax the next day. Although she insisted on doing her household chores, I told her that I would take care of them. I did agree, however, to let her continue with the cooking duties, as I had never done so much as boil a pot of water in my life.

She seemed pleased with this agreement, and I even gave her one of my magazines to read. She flipped the pages, her eyes becoming as big as saucers when she came across a photo of Clark Gable.

"He is handsome!" Flora gushed. "I miss going to see a picture. He was quite dashing in *It Happened One Night*."

"If you think he's something, just wait!" I said, taking my attention away from feather dusting the lamp for a moment. "Turn to Guy Madison on page forty-two."

Flora licked her thumb and turned the pages, her eyes nearly falling out of her head. "Oh my!"

A knock came at the door.

I stopped dusting and walked into the foyer to answer it.

Clark stood on the porch with his cabbie outfit on. He smiled instantly.

"Hi, Maggie." He took his cap off. "You sure look nice today."

"Oh." I looked down at my outfit—a long sleeve, plaid blouse and dark brown, wide legged trousers. It was nothing special, but I could help being flattered by his compliment. "Thank you, Clark. Would you like to come in?"

"No, thanks. I have a few more runs to do." He gestured to his cab. "I was driving by and wanted to check in."

"Is that Clark?" Flora called out from the den. She walked in and gave him a kiss on the cheek. "Hi, honey. How are you doing?"

"I'm fine, Flora," he said. "How are you?"

"Oh, I'm wonderful!" She smiled. "Come on in. Are you hungry?"

"I'm sorry, I can't." Clark shook his head. "I'm just checking in."

"Well, isn't that thoughtful?" Flora said. "Are you sure I can't fix you something to go?"

"No, thank you." Clark smiled at Flora. "I appreciate it, though."

"It was nice seeing you, then," Flora said.

"You, too," Clark said. "Take it easy, Flora."

"I am!" Flora beamed. She leaned in close to Clark and added in a delighted whisper, "Maggie's making me relax! She even gave me one of her magazines to read!"

Clark turned to me and smiled. "Well, isn't that nice!"

"I just wanted Flora to take a day for herself, that's all," I said, trying to hide the blushing that had appeared on my cheeks. "She deserves it."

"That she does." Clark nodded. "Listen, Maggie, can I talk to you for a minute?"

"Sure." I followed Clark out onto the porch. "What's the word?"

"I heard that you were able to get Mr. Winston to come to the Harvest Festival," he said.

"Gee, swell news sure travels fast. How did you find out?"

"Clarabelle told me."

"Clarabelle? It literally happened yesterday. How did she tell you?"

"I saw her down at the post office," Clark said. "I think it's great that you were able to talk him into it!"

"Yeah, well, it wasn't easy. Let's hope he keeps his word."

"I'm sure he will," Clark said. "He may be a difficult man sometimes, but when he agrees to something, he sticks to it."

Clark put his cap back on and headed down the steps, toward his cab. He opened the door but stopped before getting in.

"You've done a great job, Maggie!" he called out to me.

My cheeks warmed up again. "Thanks, but I couldn't have done it without your help—and Clarabelle's."

"Anytime," he said. "I hope you'll be at the Harvest Festival as well."

"With bells on!"

"Great!" Clark smiled. "I'll see you around."

He tipped his hat, giving me a small wink before getting into his cab and slamming the door shut. As he backed out, he waved to me.

I waved back, finding myself unable to stop smiling until he was out of sight.

Flora, Clarabelle, and I packed together in Flora's truck the next day and went over to the pecan farm one last time before the Harvest Festival. Clark stopped by again to bring more pecans over to Farmer's. Even though Flora had enough stored to get her through the next few months of distributing, she still wanted to make one last visit before harvesting season ended. After the Harvest Festival was over and done with, Flora said that she would begin preparing for next year's harvest season, saying it never hurts to get an early start.

"Give yourself some time," I said. "It's not even Thanksgiving yet."

"I know, but I like to at least prepare," Flora said. "The weather doesn't get too cold around here, and even if it does, I still have to make sure the trees don't dry out."

"It's not like you get snow down here," I said. "You haven't even seen what a real winter is."

"Not true, Margaret," Clarabelle said. "We've gotten snow. It only happens every once in a blue moon. It's usually just a dusting if anything, but I remember when I was six years old, and it snowed here. Quite a bit, too."

Clarabelle leaned forward and craned her neck, looking at Flora who kept her eyes on the road ahead.

"Remember that, Flora? That snow storm Savannah had when we were youngin's?"

Flora nodded. "I remember. It was beautiful. Although, no one knew what to do with themselves."

"When you were six?" I said. "What year was that?"

"Never you mind," Clarabelle sniped at me. "The point is, we've gotten snow. Just not as much as you're used to."

"I can bet you it's probably snowed in Boston by now," I said.

The grin from my face dropped, and the image of my lovely hometown coated in beautiful white blankets of late autumn snow flashed in my mind. For some reason, snow seemed to come early for Boston sometimes. Even though my dad had always griped about it, I couldn't help but love it.

The feeling of homesickness swelled in my chest again. I thought of how when I was little, Uncle James would take me out for the first snowfall, and we would run up and down Beacon Hill, tossing dustings of snow at each other and laughing until we practically lost our voices. This memory made my cheeks flush, and I smiled again.

When we arrived at the pecan farm, I was astounded to see how many pecans had fallen off the trees since Flora's and my last visit. The ground was coated in a mixture of pecans and leaves. Most of the branches were completely bare. To be honest, it was a little bittersweet to see the harvesting season come to an end. I thought back to how green and lush the leaves looked in the beginning. How the pecans hadn't even emerged from their shells yet. Now it was almost over, and I couldn't help but feel a little sad about it.

Gazing out at the endless trees, my heart swelled with regret over my lack of appreciation and attitude towards this place when I first arrived. I only wished I could travel back in time and knock some sense into my silly former self.

We gathered our supplies and headed over to the trees.

Flora, as usual, walked quicker than any of us, unable to wait one minute longer to get to her beloved pecans.

She bent over, inspecting the pecans and throwing them in her bucket. She reached out and lost her footing, falling over and grabbing onto the tree trunk for support.

"Oh, good Lord," Clarabelle said. "Margaret, go help her out before she breaks her neck."

I hurried over and helped Flora stand straight up again.

"I'm fine," she said. "Just lost my balance."

"Be careful," I said. "We don't want you getting hurt."

"Thank you, Maggie. Why don't you and Clarabelle gather the pecans from the other side, and I'll work on this?"

"All right," I said. "But let us know if you need any more help."

"I will." She bent over, getting back to work. It was as if nothing happened.

CHAPTER THIRTY-FIVE

After Flora and I dropped Clarabelle off at her house, Flora told me to stay in the truck while she brought the pecans into her basement. I was curious as to why she didn't want me to go in with her.

When she came back, she hopped back into the truck and drove off again.

"Where are we going?" I asked.

"Just one more stop somewhere," Flora said.

I admired the scenery out the window as Flora kept our destination a secret. The sun shined brightly through the beautiful golden hues of the trees. I cranked down the window, leaning my elbow on it and enjoying the warm, crisp air on my face.

Flora turned into Forsyth. She turned to me and smiled. "I thought it would be nice to bring you here again."

"Why did we drop Clarabelle off at home? She could've come with us." I stopped short at the words I had just uttered. "Wow! I never thought I'd say that!"

Flora chuckled. "To be honest, Clarabelle has never come here with me."

"You mean I'm the only one you've brought?"

Flora nodded. "Yes."

The fact that I was the only person Flora decided to share this place with besides her husband and son made me feel quite special. A warmth spread through me, and I smiled lightly. I felt as though she trusted me with sharing her precious memories.

As we strode down one of the pathways, I noticed Flora humming that song she always did whenever she was lost in thought.

"What song is that?" I asked.

"Hm?" Flora said.

"That song you're humming. I've heard you hum it before."

A quaint smile curled at Flora's lips. "It's called *Georgia Lullaby*. I used to sing it to my son when he was little."

"Could you sing a little bit of it for me?"

Without hesitation, Flora began to sing. She kept her voice clear and soft, and at times, it almost seemed as if she were singing to herself. I saw what kind of a mother she must've been when her son was alive. I pictured her tucking him into bed and singing him to sleep, stroking his little cheek as he fought to keep his eyes open just so he could hear his mother's special lullaby to him.

"I like it. It's pretty."

"It always made little Alfred Jr. so sleepy," she said. "But he loved it. I even sang it to him the last night he was home before he went off to the Navy. I was afraid I would never get to sing it to him again."

Flora's eyes shifted downward. I could tell that she was reliving the last night her son was home. I wanted to lift her spirits again.

"At least you have wonderful memories of singing to him when he was little. I'm sure those were some of his favorite moments as well."

Flora smiled again and linked her arm into mine. "You always know how to make me feel better, Maggie."

I grinned. "Let's keep walking," I said, leading the way back down the path.

"What about you?" Flora asked. "Did you have any special lullabies that were sung to you?"

I shook my head. "Never. You know about what kind of people my parents are like, and my uncle was never the singing kind of guy."

"You must really miss him."

"I do." I nodded.

The lump that would now and forever rise in my throat whenever I thought of him ached something terrible in that moment.

"I'm sure he would've been very proud of everything you've done here," Flora said gently.

A feeling of melancholy rushed through me. I only wished that Uncle James had been here to see how much I've grown in the past few months. Flora was right. He would've been proud. Of course, he would've teasingly taken credit for it.

"You know, you could talk to him if you want," Flora said. "Just because he's gone doesn't mean you still can't connect with him."

I shook my head quickly. "Oh, that's all right. I'm really not that spiritual. No offense."

"Don't worry about it, honey. Just a suggestion. But if you ever did want to talk to him, you know where he is."

That night, I took a long hot bath, letting myself soak for over an hour. I relaxed in the tub and closed my eyes, my mind wandering over the past few months and how everything had changed so much. I thought about how, if it wasn't for my silly behavior, I would never have been here in the first place. I never would've met Flora, or Clarabelle, or Clark.

Flora and Clarabelle who—in the beginning—I considered the banes of my existence had become two of the most wonderful friends I could ever ask for.

And Clark, while he was someone I never would've given a second thought or look toward, I now found myself lighting up and feeling warm inside whenever I saw him. I would catch myself thinking about him when he wasn't even here.

After I was finished with my bath, I got into my nightgown and took my hair out of my head wrap, letting my locks flow past my shoulders. I got into bed, lying there for a moment and letting all my thoughts swirl in my head.

I thought back to Flora's words about Uncle James and how he would've been proud of me. I know he would have. I could just see him now, sitting there at the kitchen table, his face bright with pride and his head nodding in approval.

"You did good, kid," he would've said to me.

I fiddled with my thumbs, fully awake and unable to sleep as my thoughts lingered on him. I thought of how he would've enjoyed seeing all the work I did to help Flora, and how I discovered I had a professional side to me that I didn't know was there. The image of him flashing into my mind made me both smile and my heart ache with longing.

"I do wish you were here," I said out loud. "I wish you could've seen everything I've done. I know you would be proud of me. I'm proud of myself. But this time, it's different. It's the feeling of knowing I've done something good for someone other than myself. You were the only one who could bring me back to reality when I was being difficult. Now, all I want to do is make Flora happy. You would've loved her. She's the best person I've ever known—other than you, of course. She would've loved you, too. I can just see her fattening you up with loads of pecan bread, and you eating every last morsel until you're stuffed to the brim because you would know what that would mean to her. I think about you every day—I guess you know that already. I will continue to make you proud, just as you made me proud when you were here. I'm sorry I never told you that. I hope you know that, though. You always made me proud. I miss you, Uncle James. I always will. I love you. Goodnight."

CHAPTER THIRTY-SIX

When I came downstairs the next morning, I was surprised to discover Clark sitting at the kitchen table with Flora.

I gasped, immediately tightening my satin robe over my nightgown. Of course, the one morning I decided to not get dressed right away. I bunched the neckline together and ran my other hand through my tousled hair. I also realized that my face was bare naked, putting my countless freckles on full display. However, Clark didn't seem to notice or care about my appearance.

"Morning, Maggie!" he said, his voice bright.

This was the one thing I was still not used to: everyone being overly chipper at basically the crack of dawn.

"Hello, Clark," I said, still keeping a death grip on my robe. "What are you doing here…so early in the morning?"

I sat down as Flora got up and handed me a freshly-made biscuit with peach jam and a cup of tea. I sipped it slowly, my chest as close to the table as possible.

"I have to run down to see Mr. Winston before work," Clark said. "I just wanted to see if Flora needed me to tell him anything while I'm there."

"I would like to come." I shifted my eyes toward Flora. "That is, if that's all right."

"Go ahead." Flora waved her hand at me. "Make sure Mr. Winston is still coming to the Harvest Festival."

"I will." I stood up, not bothering to take a bite of my biscuit. "Clark, I'll be right down."

I rushed through getting dressed, choosing my navy peplum dress and my pair of black pumps. I quickly put some rouge on my cheeks and threw on some lipstick before running down the stairs to meet Clark out in the foyer.

We used his cab as a mode of transportation. I sat in the front seat, enjoying his company during our ride.

"So, what part of Boston are you from again, Maggie?" Clark asked.

"Beacon Hill. It's right in the North End. It's a lovely area."

He nodded. "It must be. And your mama and pa live there, too?"

I hesitated, glancing down at my lap. "They do. I lived with them, but they aren't exactly model parents. They're a bit more preoccupied with my dad's grocery business."

"Oh, gee. I'm sorry to hear that."

I shrugged. "Don't be. My Uncle James was the closest thing I had to a parent. Now that he's gone—"

I stopped, a tightening in my chest taking hold of me. This was the first time I had ever opened up to a boy before. I didn't quite know what to think of it. My head swirled, and the tips of my fingers tingled. I cleared my throat, wanting to get off the subject of myself.

"That's enough about me, though. What about you? Do your parents live close by?"

"I was raised by my aunt and uncle." Clark kept his eyes focused on the road. "I was left on their front porch when I was two years old."

"Two years old?" A piece of my heart ached as I pictured Clark as a tiny toddler being abandoned.

"My mama wasn't fit to be a parent, apparently," Clark explained. "Never knew my pa, so my mama decided to leave me with her sister and husband. My aunt and uncle were good to me, though. They made sure I went to school and worked hard. They never had children of their own."

"Where are they now?" I asked.

Clark frowned. "My uncle died in the war in 1941, and my aunt died last year."

"Oh, Clark." My eyebrows etched together, and my chest tightened.

I couldn't help feeling a spark of empathy towards him. All this time, I never knew how much we had in common. There was a connection knowing that he understood what it was like to be unvalued by his parents and the great deal of pain of losing someone so close.

"I'm so sorry," I said. "I wish I had taken the time to get to know you better in the beginning."

"It's all right," Clark said quickly. "I don't like to talk about myself that much, anyway."

When we arrived at Mr. Winston's, Clark held his cab door open for me, and I held the building door open for him. I could tell he was a little taken aback by it but was appreciative nonetheless.

Mr. Winston greeted us by giving Clark a firm handshake and me my unsolicited kiss on the hand. He was in good spirits going over the recent sales with Clark and telling him that they had gone up four percent within the past week.

"Yes, we're neck and neck with Golden Hills in terms of sales right now," Mr. Winston said. "And if we can boost them up more in time for Thanksgiving, I'd say we may be able to make good for the remainder of the year."

"And after the Harvest Festival as well," I said. "You didn't forget about that, did you?"

"No, I didn't," Mr. Winston said. "I'll be there. However, you must understand that if something else comes up, I won't be able to attend the festival."

A wave of anxiety rushed through me. I kept my best poker face on, however, and gave him a compliant nod.

"Yes, Mr. Winston." I clasped my hands together tightly in my lap, silently hoping that nothing would come in the way of Mr. Winston's attendance.

"Well then." Mr. Winston rose from his chair. "I'm sorry this meeting was so quick, but Clark, I know you have to get to your job, and I have quite a lot of things to get done as well."

"Thank you, Mr. Winston." Clark stood up, holding his cap in his hands. "I'll see you after Thanksgiving."

"That you will." Mr. Winston shook his hand. "I hope to see you at the Harvest Festival too."

"I'll be there, sir."

"And, Maggie." Mr. Winston turned to me, enveloping my hands in his, "I'll see you at the Harvest Festival as well."

"I'll be sure to look out for you." I offered a courteous grin.

"I look forward to it." He kissed the back of my hand.

Clark and I waved to Mr. Winston as we left his office. Clark put his cap on his head.

"That went well," I said, putting my gloves on.

"I think that's the first time I ever heard you say that," Clark said as we walked toward the elevator.

"I never thought I would say it," I admitted. "But it seems as if Mr. Winston is going to keep his word. Let's just hope everything goes according to plan."

It was raining by the time we left Mr. Winston's office. When we got back to Flora's, Clark opened my door for me and put his cap on my head. He put a gentle hand around my waist as we dashed to the front porch, shaking the rain off ourselves. I wiped at my sleeve, which was sopping.

"I'm sorry I don't have an umbrella," Clark said. "You'd think after living here my whole life, I'd have a sixth sense of when it was going to rain."

"Don't worry about it," I said. "It's not like it'll make me melt or anything."

Clark gave me a good-natured smile, his slightly crooked teeth peeking from behind his lop-sided grin.

"Thanks for letting me come along," I said.

"Glad to have you." Clark's cheeks blushed a bit. "Well, can I?" He pointed.

My eyes widened and my stomach flipped inside of me. Was he going to do what I think he was? I wasn't sure if I wanted him to.

"Can you what?" I said, my tone cautious.

"My hat. You're still wearing it."

"Oh!" I reached up and touched it.

I took the hat off, brushing some of the rain droplets off. In the span of three minutes, I had forgotten he had even offered it to me.

I handed it back to him.

"Of course. I'm sorry. You didn't have to do that."

"It's all right." He put it back on. "I didn't want you messing up your hair."

"Thanks again."

"Don't mention it." He gave me another smile.

We stood in awkward silence for a moment.

I swayed back and forth, not knowing if I should be the first person to say goodbye.

"Well," I said. "I'll see you soon, then."

He nodded. "See you soon. Tell Flora everything went well with Mr. Winston."

"I will. Goodbye, Clark."

I waved to him as he stepped off the porch.

When I entered the house, Flora was standing right next to the doorway, startling me.

"Jeez!" I slammed my hand over my chest. "What are you doing, Flora?"

"How did it go?" she asked, following me into the foyer.

I took my coat off and hung it in the closet. "It went perfectly fine. Mr. Winston said he's still on for the Harvest Festival."

"What about the sales?" Flora asked. "Did he mention that?"

"Oh, right." I walked into the kitchen. "Mr. Winston was very pleased with your sales. In fact, you're neck and neck with Golden Hills. His words exactly."

"Neck and neck? Heavens, that is good news!"

I sat down at the table as Flora handed me a glass of iced tea from the refrigerator. She took a seat across from me.

"See?" I said after taking a sip of my drink. "I told you everything was running smooth as silk."

"And how was it with Clark?" Flora smiled, drawing out the syllables on his name.

"It was very nice."

"I saw you two talking on the porch."

"Is that why you were so close to the door? You frightened the daylights out of me; I thought I was going to have to change my girdle!"

"Well, I heard the car doors close. But when I peeked out the window, I saw you two chattin' it up. You looked so cute."

I scoffed. "We were just talking."

"You were wearing his hat." Flora smirked.

"Because it's raining. He didn't want my hair getting wet."

"He is a sweet young man, isn't he?"

"Yes, Flora." I nodded. "You've said that to me before."

"I know. I'm saying it again. I'm sure he'll be at the Harvest Festival."

"I know he will be. I told him I'd see him there."

"Maybe he'll ask you to dance."

I chortled, nearly choking on my iced tea. "Dance?"

"Yes. We have a lovely local jukebox group play music for us."

"I don't know." I shook my head.

"Then why are your cheeks turning red?"

"They're…they're not." I touched my cheek, noticing it was warm.

Flora tilted her head and fluttered her eyes. "If you say so, honey."

I took another sip of my iced tea and shook my head. Flora was being silly. My main priority was to make sure her pecan bread sold so well at the Harvest Festival, that people would flock to the stores to buy her pecans. My mind would be on that and nothing else. How we would go about advertising them was another question. I wasn't sure if I would have time to rub elbows with everyone there. I had a very important task that had to be done. Clark knew that. He understood how important this was.

Still, I couldn't help but wonder: what if he did ask me to dance? Part of me hoped he wouldn't. But the other part of me wanted nothing more in the world than to share a dance with him.

With just a mere two days away from the Harvest Festival, Flora was out and about buying all the ingredients she needed to make multiple loaves of pecan bread. I was able to convince her to leave her duties for one hour while we went out and bought dresses for the festival.

"I have plenty of dresses," she said. "I can wear one of those."

"Nonsense," I countered. "You need to look your absolute best. Not that your other dresses aren't nice or anything, but you need something perfect for the Harvest Festival."

While Flora must've looked through at least eight dresses in the store, I found mine within minutes. It was a gorgeous plum color with long sleeves and a tie at the base of the small, round collar. The wide, flared hem came down just below my knees. It would look absolutely dynamite with my black pumps. Flora finally settled on a sweet, modest floral dress with a white lace ruffled collar, saying it would go perfectly with her string of pearls. She paid for the dresses—insisting it was her treat—and we headed home where it was back to work for Flora and some house chores for me.

I hung our dresses up in the closet, keeping them in their garment bags so they wouldn't get wrinkled. I felt as if I were going to be attending a big Hollywood picture premiere and not a Harvest Festival in Savannah, Georgia.

I was both giddy and nervous. On one hand, I hoped everything would go well, even sending a quick little prayer up to Uncle James to bring us luck. On the other hand, I thought of Clark, and how Flora was convinced that he would ask me for a dance. The dress I bought would certainly do wonders for twirling, but I couldn't harp on that. I had to keep my mind focused on helping Flora.

As I came down the stairs after dusting the hallway, the aromas coming from the kitchen were heavenly. Flora was making chicken and dumplings for dinner and a hummingbird cake for dessert. I had no idea how she found the time to whip up two homemade meals from scratch, all while preparing to make a ton of pecan bread in just a few days.

I waltzed into the kitchen and stuck my finger into the bowl of homemade icing and took a taste.

"Hey, now!" Flora swatted me playfully on the arm. "Wait until dessert!"

"I'm sorry." I smiled. "I couldn't help it. It looks delicious."

"Your eyes are bigger than your stomach. It won't be ready for a while. Why don't you finish up your chores?"

"All done," I said.

"Really? My goodness. You work fast. Maybe I should give you more."

"Nice try, Flora." I gave her a wry grin.

A loud knock came at the door. Flora and I nearly got whiplash from turning our heads toward it.

"Who could that be?" Flora wiped her hands on her apron; however, I held my hand out in front of her.

"I'll get it," I said.

Another eager knock pounded on the door, and I hurried my steps so as to not keep whoever it was waiting. When I opened the door, I gripped onto the knob and nearly fell to the ground.

It was my parents.

CHAPTER THIRTY-SEVEN

My dad and ma stood on the porch, huddled so close to each other; they looked as if they could have molded into one being. Judging by their clipped expressions, this was clearly the last place they wanted themselves to be—and I couldn't help but agree.

The brim of my dad's fedora was slanted downward, as if wearing it that way would somehow magically turn him into Humphrey Bogart. My ma, as usual, wore a business suit peeking beneath her black wool coat. Her cheeks were rosy—and not from rouge. They stared at me expectantly, as if I were a hostess at some swanky restaurant in the North End.

"What are you doing here?" I asked after being able to finally find my voice.

"So much for Southern hospitality," my dad sneered.

"How..." I stumbled with my words. "How did you find me here?"

"We knew the address," Dad said. "I had written it down before you even came here. Although, I did have to phone Siobhan to double check. Finding the place, now that was a different story. We had to call for a cab, and then the driver wouldn't stop talking to us the whole way here."

A car horn honked, and I craned my neck to see Clark driving away, giving me a wave as he backed out. I rolled my eyes. I hoped my parents weren't rude to him; however, given how rude I was when I first met him, it wouldn't have shocked me if my parents were the same way.

"Well?" Ma said. "Aren't you going to let us in? Or are we just going to stand out here like gargoyles?"

"Maggie, who is it?" Flora's voice called from the kitchen.

Her footsteps pattered about. She came trotting down the hallway, wiping her hands on her apron. She smiled politely upon seeing my parents. I winced, not wanting Flora to be the next target of their hostility.

"Hello," Flora said, her voice sweet as ever.

"Flora," I said, dreading the introduction process, "these are my parents. Ma, Dad, this is Flora."

"How do you do?" Ma said, her voice monotone.

Flora paused for a second. A flash of bewilderment crossed through her green eyes.

However, she straightened up and gave a light, cordial smile.

"Well, this is nice! Why don't y'all come in?"

Ma and Dad stepped into the foyer. It was then that to my horror, I saw they were each holding a suitcase. They looked around, scoping the house out. They appeared neither impressed nor disgusted, just banal.

"Isn't this a surprise?" Flora said. "Maggie, you never told me your parents were coming."

"Believe me," I said, my eyes never losing their glare for my parents, "I'm just as surprised as you are."

"I'm in the middle of cooking dinner," Flora said. "You can stay, of course. It's chicken and dumplings."

"Oh." I shook my head.

The expressions on my parents' faces at the words "chicken and dumplings" were almost hilarious. They looked as if Flora asked them to eat a live scorpion.

"Maggie?" Flora said. "What's the matter? I made plenty."

"Flora, could I have a minute with my parents, please?" I said.

"Of course!" Flora said. "I'll go put some tea on while y'all catch up."

Catch up. As if my parents and I were old Army buddies drinking beer together one afternoon.

Flora gave my shoulder a light squeeze before shuffling off into the kitchen.

When she was out of my sight, I twirled my head toward my parents.

"Now do you mind telling me why you're here? It certainly can't be because you missed me."

Dad let out a breath through his nose and placed his suitcase down on the ground. "We have a meeting to open a new store in Savannah."

My eyes widened. I couldn't tell whether I was hearing things or if my dad actually uttered those words. "What?"

He nodded. "Tomorrow afternoon. There is a development in the works Downtown, and the next location may be going there."

"Hold on," I said. "What happened to Tennessee? The last I heard from Ma, you were two champagne bottles away from celebrating that deal."

Dad paused. The temple in jaw clenched. He gave my ma a quick glance, who also looked as if she swallowed a rotten grape.

"It didn't happen." Dad downcast his eyes to the ground. "Last minute. They decided to not go through with it."

I couldn't help the snort that escaped from me. "So, someone actually didn't want to go into business with you. I never thought I'd see the day where the great Richard O'Hanlon didn't seal a deal."

Dad's gaze flickered up at me. His eyes held a steely glint of anger. I could see there was a mixture of failure in there as well. It was something I never knew would bring me so much glee.

"Now look." He pointed a finger at my face. "It wasn't me."

"Of course," I said, my tone laced with faux sympathy. "It never is."

"They decided to back out at the last minute," Ma offered. "They wanted to go with something a little more modest, as they put it. I've never seen such unprofessionalism."

"The point is," Dad said, "we had to start from the ground up."

"So, you decided to come to Georgia." I folded my arms across my chest. "It's not like there was that one place in Tennessee. You could've found another area there."

"We figured since you're here—" Dad started.

"Are you serious?" I retorted. "You're not here because you wanted to see me or because you felt bad about how we left things after Uncle James' funeral. You're here so I can get you an in."

Dad lifted his chin. He knew I had his intentions pegged, and yet he still showed no guilt in it. There was not one ounce of remorse or parental fiber in his body. While I wasn't surprised by his stunt, I still couldn't help but shake my head in bewilderment.

"You need to leave." I picked up his trunk and handed it to him. "Now."

Flora came into the foyer. "Tea's all ready! Supper will be ready soon. Here, let me take your things. You may spend the night if you want."

"No," my dad said a little too forcibly, clutching the handle. "We'll find a hotel…somewhere."

Flora waved her hand at them. "Nonsense! You just got here! I'm not gonna let you leave when it's so close to nighttime! I have a spare room. The bed's all made up and everything!"

"Flora," I said. "Let my parents stay someplace else. They never should have come here anyway."

I scowled at my parents. They didn't deserve Flora's kindness, much less her roof over their heads. I wanted nothing more than to push them out the front door and slam it shut behind them.

"Maggie," Flora said. "It wouldn't be polite to not offer. Why go find a hotel when there's a perfectly fine bedroom—"

"They're not staying!" I screeched.

Flora's eyes widened. She placed her hand over her chest.

"Maggie, what's gotten into you?" she asked, a tremble in the back of her voice.

Instant guilt plagued me for hurting Flora's feelings. My parents, however, I didn't care how they felt. They stood there, still holding onto their luggage, not batting an eye at my outburst. I breathed ragged breaths in and out of my nose. My eyes darted from one person to the other, eventually landing back on my parents.

"I don't want them here," I said, my voice sour with disdain. "I don't want anything to do with them."

I spun around and stomped up the stairs to my room, slamming the door with all the force I could muster.

I sat on the window seat, leaning my head against the window pane. The falling leaves which had once been bright and vibrant had now turned to a mixture of dreary orange and brown.

A light knock came at my door.

I didn't bother looking up or telling whoever it was to come in. The door creaked open, and a pair of feet shuffled toward me.

"Maggie?" Flora's soft voice said.

I defiantly kept my head turned away. I didn't want to know if my parents were with her.

Flora came into view and sat down next to me. I glanced quickly at her before returning my eyes back to the window. She folded her hands into her lap.

"Maggie, the way you acted toward your parents was very rude," Flora said.

I lifted my head up, and my eyes shot toward her. "I'm rude? What about them? They show up out of nowhere. Not even a wire saying they're coming. They act like the world owes them a favor just by existing. They barely said two words to you. I'm not the one who is being rude. They are! And besides, I can't believe you would let them stay here!"

"Of course, I would!" Flora said. "I'm not going to let them leave, after they took so long to get here to see you."

"They're not here to see me." I shook my head. "The only reason they're here is so they can build a new grocery store. Their deal with Tennessee flaked out, so they figured they would come here instead. They couldn't give two licks about seeing me. They're using me to find a new location. They just wanted to make sure I don't say anything bad about my dad's business. That's all they care about. That's all they've ever cared about."

Flora sighed. "I know you and your parents don't have the best relationship—"

"We don't have any relationship," I spat.

"But how do you know they're not here to see you?" Flora asked, ignoring my interjection. "Maybe this is a sign to start over and build a fresh start with them."

"That's baloney."

"Maggie," Flora said, her tone surprisingly tense. "You need to quit acting like a child. I know you can behave like a lady. Now, your mama and daddy are staying for dinner and for the night. I'm putting them up in Alfred Jr.'s room. Dinner will be ready soon."

"I'm not eating with them," I said.

"You'll come downstairs and have a civilized dinner with everyone. You'll be polite and respectful. Do you understand?"

I stood up, continuing to keep my glare on Flora—who had an equally firm glower on me. She wasn't backing down any more than I was. I puckered my lips and gave her a stiff nod.

"Yes, ma'am. But don't expect me to talk to them. I'm only going downstairs for you."

The tension was awkward at dinner. My parents nibbled on their chicken and dumplings as if they were being forced to eat it at gunpoint. Flora asked them questions about themselves, which my dad didn't hesitate to answer when the subject came to his grocery store. Although he prattled on about O'Hanlon's, at the same time, he sounded as if he wanted to be anywhere else in the world. I ate quietly, barely offering so much as a nod toward my parents when they directed the conversation at me. Not once did they ask how I was doing or anything about Flora.

I couldn't get over that even though Flora knew how I felt about my parents and could see what kind of people they were, she still listened with an eager ear and a smile on her face. I couldn't take it anymore. I wiped the corners of my mouth with my napkin and placed it onto the table. I stood up, my chair scraping against the floor, interrupting my dad on whatever he was babbling about.

"Maggie?" Flora looked up at me. "Where are you going?"

"I'm tired," I said. "I'm going to go to bed. Thank you for dinner, Flora."

"There's still dessert," Flora said.

"No, thanks. I'm just going to go upstairs."

"Please sit down." Flora pointed to my chair.

I narrowed my eyes at Flora and obeyed, plopping back down in my seat and scooting my chair closer to the table. I placed my napkin back on my lap.

"Well, at least she listens to someone," Dad said, then added under his breath, "About time."

I clenched my fist on the table, fighting the urge to snap at him. I didn't even want to look at him or my ma anymore. For the remainder of dinner and dessert, I kept my eyes averted from them.

My ma, who had barely said a thing the entire time, poked at her hummingbird cake with her fork, taking out the little pieces of pecans and putting them to the side. I fought off an eye roll. The least she could do was be gracious and eat the damn cake. She hadn't the faintest idea how hard Flora had worked to prepare this meal.

When everyone was finished, I offered to help Flora clean up, which my dad believed to give him another excuse at offering a snide comment towards me. While I helped Flora, my parents took their luggage upstairs to the spare bedroom, glaringly disgruntled that they had to spend the night.

"Well," Flora said, her voice breaking through the silence. "That was a nice dinner."

I stopped drying the dish in my hands and chucked the rag onto the counter.

"All right, that's it. I honestly can't tell if you're being serious or sarcastic. How could you possibly think that dinner we just suffered through was nice? They were incredibly rude."

"They're just used to a different way of life," Flora said. "I don't judge based on first impressions."

"First impressions?" I lowered my voice. "I've told you exactly how they are, and you saw it firsthand tonight!"

Flora sighed. "You're right, your parents are…different. But they were raised differently than I was. I know y'all have your troubles. Maybe you should try talking with them. It could help."

"I am not talking to them," I said, my words clipped. "They can ride home in a milk truck for all I care. Besides, tomorrow is the day before the Harvest Festival. We need to focus on that."

"I'm not worried about the Harvest Festival. What I am worried about is you."

"You don't need to be. You know I'd do anything for you, Flora. But this?" I shook my head, a circus of emotions tumbling through it. "I can't. I won't."

Flora put her dishrag down and held onto my arms. "And I can't make you do anything. I've come to learn that. But trust me, honey—and I know you know this all too well—consider talking to them. Because if you don't, it may be the last time you'll get to. And by then, it'll be too late."

CHAPTER THIRTY-EIGHT

I sipped my cup of tea while giving my parents a look of contempt as they sat across from me at the kitchen table, begrudgingly choking down Flora's homemade biscuits and gravy for breakfast, completely ignoring their own cups of tea in front of them. My ma did the little trick of scattering the food around to make it look like she had eaten more than she had.

Flora walked over to them, a hospitable smile on her face.

"Still hungry?" she said. "I have plenty more."

"No." Dad shook his head. "We're fine."

"All right," Flora said. "Maggie, how about you? You barely touched your breakfast."

"I'm not very hungry," I grumbled, pushing it away.

Flora took everyone's plates to the sink to wash them.

My parents got up from their chairs, not offering to help clean up their mess.

"We have to get going," Dad said.

"So soon?" Flora said. "What time is your meeting today?"

"One o' clock," Ma said. "But we have to be ready. So, we must go now."

"Goodness, that's not for another six hours!" Flora exclaimed. "No need to rush. Why don't you stay here until then?"

I glowered at Flora. "They need to leave. Now."

"Listen," Flora said. "I have some errands to run today. There's a few things I need to take care of before tomorrow. Maggie, why don't you show your parents around Savannah? I'm sure they would love to see the city."

"I don't think so," I said. "Besides, they're only here for today. I'm sure they have a train to catch right after the meeting is done. They wouldn't be here all that often anyway."

"Oh, you can make time!" Flora waved her hand. "Staying a little bit longer wouldn't hurt. Tomorrow is the Harvest Festival; why don't you two stay for that?"

"Harvest Festival?" Ma said the words as if they were the most repugnant thing to come out of her mouth.

"Yes! It's such a fun time! Maggie will be there, as will I. You'll even get to try my pecan bread!"

"Pecan bread?" Dad echoed, equally put off.

"Yes, her pecan bread." I turned to him. "Remember? The one I told you about?"

"I remember," Dad grumbled.

"That's a first," I snarled under my breath, but loud enough for him to hear.

His jaw clenched. He gripped his suit coat and pulled on it. "We have to go. Mary, let's get our things."

They walked out of the kitchen and through the hallway, with Flora following closely on their trails. She hurried, trying to catch up with their swift walks.

"I do wish you would stay!" she said.

"We need to leave," Dad said. "We have to be ready for our meeting."

"But it's not until the afternoon!" Flora pleaded. "I don't want you two sitting around in a waiting area for hours. You can stay here until then."

"No, we must go." Dad climbed the stairs. "Maybe they'll take us early, then we can see if we could catch an earlier train home."

"Besides, it looks dreadful out," Ma countered. "I hope it doesn't rain."

"I can already tell you, it's going to," Flora said. "I just hope it lights up in time for the Harvest Festival tomorrow."

"Forget the Harvest Festival!" Dad snapped, stopping on one of the steps and turning his attention onto Flora. "This is a big meeting for us!"

"Dad!" I scolded.

"No!" he said. "This is our career, Maggie! Not some silly harvest hootenanny!"

My eyes widened. I looked over at Flora, whose own eyes were as big as saucers.

Her eyebrows furrowed, and she nodded lightly, walking over to the hall closet and pulling out her sage green sweater.

"Very well," she said, putting her sweater on. "I'll let you two pack up an be on your way." She turned and shuffled out of the house, closing the door behind her.

I twirled around and faced my parents "What's the matter with you? How could you be so rude?"

"Maggie, she wouldn't stop pestering us!" Dad said. "She's worried about some silly Harvest Festival that doesn't even matter!"

"But it matters to her," I said. "And to me. Just like this dumb meeting of yours matters to you."

"How could this festival matter to you?" Ma said. "It's just some silly get together around a bale of hay! It seems they've turned you into a regular country bumpkin."

"Get out," I spat. "Get your things and leave! Go to your meeting. I hope they reject you."

I stalked out of the house and followed Flora, who was swiftly making her way toward her truck.

"Flora!" I ran up to her. "Flora, are you all right?"

"Yes, I'm fine." Flora hopped into the driver's seat, keeping her eyes off of me.

"I'm so sorry. My dad…even I can't believe he could say something so terrible."

Flora shook her head, sighing. "I'm sorry, Maggie."

"What? Why are you sorry? My parents were the ones—"

"I never should have tried to force you to make amends with them."

My expression softened, and I swallowed, afraid that I was going to lose whatever composure I had left right there. I shook my head.

"I don't fault you."

Flora let out another placid sigh. Her eyes floated up to mine, and there was a mixture of remorse and defeat in them.

"If you truly want nothing to do with them anymore, then I support your decision. You're right. Your parents are…"

"Terrible."

Flora gave a short, reluctant nod. "I don't like to speak ill of people, no matter what their character is."

I let out a sad chuckle. "You're a better person than I ever could be. I'm so sorry they hurt you."

Flora looked up at me again. "And I'm sorry they hurt you."

My chin trembled, and I gave Flora a hug before she slammed the truck door and drove off. After she was out of sight, I turned and stormed back into the house and made my way up to my parents' room.

I barged into the room, flinging the door open with such force, that the knob smacked against the wall.

My dad was closing up his suitcase, and my ma was applying a fresh coat of lipstick.

I slammed the door and faced them.

"What is wrong with you?" I crossed my arms against my chest.

"What?" Dad's eyebrows furrowed in annoyance.

"You were incredibly rude to Flora!"

"Oh Maggie, she's fine!" Dad turned his attention back to packing. "She was irritating the hell out of us by constantly asking to stay when she knew very well that we're busy!"

"She was being thoughtful! Not that you would know what that's like."

"Excuse me?" Dad straightened up, sending me a scolding glare.

"You're a terrible person. Both of you are."

Dad's eye twitched, and I could see the small vein protruding on his lid. "Don't you—" he started.

"No!" I screamed. "All you ever did when I was growing up was hand me off to Siobhan so you didn't have to take care of me. You never did anything for me! You never talked to me, you never held me, you never loved me! Why do you think I grew up to be such a brat?"

I no longer cared about civility. Twenty-three years of not being good enough, not feeling like their daughter. I lost my ability to keep my composure, and everything inside of me bubbled over the surface.

"Do you have any idea how I felt when Uncle James died?" I cried. "How when I got home, I never felt so awful or alone in my life? I sat by myself in his room, knowing that I would never see him again. He was gone. He was gone, and you didn't even care. You just couldn't wait to get his funeral over with so you could go off to open another damn store. And then you couldn't even take one minute to be with me. I had been gone for months, and you couldn't even muster up the decency to be a parent. I was hurting and missing him so terribly, and you couldn't even see that. And when I left again, the only reason you tried to stop me wasn't because you wanted me there, it was because you were trying to prove you had power over me. Well, you didn't. You never did, and you never will."

The temple in my dad's neck pulsed. I could tell that it was taking everything in him not to lose his own composure and strike me against the cheek. His stance was rigid, and he was wavering back and forth.

"When I came back here," I continued, gulping down a sob, "Flora did everything that you never did. She held me, she listened to me, she let me cry on her shoulder. She knew how it felt to lose someone so close to her. She was—is—the only person besides Uncle James who has ever shown that they loved me. Do you know what that's like, knowing your own parents don't love or care about you?"

My chest heaved as tears formed in my eyes again, and an explosion of grief shuddered through my body.

"And then you come here with the news that you're trying to open a new store. You don't even send a telegram letting me know, you just show up! And you expect me to help you? After everything you never did for me, you still think I owe you the favor of helping you? I will never do anything for you, just as you never did anything for me!"

The urge to pound my fists on their chests overpowered me. I clenched my hands at my sides and backed away. With a swift turn, I fled out of the room, wanting to be away from them once and for all.

CHAPTER THIRTY-NINE

I made my way out the door, fleeing down the front porch and rushing out of the awning of trees that led to Flora's house. Whether my parents saw me leaving or not, I didn't give a damn. I quickened my pace, turning the corner onto the main dirt road.

My head was jumbled and heated as I made my way towards Clarabelle's little house. I trudged up her front steps.

"Clarabelle!" I pounded relentlessly on the door. The waiting for Clarabelle to answer felt like an eternity with no end in sight.

Finally, the door swung open, and Clarabelle looked at me with anxious and irritated eyes.

"Margaret!" she said. "What in the name of—?"

The sight of me crying sent her to a screeching halt. I didn't necessarily want to be here, but there was no one else to turn to.

Clarabelle's eyes widened, and her mouth gaped open. Her shoulders clenched up, and she gripped onto the door frame tightly.

"What's wrong?" Panic tumbled out of her voice. "Is it Flora? What is it? What happened?"

I shook my head. "No," I said in between hyperventilating breaths. "It's—it's not Flora. She's—I need to come in. I can't go back there."

"Can't go back where? To Flora's?"

I nodded. "I need to come in. Can I stay here with you? Please."

"Margaret, you're scaring me." Clarabelle shot me a side glance, and her voice warbled. "What's going on?"

I gulped and opened my mouth to speak. The only thing that escaped from my lips were desperate whimpers.

Clarabelle's posture relaxed, and she cocked her head towards the inside of her house.

"Come on in, Margaret. Come in and catch your breath."

Clarabelle put her arm around my shoulder and ushered me into her house. She sat me down on her sofa and plopped down next to me.

"Now, what happened?"

I drew in a deep breath, not knowing where to begin. I couldn't look Clarabelle in the eyes. For someone I've disagreed with for so long, she was being surprisingly patient with me.

"Take your time," she said calmly. "I don't have anywhere to be."

"My parents," I finally said. "They're here. At Flora's. They came to...to open up a new store in Savannah."

"Hold on." Clarabelle put her hand up. "They came all the way out here just to open a new store?"

I nodded, finally meeting my gaze with Clarabelle's. "They showed up unannounced at Flora's. They were so mean to her and hurt her feelings terribly."

A steely glint flashed in Clarabelle's eyes, and I could tell she too wouldn't mind giving my parents a good kick in the pants. She gulped, bracing herself for her next question.

"What did they do to her?"

"They disrespected her, basically telling her that the Harvest Festival was a ridiculous get together. You should have seen the look in Flora's eyes. It broke my heart to see her that way."

Clarabelle puckered her lips. "Humph."

"Besides, they only came here because they were supposed to open a store in Tennessee, but the deal flaked out at the last minute. So, they thought they'd come here, using me as an in to see what Savannah is like." I shook my head. "I don't know what to do. Flora is out running errands for tomorrow, and my parents...I can't go back while they're still there. I don't want to be anywhere near them. Can I stay here with you until I know Flora is back?"

Clarabelle sucked in a deep breath. "Margaret, you know I wouldn't dump you out on your rear end when you're in trouble—no matter how at odds we are. Of course you can stay."

"Thanks," I sniffled.

"You want some tea?"

I nodded and we moved into the kitchen, sitting at the table with our tea and a tin of shortbread cookies. We were silent for a bit, until Clarabelle decided to be the one to speak first.

"Now, I hate to ask but...what does Flora think about all of this?"

I sighed, placing my tea cup down on its saucer. "At first, she wanted us to talk and make amends."

Clarabelle raised her eyebrows. "She did?"

I nodded. "She had this belief that even though my parents and I have been like oil and water for our entire lives and barely had a proper conversation about…anything, somehow we could find a way to connect with each other, as if everything was some damn fairy tale. But now, she sees what they're really like and thinks I should let sleeping dogs lie."

"Well, you wanna know what I think?"

I shifted my eyes at her, wary of her response "What?"

"I think Flora's right. I think deciding to cut ties with them is the smartest move you've ever made."

I raised the tea cup to my lips, Clarabelle's words sinking into my mind.

"I know it's not easy," Clarabelle continued, "and I wish everything was different for you and your parents and you were able to have the kind of relationship y'all deserve, but honey, if they're not willing to be the mama and daddy you need them to be, then you need to go your separate ways."

I expelled a deep sigh and took a sip of my tea, placing it down back on the saucer and tracing the rim of the cup with my finger.

"And if it's any consolation," Clarabelle said, "you'll always have me and Flora."

A soft smile curled at the edge of my lips. "Thanks, Clarabelle."

The front door opened, and our eyes followed the sounds of footsteps leading to the kitchen. Flora entered with a small box.

"Oh, there you are!" She walked over to us, her gaze fixated on me. "I was wondering where you went off to. I came back to find the house empty. I went upstairs and saw that your parents had gone as well."

"Good." I turned my head away from her. "They got the message."

Flora's brows knitted together, a nurturing expression crossing her features. "Are you okay?"

I let out a deep breath. "I'd be lying if I said yes, but I will be."

"I got some blank recipe cards for the Harvest Festival tomorrow. You want to help us write some out? It'll take your mind off of things."

I looked away. I wasn't necessarily in the right mind frame to write recipe cards. All I wanted to do was lie down. Flora was right, however. It would help me forget the horrible last few days I had. With much reluctance, I swallowed my grief and nodded. Clarabelle made another pot of tea, and we got to work on writing Flora's recipe.

Flora and I drove back to the house after writing out a few dozen recipe cards. Our hands were cramped, and all we could think about was having a relaxing evening. As we approached her house, however, my heart stopped.

My parents sat on the front porch with their luggage. Flora noticed, too. Her eyebrows creased together.

"What in the world?" she said.

I hopped out of the truck and marched toward them.

"What are you doing back?" I folded my arms over my chest. "I thought I told you to leave for good."

My parents stood up from their wicker chairs.

Flora plodded up the steps and formed a protective shield between me and my parents.

"I think it would be best if y'all left," she said, her voice even but firm.

Dad took a step toward us, his fedora gripped tightly in his hands.

"We want a moment with Maggie," Dad said.

"After the way you treated her?" Flora's tone took on an edge. "With all due respect, Mr. O'Hanlon, you two haven't exactly been the parents she deserves."

"Excuse me?" Dad's eyes narrowed.

Flora's shoulders straightened, and she stood tall. "You have an amazing, young lady for a daughter, and you don't even appreciate her. If I had a daughter like Maggie, why, I'd feel like the luckiest woman in the world."

Dad screwed his lips tightly, and his eyes softened. His gaze shifted over to me.

"We just want a minute." He looked away, his cheeks flushing. "Please."

That was the first time I'd ever heard him say that word. I bit the inside of my lip and stood beside Flora.

"One minute," I said, my voice thick. "That's all you get."

I brushed past them and headed up to my bedroom with my ma and dad close behind. I closed the door, folding my arms over my chest again.

"Well? Why are you here? I thought you had your meeting."

"We went," Dad said. "We couldn't think straight the entire time. We kept thinking about everything you said."

"So it's my fault your meeting was a bust?"

"I didn't say it was a bust. It went well, we just couldn't get you out of our heads."

"Oh, well, I'm so happy to hear that you may get a new precious store. Just don't expect me to give it my regards."

"Now listen, that's not why we came back."

"Sure, Dad. You just couldn't wait to rub it in my face—"

"No," Dad interjected, shaking his head.

"Why don't you leave?" I spat.

"Dammit, Maggie, listen to me!" He tore his eyes away from me. His jaw clenched as he rubbed his stubbled chin. "This isn't easy for me to say."

I shrugged. "What?"

He continued to keep his gaze away.

"What Flora said. She's…" He paused, twisting the corner of his mouth like a corkscrew. "We…we never showed appreciation for you."

"That's because you don't. You've never wanted anything to do with me."

Dad sighed, and he shoved his hands into his pockets. "I admit that by the time you were born, O'Hanlon's were starting to become so successful that we didn't see ourselves as parents."

"Unless you ended up having a son, right?" I asked.

I didn't think my dad could downcast his eyes any more than they already were. His cheeks deepened into a light scarlet.

I couldn't understand why he was expressing shame now. Even though he never said those words out loud, he knew I was right.

I nodded and motioned my head toward the door. "Thanks, Dad. Shouldn't you be catching your train back home?"

"I didn't finish what I wanted to say." His tone was quiet but flat.

"Oh, I think you've said enough."

I walked to the door and opened it, gesturing for them to leave.

My parents stayed in place.

Finally, Dad looked back up at me, struggling for a moment to meet my eyes.

"I saw how much your uncle meant to you," he said.

I rested my hand on the door frame, a light prickle tickling my spine at his acknowledgment of Uncle James.

"You're right," he uttered the two words I never thought he would say in my wildest dreams. "He was more of a father to you than I was. He was…a better father to you. When you came home after he died, I did everything to avoid you. I knew that if I took one look at you, I would've seen how upset you were, knowing how close you were to him."

"Still," I said. "You could've talked to me. Either of you! You could've swallowed your so-called pride and talked to me like any other parent would do. But you didn't."

"We couldn't bring ourselves to." He shook his head.

"That's not a good enough excuse." I folded my arms tightly across my chest. "I realize you were grieving in your own way too. But Dad, I tried to reach out to you after the funeral. I saw that you were struggling and tried to reach out, but you just pushed me away and announced that you and Ma were going to Tennessee of all places to open a new store."

"I didn't know what else to do." Dad shrugged, as if that were a good enough answer. "I was trying to push the grief away, not you."

A faint scoff slipped out. "Baloney. You pushed me away."

Dad's eyes left mine again. A mixture of what I could only decipher as shame, frustration, and guilt inhabited them.

I caught sight of my ma, who had been maddeningly quiet this entire time. She appeared uncomfortable and stiff. Not that she was ever an emotional person to begin with.

"And what about you?" I challenged.

She hesitated. Her arms were so tight across her chest that I thought they would burst through her sleeves. She kept her chin lifted.

"I thought I was being a good mother," she finally said, her voice light and raw.

I rolled my eyes, and this time, a full scoff escaped.

"Now I see," she continued, "that I wasn't even close. I wasn't raised in a warm, loving family. I didn't know the first thing about it. I raised you the way my own ma raised me—with a ten-foot pole. When you told me that this Flora lady was a better mother than me, I was livid; I thought that it was the most ungrateful thing to ever come out of your mouth. But when I saw how she was as a person, I was angry for a different reason. I realized I had missed my chance on raising and getting to know a very nice young woman."

It was my turn to look away. I never thought I would hear my ma tell me she was wrong, much less a compliment come out of her mouth. Still, for some reason, I had a difficult time accepting her words.

The fact that it took them this long to say the words I've wanted so desperately to hear all my life was borderline ridiculous.

I let out a deep sigh and brought my eyes back up to them.

"You know what? You said the right things; you just said them too late."

Dad's shoulders drooped slightly. He and my ma exchanged unclear glances.

I couldn't take it anymore.

"You should go." I opened the door further.

Dad stalled, holding his fedora. He glided his hands over the brim before putting it on.

"Fine." His voice was filled with defeat and a touch of anger.

He walked toward the door, with my ma—who couldn't even look at me—close behind.

"By the way, good luck with trying to open a new store downtown." I gripped onto the door frame and added an icy glare. "I bet it'll be a real smash."

I closed the door behind them just in time to catch a glimpse of their worn out expressions.

CHAPTER FORTY

I sat on my bed, everything my parents and I said to each other tumbling in my head until our words became a huge blur. My circus of emotions returned. While I said everything I wanted to say to them, at the same time, I felt as if I were grieving a loss all over again.

I fiddled with my locket, turning it over and looping the strand through my fingers.

A light knock came at my door.

Flora entered my room. Her face was relaxed, however, a touch of melancholy flickered across her features.

"Maggie?" Her tone was kind and careful. She sat down next to me, the edge of the bed creaking slightly. "How are you doing?"

I kept my eyes down. "Are my parents gone?"

"Yes. They left quite abruptly."

"Did they say anything to you?"

"No." She shook her head. "They muttered a quick goodbye and left."

"Figures," I said under my breath.

Flora halted my fidgeting by holding my hand in hers, giving it a light and comforting squeeze.

"How are you doing?" she asked again.

I took my hand out of hers and stood up, wrapping my arms tightly around my body and bowing my head slightly.

"You did the right thing, you know," Flora said. "If you don't mind me asking, what did they say exactly?"

I rubbed my hand up and down my arm despite my room being quite warm. I drew in a deep breath.

"They said everything I've wanted to hear." A twinge of frustration rose up inside of me, and I twirled toward Flora. "Why couldn't they have said all those things to me when I was a kid? Why did it take them

292

twenty-three years and me screaming at them until I was blue in the face?"

Flora's eyes softened and her mouth creased downward. "I'm sorry, honey."

I walked back to my bed and sat down next to Flora.

"I know that I was no better, but do you want to know why I never expressed affection to them growing up?"

"Why?" Flora asked softly.

I paused, the truth of my words clinging to my throat. "Because I knew if I did, it would've all been futile. I would've been filling the air with useless words because I knew they wouldn't return those feelings."

Flora held my hand in hers again. This time, the squeeze she gave me was with more force and motherly protection.

I turned my head toward Flora, whose eyes were slightly wet beneath the brims. She tucked a lock of hair behind my ear.

To avoid the hitch in my chest overpowering everything, I rested my head on her shoulder, letting her maternal comfort ease my spirits until everything around me calmed.

Although I remained relatively quiet for most of the afternoon, I figured it wouldn't put me in the right headspace I needed to be in to help Flora prepare for the Harvest Festival.

After we cleaned up dinner, Flora and I prepared everything for the next day. We set up as much as we could, and Flora made us each a cup of tea, which we enjoyed at the kitchen table.

Apart from the occasional back and forth conversation about the Harvest Festival, Flora decided to be the first one to speak in quite a while.

"I know I've asked you this a lot today, and I promise this will be the last time, but how are you holding up?"

I took a sip of my tea, putting it back on its saucer and staring down at the lemon wedge floating on top.

I let out a deep sigh and gave a wave of my hand.

"I'm fine. It's over and done with. They're on their way home by now, and I'm sure they're perfectly fine too."

"I realize I've been repeating myself a lot today, but you made the right choice. I want you to understand that. I know it wasn't easy, or maybe it was given the relationship y'all had, but Maggie, it's also okay to be feeling every emotion under the sun. Whether you're jumping for joy or down in the dumps a bit. In the end, it's all about what makes you happy and live the life the way you want to live it."

I rested my chin in my hand, letting out another sigh.

"I just want to move on. I don't want to swallow all the negative feelings I've had all my life. I understand it's okay to feel angry about it sometimes, but I don't want to dwell on it. I don't want to hold bitter feelings inside of me that end up blowing over some day."

"Do you think you'll ever forgive them?"

Flora's question, while not unexpected, made me stop. The answer, however, eluded me.

I shook my head.

"I don't know. I mean, what if I did and I tried to reconcile with them, and they ended up treating me the same way they always have? What, then?"

"I can tell you one thing; people don't change overnight. Some folks don't change for ten, twenty years. Some don't change at all. It's an unfortunate truth that we have to learn in life."

I sighed, letting Flora's words linger on my mind. As insightful as they were, I was still struggling with the thought of it.

"I don't know." I brought my gaze up to Flora's. "Would you?"

Flora straightened, folding her hands on the table. She paused, thinking for a moment.

"Well, as you know, I was raised to believe in forgiveness. It was something that was instilled in me, and that I honestly still carry to this day. But now, I do realize that there can be exceptions. It depends on how you look at the situation, but it's a decision you have to make yourself. You have to make the choice that is right for you. Whether you wake up tomorrow and embrace forgiveness, or you decide to ten years from now. Even if you decide not to at all, it has to come from you. Don't let me influence your decision. Whatever you choose, I will always be here to support you."

Flora reached out and held my hands in hers.

A light grin trickled across my lips, and my senses eased. It was a wonderful feeling knowing I had someone like Flora in my life.

If there was one thing about my parents I was grateful for, it was that they ended up sending me to her.

"Can I ask you something?" I tilted my head curiously. "How in the world did my dad ever find you?"

Flora chuckled softly and sat back in her chair. "I put an ad in the paper."

"But how did he come across it? I know Massachusetts and Georgia aren't on different sides of the world, but they aren't exactly neighboring states either."

Flora shrugged. "I suppose you know as much as I do, then. I put out quite a few ads saying I had a spare room and would offer it in exchange for house and farm work. Home cooked meals would be included, of course. But one day, I got word that a man in Boston was looking to send away his daughter who was—to use the term lightly—"disorderly." I thought, Boston of all places! My goodness, this man was determined."

She let out another chuckle, however, her eyes softened and her expression became solemn.

"I figured this man was very serious about sending his daughter here. I got quite a few local answers in terms of the ads I put out, but something about your daddy's persistence and how you were being portrayed made the mama inside of me choose his request. I had this gut instinct, this feeling, that I knew you had to be the one to stay with me."

I bit my bottom lip and lowered my head, reflecting back to that time when my dad was being so secretive about where he was sending me. I remember being so smug, thinking he was bluffing, when in reality, I had no idea how much my life was about to change.

"I sure am glad I trusted my instincts." Flora's voice broke into my thoughts. "I am one lucky lady to have gotten to know you."

Another grin spread across my lips. I looked up at Flora, who was offering her own smile to me. My expression fell, however, and I was immediately brought back to when I first arrived here and how terribly rude I was.

My cheeks warmed, and I dipped my chin. While there weren't enough words to express how much Flora had come to mean to me, there were certain words I had yet to say. Words that had been a long time coming.

"Flora, I've been meaning to tell you that I'm sorry for the way I behaved when I first arrived here."

I looked back up at her.

A puff of indifference escaped her lips, and she waved a hand at me.

"Oh, honey. You did nothing wrong."

"No." I shook my head. "I was a downright brat. I was so incredibly rude to you for the longest time, and you didn't deserve it. All you were trying to do was give me a nice place to stay. I was too spoiled to see just how much of a wonderful person you are. I'm sorry."

"Oh, Maggie. I don't fault you for anything. You were going through a difficult time, that's all."

"I wish you would stop justifying the way I acted. Clarabelle told me how you felt, which makes me feel even more awful about it."

Flora shrugged. "Well, I was worried that I wasn't being good enough to you."

"You were! I just didn't see it that way. And I apologize for that."

"You don't need to. But thank you for doing it anyway."

"I just want you to know…" A knot formed in the base of my throat, and my chest tightened. "That I truly appreciate everything you've done for me. Everything. I'm glad I ended up getting busted at that underground casino because by some crazy circumstances, it brought me to you. If I had known it would have changed my life for the better, I would have done it sooner. Thank you, Flora. Thank you for everything you've done for me."

Flora's rosy cheeks pinked even more, and her green eyes glistened. She gripped onto my hand again and gave it her motherly pat.

"Well…" She shook her head modestly and cleared her throat. "I can't take all of the credit."

"You can." I smiled. "Because it's true."

Flora smiled back, her lips quivering slightly. "What a wonderful young woman you are, Maggie. I'm so glad you came into my life."

I stood up from my seat and moved to the chair right next to her. I embraced her, wrapping my arms around her neck.

Flora responded by wrapping her own arms around me.

"So am I," I said.

CHAPTER FORTY-ONE

Flora got us up at five AM on the dot. While I was fully prepared for her early morning wake up call, I still had a difficult time tearing myself away from the comfort of my warm bed.

Before getting ready, we ate a light breakfast of grits with biscuits and peach jam.

After we cleaned up breakfast, I went upstairs to get ready, at Flora's urging, while she began preparations on the pecan bread.

I got dressed diligently, putting on my gorgeous plum colored dress and black pumps. I slapped my face on, observing myself in the mirror to make sure everything looked perfect. A stubborn stray lock of dark auburn hair stuck out, pestering me. I wet my finger and curled it around, sweeping it off to the side.

When I entered the kitchen, Flora was at the counter whisking the bread mixture together.

"It smells great." I walked up to her.

"Oh, Maggie! Don't you look lovely!"

"Thank you." I couldn't help but flare out the skirt of my dress, something I've always done when complimented on my clothing.

"Help me put this first batch in the oven, would you?" Flora gestured with her oven mitt clad hand.

I put an apron on and got right to work.

Flora and I had quite the assembly line going on as we took turns between mixing, slathering baking dishes with Crisco shortening, and throwing loaf after loaf into the oven.

Time was moving fast, and before we knew it, it was nearly eleven in the morning. Clark was to drive us there to meet Clarabelle, who was securing our stations for us. We were to be no later than noon. Flora hadn't even changed out of her house dress yet.

"Go get ready." I gave her a gentle push toward the foyer. "I'll take care of the cleaning."

Flora advised me to cut up the loaves of bread into little squares before scurrying off upstairs to get dressed.

I was in the middle of slicing into a loaf of pecan bread when a knock came at the front door. I wiped my hands on my apron and answered it.

Clark stood on the porch, immediately taking his cap off when he saw me. He gave me a lopsided grin.

"Hi, Maggie."

A smile spread across my own face. "Hi, Clark. Come on in."

I stepped aside to let him into the foyer.

Clark looked quite adorable. He wore a white collared shirt with a tie and a brown and tan sweater vest over it and dark brown trousers. His wavy strawberry blond hair was slicked off the side.

"Gee, you look really pretty," Clark said.

Even though I had generous amounts of pecan bread crumbs on my apron, I couldn't help but blush, thinking maybe I didn't need to put rouge on in the first place.

"Thank you, Clark. You look very nice, too."

Clark gave me another smile and placed his hat and coat on the rack near the door.

"Is Flora getting ready?" He shoved his hands into his pockets.

"Yes. I'm on pecan bread duty for the time being."

"Need any help?"

"I'd love some."

I led the way into the kitchen, giving him the quick rundown of Flora's instructions.

We stood at the counter, cutting up the loaves of pecan bread into sampling pieces. I caught a glance at his hands. They worked with ease and care.

I reached for the dish towel at the same time he did, our fingers momentarily intertwining with one another's.

My chest fluttered, and my cheeks warmed up. I quickly retracted my hand and cleared my throat.

"Sorry," we both said at the same time, which garnered an awkward chuckle from each of us.

"You can use it," I said. "I'll just get a new one from the linen closet."

I dashed off to the linen closet, giving myself a moment to gather my composure as I grabbed a clean dish towel, quickly using it to fan my face in an attempt to calm down my flushing cheeks.

"Here we go." I flourished the dish towel in my hand as I made my way back to the counter.

"These smell great," Clark said. "I can't wait to dig into them at the Harvest Festival."

I took a square of pecan bread and broke it in half, giving Clark a mischievous smirk.

"We can have a little taste," I said, then leaned into a whisper. "Just don't tell Flora."

I popped the piece of pecan bread into my mouth, and Clark did the same.

"I don't know how she does it." Clark shook his head.

"She's the best cook, that's for sure."

We went back to packing up the Pyrex dishes.

"So, Maggie, were those folks that visited the other day, your parents?"

My stomach dropped a bit, however, I didn't want to lie to him. After all, he knew my parents and I weren't exactly a model family.

"Yes, they were." I nodded.

"That's nice. How did it go?"

I paused, averting my eyes away from him.

"Well, it wasn't exactly those heartfelt reunions you read about in great literature. It's kind of a long story."

"Oh, I'm sorry." Clark's eyebrows furrowed sympathetically. "Yeah, now that I think of it, I remember you talking about how they were more into your pa's work."

I nodded again. "Yeah. Anyway, everything is fine. I had Flora here with me, and she made me feel better."

"I'm happy to hear you're doing fine."

"Thanks." I smiled again.

Flora's feet pattered down the staircase.

"Clark's arrived?" Her voice rang out.

"Hi, Flora!" Clark called, causing me to giggle.

Flora entered the kitchen and gave Clark a hug and kiss on the cheek.

"So, what else is left to do?" she asked.

"Not much, really." I shook my head. "Why don't you take a load off? Relax a little."

"Are you sure? I don't mind helping."

"I'm sure."

"All right." She shrugged, plopping down into a chair at the table.

"You look very nice, Flora," I said.

"Oh, stop." She waved her hand at me.

I walked over to her and leaned down a bit. "Are you wearing rouge?"

"What? No." Flora put a gentle hand to her cheek.

"Your cheeks look rosier than usual." I tilted my head to the side.

"Well, I may have borrowed some of yours. I hope you don't mind."

"Of course not, it looks great on you."

"We're pretty much done," Clark said. "All we really gotta do is load up the truck and head off."

"Are you ready?" I asked Flora.

She gave a confident nod. "Yes."

"All right." I threw the dish towel onto my shoulder. "Let's pack up and get this show on the road."

We couldn't have been luckier with the perfect day that graced us for the festival. Pumpkins, gourds, and beautiful late autumn foliage lavished the quaint little park, and the smells of baked goods and crisp air was just the icing on the cake.

Clarabelle stood behind her serving table and greeted Flora, who went over to her table to set up with Clark.

"Hello, Clarabelle." I walked over to her.

"Margaret." She acknowledged with a nod.

As I walked past her, she grabbed my attention, gesturing for me to join her.

"How are you doing?" she asked.

I gave her a humble half-grin. "I'm fine. Thank you again for yesterday. You really helped make me feel better."

Clarabelle puckered her lips and gave a curt nod. "I was just looking out for you, Margaret, you know that. I hated seeing you that way."

"I know, thank you. But actually…" I turned my head toward Flora, who was in the middle of setting up. I looked back at Clarabelle. "My parents returned yesterday."

Clarabelle's eyes blinked rapidly. Her shoulders hunched forward, and her eyebrows raised quizzically.

"Come again?"

I nodded. "When Flora and I returned from your house, they were on the front porch. They wanted to talk to me in private."

"And?" Clarabelle was champing at the bit.

I sighed. "Long story short, they said everything I've always wanted to hear. But it was just too late. So, I told them to leave. And I feel good about the decision I made. Now, I can surround myself with people who truly care about me."

Clarabelle's mouth relaxed. Although her hand was still placed firmly on her hip, her shoulders eased.

"I can understand that mustn't have been easy for you," she said. "But you did the right thing."

I gave her a faint grin. "Thanks, Clarabelle."

She returned the gesture with a light smirk of her own. "Now go help Flora set up. You got lots of work to do today, little missy."

Clarabelle swatted me playfully on the arm as I made my way back to Flora, who stood behind her little table looking prouder than I'd ever seen her.

People were starting to come in droves. With everyone mingling about and visiting each other's stations, it seemed as if the Harvest Festival was shaping up to be quite the gas.

I found myself anxiously nibbling on a piece of pecan bread. I glanced around, trying to see if Mr. Winston was among the people making their way in. I hoped that nothing unexpected came up that would result in him no longer attending, even though he warned me that could very well happen.

I shook my head, putting that possible scenario out of my mind. I had to be optimistic that he would indeed show up—for Flora's sake at least.

I wiped the pecan bread crumbs off my hands before she found out that I was snacking away on it. I had to be focused and keep my mind clear of any anxieties. I rejoined her in handing out pieces of bread to passersby.

Clarabelle had roped Clark into helping her hand out her peach cobbler when her table got swarmed by hungry folks.

Flora was eventually summoned over by Clarabelle as well.

"I'll be right back," Flora said. "You all right for a minute?"

"I got everything covered." I nodded.

Flora walked off to assist Clarabelle, and I placed a canister of Alcott's Pecans on her table.

Despite Mr. Winston's objections to me selling the pecans, I couldn't help but run off a bit of a sales pitch to Flora's customers. I even filled another traveling Pyrex dish with pecans so people could sample them and see what they tasted like on their own.

"Maggie? What are my pecans doing out on the table?" Flora's voice came from behind me.

"Oh, I just thought people need to know about your product itself."

Flora waved her hand. "They already do."

"Still." I shrugged. "You never know who may mosey by. I even brought some pecans so people could try them."

I held up the Pyrex dish in my hand, and Flora shook her head.

"Are you sure Mr. Winston would agree to this? It seems awfully sneaky."

I shrugged. "Why wouldn't he? You're technically promoting his company too, right? And it's not like you're actually selling the pecans. You're just letting people have a little taste."

A woman who looked to be around my ma's age approached us. She lingered for a moment, inspecting the canister.

"Alcott's?" she said.

I gave Flora an encouraging nod, and she jumped into business woman mode, her voice clear and confident.

"That's right, Alcott's Pecans. They're distributed by Farmer's Food Company. You can get them at Minton's Market and other food stores all over Georgia, and they are only fifteen cents a canister."

"Which, if you ask me, is a real steal!" I piped in.

"Would you like to try a piece of my pecan bread?" Flora held it out.

"Thank you very much." The woman smiled graciously and took a bite, her eyes widening with pure joy. "This is delicious! What's in it? I taste something sweet."

Flora grabbed a recipe card from out of its box and handed it to her. "Well, actually, I wrote the recipe out. You can make it yourself!"

"Looks easy enough." The woman scanned the recipe card. "I may have to try this."

"And Alcott's Pecans are the only ones to use for Flora's pecan bread recipe," I offered. "Any other pecan just wouldn't taste the same. Here, see for yourself."

I took a small handful of pecans and gave them to her. She popped one in her mouth and nodded, seemingly pleased with the taste.

"I grow them right here in Savannah," Flora said.

"Alcott's," the woman said again, as if locking the name into her brain. "I'll be sure to grab a canister the next time I go to the store."

She gave us a polite and intrigued nod before heading off.

The amount of pride I had for Flora nearly burst out of me.

"Look at you go!" I nudged her shoulder with my elbow. "You're doing great."

"So are you! Hey." She brought her tone down to a whisper and gestured to Clark, who was still assisting Clarabelle. "Look over there. Doesn't he look sweet helping Clarabelle?"

I nodded. "It's very nice of him."

"He looks handsome today, don't you think?"

I blushed and offered another quick nod. "Yes, he does."

The Jukebox band Flora had mentioned entered the stage carrying various instruments.

"The Vern Preston Band is setting up. You got your dancing shoes ready?" Flora winked and gave me a teasing smile.

"Flora!" I blushed harder but couldn't fight off the anticipative smirk that curled at the edge of my lips.

CHAPTER FORTY-TWO

There's always something so joyous about the comfort that autumn brings, and today was no exception. For every lovely moment the Harvest Festival was bringing, I wished I could keep adding an extra hour to the day just to make it last longer.

Flora was on a roll with serving her pecan bread. She dished out an equal amount of recipe cards and pecan samplings, as well as her sales pitch for Alcott's and Farmer's.

Dr. Meadows even stopped by at one point, along with his wife, Ada. He was absolutely delighted to try Flora's pecan bread again.

"You really know how to make a great pecan bread!" Dr. Meadows said, wiping the corners of his mouth with a napkin.

"You must give me the recipe!" Mrs. Meadows raved.

"As a matter of fact, I've written it out!" Flora handed a card to her.

"Wonderful!" Mrs. Meadows said. "I'll be sure to make it sometime!"

I couldn't hide my amusement at Dr. Meadows' eyes growing like saucers at the prospect of enjoying Flora's pecan bread at home.

The Vern Preston band announced they would be taking a break from the stage so the Harvest Queen could be crowned.

"Maggie, why don't you and Clark go watch?" Flora said.

"Oh, well, I'd like to be here with you when Mr. Winston arrives." I craned my neck to see if he was, in fact, here yet.

"Don't worry about it." Flora gave me a gentle pat on the arm. "Go have some fun. If he comes, I'll send Clarabelle over to get you."

I nodded and walked over to Clarabelle's table where Clark was.

We exchanged a quick glance, and I could tell she'd been dealing out instructions to him the whole time, which made me chuckle.

"Clark, want to watch the Harvest Queen get crowned with me?"

"Sure." He wiped his hands and looked over at Clarabelle. "What do you say, can I take five?"

"Yes, that's fine. Thanks for your help, Clark. I know you were supposed to be helping Flora out, but folks just clung to the cobbler like flies on honey."

"Well, it's equally as delicious as Flora's pecan bread, so, I don't blame them," Clark said.

"It's almost like there's a secret ingredient in there that people seem to go wild for." A teasing grin curled at the corners of my lips.

Clarabelle's eyes screamed death, and she puckered her lips together. "Don't you gotta go watch someone get crowned?"

She gave me an aggressively playful swat on the arm before Clark and I walked off toward the stage, where everything was being set up.

A well-dressed man with an equally slick hairdo to match entered the stage holding a large, beautiful bouquet of autumn flowers.

"How come you're not up there?" Clark smirked, his eyes holding a joshing glimmer.

"Very funny," I responded, my tone equally good-natured.

The crowd applauded when the man, who Clark informed me was named Mayor Dodger, approached the microphone and tapped it.

"Thank you for coming out on this beautiful fall day," he announced. "This is turning out to be the best Harvest Festival we've had thus far!"

"He always says that." Clark leaned in close to my ear and applauded along with everyone else.

When the young woman who was declared the Harvest Queen appeared on the stage, I tilted my head. She looked so familiar. I wondered where I had seen her before. It dawned on me when Mayor Dodger said her name. Essie. She was the same girl who was at that honky tonk I went to what felt like a lifetime ago.

I clapped awkwardly, hoping her husband that I had carelessly flirted with wasn't anywhere around me.

Essie was given the bouquet and a sash that she wore over her pretty navy-blue swing dress. The mayor presented her with a small tiara, putting it on her head. He followed up with a few kind words about her contribution to the city. She responded by offering a few short, grateful words and gave Mayor Dodge a cordial hug, followed by a gracious wave to the crowd.

When Essie exited the stage, the mayor returned to the microphone.

"Thank you once more, Essie Nevins, we hope to see you in the running again next year. And now, everybody continue to enjoy yourselves. The Vern Preston Band will be back on stage in five minutes!"

Mayor Dodger stepped off the stage to mingle with some folks.

Clark turned to me, shoving his hands into his pockets.

"Want to head back to Flora?"

"Sure." We walked side by side with one another. "That was quick. From the way Flora and Clarabelle described it, I assumed the Harvest Queen crowning would have a little more fanfare."

Clark shrugged. "It's just a silly little thing the mayor likes to do. Folks seem to enjoy it."

"Oh, I thought it was lovely. Essie seems like a very nice girl." I shifted my eyes, my memory recalling back to her genuine concern for my well-being at the honky tonk.

"She's fine. I went to school with her and her husband, Beau. They're high school sweethearts. She never had a bad word to say about anyone."

"I guess that's a good quality to have."

"It is. I bet that if you were born and raised in Savannah, you would surely be crowned Harvest Queen."

My cheeks flushed for what felt like the one-hundredth time that day. While I've had many young men offer sweet nothings to me over the years, that had to be the nicest thing anyone could have ever said.

Flora was still serving out pieces of pecan bread when Clark and I returned to her. When we approached her table, I was both pleased and nervous to see that her pecan bread was near gone, and there were only a few recipe cards left. While I was glad she was doing well, I hoped she didn't completely run out of everything by the time Mr. Winston arrived.

We got there in time to meet a young woman and her little boy, who both enjoyed the pecan bread.

Flora handed the woman the recipe card, who in turn expressed interest in making it at home.

After they walked off, Clarabelle moseyed over.

"Well, that's that for my peach cobbler. Folks clambered for it. You'd think they'd never eaten a day in their lives."

"Your cobbler is always a wonderful turnout. I don't know why you seem so surprised," Flora said.

"Not as wonderful as your pecan bread," Clarabelle retorted. "I see your marketing skills have paid off."

"It's been very successful." Flora smiled. "I only hope it's good enough for Mr. Winston."

"Speaking of, where is he?" I searched around, unable to seek out his balding head among the crowd.

"He's still got plenty of time." Flora waved off my concern.

"Yeah, but your pecan bread and recipe cards are flying off the table like hot cakes. That was the whole point, for him to see how well you're doing."

"Honey, stop fretting." Flora enveloped my hands in hers. Her eyes were comforting, yet they held a firmness to them. "He'll show up."

An impatient sigh that I couldn't help, escaped out of me. I nodded, however, and complied with Flora as I got back to work next to her, handing out her pecan bread.

I stared out at the mingling crowd and noticed a heavy-set man making his way through everyone. I nearly knocked the table over with excitement when I realized the man was indeed Mr. Winston.

"I see him!" I announced, wiping the pecan bread crumbs off my hands. "I'll bring him over."

I walked off, charging swiftly over to Mr. Winston, who looked around the festival like a lost kid searching for his mother in a department store.

"Mr. Winston!" I waved my hand at him to grab his attention.

I quickened my pace and made sure the smile on my face was friendly.

"Well, Maggie!" He grinned as I approached him. "Good to see you! Don't you look lovely?" He took my hand in his and gave it a quick kiss.

"Thank you, Mr. Winston. It's good to see you, too. So, what do you think?" I gestured to all the people having a swell time around us.

"It certainly is a turn out." He nodded. "Is everything going well?"

"Like clockwork!" I gestured for him to follow me as we parted our way through the growing crowd of people.

Small children ran by us in sailor dresses and suits carrying pinwheels and letting out joyous cries of fun.

When we arrived at Flora's table, Mr. Winston greeted her with a warm hug.

"Looks like you're doing well." Mr. Winston smiled at her.

"Very!" Flora said. "People are just gobbling up the pecan bread!"

Mr. Winston nodded. "I figured they would."

"I even wrote out recipe cards to entice everyone." Flora held up what was left of the recipe cards in the box.

"I'm glad to see everything is working out." He smiled, taking everything in before him.

His face shifted quickly, however, grimness overtaking the charm he was expressing not moments ago.

I wondered what he was looking at until my gaze trailed down to the canister and the Pyrex of sampling pecans on the table.

He brought his eyes back up to us. They were sullen beneath his narrowed, bushy eyebrows.

"What's this?" He pointed to the pecans.

I realized it looked like I was doing what he told me not to, however, it's not like I was taking people's money and pocketing it.

I took a deep breath, fully intending on telling him the truth.

"Mr. Winston, I—"

"I thought I told you, you couldn't sell my pecans here."

"Flora's pecans." I had to correct again, my tone taking on an edge that rivaled his.

"Maggie?" Flora stepped up next to us. "What is he talking about?"

"Okay, look," I gestured to the table, "I know this looks like—"

"I know exactly what it looks like!" Mr. Winston interjected again. "You thought you could go behind my back and sell the pecans after I told you not to."

Flora, Clarabelle, and Clark's eyes all fell on me. They were collectively silent as Mr. Winston's gaze had a standoff with mine.

"If you would let me finish talking, I could tell you." I placed my hands firmly on my hips. "You're jumping to conclusions."

My attempt to remain cordial was floundering. I was using every last piece of composure inside of me to not blow over at Mr. Winston's interruptions. I needed to get my words out before I ended up looking like a complete heel in front of everyone.

"I don't think I am." Mr. Winston shook his head, his voice low and grave. "You went against my orders."

Without another word, he turned around and walked off, making his way through the crowd of festival goers.

CHAPTER FORTY-THREE

Flora, Clark, and Clarabelle all chattered about, questioning me over what exactly was going on. Their words all overlapped one another's until their voices became a tangled mess in my ears.

I couldn't answer them, let alone think straight as Mr. Winston got farther and farther away.

Desperation clung to my chest, and I dashed after him, scurrying past people, trying not to knock anyone over in my haste.

"Mr. Winston!" I called after him.

He walked with a determination to get the hell out of here, his arms swinging back and forth.

"Mr. Winston, please!"

I caught up with him and clutched his arm to get him to look at me.

He stopped, his face still set in disappointment.

Everyone else had followed. They stood, forming a small circle around me.

"I know you said not to sell the pecans, and I didn't! All I did was bring a canister to show people what it looks like. You said I could mention your company to everyone, which I did. As for the pecans, I only wanted people to see what they tasted like on their own. I never took any money from anyone. I didn't charge a penny for them, and neither did Flora."

Mr. Winston remained silent, his face still as stone.

The frustration that had bubbled over earlier was fizzling out, and all that lay inside of me was a determination to make Mr. Winston listen.

"You should have seen her today," I said, the immense pride I had for Flora returning. "She did great. She handed out her pecan bread and recipe cards to nearly everyone that came by. She was everything a business person should be. And yes, I know that this day is purely for leisure, but let's say it wasn't. For a moment, let's say the people enjoying the Harvest Festival were potential clients or investors interested in working with your company. Flora had nearly everyone she encountered interested in her recipe. She had people asking about Alcott's and where to buy them, which if you ask me, very well could lead to a potential sale. If you could have only seen her in action, how well she did, I'm certain you would be just as proud of her as we are."

My heart was racing, and I realized I was clenching my fists. I uncurled them, allowing my fingers to relax.

Mr. Winston shook his head lightly. "All of that still doesn't excuse the fact that you went against my orders."

"Excuse me, can I say something?" Flora's voice lilted from behind me.

She put a gentle hand on my shoulder and looked at me; her eyes were soft and shining.

"Thank you for those kind words, Maggie. I really appreciate it."

She took her hand off my shoulder and faced Mr. Winston, hesitating momentarily before lifting her chin slightly and holding her shoulders back.

"Mr. Winston, don't be too hard on Maggie. She was only trying to help. I know at first glance it seems like what she did was wrong, but she did it with the best intentions. She would never do anything to jeopardize my business or your company."

Flora stopped, pausing to take a light breath. Her mouth drew downward, and a sadness crossed her features. However, as quickly as it came, the sadness left her face, and a gentle confidence settled in. She looked back up at Mr. Winston.

"I know I'm getting older and probably don't have a lot of years left in me, but I'd rather spend those last years doing what I love, which is running this business and working on the pecan farm. I understand that when I eventually go, you'll have to hand Alcott's off to someone else, but while I'm still around, I want nothing more than to be on that farm picking pecans and making pecan bread for everyone. Even though my days on the pecan farm are numbered, I can still do a little here and a little there. What's not numbered is my love for this business, and my love for what my husband and his family brought. This business stood the test of two World Wars and The Great Depression, and I want to see it live on for as long as I do. I want to keep this business for as long as I can. And I want to share my pecan bread recipe with the world."

Keeping her chin lifted, Flora stood taller than she ever had, a delicate balance of grace and grit embodying her.

My eyes stung. I couldn't understand how anyone would want to take her greatest passion away from her.

Mr. Winston's expression softened, however, there was still a twinge of irritation set in.

"Flora," he said, his tone mollifying, "you know how much I care about you. But unfortunately, I too know that you won't be around forever. And like you said, your time spent on the pecan farm is getting limited, which is a crucial part of this business."

"I can still do a small amount of labor," she said. "I may not be able to walk acres and acres like I used to, but I can still pick pecans."

"Besides, she's got me." I stepped forward. "I've worked on the pecan farm with Flora and can continue to do so. I'm able to handle heavier lifting and longer working hours. I can work side by side with her on the farm to make sure she doesn't overwork herself but still gets to harvest."

"Yes, but there's the fact of the matter that someday, this business will have to go to someone else," Mr. Winston said. "And in order to prepare for that, I need to seek out potential prospectors that can take over."

"No, you don't." I raised my chin. "Because I want to go into business with Flora."

Mr. Winston's wide-eyed stare sobered into a mixture of puzzlement and skepticism.

"You?" His eyebrows raised.

I offered a confident nod, brushing off his condescending tone. "Yes."

"You don't even know the first thing about running a business."

"No, but if you recall, I am the daughter of a successful business man and woman. I may not have a lot of business experience, but that doesn't mean I can't learn. And I think I can learn a lot under Flora's tutelage, and yours as well."

"It would never work!" Mr. Winston shook his head, his mouth sputtering for excuses. "You're much too young anyway."

I tilted my head and folded my arms across my chest. "How old were you when you first started out?"

"That's different, I—"

"How old?" I probed

"Twenty-four," he answered reluctantly.

I smiled. "Oh, what a coincidence. Because I am just two months shy of my twenty-fourth birthday."

Mr. Winston's lips twisted like a corkscrew, and he gave a not-so-subtle eye roll. He shook his head hastily.

"There's also the fact of the matter that this has been an ongoing business for over forty years."

"And yet, you couldn't be quicker at handing the business to someone else when you thought she was no longer able to work."

"That is a whole other matter. We're talking about adding another partner here."

"Exactly! I want this to be a true partnership. I want to work side by side with Flora. I know it won't be the same as it was with her husband, but I think she and I could make a great team. Although, it's still her business first and foremost. While I'd be involved with business making decisions, I still want her to maintain control over foreseeing everything. It's her name, after all."

"And would you be adding O'Hanlon's to Alcott's at some point?" Mr. Winston asked.

"No. The name should remain Alcott's, plain and simple." I took another step forward. "Mr. Winston, I wouldn't be doing this if I didn't think I could. But nobody starts out knowing everything they set out to do. A new nurse doesn't just walk into a hospital and start tending wounds; they learn to first. They grow. And with each wound, they become more experienced. Until they're sure enough they can do it in their sleep."

My chest heaved, and I drew in a deep breath.

"I know I have a lot to learn, but I can do it. And who better to teach me along the way than Flora? Mr. Winston, if you give me a chance at this, I think I will surprise you."

Sincerity surged through my gaze.

Mr. Winton's eyes no longer held such antagonism, however, a flicker of apprehension still lingered.

The cool, quiet breeze cut through the awkward silence that fell between us for several moments.

Mr. Winston gave an impartial shrug and shoved his hands into his pockets.

"Well, that was a convincing speech. But what about when the day comes that Flora is no longer with us?"

A heaviness sat in my chest at the reality of that happening someday. However, I swallowed down the premature grief and regained my confidence.

"By then, I'll have gained experience. And I'll make sure that Alcott's continues to honor Flora and her husband, and that includes having her pecan bread recipe on the label. I truly believe that adding her recipe would be the best thing for her business."

Flora's eyes glistened, and she clasped her hands together, pressing them gently against her mouth.

"I care so much about Flora and Alcott's," I continued. "I know you do as well. Deep down, I know you do. And if eventually you're going to have to have someone take over, why not someone who knows Flora? Someone who's spent time with her and understands how Alcott's works and how she conducts business?"

Mr. Winston hung his head and shook it lightly.

I understood that we'd all been through this song and dance before, but I was willing to fight Mr. Winston tooth and nail over this. I'd stand here until sunrise if I had to.

"Can I say something?" Clark piped up.

Everyone's heads turned toward him, and he stepped forward.

"I agree with Maggie. I think her going into business with Flora would be the best thing for Alcott's. I know I don't have a lot of say in this, but sir, with all due respect, I think it would be a great missed opportunity not seeing what she can do."

My chest fluttered, and I couldn't hold back the smile that spread across my face.

"The boy is right," Clarabelle offered. "If there's anyone who could go into business with Flora, it's Margaret. She may be stubborn as all else, but you'd have to be blind not to see that she knows what she's doing. She's one smart gal, and we couldn't be any more proud of her if we tried."

While Clark's words made me feel ten feet tall, Clarabelle's shot me out of the universe. Immense gratitude swelled inside of me, and I looked back at Mr. Winston with hopeful and pleading eyes.

"Mr. Winston." Flora spoke before he had a chance to open his mouth. "There isn't anyone I'd rather work with than Maggie. I can see myself working side by side with her until my last day on Earth. I trust her. She is a wonderful friend, and I know she would be an even more wonderful business partner. I ask that you give her a chance. If there is anything I should have a say in, it's who I work with and who should carry on my name."

I stole a peek at Mr. Winston. His shoulders drooped, and he had lost all superiority in his expression. I couldn't tell if he was beginning to crumble or if he was chagrined. He drew in a deep breath.

"Why don't we continue this in my office on Monday? We'll examine the process of adding Maggie as a business partner."

Flora and I nearly fell over. I had honestly wondered if I heard him correctly.

"Wait, what?" My eyes widened.

"There is still a great deal to discuss." Mr. Winston's words were positive, but his expression was still serious. "I want to go over everything in further detail without all of this hullabaloo around us." He motioned toward the Harvest Festival that was still in full swing.

"Oh, thank you, Mr. Winston!"

Flora threw her arms around him.

Mr. Winston couldn't help but reciprocate and give her back a gentle rub.

"I expect to see you two at ten o'clock Monday morning." He pointed to me and Flora.

"We'll be there." I beamed, giving him a genuine smile. "Thank you, Mr. Winston."

I held out my hand, and he gave the back of it a kiss, which, for the first time in my life, I didn't wipe off on my dress.

"Would you like to stay?" Flora asked.

Mr. Winston shook his head. "I'm afraid I can't. I still have quite a bit of work to get done before our meeting."

Flora tilted her head and gave it an accepting nod. "Thank you so much again. You have no idea what this means to me."

"You're welcome, Flora." Mr. Winston smiled lightly. He offered one final wave before leaving.

Flora and I embraced immediately.

"Oh, Maggie, I cannot wait to work with you." She squeezed me so tight, I thought the buttons would pop off my dress.

"We're going to make a great team." I hugged her equally tight, burying my face in her shoulder.

We let go, and she brushed underneath my eyes with her thumbs.

Clarabelle moseyed up to us. She wrapped Flora in her arms and offered a few quiet words in her ear, to which Flora responded with a tearful nod.

When she came over to me, she gave me a light punch on the arm and winked, following it up with an affirmative head bow.

"Shall we return to the festival?" Flora took off her glasses and wiped under her eyes with a handkerchief. "It should be winding down soon."

Clark fell into step with me. His earthy cologne tingled against my nose, and I turned my head to smile at him.

"Thank you for what you said to Mr. Winston."

"Well, it's the truth." He grinned back. "You're the perfect candidate. As much as I respect Mr. Winston as a businessman, I was ready to tell him he was crazy for not seeing what was right in front of him."

I blushed. "You've really done more than Flora and I ever could ask for. I really appreciate it."

We stopped walking, and Clark's hazel eyes crinkled at the sides.

He looked over at the stage and cocked his head. "You wanna dance?"

My wide smile spread even further, beaming across my face. I linked my arm into his, and we moved in front of the stage and began bopping to the music.

Clark was pretty good on his feet, if not a little goofy. He definitely had some nice moves about him. He took my hand and twirled me around, and when I came back to him, I leaned in and kissed him on the cheek. Their pink hues deepened, and he gave a bashful grin. I smiled at him, and he twirled me around again.

I glanced over to see Flora and Clarabelle tapping their feet in place. Flora's gaze caught mine, and she looked at me as if I gave her the world. I reciprocated with a thankful nod.

As Clark twirled me around and dipped me, I let out a joyous laugh, embracing him tightly, wishing that this moment would never end.

CHAPTER FORTY-FOUR

M r. Winston was in a better mood than when we last saw him as he warmly greeted me and Flora into his office on Monday morning.

He wasted no time getting down to brass tacks, putting me in the hot seat first and foremost.

"I understand your visions for changing the presentation of the labels, Maggie." He took a puff of his cigar. "But before I can fully agree to it, I want to know what you have in mind for Alcott's as a whole."

I smoothed my dress out and cleared my throat. "Well, I'd have to say I have the same ideas as Flora. Meaning, I want to see this business go on for a long time. Maybe someday down the road, Alcott's and Farmer's can be featured in stores outside of Georgia. I know you're keen on expanding where your products are sold."

Mr. Winston blew out his last big of smoke and stubbed his cigar out in a crystal ashtray.

"That is true." He nodded, squinting his beady little eyes. "But is that it? When the day comes for you to fully take over, where do you see yourself? Where do you see this business?"

I swallowed the anxious ridden lump in my throat. I didn't appreciate that Mr. Winston was continuing to dwell on Flora's longevity, acting as if she had one foot in the grave already. Whether he was trying to make me sweat or was truly testing my business sense was something I couldn't decipher. I cleared my throat again and decided to go with the latter. I straightened in my seat and lifted my chin.

"For one thing, I hope that certain day doesn't come for a very long time. I'm looking forward to forming a partnership with Flora, and I hope I'm able to do so, and that it lasts many years." I smiled lightly at Flora, who returned the gesture. I brought my attention back to Mr. Winston, regaining seriousness. "But to answer your question, as I've said, I see myself having gained experience. I understand I still have a lot to learn, and honestly, will probably continue to learn and grow as a business person every day. But that's okay. Nobody changes overnight, you know."

There was an eerie quietness to Mr. Winston as he gazed at me. His fingers pinched the bottom of his lips. I was beginning to worry that I was losing him.

"What I mean is," I continued hastily, "it's okay to learn new things about the business as you gain more experience. I'm sure there are things you know today that you didn't know a week ago."

"That may be," Mr. Winston said. "Of course I don't expect you to know the ins and outs of being a business owner right away. You're right, though. You do have a lot to learn."

His tone lowered, and worry set into my chest again that he was still doubtful about my potential. I was coming to the realization that I would have to once and for all accept his hot and cold personality. As much as it still grated me, this was who he was, and I had to find a way to meet common ground with him.

I was about to further plead my case when Flora cleared her throat and leaned forward in her chair.

"Mr. Winston, I understand that we went through all of this the other day, but you can't tell me that you don't see the promise in Maggie. I, for one, do, and that's not only because I've had the pleasure of getting to know her for the last few months. It's because she is a smart and determined young lady. I'm sure you can see that when she sets her mind to something, she doesn't back down."

"No, that she doesn't." Mr. Winston shook his head.

"Isn't that what you want in a business owner? Isn't that what you want in someone who works for you? If this is what she's like now, just imagine how she'll be five or ten years down the road." Flora inclined her head modestly. "I sure wasn't as courageous as she is when I first started out. I'm still not, but I've gained a lot of confidence in myself, and that's all because Maggie has helped me see that I am good at this. I am a good business woman, and my love for this business that my husband and his family started is what drives me every single day."

Flora pointed at me.

"I see that in her. I see that drive and that love. And I know she will carry that on long after I'm gone. She will carry on my name and the meaning of what this business is. Alcott's isn't just about pecans. It's about family." Flora grabbed my hand, wrapping her fingers around mine. "And Maggie is family."

I squeezed Flora's hand and smiled at her.

Mr. Winston clasped his fingers together and placed them firmly on his desk, still seemingly dubious.

My patience was waning, and I had to physically restrain myself from telling him to make up his mind. I was about to when his gaze fixated on mine.

"You understand that this is a serious and long-term decision to make," he said.

I nodded, fighting off the retort that I acknowledged that not moments ago. "Yes."

Mr. Winston responded with a head nod of his own. "All right, then. There are still a lot of ground rules to go over, legally speaking that is. I hope you two don't mind discussing those today, if you have the time."

"We don't have anywhere to be," I said.

"Wonderful. We will need to go over some paperwork for you both to sign. Once we get everything squared away, I want to start the process of changing up the labels." Mr. Winston turned his attention to Flora, giving her a smile. "Are you ready to put your pecan bread recipe out into the world?"

To our surprise and delight, Clarabelle and Clark were sitting on Flora's front porch when we arrived back home.

Clarabelle leapt off her wicker chair.

"How did it go?"

I never thought Flora's smile could go any wider than it already was. Pride was bursting out of her as we climbed up the front steps.

"Let's go inside, and I'll tell you everything." She squeezed Clarabelle's shoulders with such joy.

Flora served slices of pecan bread and tea as she explained everything Mr. Winston went over, as well as the forthcoming ideas Flora and I had for Alcott's, and how we were going to get the ball rolling with putting her recipe on the labels.

"Maggie conducted herself with such professionalism and grace." She beamed, bringing a cup of tea to her lips. "She's a natural."

"Don't sell yourself short," I said. "It was your words that finally got Mr. Winston on our side."

"I still can't believe everything you two pulled off." Clarabelle shook her head. "I gotta say, well done."

"I can't wait to see what y'all have in store," Clark said. "Consider me your first customer when the new labels are printed out."

My chest fluttered, and I smiled, instinctively grabbing Clark's hand, holding it in mine. Our fingers clasped together, and Clark met my gaze, glee spreading across his face.

Clarabelle gawked at us over the rim of her tea cup, her left eyebrow twitching as it arched up.

When Clark was ready to leave, I walked him out to his truck.

"Thank you." I smiled at him.

A soft chuckle escaped from his lips. "For what?"

I shrugged. "Everything. For believing in Flora and me when no one else did."

"Don't mention it." He gave me a soft, crooked smile.

"I don't think I'll ever be able to stop mentioning it. Really."

Clark's eyes softened as he gazed into mine.

I took every piece of him in, and the fluttering in my chest returned. I stood on my toes and kissed him on the lips.

When I let go, I found that my cheeks were warm. The fluttering turned into hammering, and I grabbed his hands, holding them in mine once more.

Clark rubbed his thumb gently over my hand. It was warm and comforting. I didn't want to be the first to let go.

"I'll see you later, Maggie?" he said.

I nodded, already counting down the seconds to when I would get to see him next.

"I'll see you later, Clark."

Later that evening, I sat in between Flora and Clarabelle on the porch swing out back and breathed in the mid-November air.

Dusk was settling in across the sky. Beautiful shades of purple, pink, and a splash of orange made it look like something out of a painting.

"I'd have to say this was one of the best days I've ever had," Flora said, her voice soft like a lullaby.

My head bobbed in agreement.

Flora linked her arm into mine.

"So, what do you think, partner?" She turned toward me, her eyes twinkling with anticipation. "We need to have a celebration."

"What do you think today was?" I giggled.

"I mean a real one." Flora waved me off. "With Mr. Winston too."

I shrugged. "I suppose that would be fun. Maybe I could pick up a bottle of champagne?"

"Huh." Clarabelle touted. "Let's not go too wild, Margaret."

"All right. Something a little stronger, then?" I smiled teasingly at Clarabelle.

"Never mind." She swatted me playfully on the knee.

"It won't be terribly big anyway," Flora said. "Just the usual folks."

"So, us three, Clark, and Mr. Winston?" I raised my eyebrows.

"Yes." Flora nodded. "Oh! Maybe Dr. Meadows and his lovely wife."

I chuckled. "That sounds very nice. We'll have a real soiree."

I suddenly thought of my parents, and all the shindigs they held. My face fell, and I lost myself in those memories that felt like they were part of another life.

"Maggie? Are you all right?" Flora leaned forward, her expression brimming with concern.

I snapped out of it quickly, nodding hastily.

"Yeah. I was just thinking of my parents. They always had these big parties and…" I shook my head, keeping my eyes down. "They were never that fun anyway. Our celebration will knock all of theirs out of the park."

I couldn't help the acidity that gripped my tone. Here I was, a budding business woman, and they wouldn't get to see how far I'll go.

Flora squeezed my hand.

"Maggie, it's okay. Look at me." Her comforting but firm voice made me obey. "Don't reside in the past. Your future is at your fingertips. Hold on to it."

I leaned my head on Flora's shoulder.

"Speaking of futures," Clarabelle crowed, "let's talk about Clark. I saw you two at the kitchen table holding hands like lovebirds."

"Lovebirds!" My head shot up. "We were just—"

"Holding hands." Clarabelle gave me a saucy look. "Mhm. Don't tell me what I didn't see. I've been around a lot longer than you have, Margaret. My eyesight may not be what it used to be, but I'm not completely blind! So, when's the wedding?"

"Wedding!" If I hadn't already been sitting, I'd have fallen over.

"Oh, does that mean we get to be bridesmaids?" Flora trilled.

A gut busting roar tore out of my lips, and I covered my mouth with my hand.

As Flora and Clarabelle teasingly gushed about what color they wanted their dresses to be, I continued to chuckle, sitting in between the two women I now called my very best friends, grateful that we would be a part of each other's lives forever.

CHAPTER FORTY-FIVE

November 1948

I was taking the last loaf of pecan bread out of the oven, setting the heavy baking dish down on the counter, when light footsteps entered the kitchen.

"Almost ready?" Clark's voice said from behind me.

I turned around to see my husband fiddling with his necktie.

"Almost. I need to finish cutting up the pecan bread into squares, then we can leave. You all ready to go?"

"Just about." He continued to battle with his tie. "I can't seem to get this new tie to stay straight. It's all crooked."

I walked over to him and took his hands away from his tie, smiling lightly. "I like it crooked."

He mirrored my expression, however, his face quickly fell. "Are you sure you want to go? I understand if you don't."

I hesitated, still holding his hands in mine. My gaze drew away from his. He brought me back by brushing his thumb tenderly across my fingers.

I shook my head.

"No. I want to go. Today is going to be wonderful. Despite…" I couldn't finish my sentence, and I looked away again.

Clark held me close, and I wrapped my arms around him. "It's okay," he whispered, rubbing my back.

A light, shuddered sob escaped from me, and I pressed my face against his chest.

Clark rested his chin on my head, swaying us gently back and forth.

I gulped down more tears and let go of him, wiping my eyes and sniffling. "I want to go. I have to. It's what Flora would've wanted."

Clark nodded a gentle and accepting bow of his head. "She'd be real proud of you, you know."

My chin trembled, and I gave my eyes another wipe. "Don't make me cry again. I already have to retouch my makeup."

The corners of Clark's lips curved upward, and he brought me close again, giving me a light kiss on the forehead.

We carried out the traveling Pyrex dishes of pecan bread to his truck.

I stopped in the bright foyer and examined the painting of Flora's pecan farm on the wall. I grinned, its legacy now taking on a whole new meaning for me.

Not long after Flora's pecan bread recipe had been printed and finalized on her labels, Farmer's began expanding their products to other states. Alcott's success grew like gangbusters and was now sold in stores across Georgia, Mississippi, and most recently, Alabama.

Flora and I continued to work hard together until she fell ill again, eventually losing her battle in February of this year.

We arrived at the Harvest Festival in record time. It was strange. Even though this was my third time attending, I almost felt as if I had been coming my entire life.

Clarabelle stood near the entrance and greeted us. She gave me a hug, offering a gentle pat on the back.

"How are you doing, Margaret?" Her gruff voice had weakened over time. "I know today isn't easy for you."

"I'm fine." I sighed. "How are you?"

Clarabelle shrugged. "Holding up."

I nodded. "I know it'll be hard, but Flora would want us to enjoy ourselves. Let's make today the best the Harvest Festival has ever seen."

Clarabelle nodded as well, although hesitantly. She joined Clark and me at our table, deciding to assist us this year instead of handing out her peach cobbler.

The air was crisp and cool as we lost ourselves in mingling with everyone and handing out pecan bread.

Before Flora passed, she gave me her blessing to continue on making her recipe.

Mr. Winston stopped by our table, where he acknowledged the canister of pecans placed front and center.

"I like how you have the back of the label facing everyone, so the recipe is the first thing they see." He smiled.

"It was Flora's idea last year." I smiled back. It faded quickly, however, and sadness rushed over me again.

Mr. Winston also grew somber. "She was a wonderful business woman." He paused and took in a sharp breath. "One of the best I've ever known."

As the day wore on, many people came by to express their fond memories of Flora's contribution to the Harvest Festival, including Dr. Meadows and his wife, Ada, who stayed with us until the Harvest Festival was coming to a close.

"I know we didn't know each other for a very long time," Dr. Meadows said, "but she had a way of making you feel as if you were her greatest friend in the world."

"I don't think truer words have ever been spoken." I concurred.

The small crowd of people murmured in agreement.

I took a piece of pecan bread, cupping my other hand underneath it to catch the crumbs.

"Everyone, take some pecan bread. To, Flora—" My voice cracked on her name.

I paused, taking several seconds to get past the lump that rose up. I cleared my throat, my lips quivering with a reflective smile.

"One of the greatest business women, and people, we ever could have known. There was nobody like her."

I scanned the little group in front of me. A mixture of tears, sniffles, and memorializing nods responded.

"To, Flora."

We raised our pecan bread and took a bite, savoring the taste of Flora's memory.

FLORA'S PECAN BREAD

2 1/4 cups Self-rising flour
  2 tsp lemon juice
  1/2 tsp salt
  1/4 cup cinnamon sugar mixture
  1 tsp vanilla
  1/2 cup packed dark brown sugar
  1 large egg
  1/2 cup vegetable oil
  1/4 cup milk
  1 cup buttermilk
  3 tbs melted butter
  1 cup chopped pecans
  1/2 cup honey
  1/3 cup pecan halves

Gather ingredients and set oven to 350 degrees. Grease a 9 x 5 x 3 loaf pan with Crisco shortening. Mix dry ingredients in a large bowl (excluding the pecans). Mix together the buttermilk, egg, lemon juice, oil, milk, and melted butter in a small bowl. Add the wet ingredients to the dry mixture and stir carefully. Add chopped pecans and fold gently. When everything is mixed well, transfer bread batter to greased loaf pan and smooth it out. Add pecan halves to the top and sprinkle with more cinnamon sugar mixture. Bake for fifty minutes or until center is fully cooked. Let cool for thirty minutes. Cut pecan bread into loaves or squares. Top with a drizzle of honey or any desired toppings, or enjoy plain!

ACKNOWLEDGMENTS

There are so many people to thank that helped this book come to fruition, but the first ones I want to thank are my family, especially my parents who have always fostered my love of reading and writing. Thank you for all your love and support and putting up with countless questions and reading through scenes to see how they sounded. I love you guys.

Thank you to my awesome friends for their support as well and sharing all the excitement and milestones throughout the journey of writing this book. You guys mean so much to me.

Thank you to my editors, Kereah Keller and Borbala Branch for polishing and shaping this book with their encouraging and helpful feedback. I really enjoyed working with the both of you.

Thank you to Dane and the team at ebooklaunch.com for creating the book cover. You did such a wonderful job capturing Maggie's character and the setting of Flora's home.

Thank you to my critique partner, Abigail Silver, who was the first one to read this story and offered such lovely comments and feedback and endless support. I will always get a kick out of your reactions to Maggie's antics. Also, thank you to Harlow Kelly, who was such an incredible beta reader and provided great feedback and for being a cheerleader for this story, all while wanting to give Maggie a good kick in the pants at times.

Thank you to George Beckman and the Writing Community of Twitter, especially Line By Line Time for their constant support and constructive critiques on scenes shared from this book. I always look forward to our Wednesday night chats.

About The Author

Rebecca Amiss is the author of the coming of age novella, *Summer of '77* and the short stories, *The First Snowfall of Christmas Eve* and *Down by the Bay,* the latter of which was a quarter-finalist in Screencraft's Cinematic Short Story Contest. Born and raised in Massachusetts, Rebecca loves setting many of her stories around the New England area. When she's not writing, Rebecca is an avid reader and movie buff. *South of Home* is her debut novel.

Instagram: @rebeccaamissauthor
Twitter: @RebeccaJAmiss
TikTok: @rebeccamissauthor
Goodreads: Rebecca Amiss
Website: www.rebeccaamiss.com

Made in United States
Cleveland, OH
25 August 2025

19733913R00198